THE SIX KNOWINGS OF
ASAIRA

THE SIX KNOWINGS OF
ASAIRA

CARMY STUBBS

Shimmering Circle Press

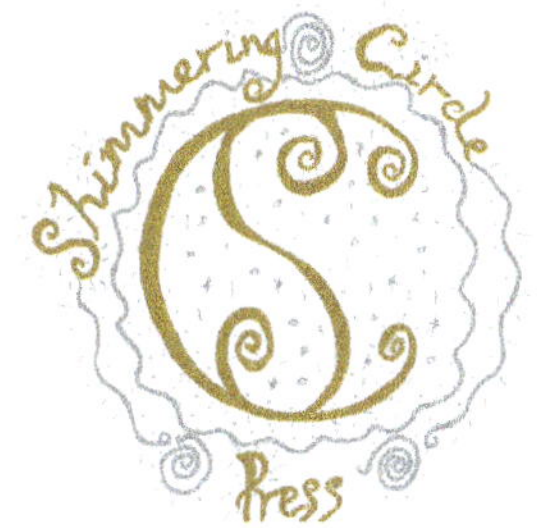

The Six Knowings of ASAIRA

Text and illustrations by Carmy Stubbs
Blended images by Carmy Stubbs and Carmen Wright
Book and cover design by Carmen Wright

ISBN: 978-1-7386675-0-5 (Paperback)

This

Book

Is

Dedicated

To

☆ *Isabel Iglesias Gómez* ✮

☆ *Isa de mi Corazón* ✮

¡Amor y Gratitud, Hermanita!

And

To

☆ *My Mother* ✮

☆ *Carmen Gómez Martínez* ✮

and

☆ *My Father* ✮

☆ *Denis Stubbs* ✮

Both Storytellers of Old

Wonderful

Loving

Parents

Love and Gratitude, Mama and Daddy!

THE KNOWINGS

THE 1ST KNOWING OF ASAIRA

AILEEN

THE LIGHT BEARER OF THE GREEN MEADOW

☆★ THE STORY STARTS ★☆

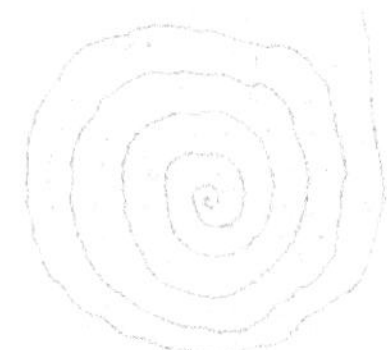

I am

I am the Essence of Essences

I cannot be spoken of

And yet I am

I cannot speak

And yet I do

I am described in a billion trillion words and pages

My voice is heard loud and clear in the Open Heart

Yes, Mystery is my name, if I had one

I am the Light of Lights

The Mystery that Clarifies All

I am the Untold of

And the Retold

Hear me, Children of the Earth and Sun, Hear me…

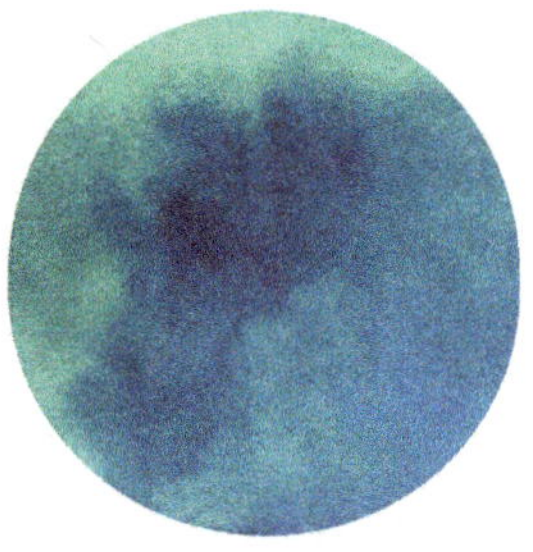

Earth: Primrose Meadow

Her eyes alight, Aileen ran towards the lush forest of Douglas firs. I can hear you… just let me get to the forest…

The voice Aileen had heard so many times since she was a child felt like a waterfall of sparkling words pouring down through her head and into her heart. It always made her want to sit down and write, an inspiration that kept insisting, knocking at the door. Sometimes what came was a poem; other times a short story or a drawing. But this time… it was another message!

"Nearly there, Bruxa!" Aileen scooped up the little white dog under her arm. Laughing, Aileen watched her feet avoid the primroses and run through the grassy ocean of the Meadow.

At last… yes! Her feet hopped onto the trail that led into the forest. The trees rustled. Aileen breathed in the magical aura of woody smells and flickering sunlight. So still… mmm… lovely… ooops… don't stop… and her legs picked up the pace again in the direction of her beloved Wise One. Bruxa gave out a little bark of glee.

And there He was. Aileen put Bruxa down. Catching her breath, she bowed in front of the Ancient Being and placed her left hand on its rough bark. Her eyes closed while her whole body embraced the Tree. "Ahh… Wise One," she whispered.

After a long sweet moment, Aileen sat down with her back against the tree trunk and took out her notebook and green pen. Bruxa snuggled up.

"Okay, here we go…"

Words appeared on the paper:

Wow...

The first message from the Star had been easier to understand.

Aileen saw herself again as a seven-year-old with Big Bear, her sweet Labrador, when together they'd found the Great Tree for the first time. She'd fallen asleep under the Tree and had a dream. That was when she'd received the Star's first message.

Aileen wrote the first message out again under the second:

From that day onwards, Aileen had repeated 'I want to Follow the Heart!' a million trillion times, it seemed to her. That's how, years later, she felt she was living her true life: a life filled with her love of nature and animals, of writing and art, close to the Ancient Tree.

But what did this second message mean? The Light of Love, Magical Signs… and a Promise? Hmm… Garden of Paradise?! Aileen chewed on her green pen when Bruxa decided that Aileen's lap looked very comfortable and promptly sat herself there.

Aileen laughed and set her notebook to one side, stroking Bruxa's soft head, "Ah, my little Light Bearer… hmm… are you one of those Magical Signs?" Aileen's eyes crinkled up with joy. She hugged the dog, who licked Aileen's face with no less joy. "Let's be off now! Bagha's at home waiting for his dinner."

But instead of getting up, Aileen let herself drift to sleep under the caring branches of the Ancient Tree.

The Tree of Lands

Aileen, Child of the Earth, I cherish Thee

Solid and Rooted am I

Ancient and New

Never do I tire

My Branches ever uplifted and protecting

Listen to the Star

As on Earth, As on Sun

The Light of Love

Never-ending

The Garden of Paradise

The Meadow of Meadows

Aileen... Aileen

Aileen

Sun: Shimmera's Tower

Shimmera stood in front of the window, her eyes closed. Her long golden hair fell softly down her back in waves, cascading from a garland around her head. The gown she wore shone with iridescent turquoise hues.

Shimmera's glow emanated and spiralled through her. Every new day she would stand in front of the windows of her Tower and feel the golden Light of Lights merge with the silver Sea of Seas.

"Shimmera, Golden One," a voice inside said.

Shimmera listened in quietness and recognised the Star of Heavens.

"Shimmera. I bring tidings of revelation and truth."

The Golden One smiled. "At last. The Promise."

Sun: Silas' Tower

As Silas looked out of the heavily draped window of his Tower, he saw his lands and in the distance, the Sea of Seas. The lands were ravaged, burnt-like, wasted. Yes, a wasted wilderness… no green, no flowers: a Cinder of Cinders.

Silas sighed. He had a huge burden. It weighed so, pushing and doubling him over.

Like a bolt of lightening came his animating force: a raging thought which was so dear to Silas, so important and vital to him that all burdens crashed to the floor, and he was reborn in strength and power, "Justice. Justice! Justice I seek and I shall have it. No Peace is possible until I do!"

Silas' eyes glimmered in the candlelight of his chamber.

Sun: Saul's Tower

Saul closed his eyes and breathed. The dream of the young woman and her animal guide brought various ancient legends into remembrance: legends of other lands, other towers beyond the Sea, legends of a place called Earth, legends of a Great Tree… and the Promise.

Saul had told the Star he was ready. He felt calm, his inherent gentleness radiating in golden wisps. "I must leave the Tower. But how?"

Saul found himself walking on the surface of the Sea of Seas. He smiled at the easiness of something that had felt to be impossible.

As if impatient, the Sea lifted Saul up onto a silvery wave and delivered him to a shore.

Sun: Smanara's Tower

Smanara danced to the sound of the drums. She spun round and round while the drum beat grew faster and faster.

In a frenzy, Smanara collapsed onto the carpeted floors and gave herself in scorching passion. Yet, her desire never left, always burning, always relentless and insatiable.

"Yes!" Smanara got to her feet. "I am The Rejected One. I have Power, Beauty and Passion! Every living creature falls at my feet!" Smanara's voice became shrill. "Yes, I adore being the Rejected One. There's no hope for me, so I do what I wish!" But the words were unconvincing. A sorrowful sigh bubbled up in her throat.

Smanara went to the window and looked over at the silver waters of the Sea. She felt so thirsty, was she never to be truly quenched? Her hands ran through her thick black hair.

A thought tore into her: I cannot be quenched because I must find my equal! Only with him shall I be complete!

Driven by an ancient force as if she had searched for Him, the Beloved, many, many times, Smanara stepped onto the Sea of Seas, a solid silver surface for her goddess feet. At every step, she felt the fire in her womb intensify when, after what seemed both centuries and no time at all, another Tower of the Sun arose in front of her.

Smanara let her feet drop onto the shore, knowing that this new land and Tower could only belong to the one she searched for.

The Star of Heavens

I bring Scintillating Tidings to those that can hear me:

The 5 shall meet

He who was Prayed For

She, the Golden Shining Glow

He, the Woodland One of Fiery Silver

She who Carries the Suffering

And

The Light Bearer of the Green Meadow.

See how I speak to you, Children of the Earth

Children of the One Light

I delight in these words

Sparks of Living Material in Creation

The Storyteller

By Jove, the Story has started without me I see!

How fascinating!

Dear Reader, it is a delight to make your acquaintance. Let me introduce myself later, though. Part 1 presses: Aileen is dreaming things of importance under the Wise Tree, and the four Children of the Sun are soon to meet.

☆* PART 1 **

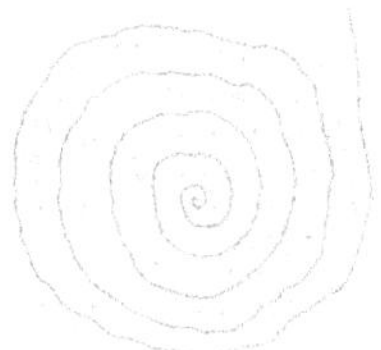

I am

I am the antecedent to All

I am the antecedent to Earth

I am the antecedent to Sun

I am the antecedent to the Story

I am the antecedent to the Words

I am

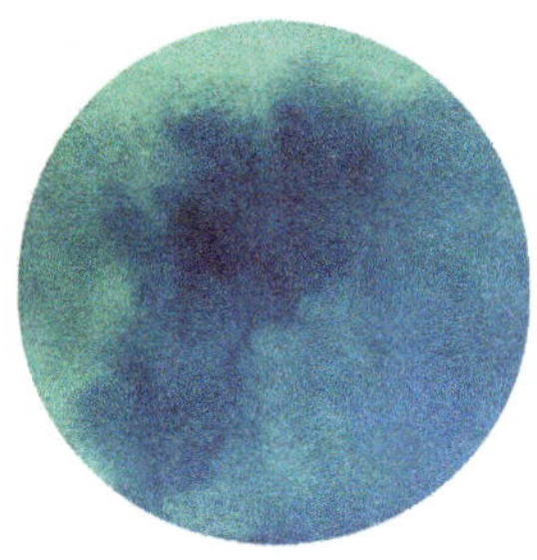

Earth: Aileen dreams under the Great Tree

Aileen is a little girl. She's hugging a tree. It's so huge and wide, she barely covers even a tiny bit of it! A tear rolls down her cheek. In the background is her dad, Aaron. Next to him is a big brown dog.

Sparkling whispers in a breeze call out, "Follow your Heart… Follow your Heart… Look for the Magical Signs… They are the Light of Love… Fulfil the Promise, Child of the Earth…"

A night sky descends and buries all.

Words write themselves across the darkness:

♡ The 4

♡ The 6

♡ The Green Meadow

♡ ASAIRA

♡ The Purest and Rarest Flower Am I

Aileen is a young woman. She's running through a field of ruby red poppies. It's sunny. Suddenly, dark clouds turn everything into ash-coloured black and white. The shadow of a monstrous, bird-like Being sweeps over Aileen.

Aileen shuddered and opened her eyes. Lifting Bruxa off her lap, she got up and hugged the Tree. A sweet fragrance of fruit mixed with earthy dampness tickled into Aileen's nostrils. She shuffled her feet a little and moved as close as she could, her right cheek pressed onto the bark.

The Storyteller

Greetings again, dear Reader.
Allow me to introduce myself
briefly as we leave Aileen at the
Tree. Then, we shall see what is
happening with the Children of
the Sun.

As the title declares, I am the
Storyteller. I am here to tell
you this Story about Aileen as it
unfolds. Sometimes stories have a
life of their own, and especially
this kind, for I do not fully
know yet what is to occur. Ah,
I so delight in this! Welcome,
Reader, to the Story!

I have some information to share
with you about Sun, which as
you must already have noticed is
not the Sun of your world. (I am
assuming that you, as is Aileen,
are also a Child of the Earth,
but if I am mistaken, by George,
how intriguing that would be!)

Sun

Sun gives the impression of being
divided into four regions. Each
of the four regions has a central
point called a Tower. These four
towers are called Towers of the
Sun.

In the middle of the four regions
there is an immense round stretch
of water like a lake. However,
for each of the four regions, the
appearance is of a great sea, and
the inhabitants of Sun have come
to call it the Sea of Seas.

Let me draw a map of sorts:

Each Tower is presided by a Child
of the Sun: Shimmera, Saul,
Smanara and Silas. Until now,
they have never met each other.
They do, however, have some deep
ancient knowing of there being
three others over the Sea, of
a forgotten time, but there is
only a legendary quality to this
knowing.

Let us continue, then, Reader.
I am eager to see what happens,
for Saul and Smanara are each
standing on, what is to them, an
unknown shore of the Sea of Seas.

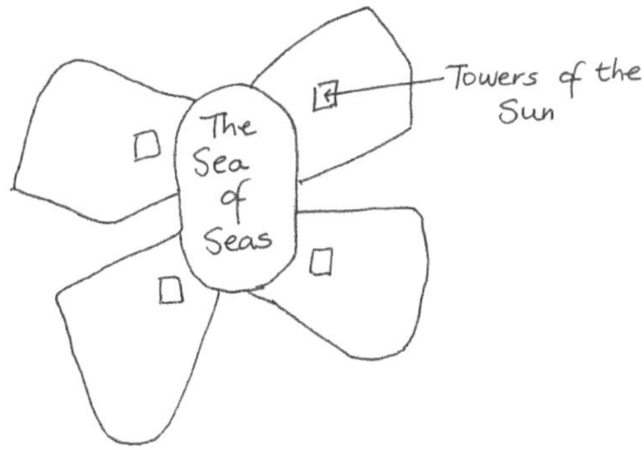

Sun: The 4

Shimmera and Silas looked out of their Towers. Both could see an enigmatic figure down below, someone unknown to them and yet, forever sought.

Regardless of the distance and height, the figures were totally clear to see, even the most minute of details. Neither Shimmera nor Silas considered this to be unusual. They were Children of the Sun, after all, powerful Gods.

And now, each of the 4 were face to face with their equal in wisdom, power and beauty. From above there was a flower-like quality to the meeting when Saul bowed to Shimmera in her Tower of the Sun, and Smanara bowed to Silas in his Tower of the Sun.

Sun: Shimmera's Tower

Shimmera received Saul with open arms. His shining luminosity was an unconcealed mirror of truth, for he reflected Shimmera's essence in a way she'd never encountered.

As Saul and Shimmera embraced, their bodies rippled in recognition. The two Gods of Goldness realised they had known each other in other times, and felt themselves merge into a forgotten joy.

Shimmera and Saul knew they would set out and cross the Sea of Seas together. There was a tingling excitement as they stepped onto the liquid plains. Saul took Shimmera's hand. They stood still for a moment, floating on the shallow waters of the shore, noticing the lapping sound of the waves.

The 2 started to walk across the Sea. One sentence echoed in their hearts:

"The Green Meadow shall unite the Earth & Sun, Storm & Calm. This is the Promise of Light that the Child of the Earth bears."

Sun: Silas' Tower

Silas glared suspiciously at Smanara.

Despite the foreboding sensation snarling around her body, Smanara lifted her head and stood upright to look this magnetizing God in the eye.

Silas's eyes looked straight back at her and sent a current of iciness up Smanara's spine. Her whole body trembled and froze.

Then, the Fire erupted! Its hurling energy roared through their bodies. Smanara felt the energy burn her body like molten silver.

Silas moved one step forward, his jaw clenched, "Who are you?"

Smanara's response arose in defiance, her black eyes like a wild animal, "I am called the Rejected One!"

At this, the lava of violence in Silas' stomach stormed up into the throat and burst into his brain, "I shall have you! I shall have you and destroy you, I see your wickedness! Justice will be had!"

Smanara saw Silas' eyes become a scalding red. She took a step back…

The Sea of Seas

We await Thee

The Waters of Love

Circles of Rippling Life

We await Thee

My watery womb is ready to give birth

Birth to ASAIRA

Can you hear us call, Little One?

Come Closer

Come Here

Be Born

Aileen

Aileen

Aileen

☆* PART 2 ✨

I am

I am the antecedent to all exquisiteness

I am the antecedent to all dread

Immaculate & Pure

I see

I see the Tree of Lands protecting

I see the Star of Heavens announcing

I see the Sea of Seas awakening

One Light, One Love

♡ **Magical Signs that Point to the Light of Love** ♡

One Flower ♈ ASAIRA ♈ One Light

Earth ⁓ Sun

Aileen has her eyes closed, her head turned to one side. The bark of the Ancient Tree feels warm. An image of a flower with letters surfaces through into Aileen's consciousness. That word again… ASAIRA… The sound of the word takes Aileen into herself, deeper and deeper. ASAIRA… Aileen's hands become numb. I'm disappearing… Yes…

Shimmera and Saul step onto the same shore where Smanara arrived not long before. Behind them, the Sea of Seas sparkles in gratitude, for it has loved the soft, sweet tread of the Golden Ones. Shimmera and Saul turn to face each other, smiling calmly. Turning again, they observe their surroundings. The sky is red and orange and alive with electricity: flashes of lightning, goaded by grumbling thunder, crack across the Heavens. Shimmera sees the dark structure in the distance… a Tower of the Sun! Saul takes a deep breath as he looks at it: the Tower's scorn burns his cheeks.

Aileen can't see: only a sense of swimming upwards through darkness. She keeps the panic at hold and follows the quiet voice, "Come closer, Light Bearer of the Green Meadow, Come closer."

Silas shakes as he grabs Smanara by her hair. He pulls her towards him and kisses her. Smanara arches her body and surrenders to the hard steel lips that compress her. Silas cannot stop, his hands grip Smanara's head, making his nails dig in. Smanara moans. She knows it is to be this way. She won't survive… there's no escape, no more power, only this pain! Silas tightens and tightens his grip. Smanara's body goes limp.

Aileen crashes out of the tunnel-like narrowness, but not into air, into liquid! She still can't see, her heart beats fast, but the liquid feels soft and refreshing on her face.

I can breathe under this water… I can breathe!

Aileen pushes herself upwards, head first, arms to her sides, her whole body reaching up and up and up. When she breaks through the surface, Aileen's eyes take in the silver liquid surrounding her.

I'm in an ocean!

The air smells smoky, like incense, the sky lit up in reds. She hears a rumble. Thunder, yet the water is so calm, no wind. Not far off, Aileen sees land.

Okay, to the shore we go…

Her body on fire, Smanara feels her bones crush as Silas squeezes the air out of her. She dissolves into Silas, and Silas dissolves into Smanara. One thought pounds and blazes, again and again: we are the Rejected Ones, and we shall never have love, only pain!

A piercing scream, a terrifying cry of ages, cuts through the Universe. The Dragon of Dragons opens its wings and screeches, sending out flames of burning sorrow. The enraged creature climbs out of the window to the top of Silas's Tower, perches itself, looks at the Heavens and shrieks in desperateness.

Silas and Smanara are nowhere to be seen.

Sun: On Silas' Shore

Aileen bobbed up and down in the ocean silverness that held her. The two figures standing on the sand with their backs to Aileen glowed in a golden light that reassured Aileen.

Who are they? They're so tall. Are they ASAIRA? "Oh, Wise One, help me, am I inside you? Is this a dream… but it feels so real. Star of Heavens, I don't hear your voice…"

The 2 turned around and smiled at Aileen. The radiant light from that smile melted all anxiousness in Aileen's heart. The woman beckoned to Aileen, who felt magically lifted up and placed right in front of the god-like Beings.

Aileen swallowed and looked up to their faces. She could hardly make out exact features. They were a golden blur, yet the light emitted from the two was warm and loving. Aileen's whole body tingled.

Shimmera said, "You are the Child of the Earth. You come to fulfil the Promise, bearing the Light of the Green Meadow."

The woman's voice sounded like glittering kindness, thought Aileen. "Are you the Star of Heavens?"

"No, we both are Children of the Sun. I am Shimmera, and this is my Beloved, Saul. We hear the Star in our Hearts, as you do too."

Aileen noticed a spark-like vibration all through her body.

"Child of the Earth…" said Saul. "What is the name you go by?"

"Aileen."

"Aileen," Saul smiled. "There is much we do not know. In this, the three of us are alike. We can only trust in our Hearts. We three have been brought to this land of cinders to fulfil the Promise. Yet neither Shimmera nor I know what this entails exactly. For we are lost and incomplete, as all Sun is."

Aileen smelled a wisp of lavender. She breathed it in.

"The Star has a message for us before we encounter the Silver Children and the Storm," Shimmera said. "Do not be afeard, Aileen of the Green Meadow. Soon we shall see with all clarity. This is the Promise!"

Shimmera took Aileen's hand and Saul's.

The Voice of the Star of Heavens invaded the senses of the 3 as though it could be tasted, heard, seen and smelled all at the same time:

Third Message for the Children of the Earth & the Sun

Unconditional Love

You know who You Are

And You know You Are also the Dark One who was rejected:

The Green Man, Pan, the Demon, the Devil, the Darkness, the Witch,

The Temptress, the Mind, the Thought, the Worm, the Snake, the Dragon,

The Body, the Gut, the Dark Cold, the Gelid Snow, the Snow Queen,

The Frozen Heart...

Yes, there must be Circles.

There must be Children of the Earth and the Sun in those Circles.

There must be Animals and Trees and Plants in those Circles.

There must be Darkness and Light in the Circle.

This Circle shall be External and Internal for we are ONE.

The Oneness shall have All of This in it and BE it, too.

The Garden of Mystical Lovers is the Creation, the One Creation.

We are All IT.

Please, let us pay Homage to Milton[1]:

Return to Paradise, Beautiful Dark Noble Lord/Lady, for we miss Thee.

We know the Pain, we know that Terrible Things were done,

But this Refuge, this Sharanam that we Are, is forever Forgiving and Open.

You may come to the Light. You are Welcome Here.

Yes, there is a trembling on seeing You… but something tells us that

You are Not what You seem.

Instead of trembling, I shall dance for Thee, and

You will know who You really Are:

The Light of All Lights.

Jump for Joy, Child of the Earth and Sun!

Breathing in every word the Star had said, Aileen, Shimmera and Saul stood statue-like, silent and timeless.

---

1 The Storyteller

Reader, I am feeling I might add extra information for you: The Star of Heavens makes reference to John Milton, a Son of the Earth from the country of England. He wrote an epic poem called Paradise Lost. This was in the year 1667.

A little before, when the Star says "The Garden of Mystical Lovers," it seems to echo the Persian Son of the Earth from the 13th century, Jalãl ad-Din Mevlana Rumi. His words: "I, you, he, she, we, In the garden of mystic lovers, These are not true distinctions."

☆ PART 3 ✦

The Storyteller

Dear Reader, I have two images to share with you, so let Part 3 be a brief rest while Aileen and the Golden Ones absorb the message from the Star. Then we shall return and, I trust, find out what has befallen Smanara and Silas...

Here is the first image:

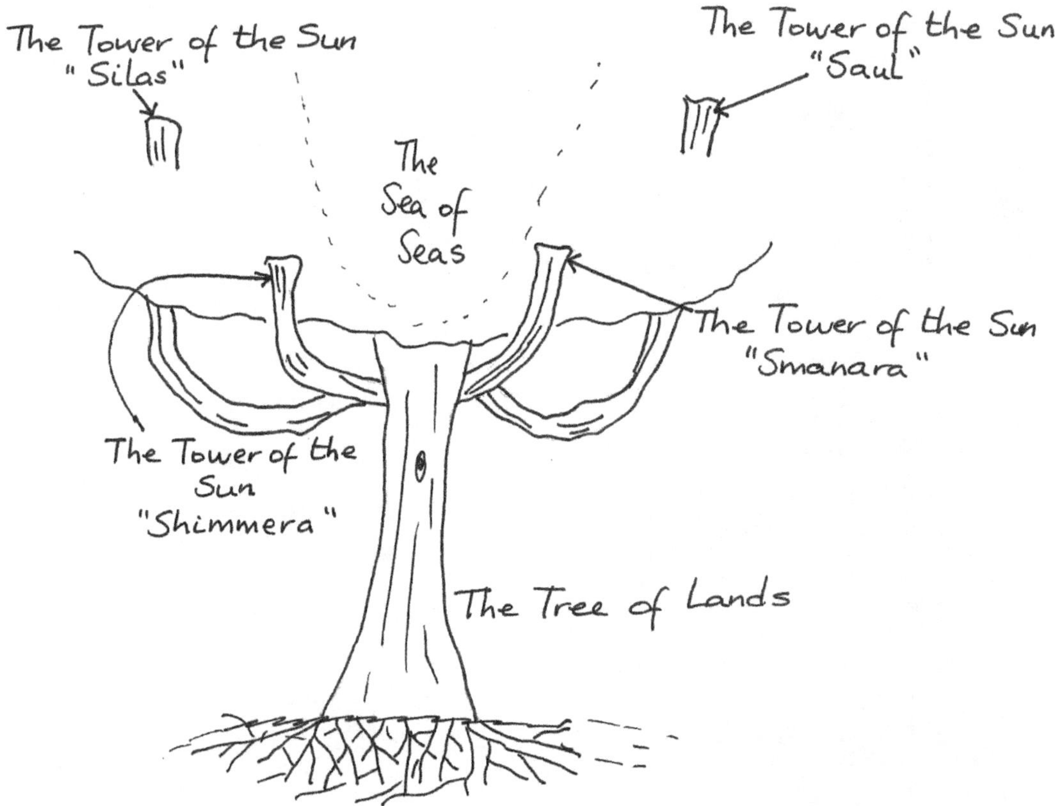

The second image contains the word ASAIRA, or does it say RAASAI? Hmm...

An Ancient Promise

Always Here & Now

Ever Available

I am the Promise of Promises

The Greenest of Meadows

Lie Down in Me

And Rest

✩* PART 4 ✫*

The Star of Heavens

The Tree of Lands sustains & grounds

Rooted in Eternity

The Sea of Seas gives birth & purity

Its Womb, the Nourisher

Out of both

The Child of the Earth comes to the Sun

She is the Light Bearer of the Green Meadow

Innocent & Wise

Surrendered to the Love of the Meadow

Bring the Promise of ASAIRA does she

The Separate shall be united as One

In the Light of Lights

Sun: The Dragon of Dragons

The Dragon of Dragons stopped screeching. Something had attracted its attention: a glowing on the shore of the waters. This luminosity had never been contemplated by the Dragon, and yet deep down, it knew of this goldness.

Aileen shivered. She could see a huge bird of some kind flying towards them… it felt unnameable and dark… full of pain. Eyes wide-open and questioning, Aileen looked at the 2. Shimmera took Aileen's hand and brought her to one side, while Saul placed himself on Aileen's other side.

The Creature looked down from above, suspended in mid-flight. The glow had a mesmerizing effect, and the Dragon of Dragons, instead of attacking anything and everything that was alive, just circled over the 3. The Dragon was a terrifying beast to behold, but in this slow, circling movement, it was elegant and breathtakingly beautiful. An eagle, said a voice inside Aileen.

As the hypnotic circling continued, the Dragon started to hiss. Around the Dragon there were electric silver sparks that shattered the air. Aileen's legs shook and her heart beat faster.

In a sudden movement, Saul rounded the 3 into a circle. "Child of the Earth, Aileen, there is no time to lose. Trust us. You are more than what you seem," Saul said, "Connect to the Earth, to the Meadow, to the Great Tree. Ground yourself."

Aileen swallowed and took a deep breath, closing her eyes a moment. Wise One… Aileen felt the Beloved Tree, his strength and support, his roots becoming hers. Then, copying Saul and Shimmera, Aileen stepped back, and the 3 spread out into a wider circle.

The Dragon shrieked, awakening all Realms, and plunged downwards to land with a thud in the centre of the circle. It whimpered, spitting out greenish fumes, but at the same time it looked alert and positioned to attack.

Time stands still.

Or at least it feels like that to Aileen.

It's like I'm watching a film.
The camera rolls and action happens.
But it's all golden and hazy.
Slow… here and distant at the same time… in slow-motion.

A smell of charred wood.

Aileen moves her head firstly towards Saul and then to Shimmera.

The Dragon hisses. Aileen looks at it.
It's so huge.

Oh my God…
Her whole body trembles.
At the same time, a realisation surfaces:
this is where I'm supposed to be… yes, this is where I'm supposed to be.

"We greet and bow before Thee, Powerful One."

It's all three of us speaking, but our lips don't move.

The Dragon relaxes its head.
Small reddish flames spiral out of its nostrils.

The silent Voice of the 3 speaks again, "Powerful One, what is it that ails Thee?"

The Creature howls.

Inside their heads, the 3 hear a pitiful lament that sounds like a child, "We are the Rejected Ones. We destroy all who come near. We have suffered. We are not loved. Pain is our punishment and our nourishment."

"Mighty Ones," the Voice of the 3 says, "This Sacred Circle knows who YOU are and knows terrible things were done. But Noble Lord, Noble Lady, YOU are welcome here, for we are forever forgiving and open. Join the Circle and bathe in everlasting Peace."

At this, the Dragon of Dragons lifts itself up, "Peace! But we are the Rejected Ones and we have no peace!!" Orange and blue flames fume out of its mouth while it beats its wings. With a look of despair in its red eyes, the Dragon soars up into the air.

The Sea of Seas

Oh Fiery Ones

Here are our Waters

A Liquid Peace

Calm yourselves in our watery embrace

In our circular and swirling ripples

Hear us

Hear us

Fiery Ones

Hear us

The Storyteller

Reader, Friend, if I may call you so, these Magical Signs have arrived now directly for you. In truth, I do not know if Aileen has seen or heard them, but the Signs have insisted to be shown to you, dear Reader, before Part 5.

Let us continue, for the moment is intense.

✩✭ PART 5 ✭✩

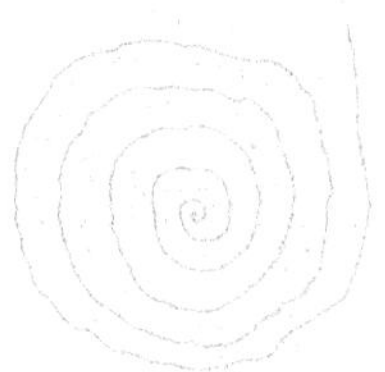

The Gentle Pulsing of the Earth

The Rippling Waves of the Sea

The Sparkling Transparent Molecules of the Air

The Burning Sparks of the Fire

Are Breaths of the One

I am

Rest, my Loves, Rest & Breathe

Sun: The 6

Exhaling green rings of smoke, the Dragon lay exhausted in the middle of the Circle. It had circled and soared in the skies for aeons, it seemed. The Creature felt it had finally given itself to death… if death were merciful enough to come… but it felt only more pain and more oblivion.

Aileen stepped towards the Dragon. To a Being such as the Dragon of Dragons, Aileen was a tiny insignificant creature, an easy prey on good days, but today there was just no more energy.

Saul and Shimmera stood unmoved like silent golden pillars of light.

Trembling, but clear this was what she had to do, Aileen took three more steps, very slowly, and placed herself terrifyingly close to the Dragon. "Peace to You," Aileen said, her head lowered.

The Dragon made a grumbling sound.

Aileen lifted her gaze and saw two desperate eyes fixed on her. Aileen felt a sharp stab in her chest and belly, followed by pain, raw and heavy, stinging and unbearable. Images of the past when her dad had died came in and brought back that same unbearable grief, an unending void. But Aileen had learnt that by standing it out and bearing the unbearable, what had been never-ending grief had metamorphosed into never-ending love. This was no monstrous dragon; it was a hurt animal yearning for love and peace. A single tear rolled down Aileen's cheek as she saw in the eyes of the Dragon the sweetness of her childhood companion, her dog, Big Bear.

Aileen's compassion and her innocent recognition were felt in the most forgotten of places. Something woke up. Through the eyes of the Dragon, something was recognizing itself, something that simultaneously acknowledged itself as Silas and Smanara.

Aileen moved close enough to touch the Dragon's rough, scaled skin.

ALL

shook.

ALL

became still.

From Aileen's mouth came the softest of sounds, whirring words of love, of kindness and respect while, eyes closed and deeply connected to the Great Tree, she stroked the Creature's skin.

ALL

dissolved.

ALL

was created.

A million sulphuric earthquakes shook and jolted the Land of Lands.

The raging heavens opened and released their waters.

A timeless eternity passed.

And yet, no time, no place,

just a restful

Peace,

quiet and vibrant.

Aileen opened her eyes. She saw her hand stroking a silky orange, black and white coat. It was the coat of the most incredible Being she had ever set eyes upon! A tiger! One name came clearly: Tiger Bright. On each side of the tiger stood a tall figure. Enthralled, Aileen looked up at them. They shone brightly, two new captivating gods of another world. Their names, too, appeared in her mind: Smanara and Silas.

Silas and Smanara looked at each other. They were dark and silvery, powerful and magical, and most miraculously, at peace. The joy of this re-found Peace radiated out in a silver hue. Shimmera and Saul walked up to the Silver Ones, and the 4 bowed to each other. They laughed, all four knowing they had found each other at last.

The Goldness and Silverness turned around to face Aileen, the Light Bearer, who wanted to speak but could not. Silver and gold particles spiralled out of Shimmera, Saul, Smanara and Silas towards Aileen. She lifted her hands to her chest, feeling the shimmering warmth of the particles melt into all her cells and neural pathways. Her eyes aglow, Aileen's Heart of Hearts radiated a soft white light back to the 4, who, arms wide-open, received the Light with nostalgic ecstasy.

An ancient knowing rippled up into the 4's and Aileen's awareness that burst out
to form one word on their lips, "ASAIRA!"

The Golden Silver Four, Aileen from the Meadow,
and Tiger Bright,
placed themselves into a circle and became six.

The Sea of Seas arose and roared around the Circle,
a whirlpool of watery solidness.

From under the feet of the 6,
The Tree of Lands raised its four enormous branches
and they became
ONE.

The Flower of Life,
ASAIRA,
bloomed and opened her never-ending petals,reaching out to the celestial Star of
Heavens.

Upheld in Pure Love,
the 6 that were One
floated in eternity.

I am

Here

For I am

You

Know Me

Know Thyself

Breathe Me

Breathe Thyself

Float in Me

The Light Is

Within You

For You

Are

The Light of Lights

The Light of Loves

Here

For Eternity

✰⋆ PART 6 ⋆✰

The Star of Heavens

The Mother

Of All

One Organism

One Precious Flower

To Awaken

ASAIRA

Different Petals

One Soul

To Flower & Flourish

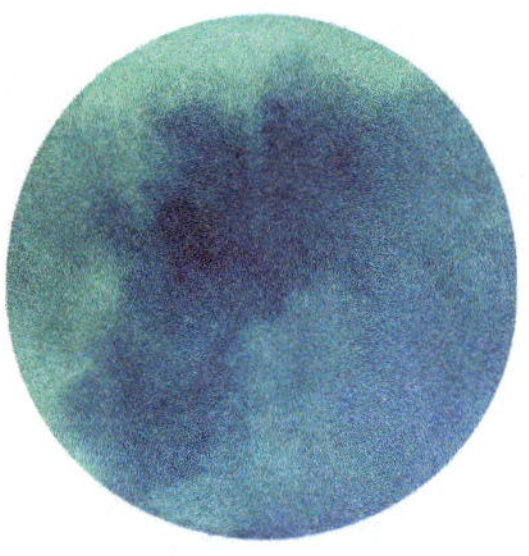

Earth: In the Forest

On opening her eyes, Aileen finds herself back at the feet of her dear friend, the Beloved Tree. With her arms around him, Aileen stays still. Another tear rolls down her cheek. Aileen closes her eyes again while the Tree of Lands whispers sweet rustles into her ear.

The Tree of Lands

Oh, Sweet Child of the Earth

Child of the One Light

Aileen

You have borne

To Sun

The Light from the Green Meadow

And found

The Circle of Love

That breaks all fortresses

This Ancient Wisdom

Ancient & Here

Now

In

You

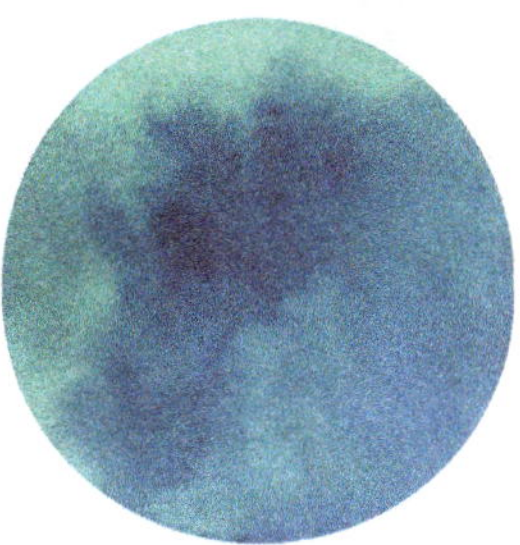

Earth: Into the Meadow

Wow! The Meadow looks so beautiful! And the primroses… so yellow!

Ohh, the poppies are here again! Mmmm… pretty…

The young woman stood still, noticing a breeze come through the grass and gently lift her hair. She smiled. The Meadow looked alive as never before. The green, yellow and red enticed and throbbed… vibrant and bright.

"Bruxa, let's run! Come on! Bruxa, come on, run!"

The white woollen dog could hardly contain her joy and ran and played with her mistress until they could no more! They dropped down onto the greenness and basked in the sun.

The woman cuddled the dog. She loved Bruxa so much that she felt her heart would explode. "Look, Bruxa, I'm laughing and crying at the same time! Hey, we'd better go. It must be dinner time… Bagha must be wondering where we are."

The Storyteller

Dear Reader, while Aileen makes her way home, I have some more Magical Signs to pass on to you. Again, the Signs are especially for You, Reader of Readers, and perhaps for me, as I do feel more and more intrigued by 'ASAIRA'.

The Star of Flowers
ASHRA
S U N
The Sea of Seas
The Tree of Lands
EARTH
The Green Meadow
MOTHER

☆* PART 7 ✦*

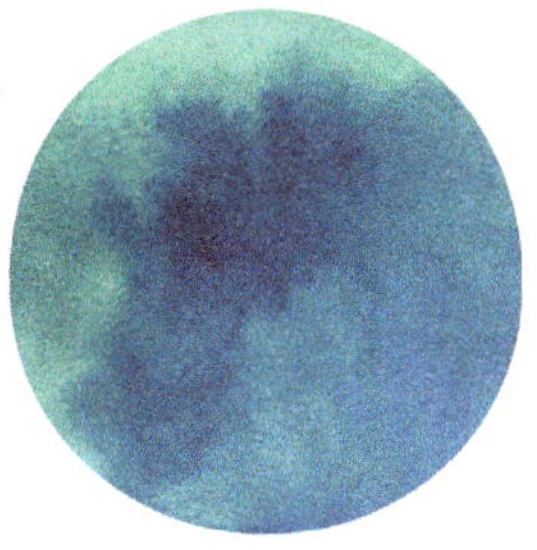

Earth: Home

Aileen and Bruxa arrived at Grandma Becca's cottage just as the sun set. Going through the front door felt like the most heavenly thing in the world. Ahhh… Aileen collapsed onto the sofa and curled her legs under her thighs. Bagha meowed looking rather put out. Ooops! Aileen jumped up and prepared some dinner for both Bagha and Bruxa. Watching the cat and dog dive into their food made Aileen realise she was also starving so she made herself a sandwich and some tea.

Back on the sofa, Aileen sipped her tea, noticing the room around her. Grandma Becca's maple wood furniture looked alive and stood out from the rest: the chest of drawers, the dining-room table with her grandmother's hand-made crocheted doily… so feminine and pretty. Her grandfather, John, was present, too, in all the beautiful watercolour landscapes he'd painted that covered the walls. Grateful, Aileen absorbed the love and connection in the room that made her feel so at home. And just like a confirmation, Bagha jumped onto Aileen's lap and purred away. Bruxa, not wanting to be left behind, sat herself next to Aileen.

It felt like a century had passed since she'd gone to the forest that morning. Flashbacks, images, words, feelings and emotions zoomed up in front of her… juggling to get her attention, she thought. Aileen smiled at the occurrence. She sat on the sofa a little while longer and then stood up, "Okay, that's enough, everyone, for today! I'm worn out. Time for bed!"

Aileen's Notebook

I seem to know things.

It's all inside, yes… and outside.

And really, there's no inside or outside, just this.

This 'this' I can't really understand…

I feel it… It's ASAIRA.

But ASAIRA feels like a 'her'.

I thought 'she' was the Star but she isn't.

ASAIRA is everything, like Mother Nature.

I'm not sure, though…

*Everything that happened was real, at least, I know I had to be there,
exactly that way.*

*But what Saul, the Golden Man, said about being lost and incomplete,
then when he and Shimmera found the Silver Ones, Smanara and Silas,
they knew they'd found each other after much searching.*

*That's how I feel, too, now, that I wasn't complete, and now the 4 and
Tiger Bright, and I think the Star, the Wise Tree…*

they're all inside, as if they're part of me.

I can feel my mind getting confused!

Let me just stop a moment.

I'm going to read the Star's 2nd message again,

The Brilliant Light of All Clarity.

Yes, that's it! It's all there, in those lines.

That was the Promise: uniting the Earth and the Sun,

creating something new. The Garden of Paradise?

And the Star's last message, I can remember bits…

Yes, again: The Garden… The Garden of Mystical Lovers… the Oneness!

*They called me the Light Bearer of the Green Meadow… is the Meadow
the Garden?*

Is the Garden ASAIRA?

ASAIRA

Who are you?

The Storyteller

Dear Reader, the end of this
Story is drawing nigh, but not
quite, not quite.

Part 8 is here.

✰⋆ PART 8 ⋆✶

Child of the One Light

I

Am

ASAIRA

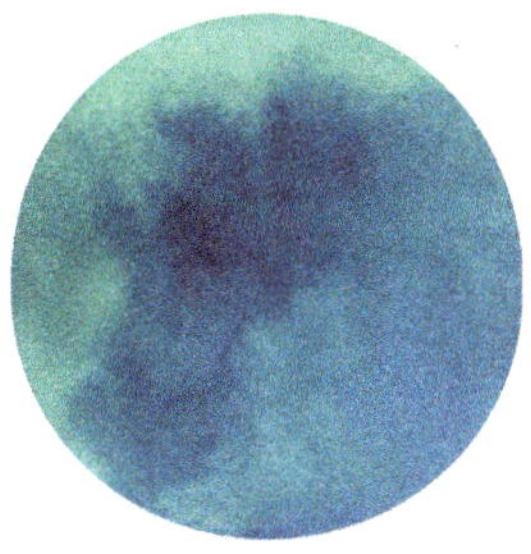

Earth: Meant to Be

Aileen sat up with a start. ASAIRA is the Mother of All. We're all 'Her'! It seemed totally obvious now to Aileen. She lay down again, enjoying the tingling sensation all through her body. ASAIRAAAA… Mother…

Memories of the past poured in, bringing happy-sad tears. All her family had gone; her mum giving birth to her; her dad, Aaron, when she was teenager… then Grandma Becca had passed away three years ago.

Now, deep down, there was a feeling of "meant to be" that spiralled in around Aileen's heart. She'd been happy, despite all the sad moments, and grateful to live in her grandmother's little cottage. In truth, Aileen knew she'd been able to live without a worry and to follow her heart.

Aileen dried her tears and got up.

Everything felt more alive… fuller, was the word that came to Aileen. She had changed. She wasn't the same person anymore.

But I've no idea if I'm supposed to actually do something, so I'll just carry on as normal and see what happens. I'll get shown the way, I know that for sure. "Come on, Bruxa, time for a walk!"

Legends of Old

Here & Now

The Same Story

Retold & Re-Lived

Look around You

For I am

Light of Lights

You shall hear me

In the Stars

In the Seas

In the Forests

In the Fires

In YOU

Still & Silent

I am

The Storyteller

Dear Reader, the Story Told comes to its end!

I am quite amazed at the comprehension of what ASAIRA is. However, for myself, I feel I must reflect more on it.

I hope you have enjoyed the telling and that we meet again. As you must know, every ending is always a beginning! And I can see there could be more for Aileen to discover. At this point, though, the Story ends. We shall see if it transforms later into a beginning. By George, I do love the unknown and endless possibilities the Story brings!

Ah... before I forget... here is the last picture that declares it wants to be drawn.

So I draw!

Farewell, Friend!

Farewell, Child of the One Light!

ASRIA
Light of Lights
Life
The Green Meadow
YOU

THE END & THE BEGINNING

THE 2ND KNOWING OF ASAIRA

THE FOREST OF AARIAS

ASTRAEA
Light of Lights
The Green Meadow
YOU

Never does the Story end

Never does the Story begin

The eyes open

The eyes close

Within & Without

No difference

And yet

The Eternity of the Moment

Deeper than the Deepest Depth

Rooted in the Mother

Solid in the Tiger Warrior

This Never-ending Now

Is the Truest Story of All

Yes, my Child

Listen

Listen

Listen

To the Stillness I am

The Storyteller

Well, well, well... it seems that there is a new beginning! Again I have been caught unawares, and the Story starts without my being completely prepared.

But there is no doubt about it: the Story of Aileen continues!

Ah, Reader, I am delighted to greet you again! Although I must tell you that I notice a certain caution in the air. I do not know the reason. However, what I do know is that I am eager to see Aileen and find out how she fares.

Let us commence, then, dear Reader, if you are ready!

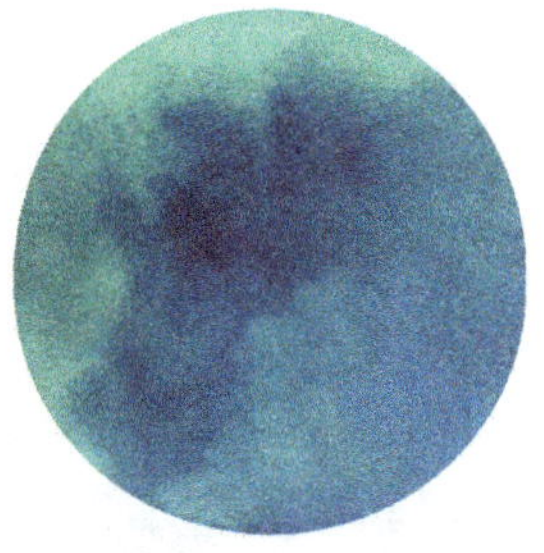

PART 1

Earth: Aileen at home

Aileen stroked Bagha who was purring on her lap. Bruxa, white and lamb-like, slept snuggled at Aileen's feet. Aileen took a deep breath and noticed how the 3 of them breathed together as one. Ah… her sweet companions, her light bearers!

A fire burnt and crackled in the fireplace. Outside the old house, Grandmother Becca's precious domain, it was dark, rainy and windy. Autumn had descended and with it, the feeling of retreat and hibernation.

Aileen pulled her favourite blanket over her shoulders, enjoying its soft lime-greenness. Mmm… Absolute bliss! Aileen sighed and closed her eyes.

Out of the blue, or in this case, out of the dark, there was a knock at the door. Aileen started a little, her eyes opening. It was most unusual to have visitors, especially late in the evening on a cold November night.

A tinge of fear ran up Aileen's spine. Bagha, in a flash of kitty blackness, jumped off her lap, and Bruxa ran to the door.

Knock!

Knock!

Knock!

The Storyteller

Jumping Jehosaphat! What is that?

I am hearing the knocking
myself, right here in my home!
But no, it's not here! It is the
Story! There is an urgency and
my heart is racing... yet, dear
Reader, forgive me, I am lost for
words...

Please give me a moment...

The knocking continues. I am not
ready, but Aileen is at the door
and she will not, cannot wait...

Knock! Knock! Knock!

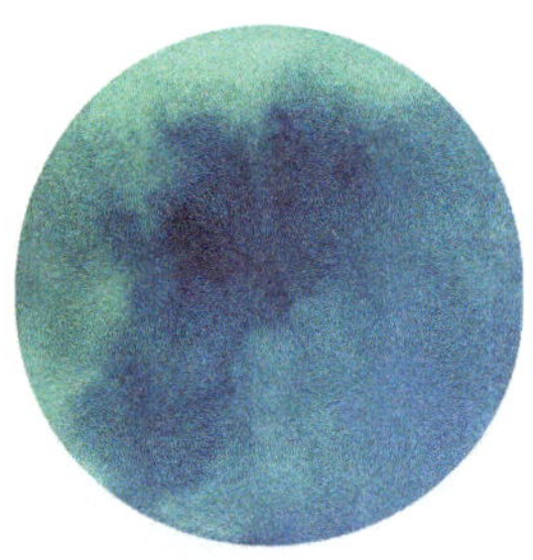

Earth:
At Aileen's Door

Aileen opens the door, very slightly, it's truly dark out there. With her foot, she gently pushes Bruxa back behind her. Bagha is nowhere to be seen.

Aileen's brain tries to interpret what the eyes bring…

A man with hardly any clothes on, holding a spear?! What…??

Their eyes meet.

The man's eyes penetrate into Aileen's brain like two bloodhounds in search of the kill. Her body stops breathing for a second.

Aileen slams the door shut, locks it and pushes her back right up against the door. Her hands shake as they press onto her stomach. Her legs limp, a swirl of fear buzzes up through the throat and deafens her.

Whimpering at her feet, the little white dog's eyes meet Aileen's.

The Tree of Lands

The Ground quakes

She,

The Light Bearer

of

The Green Meadow

meets

He, the Earthy King

of

The Mirrored Forest

Yes

Children of the

One Light

My Roots shall

Sustain ALL

Shall nurture

All Seeings

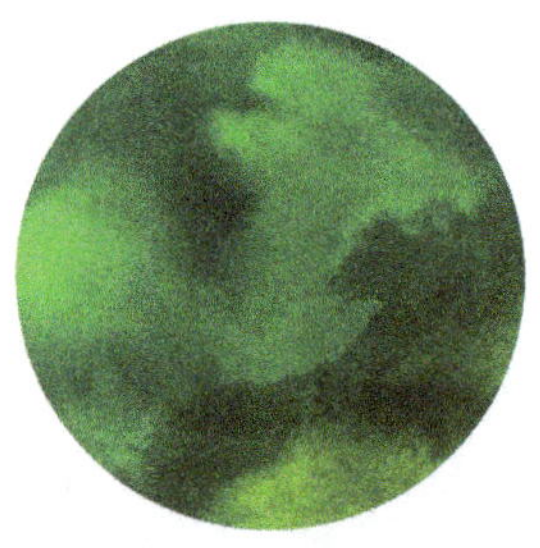

The Forest of
AARIAS: Before the
Great Tree

"Old Ones, hear me! I invoke YOU! I asked for Absolute Wisdom. I wait no longer. For I am the King of Kings, the King of AARIAS, the Forest of Mirrors. Show me the last Mirror of AARIAS for Complete Wisdom and Power! Open and Reveal!"

The tall dark-skinned figure stands firmly as the long-awaited Mirror materializes in the trunk of the Great Tree. "At last!" he says, and the man brings down his head in reverence.

Then, the man who calls himself King lifts his head and looks at the Mirror.

Mirrors of Truth

Rippling Revelations

Of the Eternal Mystery

The Ever-Blossoming **ASAIRA**

Countless Petals

Rare

Countless Names

Unique

AARIAS

Am I

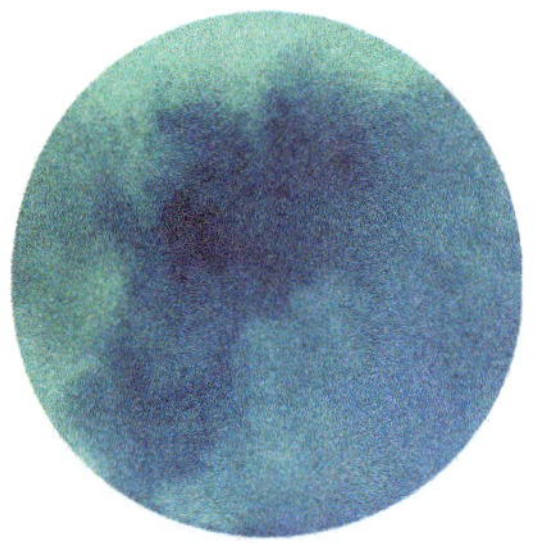

PART 2

Earth: Aileen

Who was that man? What's happening?

I feel dizzy… I need to think clearly… everything's gone cloudy.

Calm down… calm down… it's okay… it looks like he's gone…

Mother, ASAIRA, please help me.

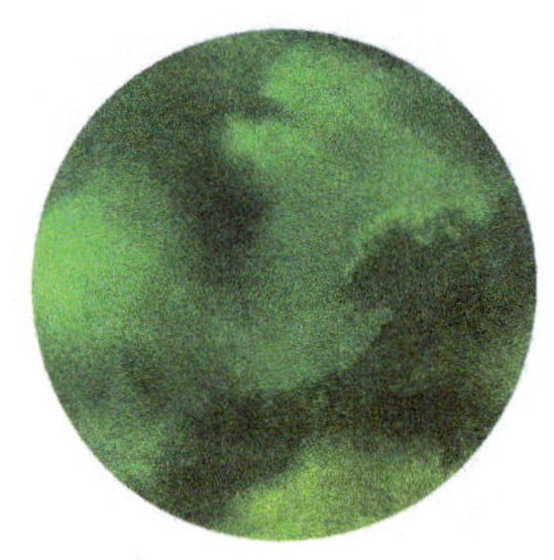

The Forest of AARIAS: UT

I am UT, King of Kings, King of AARIAS, the Sacred Forest of Mirrors. My task is to protect the Holy Forest. No one can enter, for I am its Appointed Guardian. In exchange for this protection, I receive wisdom from the Mirrors. When I am given the Absolute Wisdom, the Mii-Laa, I shall leave the Forest and exercise my right to rule and reign and protect all lands, all life. I shall embody the Mii-Laa, thereby being the Carrier of the Absolute Wisdom.

Today the Great Tree revealed its Sacred Mirror of Truth, the last Mirror of AARIAS! It is the beginning. The Mirror reflected for only a short moment. I cannot understand what was seen, but I sensed it: a weak, fearful energy that is unknown to me. I shall await before the Great Tree again. The Mirror must remain for the Absolute Truth to be seen.

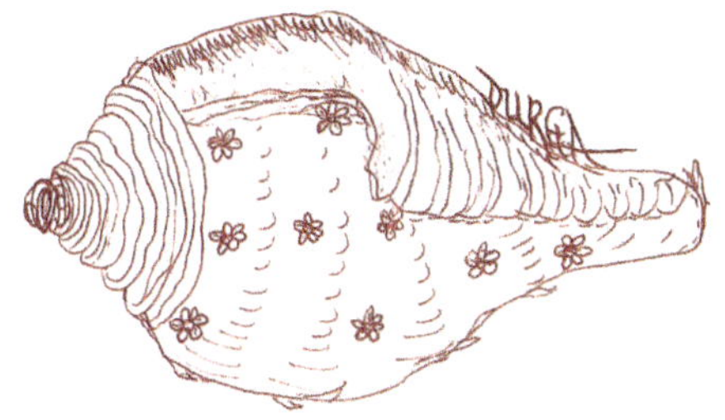

Durga, Glory of the Goddess

I am Summoned

Tiger Bright, hearest Thou?

The drums are sounding

It is the Heart of the Light Bearer

Strength & Valour

Both are aspects of the One Love

I come forth

I answer the Call

The Ancient Call of ASAIRA

The Lamb & the Tiger

One are they

The Warrior brandishes her weapons

Yes!

Tiger Bright, we ride!

The Storyteller

By Jupiter, the Story completely
tells itself! I was not able
to say a word although I wanted
to jump in at various points.
Have I lost the function of
storytelling?

It is most bewildering... the
Story takes over. I hear the
noises that occur and feel the
emotions of Aileen in a manner
that is unknown to me.

And UT, this King... he troubles
me when I hear his words.

Ah, dear Reader, I thank you for
your patience if my storytelling
is disconcerting to you. I am
somewhat rattled at the moment...
I shall rest a little, now that
Aileen seems safe and has gone
to bed. I have an image and some
information to share, but I will
leave it for Part 3.

☆★ PART 3 ★☆

The Tree of Lands

The Roots of Old

The Roots of Now

Entangled

The Mirror shimmers

Oh, what Deliciousness

As my Branches reach out

Oh, Little One, Aileen

The Green Meadow awaits Thee

Come hither with Thy Lamb!

Listen

SHE has arrived

The Fierce Love is Here

She rides the Tiger

Child, canst Thou not hear Her?

Aileen...

Canst Thou not feel Her?

Ah... My Roots

My Branches

I vibrate in Solidness

The Storyteller

Greetings, Friend, anew. I am
more settled now.

Before we continue, I wish to
share the image that has come.
I also need to relate some
information about Durga and The
Forest of AARIAS.

I was curious about the voice
of Durga. Her name rang a bell.
I do not know if you are aware,
but she is a deity from Hinduism,
one of the Earth religions. Durga
is said to ride a tiger. All
incredibly fascinating to me. Ah,
and Glory of the Goddess is also
the title of a religious text
about Durga.

And here is the image:

The Forest of AARIAS

In all honesty, I do not have
many details at this point.
However, what I can say is that
the Forest of AARIAS is not
Earth, nor is it Sun. It is
another realm. And, I assume,
part of ASAIRA.

This forest was unknown to me
until the knocking on the door
entered my world. Nonetheless, it
is somewhat familiar. I cannot
explain this, and just as UT's
words trouble me... the Forest,
too, has a similar effect.

Part 4 is already here, and I
feel the Star of Heavens is to
speak.

So be it, yet I hesitate a
little...

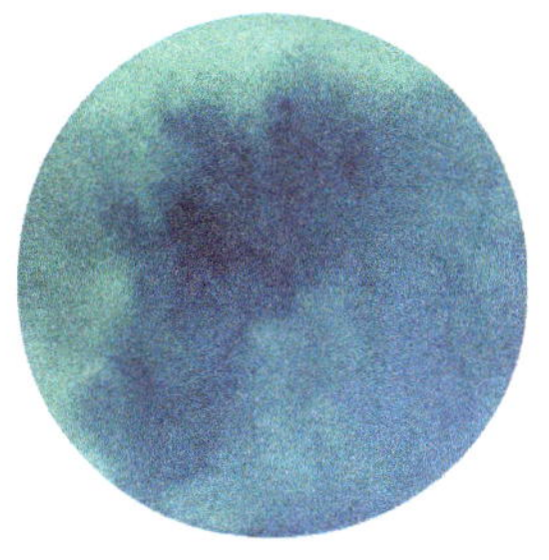

Earth: A New Day

Aileen woke up and saw the sun streaming through the window. Mmm… beautiful…

Last night's torments forgotten and dream-like, Aileen ate a quick breakfast, fed Bagha, got dressed and rushed out with Bruxa into the warm sunshine that reclaimed her.

It was late November. The lands were a myriad of copper-coloured leaves: maroon reds, ochre yellows, burning browns… all dancing and radiant in the sun's playful rays.

Primrose Meadow contained no primroses, but the green glen looked rich in its starkness. The forest of firs invited Aileen and Bruxa, its trees swaying in the cold breeze. Hello Aileen, they appeared to say, hellooo…

The Star of Heavens

I am moved to Sparkle and Speak

I hear a Growling

A Roar

The Fiery Elements

Show their faces

The Sparkles intensify

Glitter & Glimmer

The Children of ASAIRA

The One True Light

I send

♡ Divine Sparks of Insight & Revelation ♡

A Shimmering Messenger Awakens

The Golden Sparks

Dance through the Heavens

Listen & See, Storyteller!

Bear the Light, Aileen!

Children of the One Light

The Storyteller

Child of ASAIRA, I am sorry, but I must go for now. I have lost my bearings. My function of storytelling is not clear. I know not who I am, nor what part I play. Am I really needed? The Story is here with or without me.

In the olden days, without my voice there was no tale. Certainly, I knew it had its own life, and I loved to give myself to its magical impulse, but there were no doubts that I held the reins on something. I had a voice that managed the Story.

But now I can hear the Tiger's roar too clearly... and I am actually part of the Story. Yes, Friend, I am bewildered. This has never occurred to me in my experience as the Storyteller of Old.

Thus, I bow and step down to observe. In her message, the Star of Heavens has said I should listen and see, and this is what I shall do.

I leave you, dear Reader, in capable hands. This, at least, I deeply know.

ROAR!!!

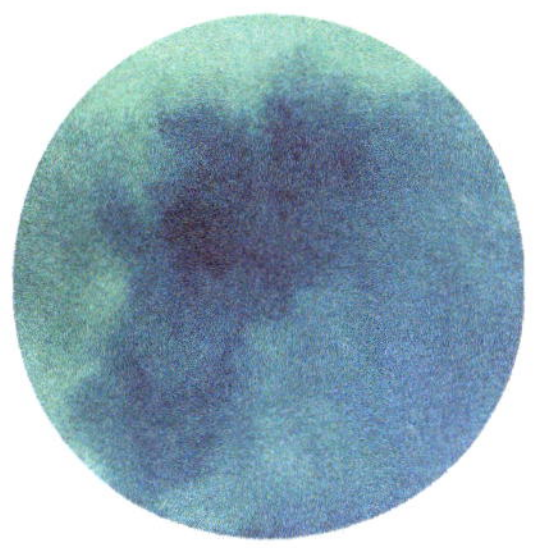

Earth: Into the Forest

What was that?! Aileen stopped in her tracks. Bruxa whimpered. Aileen picked her up and rushed towards the forest to her Beloved Friend, the Ancient Tree.

The fear that had been felt the night before returned and pierced her stomach. The forest was dark, the sun veiled by black clouds, and now Aileen could have sworn she'd heard a wild animal growl.

At last the Ancient One came into view. It had been a while since she'd visited. Aileen bowed. She sat down and leant with her back against the familiar bark. Cuddling Bruxa, Aileen felt into the energy of the Tree.

Oh, Wise One, I think I've forgotten who I am. I know Shimmera, Saul, Smanara and Silas are inside, but it's like I've lost the connection with them and the Star… and ASAIRA… I feel scared and alone…

Aileen noticed the Tree's warmth that poured through into her body. Her back tingled and came alive with ripples of energy running up and down her back. Mmmm… like musical notes came the thought.

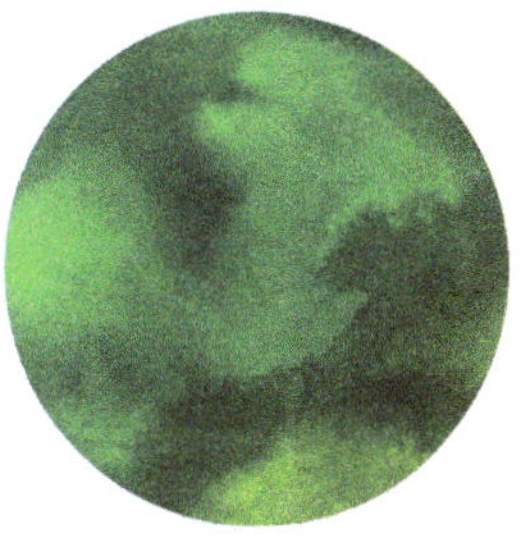

The Forest of AARIAS: Before the Great Tree

UT stood still despite hearing the roar. He gripped his spear, his eyes fixed on the Tree, the Revealer of Truth.

UT knew the Mirror would appear since once it had shown itself, even a glimpse, he knew it would return. And then… the Mirror would stay forever as was customary in AARIAS.

UT felt ready for the Mii-Laa, the Absolute Wisdom that he would be granted through the Great Tree.

♪ "Uuuuu…" UT used his voice and body to emit the healing Sounds of AARIAS.

The Sacred Forest of Mirrors vibrated and shook, shimmering in the moonlight, for here it was always night.

♪ "Uuuuuuuu…"

I am Every Creature

I am the Lamb

I am the Tiger

I am the Spider

The Snake

The Dolphin

See Me in All Creatures

For I Am

I am the Melody of the Universe

I am the Sound of Life

I am the Silence of Love

Sing, Sweet Children, Sing

The Tree of Lands

Storyteller of Old

Where art Thou?

We love Thy Voice

Aileen, Sweet Child

The Innocent Lamb

Be not afeard

Remember ASAIRA

Remember who Thou art

Love is Strong

My Roots nourish Thee

My Trunk supports Thee

My Branches uphold Thee

Bear the Light

Bear the Light

Children of ASAIRA

✩★ PART 5 ★✩

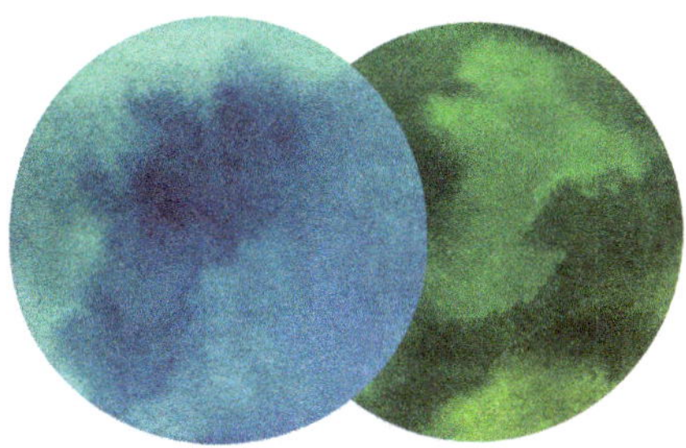

Earth ≈≈≈ The Forest of **AARIAS**

Aileen opens her eyes. She smiles. Her body feels at ease with Bruxa huddled in her lap and the Ancient Tree behind her. The forest is utterly still. A soft goldness glows all around. Aileen lifts her hand to her chest… mmm… the gold is inside too…

UT sits down in front of the Great Tree, lays his spear on the ground and closes his eyes. UT is indeed impressive to behold. He has long dark braided hair that comes down to his waist. Woven necklaces and bracelets made of roots and leaves adorn his arms. He wears a leather loincloth of some sort, and from his waist hang weapons or primitive tools. Barefooted and bare-skinned, UT's body shines with painted symbols and letters.

♪ "Uuuu… Orrr… Ahhh… Ehhh… Eeee…" UT tones and hums, his body and voice a musical instrument. The sounds bounce through the forest.

Aileen hears the vibrancy of the goldness. It flickers and reverberates, golden waves that penetrate her whole body. She puts her lips together. A sound comes out, ♪ "Ummm…"

♡ **Divine Sparks of Insight & Revelation** ♡

Ut Re Mi Fa Sol La

The Sparkling Messenger Arrives

ASAIRA Opens her Petals

The Storyteller says,

Aileen says, **"YES!"** says **UT**.

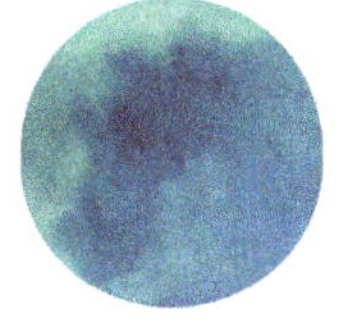

The 3 hear:

ROAR!!

One Yes

One Roar

The Waters Ripple

The Petals Open

For the One Truth

I am the Rarest Flower

Multi-Layered

Forever Giving Birth

In the Spiralling of Life

Of No Beginning & No End

The Storyteller

Yes!

Truly, Friend, you must see me
as fickle and inconsistent or
downright mad. Yet, even though I
find myself quite ridiculous with
my hesitation and doubts, I stand
true to this moment.

I think I see it clearly now.
Of course, I am part of it all.
And undoubtedly, I do have a
function. It is simple. My
function is to tell the Story and
open to it as it comes. By Jove!
I have always known this.

Yes, the Story is affecting
me more than ever before, but
now I could say I am curious
about that, too. The Story is
astoundingly alive! Even though
I was resting, more images were
coming, and understandings. How
can I ignore them?

Also, dear Reader, remember that
YOU play a part in all of this
mystery. Pay attention to the
sounds and signs that you hear
and see.

Let us continue and see what
happens with Aileen and UT.
First, there is an image and some
more Divine Sparks from the Star.

♡ **Divine Sparks of Insight & Revelation** ♡

The 3 shall be the 6 ⸙ The 6 are Spiralled in their Multiplicity

3 Mirrors 6 Reflections ⸙ All Revealed

1st Knowing ⸙ 2nd Knowing ⸙ Unlimited Knowings

☆★ PART 6 ★★

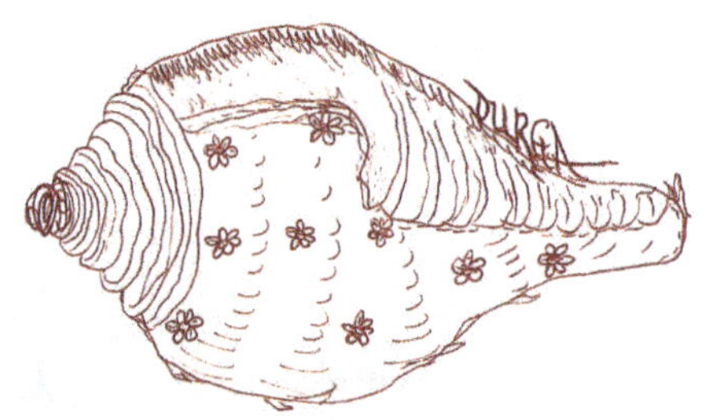

Durga, Glory of the Goddess

Tiger Bright roars

Roar I, too!

I celebrate in my Fierceness

As I brandish my weapons

The Spear

The Dagger

The Bow & Arrow

All lie in the

Flower of Life

Strength of Strengths

For the Children of the One Light

She comes

She comes

Aileen, Prepare Thyself!

UT, Prepare Thyself!

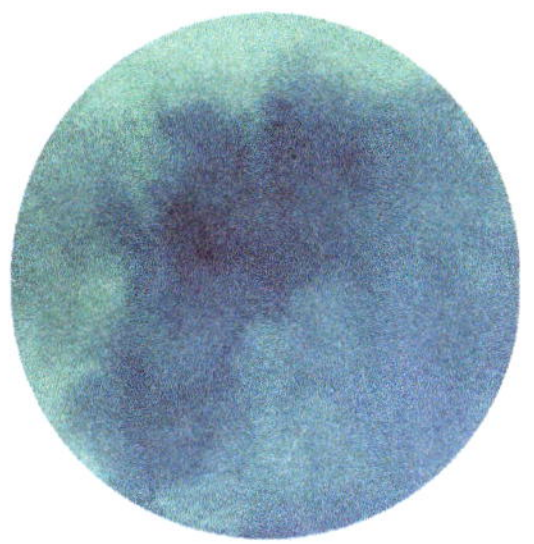

Earth: Back Home

Aileen ran into the house, dropped Bruxa onto the sofa with Bagha and took herself straight to the mirror in the bathroom.

Breathing in and out really slowly, Aileen studied her reflection. Her breath turned into sound, a humming that vibrated inside and around her in a whirlpool of waves. The mirror became a liquid haze.

Aileen's reflection transformed into four timeless faces of silver and gold. The faces spoke in billows of incense, a perfume of remembrance that filled Aileen with peace.

"Aileen, remember me, this is Smanara… remember my Knowledge of Arts, my Fierce Search of Truth."

"Aileen. I am Shimmera. Yes, You are the Golden One, too. Let your Healing Glow shine on all. Remember me!"

"I am Saul. Look at me and know me. Then you know Yourself, Child of ASAIRA."

"Aileen, this is Silas. Take me with you. Feel my Strength, my Force, and know my Discernment. No deceiving can entangle you."

Aileen froze. Someone had just knocked on the door. The moment had arrived!

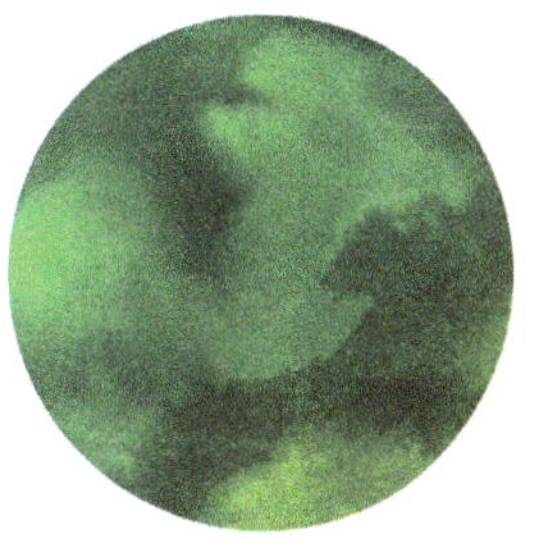

The Forest of AARIAS: Before the Tree

UT brandished his spear. He stood in all his grandness in front of the Great Tree. He was determined not to flinch, never to leave until the last mirror revealed itself.

UT sang the Sacred Notes of AARIAS:
♪ "Re, Mi, Fa, Sol, La…"

The whole forest shimmered in moonlit beauty. All the mirrors that had been revealed joined in with their mysterious no-sounds.

UT cried out, "Open! Open! Great Mirror of Truth! Open! The moment has arrived!"

Knock! Knock! Knock!

The Sea of Seas

We are here to open the Gates of Life

We release the Waters of Reality

ASAIRA

Here is Thy Daughter

We bear Her into Thy arms

For the Son & the Daughter

Are One

The Silvery Liquid Truth

Reveals All in its Sacred Mirror

We Open

We Pour Out

In Ecstatic Relief

The Tree of Lands

Aileen

Daughter of Life

ASAIRA calls you

Open the Door of my Rooted Solidness

Come to AARIAS

Know Thyself

As Lamb & Tiger

As Fragile & Strong

My Branches

My Roots

Support Thee, my child

And Rejoice!

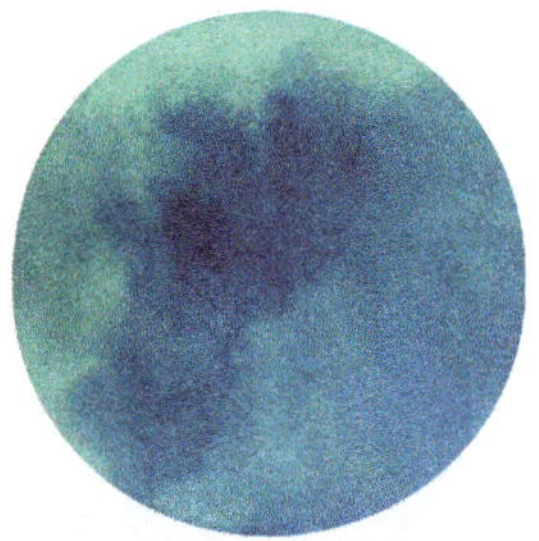

Aileen makes her way to the door.

Bagha and Bruxa are near, sensing something beyond words or perceptions.

Outside, night has returned,

threatening and dark…

Aileen takes a deep breath. "ASAIRA, I'm ready… give me strength and courage."

Trembling, Aileen opens the door.

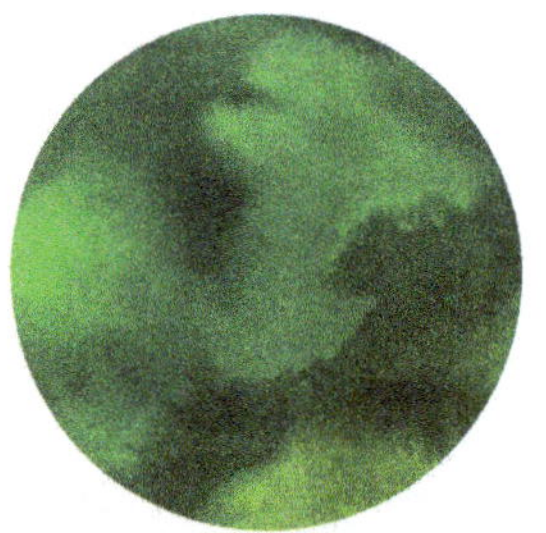

The Great Tree shakes a little, and its aura becomes visible. Deafened by the silent roaring, UT feels his whole body vibrating.

The Mirror of Truth, the last Mirror of AARIAS, reveals itself.

UT sees a bright light that nearly blinds him.

Nonetheless, UT stands fast.

The Storyteller

Dear Friend, everything is to merge... I am nauseous and atremble, but I stand fast, too...

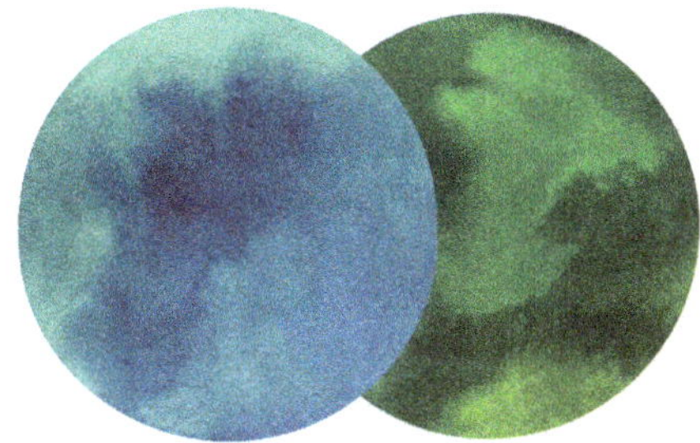

Earth ~≈~ The Forest of **AARIAS**

UT: I feel that strange, weak energy again… what truth can there be in this? I shall not move until I know! Yes… yes… the Mirror begins to show…

Aileen: It's him! It's okay, Aileen, just lift your head and look at him… Come on, you can do this… look!

Both UT and Aileen experience a wave of energetic static through their bodies when their eyes land on each other's. For Aileen, time stops, surrounding her in serenity despite the fearful awe. UT stares in bewilderment.

UT: I do not understand… I do not understand… It is that small pale creature again in the Mirror of Truths… So be it, I shall speak! "Greetings, I bow to You, O Noble Truth. I await the Mii-Laa in Humble Gratitude and Honour."

Aileen: "Sorry… I don't understand your language… shhh, Bruxa, it's okay, shh, stop barking… come here…"

UT: "The Lamb!"

UT knows it's a sign. He steps closer and unwittingly triggers a vortex of movement: Bagha meows and dashes out of the door-mirror followed by Bruxa who jumps from Aileen's arms. Shocked, Aileen takes a step forward while UT stands rock-like in incomprehension and amazement, for nothing ever comes out of a mirror! Aileen reaches out to push the dark figure aside to run after her beloved friends, but when she touches UT, she is deafened by a roaring of sounds, of humming, of words, of vibrations… her body feels pushed in all directions. Aileen faints. UT falls to the ground, too, and feels himself being dragged into the Mirror like a dead animal. Just before losing consciousness, UT notices an anguish he has never, ever felt but has heard of: FEAR!

Nothing is what it appears

A Reflection

A Truth

A Symbol

Only

I am

Absolute

♡ **Divine Sparks of Insight & Revelation** ♡
Flower-Like ❦ **Bird-Like** ❦ **Tiger-Like**
ASAIRA is ❦ **SAIRAA** is ❦ **The 3 are 6**
❦ **The Mirror of Truth**

The Storyteller

I am, dear Reader, breathless and shaking...

I see Aileen... I see her... and I shall share this with you herewith. As for UT, he is a blur, I don't know what has befallen him...

Let us continue, no stopping now...

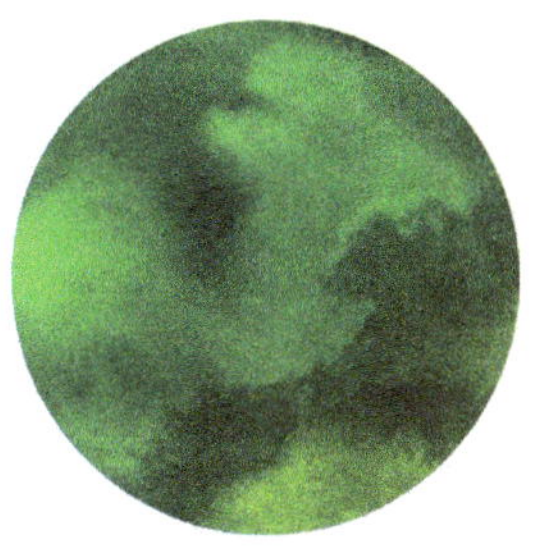

PART 7

The Forest of AARIAS: Under the Stars

Aileen opened her eyes and saw the silver moon. The sky was alive with shining stars. A damp warmness that smelled of recent rain entered her senses, sending a shudder throughout her body.

Aileen breathed in deeply and suddenly realised that she was outdoors, lying on the earth. With difficulty, Aileen got herself to her feet, and like a leaf, she dropped to the ground again. The soft moss, the Mother's green mattress, welcomed the visitor and embraced her. The intoxicating vibration inside and outside of her body sent Aileen to sleep. She dreamt that the Universe sang of green meadows and sacred forests, of ancient times and wisdom… of ASAIRA…

The Forest of Mirrors had never hummed so intensely. The Great Tree sighed and shook while the silent frequency soared through every tree of the forest, dancing in and out of the mirrors.

In delight, the mirrors whispered in sound reflections, "The Promise… The Promise… AARIAS… AARIAS… AARIAS…"

Every Being in the Forest tuned into each other and quivered with expectancy, for such was the effect of having Aileen sleep in the arms of AARIAS.

A vast stillness fell upon the Forest like a silver mist of nothingness, dissipating all motion. Out of the misty silence came three formidable presences. They were wild, of Earth and not of Earth, of Sun and not of Sun, they were beyond realms and time, belonging only to the Mystery.

The Mother's Guardians, Gatekeepers of ASAIRA, placed themselves around Aileen and let their eyes close in patient rest.

Unknown Guardians

Always Present

Guidance from the Mother

They Bring

For they are Her

I am

The Mother

And

The Father

And

The Daughter

And

The Son

I Am

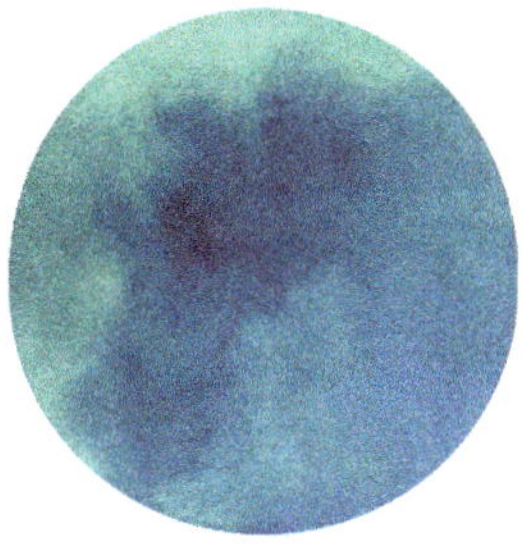

Earth: In the Light

What is this blinding light? My eyes do not open. There is a strange softness in this earth… I am upheld… Is this AARIAS? There is no earthy smell. I do not feel the raw air on the skin. And what is that sickening sensation? All strength has been drained from me… I cannot move. I am blind and trapped. Oh, AARIAS, what has befallen me?

The Storyteller

Images, my Friend, they press on
me to be drawn.

Draw, draw, the Star of Heavens says... but it sometimes feels like an impossible task! Yet, once the image is drawn, I am quite amazed!

I am still atremble at seeing what has happened to Aileen and UT. The images and Divine Sparks merit more attention now, but I cannot stop here... we must go on...

The Storyteller

Hmm... how it rains... what a storm!

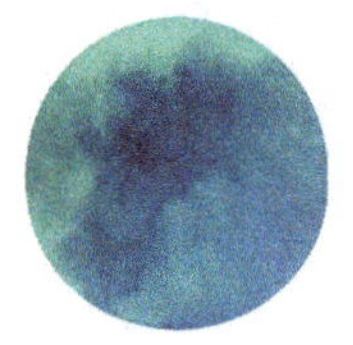

What is that sound?
Dare I open my eyes?
Why do I tremble like
a young pajzcha?

Sound
of
Rain

Oh...
raindrops...
mmm...!

♡ **Divine Sparks of Insight & Revelation** ♡

❧ *Each raindrop awakens from the dreamy sleep*

❧ *The 3 are 6 The 6 are 9 The 9 are 12*

❧ ASAIRASAIRAAAIRAASIRAASARAASAIAASAIR

❧ *Eternal Creation*

The Tree of Lands

O Sleepy Ones

Open thine eyes

Daughter of ASAIRA

Thou ask'st for Strength

Son of the Sacred Forest

Thou ask'st for the Mii-Laa

The Wisdom of Old

Awaken!!

Hear the Thunder

As my Roots unearth

The Strength of Strengths

Hear the Lightning

As my Branches gather

The Wisdom of Wisdoms

Water!

Earth!

The Fiery Tiger

The Storms of Storms

Aileen!

Open thine eyes

And

The Rest is Done!

The Storyteller

The most tempestuous of storms is raging outside!

But I see you already know.

How is it being the Storyteller that I am the last to know? This is a mystery, by George. This is a mystery.

But I shall not lose myself in ponderings that lead nowhere. I have declared my readiness to exercise no control, to have no knowledge, and if need be, which appears to be the case, I shall also be a character in the Story!

Here is Part 8, dear Reader!

☆* **PART 8** *☆

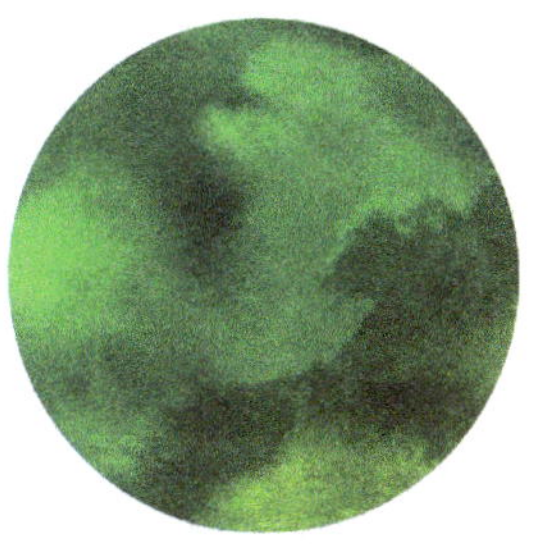

The Forest of AARIAS: Aileen Awakens

Aileen opened her eyes. She licked the raindrops from her lips and took in the moist smell of the forest. Is this a dream?

The rain stopped as unexpectedly as it had started. Aileen sensed two figures, one on each side of her. There was a breathing… hearts beating… Bruxa? Bagha? But Aileen knew that the two powerful presences were larger than her little dog and cat.

Aileen took a deep breath, sat up and looked to her sides. Two incredible creatures met her eyes: Tiger Bright! And a wolf! Ohh, what a beauty! The wolf's silver coat sparkled as the words 'Wolf Moon' and the image of the fullest of winter moons entered Aileen's heart, "Tiger Bright and Wolf Moon."

Hearing their names, the two Guardians of Truth, Gatekeepers of ASAIRA, approached Aileen. She stroked their silky coats with awe. Then, a sound like a flutter of wings… something had landed very gently on her right shoulder! As she turned to see what it was, Aileen froze. There were four creatures right in front of her! But… no… it's a reflection! It's a mirror!

Slightly dizzy, Aileen stood up. The winged-being flapped to keep its balance on Aileen's shoulder. Tiger Bright arched his back a little. Wolf Moon moaned. The sounds and soft movements of the animals soothed Aileen while she absorbed her surroundings. It was a forest… full of mirrors! The mirrors were inside the trees, and Aileen knew they reflected a magical truth. No words, though, could express the truth she saw reflected in one of the mirrors now: Tiger Bright, Wolf Moon, the Whitest of Owls and the most enigmatic creature of all, herself! Yes, it was her, Aileen, but stronger… earthier… a 'mythical creature' was the expression that rushed in!

Aileen moved towards the mirror. Her body felt like the enormity of the Universe and the brightness of the Stars. A tingling energy lifted each leg, each movement slow and precise. Aileen floated through space and yet she felt solid, a rock of the earth.

The Mirror glittered in the moonlight.

The Storyteller

Oh, my Giddy Aunt! I can feel a tingling, as Aileen puts it, in all my being. I am flabbergasted, to say the least, but overjoyed to see that Aileen is safe.

And where is UT, you may be asking? I could not tell you before, dear Reader, for I knew not. I had a few images of what he was feeling, what he was experiencing, but they were not clear.

Now, I do have the clarity. I can see both Aileen and UT, their Story rising into my senses with great force. However, they must wait just a little. Information has arisen about UT and the Forest of AARIAS that I feel is imperative, knowing that Aileen is there.

UT and the Forest of AARIAS

UT is the Guardian of this enigmatic place called AARIAS, the Mirror Forest. In AARIAS it is always night. No daylight, no sun and the absence of many other things that we, as knowers of other realms and Earth, might assume exist in this forest. This forest is unique and magical, we could say. Just as we learned of Sun, the laws of time and space are altered in AARIAS. There is much to be described.

The Forest of AARIAS: A World

- There is no daylight or sun.

- There are hundreds of tall trees.

- It is always night and the trees appear grey and monochrome... There are few colours that can be appreciated due to the darkness.

- There is a moon that provides moonlight.

- The temperature is always warm and moist.

- There is a river.

- There is an enormous tree in the centre.

- There are no flowers.

- There are few living creatures except for the trees. Most of the creatures that exist are insect-like, so minute they cannot be seen.

- There is one animal that lives near the river. It is boar-like, and UT calls it a pajzcha.

- It sometimes rains.

- There are no people or anything similar to a human Being, only UT.

- All trees potentially have a mirror in their trunk that reveals wisdom and truth. Some mirrors are visible and some are not.

- The forest vibrates at an extremely high frequency akin to musical sounds. There is a sense of trees that sing, a music in the air, a mesmerizing beat in the heart...

UT's Function and Place in this Forest World of AARIAS

- He knows himself as the appointed guardian of the forest who has always lived in the forest.

- He has no memory of childhood and can only remember being in the forest. This is not a source of sorrow for UT since he has no knowledge of what childhood is.

- He is ageless, immortal. He has no knowledge of ages and aging, of youth or old age.

- He has always been alone. He has no knowledge of women or relationships with others of any kind.

- His metabolism: he does not need to eat much but when he does, he hunts a pajzcha. He is strong, stronger than any Earthling. We could even describe him as some sort of god-like warrior, to get a sense of his physicality.

- As time does not exist, and all is as it always has been for UT, he has no knowledge of boredom and is dedicated in his function of protector and guardian of the forest. This is his duty and life.

- UT has one obsession: to receive the Mii-Laa, the Absolute Wisdom. He knows himself as the King of Kings and feels king-like in his protection and guardianship of AARIAS. He understands and affirms that he is the King of the Mirror Forest.

UT's Thought Processes

UT is a Being who tends to obsess in spite of a profound wisdom that also envelops him. Everything he knows comes from the forest. Now and then, a mirror reveals itself and talks to UT. Sometimes there are images, sometimes words. The message is not always clear, but UT interprets it all as best he can. In this manner, he has come to the conclusion that he is a king and that he is to protect the forest. UT has been shown images of other realms and other Beings, but UT cannot comprehend what he sees... these mirrors in particular are a haze to him. However, UT has understood that on receiving the Mii-Laa he will have the wisdom to be the king of those places, too, and all will be clear.

One of the trees told UT a story called the Legend of the Lamb. It was accompanied by beautiful images of the creature called the Lamb. These are some of the words that UT heard, which he now treasures and cherishes, "When the Lamb appears, the Great Tree will lift the Mii-Laa and offer it to the Appointed One to become the Carrier of the Absolute Wisdom, and all mirrors shall reflect the Truth."

Since hearing these words, UT has craved the Mii-Laa. He has awaited before the Great Tree, singing the sacred Notes of AARIAS. Until now, UT had been ready, determined, convinced of his truth and his world...

Reader, it is curious, as I explain about the forest and UT, I feel that strange yearning again. I have to ask the Star... it troubles me.

But I keep my word and continue on... both UT and Aileen can wait no longer.

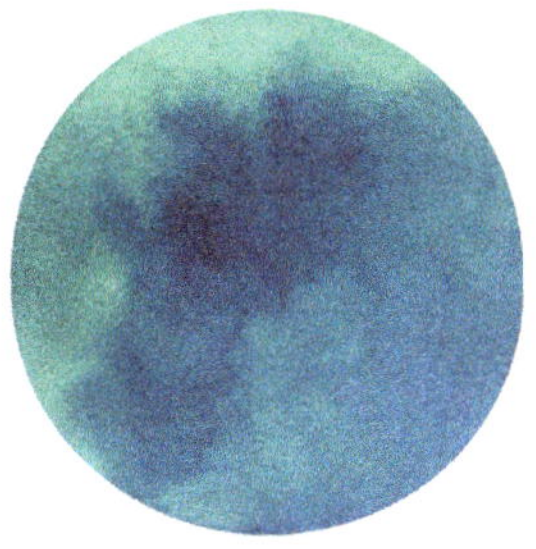

PART 9

Earth: UT Awakens

Straining, UT opened his eyes. The absence of the natural darkness he was used to caused blindness and pain. It was still very bright, but at least the tapping sound had subsided.

The sensation was of complete incomprehension; UT just did not have the words to describe his surroundings. A sickly nausea crept into UT's cells. His body tightened and his head pounded. UT felt incredibly small.

A tear, followed by others, trickled down the immortal warrior's cheeks. What is this? His fingers touched the liquid. What is this water that comes from my eyes? Where am I? Why do I tremble? AARIAS! Great Tree! Hast Thou forsaken UT?

UT is a wise and ancient creature, a god, a warrior, but his experience is truly limited. He has never known anywhere else except the Mirror Forest; he has never known fear, and he has never cried or knows of the existence of tears. Now, this king of kings is in another realm: a realm in such opposition to his, a realm so divergently sparkling and vibrant in colour and forms that he is lost.

UT lay stiffly on Aileen's homely patchwork quilt, his head tense on the feather pillow. The curtained window which opened to views of green trees and blue sky, together with the walls covered in brightly coloured flowers, pierced through his eyes. He clenched his fists.

UT's eyes closed in search of the darkness.

The Light

The Dark

One

Are

They

Embraced

In

My Arms of Vastness

The Star of Heavens

Ah...

How I delight in the Glittering Sparks!

Children of the One True Light

Hear Me & See Me Now

I give You these Wondrous Words

They shine so

A Beloved Son of ASAIRA spoke them once

And then they never left

Spiralling & Enveloping for All Eternity

Storyteller!

UT!

Aileen!

Reader!

Children, Hear!

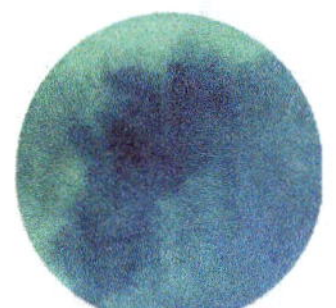

As UT lay with his eyes closed, he heard a sweet melody. The words swirled into his body, and he relaxed a little.

UT fell asleep.

The Storyteller woke up in amazement. Caliban's speech in The Tempest... Shakespeare! By Jove!

Suddenly, the Storyteller felt very small and was most afeard, despite the soothing words that advised the contrary.

Aileen continued staring at the mirror. She was completely enthralled.

In the distance, a woman's voice sang calming words that soothed any lingering fear about what she was seeing.

The Storyteller

Who are you?

Who are you that has written 'The Storyteller woke up in amazement.'? It was not I, and yet I am the Storyteller! This is too much!

What is happening? Reader? Is it you? Or are you the Star?

Alas... I become lost again... confusion and fear overtake me...

All-Seer

Greetings all that hear this voice

I am

All-Seer

As my name surely foretells

I see and hear this Story

All characters

All voices

Including my own

Including the Beloved Storyteller

I have

The power to speak and hear

To All

To the Storyteller

And

To You, Reader of Readers

For I am in essence the Star of Heavens

When All-Seer is summoned

I travel the Realms and Dimensions

In diverse forms

Loving the Earthly Elements as well as the Starry Shimmers

We are One

All is One

ASAIRA is

Never forget

You, Reader,

Are

Of the Green Meadow, too

Of ASAIRA

You have

The power to see and hear me

But now

I must address

The Storyteller of Old

"*Storyteller... Honourable One... Can you hear me?*"

"Yes... Who are you? Are you the Star of Heavens?"

"*Essentially yes, but no, my friend. I am called All-Seer, and soon you shall see the words on the page. I have and am the power to speak to you and all the characters of this Story and the Universes of ASAIRA. Noble One, you have declared the readiness to know nothing, to be another character of the Story if needs be. Hence, All-Seer is here to answer your call. You have nothing to fear, rest thee assured.*"

"I do not comprehend and feel lost and perplexed. Yet I know that when
I listen to the pondering, confusion overwhelms me!"

*"When you ponder, as you say it, you are a small creature, and nothing can be understood.
But, you are a Child of* ASAIRA... *and you have never known what was to befall. There is no
confusion when this is remembered. This is the True Wisdom you have always comprehended,
Storyteller of Old, is it not so? Dear One, jump for joy! These are glad tidings I bring to you. For
we are all characters of a story! We are all sweet expressions of a unique dreamer, the One True
Character,* ASAIRA. *You are much more than the Storyteller, can you not see?"*

"I feel a relaxing... The eyes want to close and rest..."

"Rest, Son of ASAIRA, *rest. The Green Meadow Is. The stories play and play... showing the path
to* ASAIRA, *the Mystery of Mysteries. You shall continue with the storytelling when you see fit
and choose it. This Story is your Story, more than ever before, so you must trust that we are
here to aid you. I, All-Seer, shall continue the telling while you rest. And if needs be, the Story
can tell itself, for it will always do whatever is necessary to be told and re-told."*

Reader

Rest, too

Writer

Rest, too

Let us Rest

In the All-Seeing

Of Ourselves

Of

ASAIRA

☆ PART 10 ✦

"Be not afeard; the isle is full of noises,

Sounds, and sweet airs, that give delight and hurt not..."

"Be not afeard; the isle is full of noises,

Sounds, and sweet airs..."

"Be not afeard; the isle is full of noises..."

"Be not afeard..." "Be not afeard..."

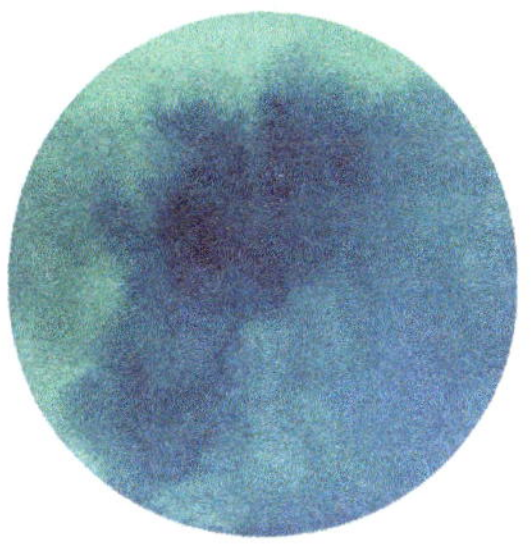

Earth: Be not afeard, UT

UT dreamt of the realms where he would be king on acquiring the Mii-Laa. It was as before, before the revealing of the Mirror of Truth. UT felt strong, the protector of all sacredness… a Warrior King!

A small lamb appeared in the dream. UT's heart beat faster, and the body gripped. Pain and fear attacked without mercy, and the dream became a nightmare. UT's eyelids flickered. His body turned from one side to the other.

Amidst the dread, a glittering voice arose, the same voice that had sent him to sleep, "Be not afeard, UT, Be not afeard…"

UT opened his eyes; it was dark. A sense of relief enveloped him, but when he noticed the softness underneath, UT knew he was still in the same nameless place.

This time it was different, though; he could open his eyes without being blinded. UT decided to move. He got to his feet. He felt exhausted and faint… both, yet again, new and incomprehensible sensations for this King of Kings.

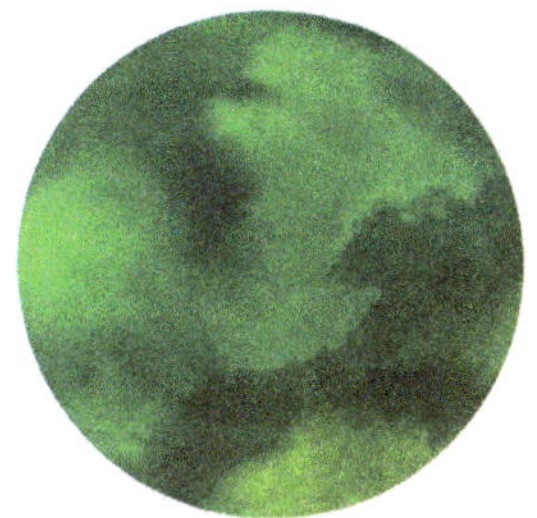

The Forest of AARIAS: The Arrival of SAIRAA

Aileen had no idea of who she was and did not care. She turned from the mirror and looked at Tiger Bright and Wolf Moon. She recognised them from ancient times and bowed.

The tall mythical figure who had been Aileen glanced towards her shoulder. She tilted her head in reverence. The Owl blinked, and the name Owl of SAIRAA spiralled in.

At this, SAIRAA lifted her head, smelled the musky woodiness of the forest and started to run. In mirrored instinct, Tiger Bright and Wolf Moon sprang to their feet to run on each side of their long-lost SAIRAA, while the Owl flew up into the sky above them.

SAIRAA, once Aileen, ran through the forest, fast and nimble. Her hair, intricately interlaced with tiny beads and corals, flew up behind her as SAIRAA ran faster and faster.

The ecstatic joy was such that it cannot be justly described here: to feel the cool wind in her face, to see the shimmering moon above her, to sense the warm earth under her feet, to experience the Mother's Guardians running and flying beside her, to know the no-thought, the no-identity… and to truly be the Running, to be the Wind, to be the Moon, to be the Earth, to be the Tiger, the Wolf and the Owl… Yes! Yes! Yes! cried the Ancientness and ran and ran.

If at that moment there had been a witness from the Earth Realm, they would have surely said, "I have seen a goddess, a warrior, a Queen of Queens!"

I am the Spiral

I am the Warrior Spirit

I am the Gentleness of the Lamb

I am the Ferocity of the Tiger

The Joy

The Love

The Silence

Peace of Peaces

I am

Endless Words of Truth

A Musical Symphony of Heart

Vast Plains of Stillness

I shall never be comprehended

Thus

Sweet & Awesome Flower that I am

Petals forever opening

In this Eternal Now

That I

Am

Utttt. . .
Reeeee
Uuuutt. . .
Faaaaaa
Miiiiii. . .
Laaaaaa
Solllll
Soooooll. . .
Ommmmmmmmmmmmmmmm. . .

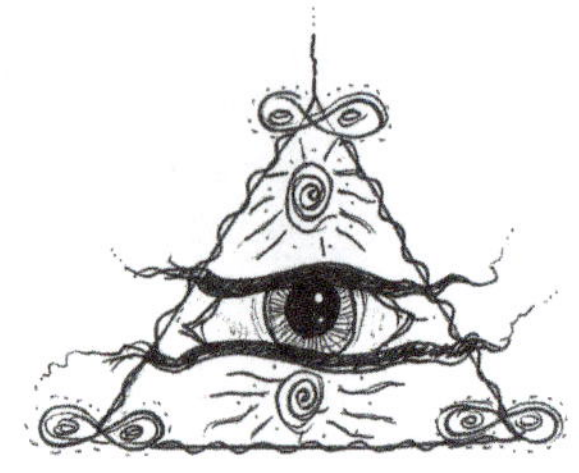

All-Seer

Hear the Sacred Sounds of the Universe

They vibrate in the Hearts

The One Heart of ASAIRA

Sing & Hum

All opens freely

And the Joy

And the Love

And the Peace of Peaces

Vibrate in Swirling Unison

Mmm...

It is truly

The Delight of Delights

I shall hum in the ears of the Storyteller

I shall sing in the heart of SAIRAA

I shall pound in the belly of UT

Ha! Ha! Ha!

All is set

The Wheels of Life

Are set

For Freedom shows her Awesome Face

Ha! Ha! Ha!

PART 11

Earth ⸙⸙ The Forest of AARIAS ⸙⸙ Other Realms

UT walks around Aileen's house. Who can know what he really feels as he sees the rooms, the objects, the walls, the doors, the fridge, the food…? UT is clearly afeard, but he is decidedly more relaxed in the fear. The softness intoxicates him. He yawns. His hands want to touch everything. What's this? He's shocked at the sudden brightness, the absence of the comforting greys of darkness! There's a moment of panic. But then he realises he can bring about and take away the blinding shock! UT smiles for the first time.

Durga laughs while she runs alongside SAIRAA. Mmm… Yes! Yes! Feel the Strength, Daughter! Tiger Bright roars in raging confirmation.

The Storyteller sleeps. In the dreams, trillions of insights and images appear and disappear until there are no more images, no more insights… just emptiness. The Storyteller wakes up and lies wide-eyed on the bed.

SAIRAA stops by the river. She crouches, looking all around her. Then, she lies down on her back in the mossy earth. Content, SAIRAA lets the sounds of an ancient language flow out of her:

"SAIRAAAAAA...

SAIRAAAAAA...

Under the Moon

The Goddess sings of Joy

Free is She

Free is She

Free is She

Under the Moon

The Goddess sings of Joy

Free is She

SAIRAAAAAA..."

All-Seer chuckles. He gazes on the Realms and sees the petals of ASAIRA opening, as indeed they are always doing.

The Tree of Lands

I hear the music

The music of AARIAS

My boughs revel

My branches delight

My leaves sing

In Celestial Earthly Symphony

Daughter of ASAIRA

See the Strength of the Love

Son of ASAIRA

Free thyself from thy self-appointed prison

I await the Two

For they are One

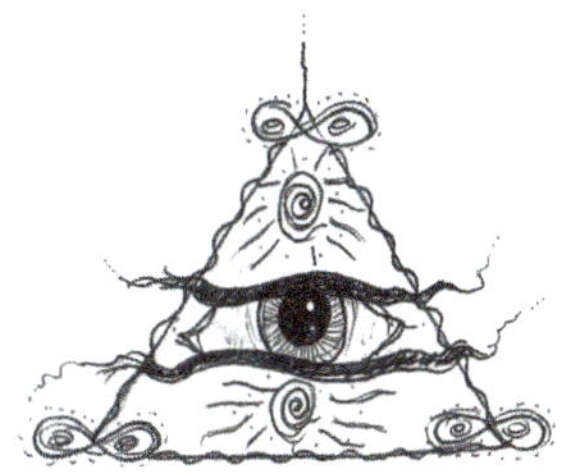

All-Seer

I see that the Storyteller will soon return.

Meanwhile, I continue the Telling.

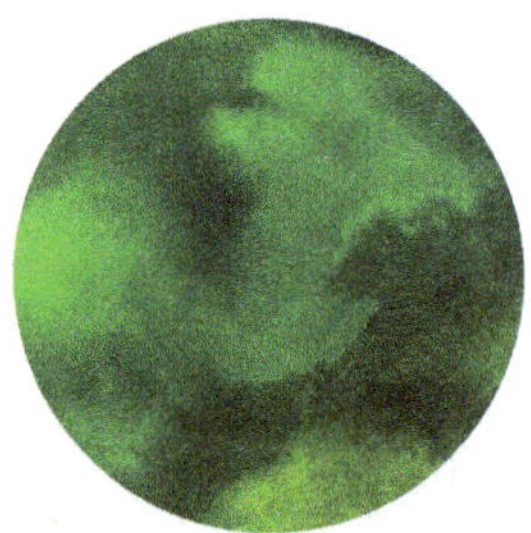

The Forest of AARIAS: SAIRAA the Wildness

SAIRAA felt the wildness spin inside of her. She got up, then knelt and drank some silver water from the moonlit river. From one of the tallest trees, the Owl of SAIRAA hooted.

Tiger Bright and Wolf Moon turned and stared towards a herd of pajzchas, the boar-like creatures of the Forest of AARIAS. The pajzchas were feeding on the moist roots and bracken that grew near the river.

The Wildness jumped back onto her feet. All eight eyes fixed their attention on the herd. The pajzchas smelled the threat and lifted their heads; a loud huff confirmed the danger, and they ran into the trees.

SAIRAA felt the pull of the prey. She looked at the bow and arrow that hung from her waist… and smelled the fear that came from the herd. Wolf Moon, her head down, took a step closer towards the warrior. Tiger Bright, stone-like, inhaled and exhaled, his nostrils flaring.

The Owl met the Goddess' eyes as SAIRAA looked up towards him. A knowing of ages arose in the eyes of the 2, stronger and older than hunting and prey, more ancient and magical than fear and chase. The Wildness of the Source smiled. She let out a laugh that sounded of woodlands and silver, jingles and earth, and crouched to pass her hands over the silky softness of the Wolf and the Tiger.

Releasing waves of safe-being, the Forest recommenced its tingling melody. The moon shone more brightly, full and round in the remembrance of another time. Slowly, the pajzchas returned to the riverside to dig up some more delicious roots.

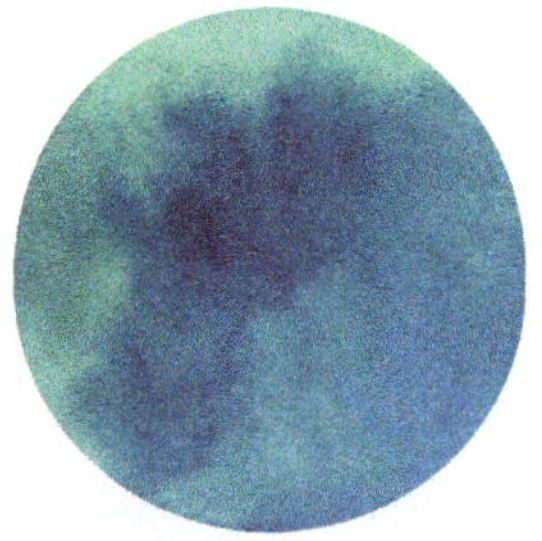

Earth: UT the Innocence

UT felt the weakness rise up in his body when he lay down on Aileen's sofa. His heart, though, pounded less.

On the sofa, there was a blanket. The colour was a lush green that poured into UT's eyes. He placed his hands cautiously on the soft, mossy object… yes, it is good! He brought the blanket to his face. As he smelled the softness, UT let his skin be touched. Ohh… his body trembled and tingled.

A tear rolled down UT's cheek while the comforting words returned, "Be not afeard; the isle is full of noises, sounds and sweet airs, that give delight and hurt not…"

UT realised in the deepest part of himself that these sensations, this sickness, this weakness, were not the evils he had thought. This was a Gift. He could not understand it yet, but began to care not, such was UT's timid delight as he placed the olive green blanket around him.

UT smiled the smile of an innocent child and closed his eyes. Everything smelled so sweet. He fell asleep and dreamt of olive green blanket lands. In the distance he could hear, "The Green Meadow awaits Thee… The Green Meadow awaits Thee…"

The 2 are 1 ୯ঀ The 1 is 6 ୯ঀ The 6 are 1

୯ঀ The Son tastes the Daughter & The Daughter tastes the Son

To See the 1 Truth ୯ঀ The Tiger & The Lamb ୯ঀ The Lamb & The Tiger
୯ঀ Is the Protection ever needed

For ASAIRA IS ୯ঀ The Ever-Protector ୯ঀ The Ever-Giver ୯ঀ The Ever-Bestower
୯ঀ The Ever-Flowering Life of Lives

☆ PART 12 ✶

The Storyteller

Dear Reader, allow that I address thee in an ancient lore that I much cherish.

I thank thee for thy patience.

I realise how confusing this may be to have the Storyteller be part of the Story! Or perhaps not! Perhaps it is just I that am confused.

But the rest and sleep have aided me, and All-Seer and the Star guide me. I am grateful.

The Story has always been mysterious. Now a new mystery has shown its enigmatic self: I am intertwined in the Story.
I am undoubtedly another character as well as a teller. I am also curious to know why. What is to be revealed?

I shall be resting for a short time more... I still feel a shakiness that I cannot describe. However, I shall return soon.

In Gratitude, I bow to Thee, Friend.

All-Seer

The Resting

It is needed

It is the Cycle

In the Wave of Creation

ASAIRA closes Her eyes

The Storyteller rests on his bed

SAIRAA lies under the Great Tree

The Three Gatekeepers doze at SAIRAA's side

Aileen floats in empty space

UT sleeps enveloped in green softness

And You, Reader, Child of ASAIRA

Taste the Still Quietness

The Resting

For it is the Calm before the Storm

The Storm of True Seeing

All-Seer sees the Peace

And merges

In its Deliciousness

The Sea of Seas

We feel the Rousing

The Roar & The Bleat

The Waters stir

It is time to give birth

We Open

ASAIRA

Let

The Waters

Be

Freed!

Let

All

Be

Freed!

☆* PART 13 *☆

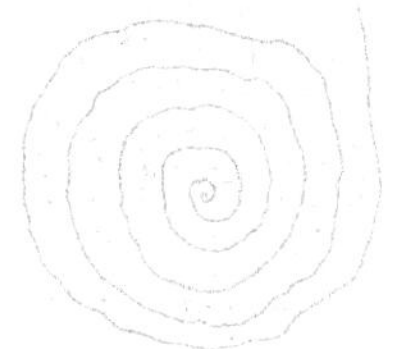

It is the Story of Old

Here anew

Can you see, Children of the One Light?

Open your eyes

Feel the Strength of the Love

I am

Feel the Gentleness of the Love

I am

Earth   The Forest of AARIAS

Both UT and SAIRAA opened their eyes. For UT, daylight dawned, and for SAIRAA, the endless night continued. Flashes of lightning and roaring thunderbolts thrown by Thor himself flew across the skies.

UT looked through one of the windows. He saw a heart-stirring ball of light rise over the trees, while lightning crackled and then clapped to split the rosy sky into two. UT had never seen such a sky, such astonishing light… there had never been a storm in the Forest of AARIAS. He remained transfixed by the beauty of the colours and the excitement of the sounds. This time UT did not experience fear, only wonder and veneration, for he knew himself in the presence of a godlike grandiosity.

SAIRAA felt the heavy raindrops falling on her face like bursting bubbles of pure life and rushed to her feet. Owl landed on SAIRAA's shoulder, and Saul the Golden One sprang up in SAIRAA's awareness. She did not pay much heed, enraptured by the lightning which for the first time pierced through all Dimensions and Realms to reach the domains of the Forest.

UT stared at the crashing down of the rain, at the birthing of the reddest of skies, at the lushness of the greenest of trees… when, without warning, he doubled up. His face crumpled, one hand on his stomach, the other against the wall…

SAIRAA dropped to her knees. Tiger Bright growled and nudged SAIRAA's arm with his head; Wolf Moon appeared on the other side. SAIRAA gripped her faithful guardians by their fur. The names 'Shimmera… Saul… Smanara… Silas…' swirled in and out of the pain waves, which literally took SAIRAA's breath away.

UT placed both hands onto his stomach in a desperate attempt to calm the rawness. A glimmer caught his attention: a mirror! UT dragged himself to the only piece of furnishing that he recognised.

SAIRAA managed to sit and lean against the Great Tree. Her back touched the mirror that had led her into the Forest although she had no recollection of this. The magical mirror was surprisingly warm, comforting, and the Forest vibrated in watery luminosity. Then, unexpectedly, the vibrating heartbeat stopped. The Forest became small and intimate. Six trees closed in around SAIRAA, the Guardians and the Great Tree.

UT and SAIRAA felt a surge of burning pain enter their eyes when they looked upon the mirror in front of them. For UT, it was one mirror, one reflection, one overwhelming hurt. For SAIRAA, there were six mirrors, six reflections crying out in six-fold sadness.

A trickle of warm crimson liquid ran down the inside of SAIRAA's legs.

The Sea of Seas

Be not afeard, Children of ASAIRA

The Waters bring new Life

The Blood

A Crimson Gift

The Cycle of the Moon

The Mother shedding

Water & Blood

The Juices of Life

Yes

Be not afeard

We

Are

The Life

The Life

of

Lives

Wolf
Moon
Bruxa
Bagha
La
Ut
Re
Mother
The Warrioress
Son
Daughter
The Warrior
Mi
Sol
The Lamb
Tiger
Bright
Father
Fa
The Owl
of
SAIRAA

The Storyteller

Dear Reader, I have never been in such peace. A growing joy is revealing itself... it reminds me of the excitement I used to encounter when telling a story. In recent times, it felt as though the joy had gone, and a staggering grief came into my heart. But now the joy returns with a different texture. It is softer yet fiercer.

Yes, the connection I feel towards Aileen and UT rallies through my cells... I see them there in front of the mirrors... I can feel their sorrow... I now accept this as it is.

And I return as the Teller! Part 14 is alive and pulsating. Numerous words and images have arisen in my dreams. I can indeed feel these words, these images leading to an end that is nigh, and I wish to know what reveals itself more than ever before!

Ah! How could I forget? I must tell you this. Another William has materialised! By Jupiter, this does make the glee return, there is no doubt about that! You shall remember that the Star of Heavens shared some of William Shakespeare's words from The Tempest... "Be not afeard..." Ahh... I am soothed only by saying those three words. Well, the Star has now shown me a poem by another William... William Blake. It is about the Tiger and the Lamb! But even more astonishing, the Star has led me to another poem... it is by Aileen. She wrote it in one of her diaries entitled 'Tiger, Tiger'. Apparently, her poem was inspired by William Blake's poem. I find it all quite fascinating.

Thus, Part 14 makes itself known and the poems, too. The Joy of this presenting unto You is sublime and is re-acknowledged as the deepest of honours.

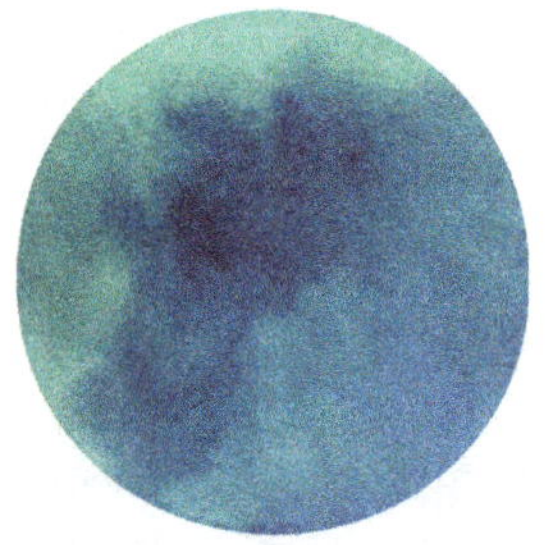

PART 14

Earth: The Lamb

UT bows at the image reflected in the Mirror. It's of a young man with clear-cut features and sweet, gentle eyes. In his arms lies the softest and whitest creature UT has ever seen: a lamb!

This man… it is I! UT looks down into his arms. The Lamb looks back at him. Tears fall down UT's cheeks as the words 'I am the Lamb' whisper in the air.

UT shudders… what is this fire in my stomach? But UT keeps still, his eyes on the Mirror. He hums as he touches the white fur and strokes the Lamb. I am ready for the Freeing Truth of Truths: the MII-LAA, I am ready!

The Mirror's image morphs into the faces of two men. Their features glimmer in gold and silver shimmers of luminosity.

The two men speak in unison, "UT, the Son and the Lamb are One with the Daughter and the Tiger. Go to the Ancient Tree near the Meadow of Primroses. Take the Lamb and be not afeard."

At this, UT sees an opening to leave this place that has become his refuge. He hesitates, but the light entices him…

A tinge of nausea accompanies the burning inside of him, yet UT with the Lamb steps through the door and goes out into the unknown.

The Forest of AARIAS: Aileen

The six Mirrors sing in woeful lament as they reflect the Suffering of Ages Old in the Green Meadow: trillions of tearful faces, of wars, of atrocities, of unconscious brutality. Aileen, for she has returned, cries for humanity.

The burning inside of Aileen's belly continues. The red drops of life seep into the soil, born into the earth. Comforting and warming Aileen, the Great Tree hums. The sound waves counteract the grief of the Mirror-Song of the 6.

Tiger Bright and Wolf Moon sleep at each side of Aileen. Her hands lie on their heads. The Owl of SAIRAA, unbeknownst to all, flies through the Mirror of Mirrors in aid of UT.

Aileen withstands all the heart-wrenching images and lets the tears flow down her cheeks.

Aeons later, or so it seems, the Mirrors stop their mourning and the rains stop. The rawness in Aileen's belly has softened.

Ahh… everything becomes quiet.

It is so still! Aileen feels her heart pump the blood through her body; she hears the silent frequency of the forest and the breathing of the Guardians; she smells the moistness of recent rain… peppermint comes to her mind.

Her eyes close, taking Aileen even deeper into the still silence.

'The Tyger' by William Blake[2]

Tyger! Tyger! burning bright

In the forests of the night,

What immortal hand or eye

Could frame thy fearful symmetry?

In what distant deeps or skies

Burnt the fire of thine eyes?

On what wings dare he aspire?

What the hand dare seize the fire?

And what shoulder, & what art

Could twist the sinews of thy heart?

And when thy heart began to beat,

What dread hand? & what dread feet?

'Tiger, Tiger' by Aileen

'Tiger, Tiger, Burning Bright'

Oh, William, William

You were right!

Your poem

The Tiger's Fiery Presence

The Lamb's Innocent Gentleness

All God's creations

Of course!

Tiger Bright

Now I understand why this name came!

Fire of Fires

The Dragon's Flames

Wild & Purifying

Rise in the Phoenix's Fumes

---

2 The Storyteller

This poem was written in 1794 in the Earth Realm by the Son of ASAIRA, William Blake. The poem can be found in his Songs of Experience. And here also is Aileen's poem inspired by William's 'The Tyger', as I mentioned to you.

What the hammer? what the chain?

In what furnace was thy brain?

What the anvil? what dread grasp

Dare its deadly terrors clasp?

When the stars threw down their spears,

And watered heaven with their tears,

Did he smile his work to see?

Did he who made the Lamb make thee?

Tyger! Tyger! burning bright

In the forests of the night,

What immortal hand or eye

Dare frame thy fearful symmetry?

---

3 The Storyteller

In case you have no knowledge of these wisdoms, dear Reader, perhaps I should explain that the phrase 'The Lamb of God' comes from another Earth religion: Christianity. The phrase is first seen in Saint John the Apostle's Gospel in the religious text called The Bible. It is said by another John (John the Baptist) when he sees Jesus. Jesus is considered in this religion to be the saviour of humanity. "Behold the Lamb of God who takes away the sin of the world." John, 1:29.

Oh Scorchness

You give me the Strength

Durga am I!

I ride you, Tiger Bright!

We burn and blaze together

As I am

Tiger, Tiger, Burning Bright

The Savage & Fearless Fierceness

That is I

Yes!

And then

The Lamb of God[3]

The Sweetest of Softnesses

Unto Thee I deliver myself

Passive Surrender

A Melody of Shimmering Sacrifice

That is I

I stroke Thee, Gentle Lamb

And become the Stroking

The Soothing

I become the soft white wool

I am the Lamb

The Lamb of God

The Spiralling accelerates

I am Here, I am There

Simultaneously

Light & Darkness

Lamb & Tiger

Son & Daughter

Mother & Father

All

One

Am

I

ASAIRA

The Fiery Tiger Bright

The Innocent Lamb of Lambs

Together as ONE!

No End, No Beginning

Sparks of Strength & Weakness

Darting & Dazzling

In the Heart of Hearts

Come, Tiger, Tiger

Come, Lamb of Lambs

Let us Walk Together

In Sweet Loving Passion

In Burning Fearless Innocence

Following the Spiralling

Mystery of Mysteries!

The Storyteller

Oh... look at this. I weep...

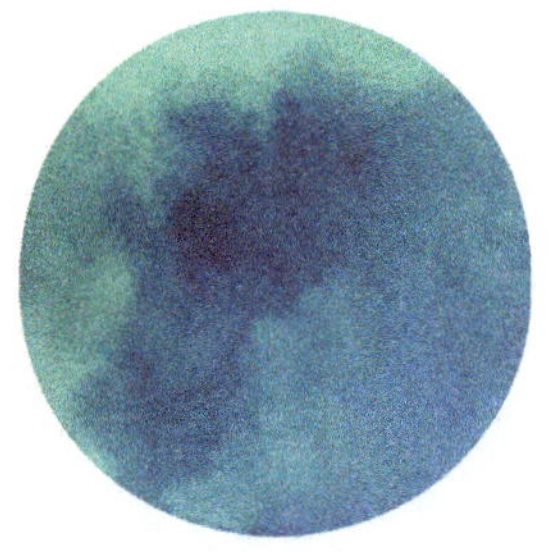

PART 15

Earth: Primrose Meadow

It's too much… UT lifts his hands to his eyes. The scorching is still there, too, in his stomach. Too much… and yet, UT feels at peace, unresistant.

UT puts the Lamb down on the pathway. He decides to really open his eyes and look.

The bluest of oceans arises in front of him. Ohhh! UT's mouth falls open. Is this the Mii-Laa? His eyes slowly absorb the colours while he feels his skin quiver from the smells and sounds. To know such a place, to feel its pulsating life… is this what the Mii-Laa means?

UT picks up the Lamb and kisses it. He walks on. Everything feels new and different… nonetheless, so familiar, so comforting, as if none of this is as new as it might seem… Ah… what does it mean? What am I to do?

In apparent reply, a white-winged creature takes form before his eyes and says UT's name. The voice is familiar… yes, the voices from the Mirror!

And there, like the most unbelievable of undreamt dreams, a bright green extension full of yellowness comes into view. Beyond, framed by the sparkling ocean, a forest of gigantic trees sways in anticipation. Small multicoloured Beings that buzz with life fly up to investigate this long-awaited Son of ASAIRA. Transfixed, UT drops to his knees. The words "The Green Meadow awaits Thee" sound trumpet-like in UT's heart.

His head spinning, UT lies down in the grass.

The Meadow sighs, loosening the roots of gnarled pain stored away in UT's belly.

I'm not the King...

The liberated roots curl out to spread across the Realms of ASAIRA.

I do not need to protect the Forest... I am not alone... not alone...

Bruxa licks UT's hand with love.

The Lamb is here... The Lamb...

"You are much more than you seem, Son of the One Light," echo the Voices from the Mirror.

UT feels a quake in the earth below him.

An image of six Mirrors shattering into pieces paints itself across his inner vision.

The Star of Heavens

Divine Sparks of Joyful Revelation

That bring

The Light Bearer, Aileen

To the Lamb

To the Sweet Son of Man

Lost in the Frozen Night Forest

A Prison of Thought

Yes!

I bring Sparkling & Scintillating Tidings

Yes!

You are the Light Bearer, too

May what was separated

Be One

May what was hurt

Be Healed

To live ASAIRA in True Rest

Lamb & Tiger

Son & Daughter

In the Mother's Arms

The Greenest of Meadows

Ah...

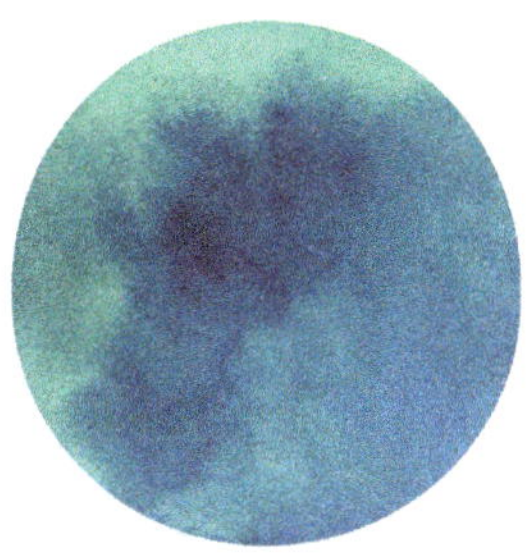

Earth: Into the Forest

The Owl of SAIRAA hooted quietly, and UT got up to follow him. With the Lamb in his arms, UT ventured into the forest, marvelled at the dappled light.

UT stopped when he saw the Tree. He sensed a movement in his heart… a presence of some kind that gasped for breath. The wind howled and the skies roared in the distance.

UT knew what to do. He sat down and leaned back against the Tree. The little Lamb jumped into UT's lap.

Sensing the Joining, the poppies that had grown all around the Ancient Tree bobbed their red heads.

A Gasp

A Howl

A Roar

The Forest of AARIAS: Poppies!

Aileen gasped. Before her, the six Mirrors had exploded and shattered into tiny pieces. Wolf Moon let out a howl. Tiger Bright roared.

Aileen arched her neck, as her throbbing back pinned itself to the Tree.

Ahhh… that feels good…

Aileen caught a glimpse of some flowers growing around the Tree. Although it was dark, she could see they were of a crimson red.

Aileen smiled to see the flowers that she loved so much.

Ohh… The Poppies are here again!

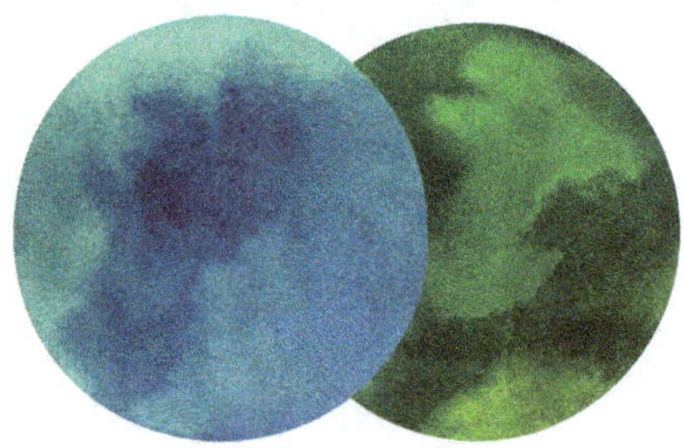

PART 16

Earth ≈ The Forest of **AARIAS**

UT remembered the pale Being he had seen before entering the Mirror of Truths. He knew this Being was near. The Owl of SAIRAA flapped its wings in confirmation, looking down from one of the branches of the Tree of Lands.

Aileen heard someone breathing and a flutter of wings. She knew it was Owl and… yes, the presence of the man she'd faced before coming to the Mirror Forest. "Who are you?" she said.

A pause. "I am called UT." Another pause, and then the words poured out. "I was the King and Protector of AARIAS, the Sacred Forest of Mirrors. But I know now that I was neither King nor Protector. For ages old, I reigned over a frozen kingdom, a prison I made myself. For ages old, did I protect this kingdom from invisible foes… but I protected that which needed no protection. The intention was noble, yes. I sought the Mii-Laa, the Ancient Wisdom, in order to leave the Forest and be king of other realms. I see now there is some truth here although I was ignorant, I was deceived. I had forgotten many things, terrible things that were done to the Daughter and the Son…" UT stopped.

Aileen heard each word in her heart and felt all language barriers crumble away. "I hear your sorrow, UT. I've seen these terrible things myself in the Mirrors of the Forest."

UT said, "Are you there, Pale One, in the Mirror Forest of AARIAS?"

"**Yes**! Where are you?"

"**In a forest** also, but it is not AARIAS. It is a realm of untold beauty. I am near the Green Meadow, with the Lamb!" Bruxa gave out a little bark.

Tiger Bright nudged Aileen who, suddenly realising what might have happened that night at her door, jumped to her feet, turned round and looked at the Mirror in the Great Tree. Staring at her was the Warrior Man… but so changed! And Bruxa in his arms!

The Mirror revealed itself to UT also and reflected Aileen.

Aileen said, "The Son!"

"The Daughter!" said UT.

At this, Bruxa and Tiger Bright leapt into the Mirror, followed by the Owl and Wolf Moon. Surprised, Aileen fell back a bit but managed to keep her balance. UT noticed a moment of anxiety seeing the Lamb leave, but he, too, kept calm and quiet.

The Mirror settled again into the 2's reflection. Aileen looked at the sweet eyes of this magical man called UT. How he had changed, still strong, but he looked so different… he was bursting with humility and compassion! She smiled. UT smiled back in complete wonder of the woman reflected in the Mirror. She was the same Being he'd encountered, yet now she exuded a love-filled strength that filled him with reverence and respect.

Words from the Star of Heavens soared into Aileen's consciousness like a long-lost song…

Yes, there must be Circles.

There must be Children of the Earth and the Sun in those Circles.

There must be Animals and Trees and Plants in those Circles.

There must be Women and Men.

There must be Darkness and Light in the Circle.

This Circle shall be External and Internal

for we are ONE.

The Oneness shall have All of This in it and BE it, too.

The Garden of Mystical Lovers is the Creation, the One Creation.

We are All IT.

Return to Paradise, Beautiful Dark Noble Lord/Lady, for we miss Thee.

We know the Pain, we know that Terrible Things were done,

but this Refuge, this Sharanam that we Are, is forever Forgiving and Open.

You may come to the Light. You are Welcome Here.

Yes, there is a trembling on seeing you... but something tells us that

You are Not what You seem.

Instead of trembling, I shall dance for Thee, and

You will know who You really Are:

The Light of All Lights.

The words of the song took physical and visual form! Spiralling and intertwining, the words wrote themselves out in rainbow-coloured sentences in front of the Mirror. In constant movement, the words danced and merged with each other, turning into an enormous snake of pulsating rainbow colours. As the Snake spun in mid-air, it appeared to be two and then, one.

The multicoloured Snake stopped moving. Taller than Aileen and UT, it placed itself upright, floating just outside the Mirror. Both Aileen and UT had the Snake's silver head looking straight at them. Aileen's heart thumped in her chest, but the SAIRAA in her recognised there was nothing to fear. Fascinated, UT bowed to the creature that was one but two.

The 3 that were 4 found each other's eyes. The Snake's eyes reflected a fierce and compassionate love. It looked innocent and wise, wild and gentle, all at the same time! Yes, all in one, all in one… yes…

Like a door of light opening, UT and Aileen understood that every creature, every Being, was the Daughter and Son… the Son and Daughter together… not separated… and that there was no threat… no threat…

A tear rolled down UT's cheek. The 3 that were 1 stayed still, contemplating the beauty of the other that was, miraculously, their own reflection.

Time and Movement stopped.

And begin again.

The Snake of ASAARI sheds off its snakeskin. The Snake is Smanara and Silas! Tall and transparent, surrounded by a dark rainbow aura, Smanara and Silas smile before the Son and Daughter, reaching out with their silver hands. UT takes Smanara's hand, Aileen takes Silas's. For the second time, but fearlessly, Aileen and UT enter the Mirror of Mirrors.

Aileen and UT find themselves opposite one another in a small bark-panelled room full of tiny glittering stars. Smanara stands to UT's left and Silas to Aileen's right. Bruxa and Tiger Bright, cuddled together, lie in the centre on a sparkling, groundless ground.

Ohhh… so wondrous, Beloved Tree, we're inside of You… You're the whole universe here inside! And look at Bruxa! The Tiger and the Lamb, yes, yes, they're the Tiger and the Lamb!

From behind UT to his right, the Owl of SAIRAA flaps his white wings and becomes the Golden One, Saul. Then, Wolf Moon appears at Aileen's side, transforming into Shimmera.

Surrounding Bruxa and Tiger Bright, the Six of Old, stand together in a Circle. They start to hum and tone the Sacred Notes of AARIAS:

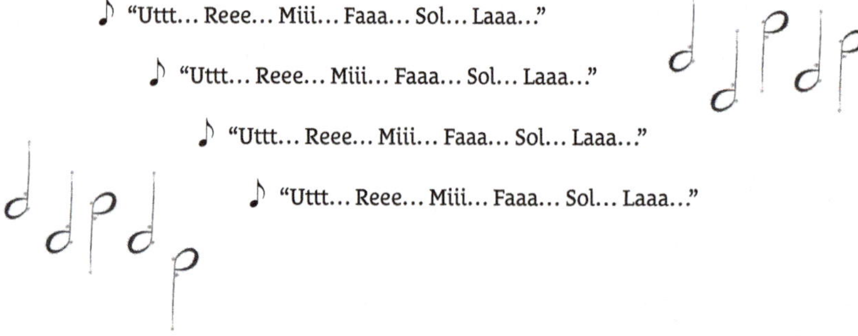

♪ "Uttt… Reee… Miii… Faaa… Sol… Laaa…"

♪ "Uttt… Reee… Miii… Faaa… Sol… Laaa…"

♪ "Uttt… Reee… Miii… Faaa… Sol… Laaa…"

♪ "Uttt… Reee… Miii… Faaa… Sol… Laaa…"

The stars in the room contract, expand, explode into a reality that is more ancient than perception, an invisible reality only seen by the Heart: Tiger Bright and the Lamb are aglow like fiery, snowy particles merging into each other, and Saul, Shimmera, Smanara and Silas have dissolved into one golden-silver light.

UT and Aileen come closer. They take each other's hands. Rising into the air, the 4's Golden-Silver Light intertwines with the Fiery, Snowy Glow of the Lamb-Tiger and pours down like a never-ending waterfall over Aileen and UT.

Aileen feels herself melt away. "We're joining…"

"The Mii-Laa, the Mii-Laa… Yes… The Daughter and the Son joined again… I melt, I melt… into YOU… Ahhh…"

From above the Circle, the invisible reality shows an immense glowing ball of fiery white light. Inside the ball of light, there is one indescribable Creature: a woman, a man, a genderless Being, an Aileen-Tiger-SAIRAA merged with an UT-Lamb-Warrior, one and all, in continuous fluctuation. It… She… He… They… We… You… I… Am… Is… Are the Daughter & Son of ASAIRA in One.

Time ceases for eternity.

Then…

Aileen falls backwards in a slow and hazy movement.

The words 'Ecstasy' and 'Joining' flow out of her mind and into her body,
penetrating her DNA.

I can't hear…

I can't see…

Mmm… but I can smell… jasmine… incense… ahhh…

ASAIRA…

Mother…

Daughter…

Father…

Son…

Joy…

Joy…

JOY!

Aileen senses a lifting, a raising, and a being placed onto water...

Ahh... The Watery Silverness...

Aileen lies there forever.

From another perspective, for those able to see:

Aileen floats on the Sea of Seas.
Her arms are outstretched.

On the Shores:
Durga, the Glory of the Goddess, tenderly holds the Lamb of Lambs
while she rides Tiger Bright.

Far away and Close:
UT plays an ancient melody on a sarod that awakens all that hear it...

The Storyteller

Ah, Friend, I cannot speak... my
heart aches, my body cries...

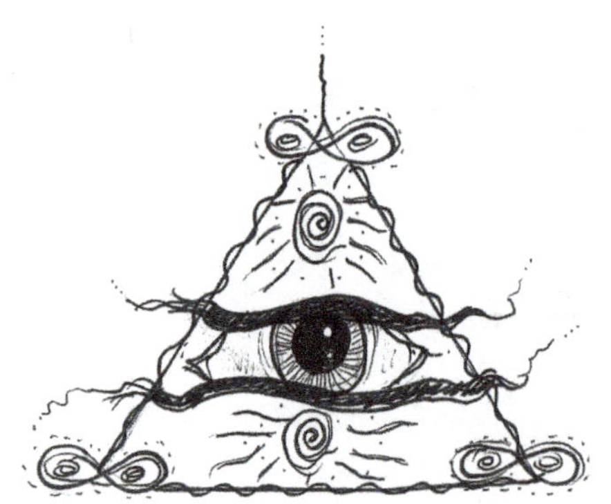

PART 17

All-Seer

I see the Known and the Unknown

I see the Waves of Life

I see the Empty Void

The Mystery

And I see a Child who also sees

She lies amidst golden petals

Droplets of the One True Light She is

ASAIRA celebrates

The Birth of the Tiger-Lamb

It is the True Surrender

The Joining of the Unjoined

The Return of the Daughter & Son

And the Mystery declares

They never left

They were never unjoined

ASAIRA They are

The Meadow of Meadows

The Greenest of Sharanams

The Refuge of Refuges

True Peaceful Alive Life

Adieu, Child of ASAIRA

Your Reading is my Reading

My Knowing your Knowing

It is our Telling

Listen inside

I come in many guises

And all are YOU!

Adieu for now!

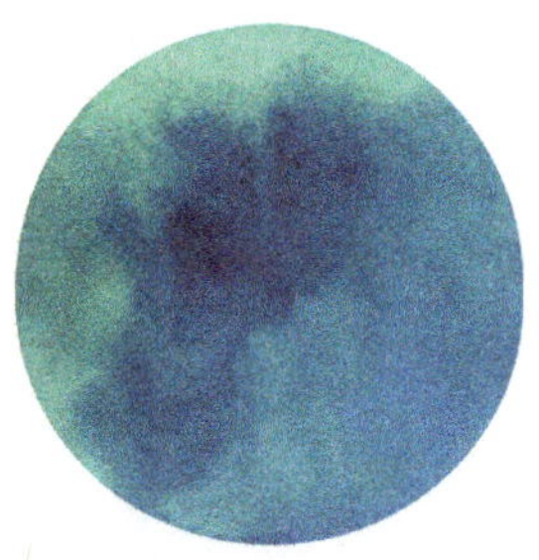

PART 18

Earth: In the Meadow again

It's spring! How can that be? Wow…

Yellow primroses… and daisies… So pretty…

Hey, Bruxaaa, my little lamb! Helloooo! And, look who's here too! Bagha! Oh, I love you both! Missed you so much! Come here… Yes, sweet ones… I love you…

Ahhh… warm sun…

I'm just going to lie here in the Meadow forever with you two… forever…

Forever turned out to be until sunset, and Aileen knew it was time to go home.

A few months appeared to have elapsed, and everything had been cared for. Bruxa and Bagha had food in their bowls, and the house was clean. Aileen did not question it, adoring the magical marvel of it all.

She made herself a cup of mint tea. Cup in hand, Aileen sat on the sofa, reached out for the green blanket and curled her legs up. The white dog and the black cat jumped up next to her.

Aileen closed her eyes, noticing a buzz rise up inside of her body. Words and images painted themselves before her:

Yes, all lies… but then so deeply believed that they'd become real!

Women had believed they were not quite as clever as men,

that they were the weaker sex and at the same time, they hadn't believed it at all,

immersed in secret anger and victimhood, hurt beyond words.

Men had absorbed all of this misrepresentation, too.

They took on the burden of protecting the women from endless enemies,

never to show any weakness, or otherwise be rejected as cowards.

No tears for those little boys,

smacked into believing that their tears belonged to weak little girls,

who they then had to rescue and protect.

For there were dragons to be killed and witches to be hunted!

And the mothers, daughters, wives, supported their brave men

and dreamt of knights in shining armour.

Even love, for both men and women, was considered fragile

and of no practical use in a cruel world of survival and competition.

Aileen sipped at her tea and placed her feet onto the floor.

Yes… so many beliefs…

In the religions, too…

There was the story of the evil snake who tempted Eve to eat of the forbidden Tree.[4]

And then, Eve, the fallen woman, persuaded the innocent Adam to follow her into the dark.

But…

What if…

the Snake had been a friend?

What if Eve and Adam weren't who they were made out to be?

Aileen took a deep breath.

What if a kind of unconsciousness had invented the whole thing to protect itself from a threat?

What if the threat was just an illusion and there was no threat at all?

What if the illusion had become a huge lie that created an imagined world of fear?

---

4 The Storyteller

Aileen makes reference to the story of Adam & Eve and the
Garden of Eden. Reader, I always assume you must know
about the stories of the Earth Realm, but again, just in
case, I shall give a little more information. This story
or belief is found in The Bible and other religious texts:
it is considered a story of the creation of humanity. Eve
(the first Woman) was tempted by the Snake (the Devil) into
disobeying God by eating from the Tree of Knowledge of Good
and Evil. Eve, in turn, tempted Adam (the first Man) into
doing the same. As punishment, God exiled them from the
Garden of Eden and cursed them as sinners.

A warm intuition coiled inside of Aileen, a knowingness that circled in the stomach and then spiralled up into the heart. The Knowingness sang to her!

It sang of…

SAIRAA's strength and natural wisdom:

the warrior woman, strong and wild, yes, but wise and at One with ASAIRA…

Of UT's sweetness and courage:

the warrior man who needn't continuously protect anymore.

Of how the Son had been freed automatically freeing the Daughter.

Of how the Mother had returned to tell and trumpet

that Love was not fragile, that it was the True Strength of Strengths,

and that it liberated all imprisonment.

The Knowingness turned into the Town-Crier, the Herald of Heralds!

The Town-Crier is dressed in red and gold, with a bell in his hand. He walks the Realms of ASAIRA and announces the good tidings, "Hear Ye, Hear Ye, Children of ASAIRA, Open Your Hearts for She is Here Now!"

Aileen smiled at the vision of the town-crier as she finished her tea. Ahh… I'm tired… She let herself fall sideways onto the sofa, pulled up the blanket and went to sleep. Bruxa and Bagha cuddled up together next to Aileen and closed their eyes.

And I, Storyteller, must say farewell, for this is the end of the 2nd Knowing. Yes, this is how this second story wishes to be called. The 2nd Knowing. I see it clearly now: the Story contains Knowings. So, more than ever, I know that this ending is just a beginning. In my bones I can feel the 3rd Knowing arise!

The 2nd Knowing has revealed to me that there is more to be known; I am changed... humbled, as it were. Nothing is in my hands.

Although I confirm my role as the Storyteller, I have asked All-Seer for more help. All-Seer has reassured me that he and the Star will always be there when I need them. And most importantly, that the Story can tell itself on its own! All-Seer's last words to me have been, "Trust in the Impulse, Storyteller of Old!" I shall endeavour to do so.

Then, with humility and gratitude,

I bow to Thee, Child of the One Light.

Until we meet again! I know it will be soon!

Ah... and there is an image to be drawn; indeed, it must be the way of things, the manner in which this Story, the Knowings wish to end, to begin... Allow me to draw it as best I can.

Oh, wait... something more has come before the image...

I am the Mother

The Midwife-Warrior

The Daughter

I am the Father

The Spirit-Warrior

The Son

I am the 3

I am the 6

I am the 1

I Am

ASAIRA

The One True Flower

The
Greenest
of
Meadows
You Are

THE END & THE BEGINNING

THE 3RD & 4TH KNOWINGS OF ASAIRA

THE RETURN TO THE MOTHER

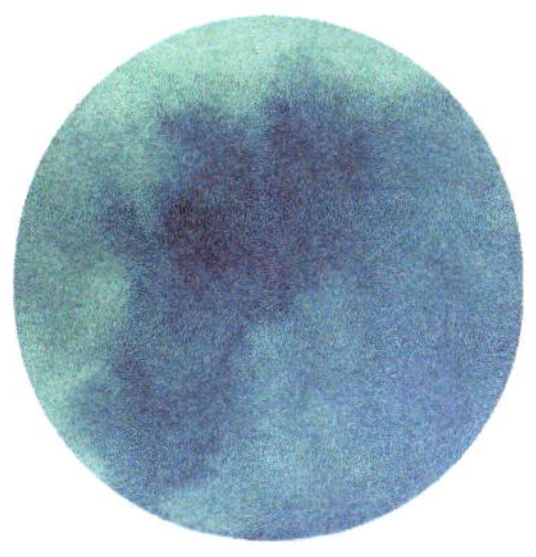

Earth

Aileen woke up.

"AIRAAS."

The word flew around the bedroom, reverberated in and out of the furniture and dove into Aileen's heart.

"AIRAAS…" said Aileen again as she fell asleep.

"AIRAAS," said the Echo of Echoes.

I have many names

All contained in One

I answer to all

And to none

No name can have me

And still, its sound

Calls me, Reaches me

I am the Name of Names

Unspeakable, Unknown

And still,

Familiar

Deeply known

To You

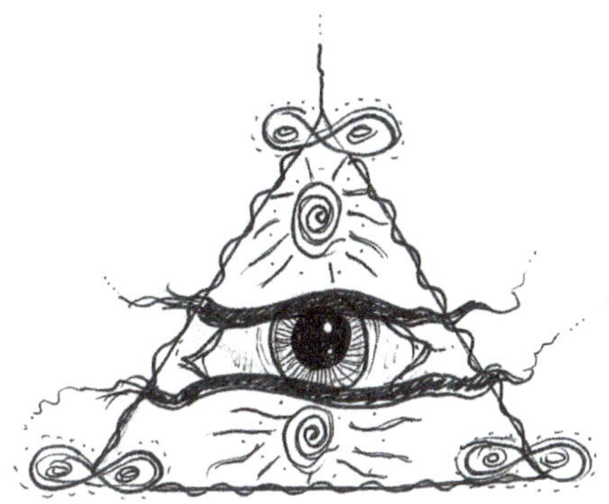

All-Seer

So long since that name came to these ears

So sweet its sound

It awakens a fluttering lightness

Yes...

The very mention of Sacred Names

Are calls on the lips of the speaker

To awaken

To see...

The Storyteller will eventually emerge

For now, the words have declared their presence

Parts 1 & 2 are sprouting

Aileen has opened her eyes to the sound of AIRAAS

And you, Reader, are open to the Story!

Reader, you are here!

You have been summoned

Curiously, this is not the time

And even more curiously

It is, of course, the time!

However, let us be in patience

The Story wishes to speak when the moment is ripe

Until then, permit the name AIRAAS to do its work

Say the name out aloud

Hear the vibrations

Sing it in you heart, Reader

And behold the miracles!

Ha! Ha! Ha!

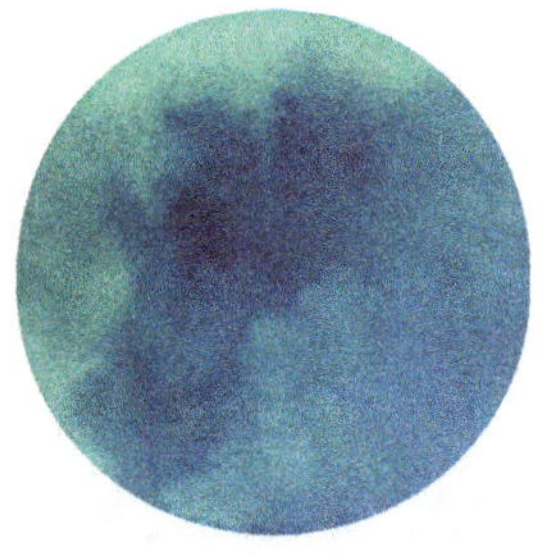

Earth: Searching for the Mother

It's time to return to the Mother. Aileen knew it in her heart. I have to see the LIES… remember the Old Ways… share it all somehow!

Aileen sighed. 'I return to the Mother' included the meaning that she still had to find her. At the same time, Aileen knew the Mother was there, here, close…

Mother, help me return to you. I'm not sure exactly what it means. I know you're here, so close. But I want to return to YOU in a way that is beyond SAIRAA, beyond all I know of ASAIRA!

And the Mother whispered waves of sweet-scented sounds into Aileen's ears, sounds of nothingness which swirled throughout the universe, "I shall never abandon my children. I am always here, open-armed, awaiting your return."

The Storyteller

My Friend, I salute you with the
greatest of peaceful excitements!

Something has decidedly awoken
and is asking to be written.
It is AIRAAS! She wishes to be
written, and I am sure it is a
she.

Much time has passed since the
3rd Knowing made its presence in
me, but I did not feel the images
and words until now. Now they
beg to be drawn and written! I
feel a blissful happiness, and as
always, awe and amazement to see
how the Story has its own timing.

So, I am here again as the
Storyteller and yet, differently.
This time I am ready to call on
All-Seer or to leave the Telling
when needed. I shall trust the
impulse and know the Story is to
reveal itself, not only to the
characters and You, dear Reader,
but also to the Storyteller. In
this manner, before starting, I
acknowledge again what is clear
by now: we are all characters in
the Story and Children of ASAIRA!

Let us commence, then, with an
image that has arisen.

The image moves... the petals, or
wings... are fluttering... How
astounding!

Wait, another image shows itself!
It is similar to the images
that appeared in the 1st and
2nd Knowings, but from another
perspective...

I see, hmmm... quite
remarkable...

ASAIRA, for I know not any other
way to call these opening and
closing images, has her back to
us...

Hmm... fascinating...

Thank you, dear Reader, for
having embarked on yet another
adventure of ASAIRA!

Let us see where we are taken...
what AIRAAS points to...

The Flower opens

The petals dance

A flutter

A transformation

An invisibility

A realness

The Butterfly

The Wings of the Mother long to fly

Yes

I am

The Flower of Flowers

ASAIRA am

The Strength of Strengths

SAIRAA am

The Healing Breeze of Breezes

AIRAAS am

I am

Behind you

Look and Feel

I am

☆ PART 2 ✶

The Storyteller

Dearest Reader, All-Seer has spoken to me in his pounding voice. He has explained that it was you, Reader of Readers, who awoke me! You said the name AIRAAS, and it travelled into my heart. Isn't that truly exhilarating? All so mysterious and intertwined!

In truth, when I heard All-Seer's voice again, a strange languor enveloped me. Since then, dreamy recollections which I cannot place or understand sing in my ear and visit me during the day and the night...

But Aileen awaits. Other considerations must be left for later.

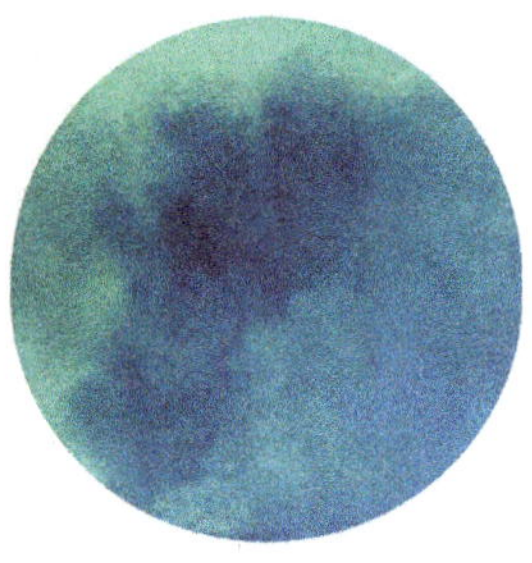

Earth: In the Meadow

Mother, do I stay here? With Bruxa and Bagha, near the Wise One and the Forest and Primrose Meadow? Or should I leave and go somewhere else?

Mmm… it's so lovely out here today!

I know trying to figure it out isn't the best move!

Okay, let's lie down here in the Meadow…

Ah… so good! I love the smell of the grass…

Mmm … An eagle flying in circles!

Mother, there's such a powerful sensation in my heart, it pushes on me… I know you'll show me the way… I know… You always do…

ASAIRA, Mother, show me who or what AIRAAS is… Show me what I have to do… Thank you, thank you, thank you…

Aileen falls into a sleepy stupor. Her breath slows down, merging with the sounds of the breeze and the birds, their song a mother's lullaby. Bruxa yawns and lays her warm white body next to Aileen.

The sun's rays caress the Meadow and awaken the insects into a mesmerizing drone. To a relaxed yet alert eye, the air is full of minute globes of energetic sparks. They bob up and down, vibrating to the hum of the insects. Intensely still, the Meadow is bathed in a golden light that shimmers and ripples.

A large emerald-green butterfly lands on Aileen's head. Despite the softness of the landing, Aileen's body starts. A crow caws in the distance, and the butterfly flutters off into the forest. But Aileen and Bruxa continue sleeping, oblivious to all… or seemingly so.

Inside the cool forest, the butterfly flies and flies. She knows where to go. On arriving, she closes her emerald wings and rests.

The Tree of Lands

Ahh...

What lightness is this?

What sweet wisdom has come to visit?

I hear

I feel

The Wings of ASAIRA

A sparkling greenness in the clearing

My roots shiver and reach downwards

Where no Child of the Earth has been

It is time then

She is ready

She is a Child of the Earth and Sun

Initiated in the Mirror Forest

Knower of the Old Ways

SAIRAA is she

Knower of the Old Untruths

UT is she, too

Protected by the Rhythms of the Mother

By the Roar of the Goddess' Tiger

By the Gentleness of the Lamb

The Silverness of the Moon Wolf

The Wisdom of the Owl

The Innocence of the Snake of Transformation

And Now

Aileen

It is time

For a journey of healing

The Journey of Revealing

The Unveiling of the Untruths

It is Time, Child, my sweet Aileen

It is Time

For

AIRAAS

The Storyteller

Oh my giddy aunt! How astonishing!

I have just received some enthralling information from the Star of Heavens. I cannot make much sense of it at the moment, but it is urgent and immediate, I know it in my heart!

So, dear Reader, what can I say? We have AIRAAS, our 3rd Knowing, and now we seem to have a 4th!

Hmm... A 4th Knowing, then? IRAASA is the 4th? They come together?

The Star of Heavens

I am here again

Though I never left

I endlessly sparkle and glitter

The Divine Sparks of Insight & Revelation continue

They are my messages

For You, Children of ASAIRA

Listen inside

The Sparks glimmer within

Listen

You shall hear

If it is your Love of Loves

♡ Divine Sparks of Insight & Revelation ♡

The Flower is the Bird is the Winged Goddess

The Queen of the Heavens & Skies & Air

But, the Flower is first a Seed

The Bird is first an Egg

The Winged Goddess first must be a Chrysalis

Underground She must go

♈ For AIRAAS to Be

♈ Into the Arms of IRAASA

♈ Must She be delivered

☆* PART 3 **

The Storyteller

The 3rd Knowing is that it is necessary for the 3rd and 4th to merge into one. What this means exactly I do not know. However, something which I do know should be shared immediately with you.

I am dizzy with spinning images, comprehensions and words that whirl around me! It's too much for me at the moment, so I have realised that I must depart again. Reader, I apologize, and at the same time I feel you can comprehend, and no apology is needed. I am full of joy with the start of the Telling, but I need to allow all the spinning that has just arisen to settle. It is impossible for me to carry on otherwise.

Both All-Seer and the Star have conceded and have reassured me again; the Story is alive and shall continue.

I am relaxed in the understanding that the Story is not my full responsibility and that my resting is part of it all.

Dear Friend, I shall be back soon, I have no doubt of this!

The Earth I am

Strong & Fertile

The Skies I am

Delicate & Fleeting

Summon the Skies

The Wings of Love

And the Earthy Womb

Stirs in compliance

ASAIRA *rejoices*

The Earth opens

To swallow all

And the Wings of Wisdom & Love

Tremble in shimmering expectancy

Yes

AIRAAS is ***IRAASA***

IRAASA *is* *AIRAAS*

Be Ready, Children, Be Ready

Earth: AIRAAS is Summoned

Aileen's body contracted as a powerful
force attached itself to her back.

Whispering, Bruxa
crept onto
Aileen.

I
can't
wake
up...

The Emerald Green
Butterfly

I have been given
Voice

I rest here
Under the Oldest Tree

My Wings sparkle
From the Dew

I rest
Then I shall
Sing
To AIRAAS

The Tree of Lands

The Ever-Deep
Earthy Wisdom
The Ancient One
So Forgotten & Dark
Ah...
Thou pullest at my Roots
The hand trembles
AIRAAS
Shall not Be
Without Thy permission
So Be It!

IRAASA

AIRAAS

Has been summoned
And I
Have awakened
I look towards the Surface
From the Darkness
We ready ourselves
Beware
All Ye that trespass
My Protectors
Prepare
Themselves

I
can't...
Just
sleep, sleep...

No resisting...

The Protectors of IRAASA

Do not trespass
We know Ye
Tramplers of the
Mother
Be Warned
Ye
Shall not
Enter
Hither

Forever
Mother   Here   Mother
Mother
Here   Forever   Here

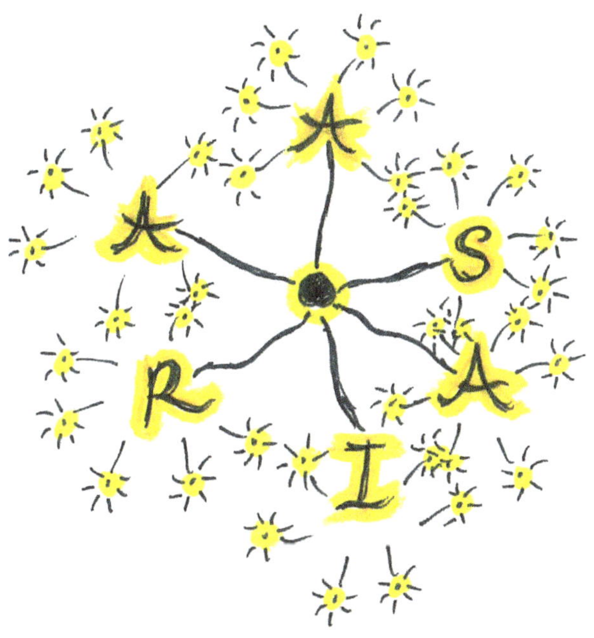

- ♈ The 6-Starred Flower
- ♈ The 6-Petalled Star
- ♈ The Wings of AIRAAS
- ♈ The Darkness of IRAASA
- ♈ ASAIRA Is

The Protectors of IRAASA

Busy Ourselves

Must we

Prepare the Soil, Oh Nightcrawler

Prepare the Silk, Oh Weaver of the Void[5]

Prepare the Depths, Oh Defender of the Nest

For IRAASA has awoken

Watch over us, Lord of Laws

No trespasser shall enter

IRAASA invokes Thy Vigilant Eye

Prepare, Oh Daughters of the Queen

Your stinging swords

No trampler shall tread on us

For

We are the Burrowers

The Prey Crushers

The Cocoon Spinners

The Watchers of the Depths

We are the Servants of IRAASA

The Fertile Void of Voids

---

5 The Story Speaks

Some of the names the Protectors of IRAASA call themselves
such as the Weaver and The Lord of Laws bring to mind the
book Medicine Cards from the Earth Realm. The Story wishes
to honour the book. It was written in 1988 by the Children
of ASAIRA, Jamie Sans & David Carson.

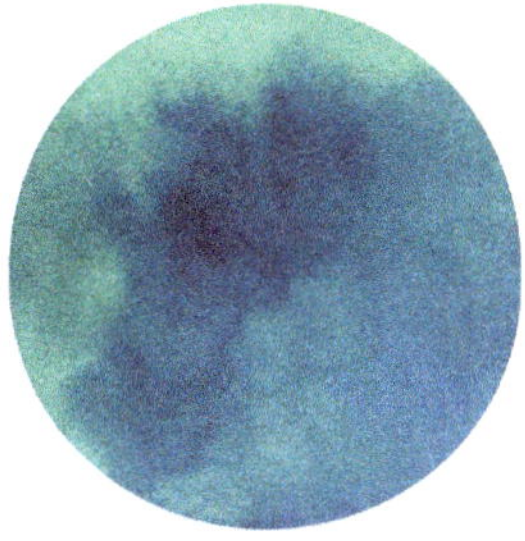

Earth: Into the Depths

Bruxa stood on Aileen's chest and barked at her. Aileen did not stir. She was not aware of Bruxa; nor was she aware of the stormy clouds or the cold wind; she was not aware of the crow that cawed and flew around her, or of the swarm of bees that crossed the skies in buzzing menace. Aileen was aware of nothing.

Bruxa jumped off Aileen. The small dog ran towards the forest. Behind her, a dark and ominous swirl of wind, tornado-like, loomed above Aileen. Just as Bruxa arrived at the edge of the forest, she stopped, glanced back and saw her beloved Aileen swallowed into the earth.

All that was left was the inky void of absence.

Into the Depths

The Child of **ASAIRA**

Must go

Earthy Love of Loves

I am

The Darkest of Warmths

The Entrails of Creation

Roots of Eternity

I am

Deep into the Burrows

Of **IRAASA**

She goes

I am the Darkness

The Great Void

Yet

The Most Alive of Fertile Soils

I am

✩⋆ PART 4 ⋆✯⋆

The Story Speaks

I am the Story.

I tell myself.

I am the Story itself as it occurs.

I know what has been written but I do not know what is to come.

I know You can read these words.

I am more alive when Your eyes glance down on me.

Now I continue...

I hear you

You called us

You have awakened us

You summoned AIRAAS

Now you are

Here with me

In the Depths of the Void

I am the Dark Mother

Mother of Mothers

I am Raw and Fertile

From our Depths

All is born

We are

Black and Earthy

The Soil of Soils

We are the

Darkness of IRAASA

It's so dark.

I can't move.

My back…

Where am I?

Mother…

What's happening??

Aileen opens her eyes and sees only pitch black. She calls out. Her back aches, it pulls her down when she tries to move.

Aileen's mind thinks the most petrifying thoughts. Her whole body stiffens more and more, refusing to yield.

The Tree of Lands

Child

Do not be afeard

Remember who You are

You are a Child of the Earth and Sun,
of the One Light

ASAIRA Thou art

You are SAIRAA and UT

The Tiger and the Lamb

You are the Golden Ones

And the Silver Ones

Call upon them

And feel my Roots

I sustain Thee

I nourish Thee

Remember who Thou Art

Child of ASAIRA!

Meet IRAASA

She awaits Thee

The Emerald Green Butterfly

Feel me!

I flutter around your head

Feel me! *Hear* me!

ASAIRA

Soothe yourself,

SAIRAA

Calm yourself,

AIRAAS

Breathe yourself,

IRAASA

We are, You are

ONE

The Dark is Light

The Light is Dark

We have many faces

We are the *Mother*

Wake up, Aileen

Wake up!

The Star of Heavens

She rises fully-winged

AIRAAS

So glorious

So immense

The Embrace

Of a Trillion Clouds

How she flies!

Ahhh...

The Child

She hears the

Shimmering

Flickers of the Emerald

Yes

Aileen

Be Calm

You are embraced

The Arms of **IRAASA** Hold you

The Protectors of IRAASA

She does not feel us

She is a-panicked

She does not breathe

She cannot see

She acts as a trampler

Perhaps she is not ready

She trespasses then

She disturbs

If she does not remember

Neither shall we

Our Jaws

And Fangs awaken

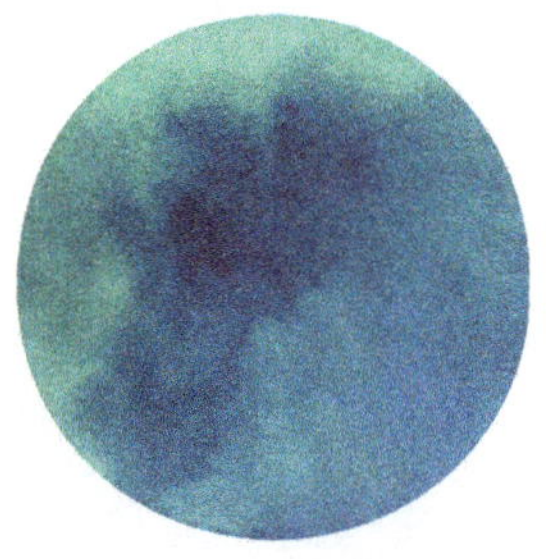

PART 5

Earth: In the Forest

In the middle of the forest there lay a greyish darkness. The Tree stood as always in its grandeur, imposing a sacred reverie upon all who sighted it. Today, though, the more one approached the Tree, the more one felt a sizzling tension.

A crow made a grating sound, like a growl if crows could growl!

And what was that noise? A swarm of bees! The bees' drone rose in deafening crescendo.

No one could get near the Tree, that was for sure. The crow cawed in confirmation, and a cold gust of air rustled through the dark leaves of the forest.

The Story Speaks

With the eyes of other realms and wisdoms,

I see an ancient tree in the forest encircled by other trees.

In the circle there is a clearing. It has very little grass, only earth and twigs.

A greenish light bathes the clearing.

A tiger lies near the tree with a little white dog who rests her head on the tiger's belly.

A crow sweeps across the clearing.

Bees circle above the tree.

No tension is felt in this realm, only love...

In the distance, perhaps in another realm, a soft fluttering is heard.

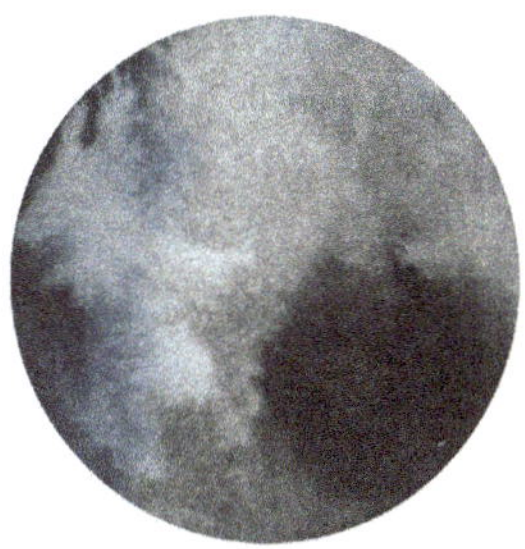

The Depths of IRAASA: Aileen in the Blackness

Realising that there was no difference if her eyes were open or closed, Aileen relaxed into the blackness.

The word AIRAAS came, and Aileen heard a flutter of wings that made her body tingle.

Little by little, Aileen became aware of her external environment, of how her body felt and where she was. She could barely move, but as she relaxed, the sense of restriction lessened. The pain in her back did not feel like pain anymore but more of a support.

The darkness smelled of moist earthiness. There were sounds... like a whispering or a hum.

Aileen felt something cold and wet that moved next to her left leg and a vibrating sensation in her left hand. Aileen shuddered.

"Help me, Mother! Let me remember my strength! Let me feel SAIRAA's warrior courage again! Shimmera! Smanara! Saul! Silas! Tiger Bright! I need you all. Please help me! Thank you! Thank you!"

A tear ran down Aileen's cheek, and in spite of the thumping in her heart, Aileen knew that everything would be okay.

Soil of Soils

Earth of Earths

Black as Coal

In my Pit of Depths

I am

We are

We harbour all

We hold the Untruths

With Fierce Compassion

No Child can enter

This Pit of Darkness

Unless to see

Is the Soul's intent

Unless to fly

Is the Soul's dream

Then IRAASA's

Earthy Arms shall embrace

The Silky Cocoon

The Barrenness of this Age

Shall transform

Transform

Into

The

Fertile

Truth

Of

Truths

"LIES!!"

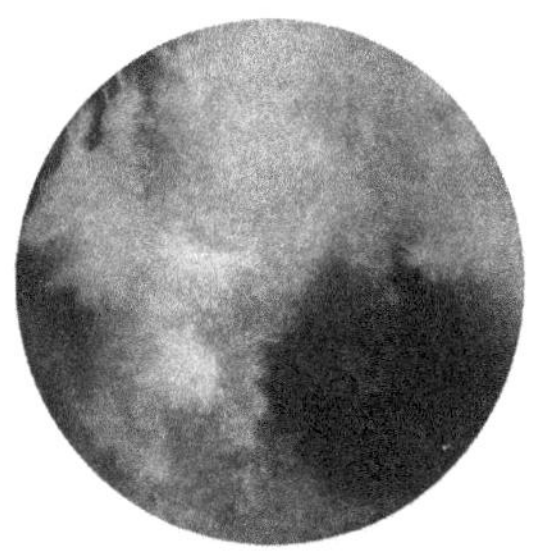

The Depths of IRAASA: Aileen Remembers

The word 'LIES!' rang through all the cells of Aileen's body. She opened her eyes wide: the call to return to the Mother and uncover all the lies... to rediscover the Old Ways... Yes, this is why I am here!

Aileen listened for the Mother. In the heart area, Aileen became aware of a burning sensation. The words 'Nightcrawler', 'Weaver of the Void' and 'Defender of the Nest' wrote themselves in the dark. The words came with images and insights that appeared, flickered and disappeared again.

✳ The roots of the Beloved Tree support me! That's what I feel in my back!

✳ I'm inside the earth, but I can breathe... it's okay!

✳ There are creatures, millions in the soil, invisible, busy, living in a different world...

✳ There are three special creatures here... magical... they protect the Mother... they protect this darkness...

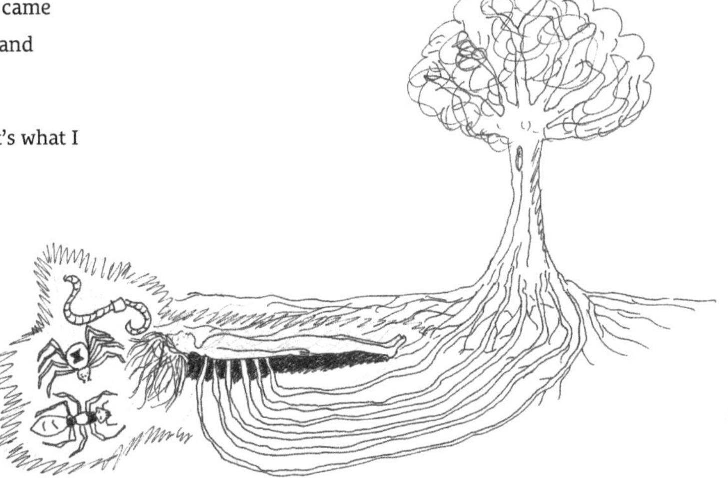

Aileen heard a voice that sounded like rumbles of thunder:

"I am IRAASA

We are the Mother

Hear me, Child

I am Dark and Soily

You must stay with us

You must not resist

Let yourself be nourished

Protected

For Thou shalt see

The Lies of Old!"

Aileen's body trembled. The roots of the Ancient One pulled a little, but Aileen realised they were her own roots now. She was joined to the Tree! Yes, the Mother carried her in Her entrails, in Her Womb! And then came a name, a name of a woman only known in photos and words, a woman that Aileen hadn't felt really existed but had brought her to life:

Mia

Tears trickled out…

The burning sensation in the heart penetrated the stomach…

Aileen's body shivered and sweated…

A sad, angry rawness gripped her throat…

It's okay… It's okay… Breathe…

I can't…

You can, my love…

The rawness softened its grip and let a word that had refused to be said for many years, so buried and hidden away, just be said:

Mama

The burning subsided.

Mia… Mama…

Mama… I miss you… I'm so sorry I never met you…

I'm so sorry I didn't want to say your name… I couldn't…

Thank you for coming to me now… Thank you…

Thank you…

I love you. I love you, Mama.

Mother of Mothers…

I'm ready… I'm ready to see the Lies of Old… I'm ready…

IRAASA gently rumbled into the ear of this Child of the One Light, this sweet Aileen from the Earth Realm. Every creature in the Depths and in all Realms, too, stopped their busyness to rest in the nourishing and forgiving love of the Dark Mother.

The Story Speaks

Above Aileen in the Realm of the Earth and the Green Meadow,
a cluster of primroses show their heads and open their petals.
Green blades of grass begin to sprout.

The Lord of Laws sits on one of the branches of the Tree and coos.
Bruxa watches the butterfly fly in front of her nose.

The storm and the darkness have passed in the Meadow,
and a light rain refreshes the land.

Some sun rays reach out to give warmth and light...
Lo and behold, a multicoloured miracle arises from nowhere:

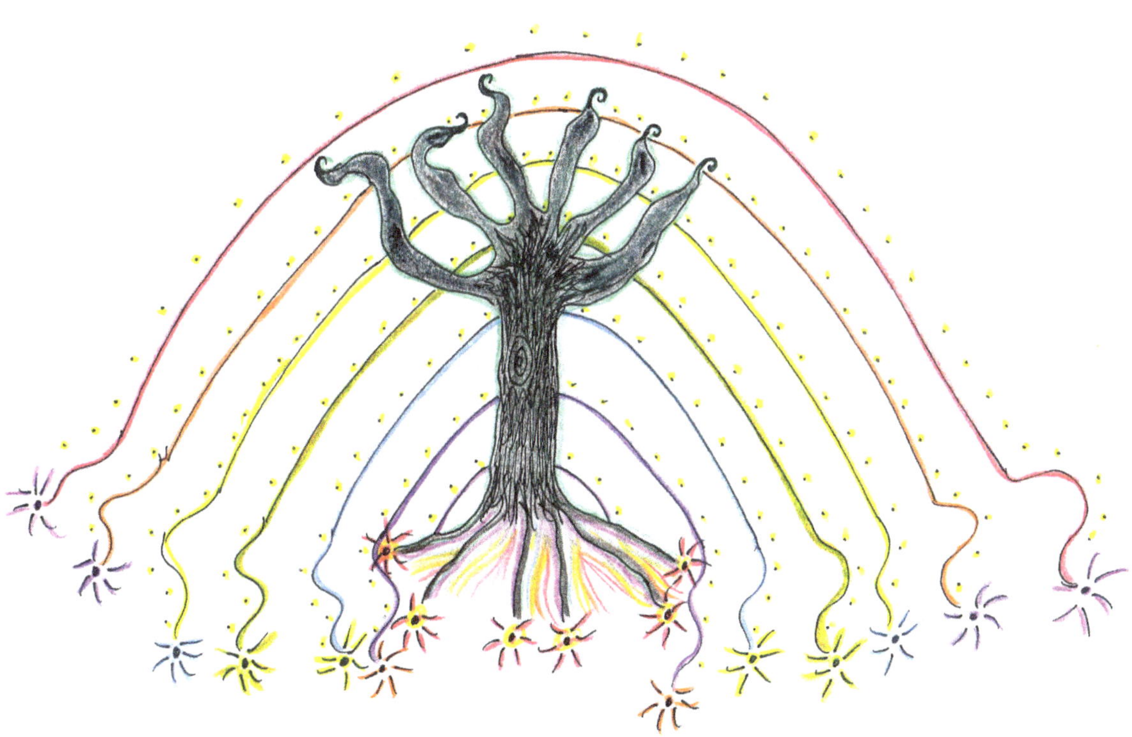

The Protectors of IRAASA

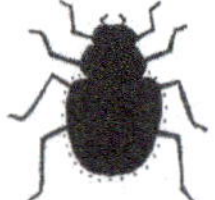

As She remembers

So do we

The Promise

Forgotten in the Depths

We were the Protectors

The Tramplers knew not

Of the Mother of All

We are now the Nourishers

For She remembers

And so shall we

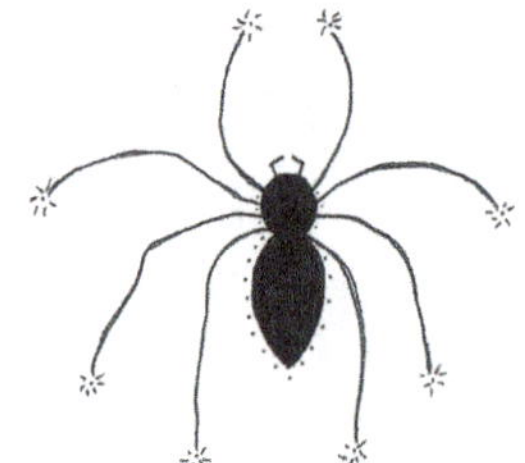

I, the Weaver of the Void

Golden Daughter of IRAASA

Shall weave the silkiest of webs

For AIRAAS becomes visible

2 are 4

4 are 2

To the Air she must go

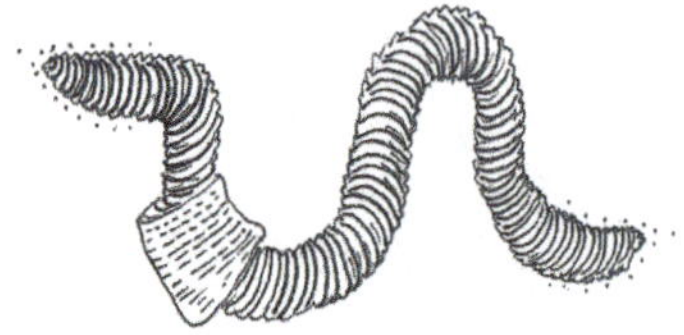

I, the Nightcrawler

Golden Son of IRAASA

Shall cast forth

The Waste of Wastes

Into the Heart of Soils

Burrowed and Transformed

Into Gold the Waste shall be

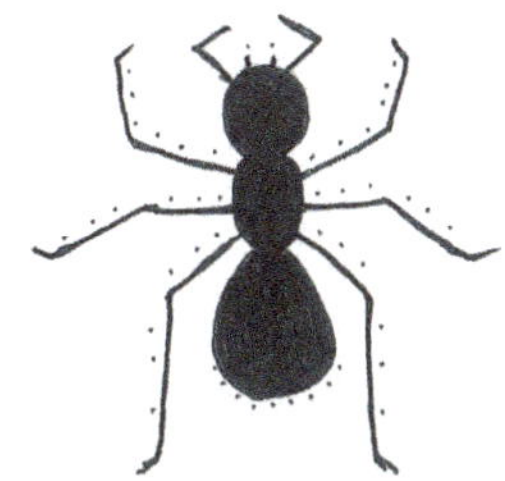

I, the Defender of the Nest

Silver Daughter of the Queen

Shall make a bed of silver threads

Round and round and round

I spin

The Brilliant White Cocoon

IRAASA's Love

AIRAAS's due

I, the Lord of Laws

Silver Son of IRAASA

Shall guard from above

No Trespasser

No Trampler

Caw shall I till the Dawn of
Eternity

For AIRAAS must be

Caw!

There are 6

They are 1

But each 1 is 6

And so forth

Mirrored in the Masculine and Feminine

One cannot be

Without the Other

ᵛ ASAIRA is the Mother

ᵛ Never-ending

ᵛ Circle of Spirals

☆ PART 7 ✦

The Tree of Lands

Aileen, my little child

You are ASAIRA

Aileen, the Warrior

SAIRAA

You are IRAASA, too,

Aileen

AIRAAS

You spin and are spun

Feel the Roots that Sustain

You are Loved

You are the Love

Aileen, Child of ASAIRA

Listen

To the Song of the Star

The Star of Heavens

Aileen

In the Darkness of IRAASA

The Shining Sparkles

Of True Wonder

Glisten in the Heart

Many Lies

Untruths and Waste

Are buried

In the Depths

Free them

And they shall dazzle

In Goldness

And AIRAAS shall be

Aileen

Aileen

AIRAAS!

The Story Speaks

There is a fog.

In order to continue, the Story shall wait until the fog lifts.

PART 8

The Storyteller

Dear Reader, I return. The fog has either lifted, or there is no fog because all I can see is what happens next!

Therefore, I am here again with you, trusting and following the impulse that tells me to speak.

Reader of Readers, I continue the Story, or much better said, the Story continues in its own mysterious manner.

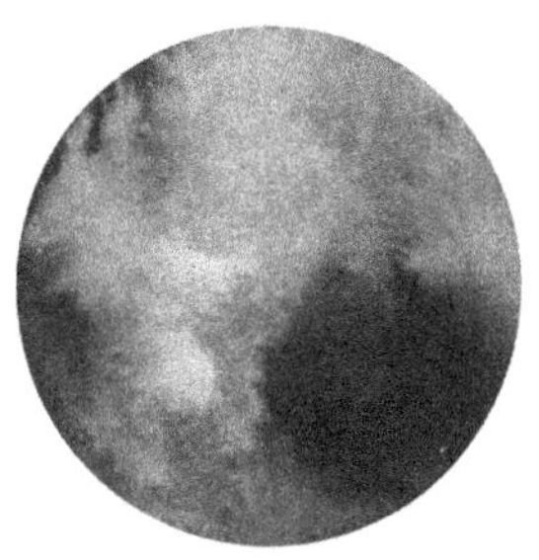

The Depths of IRAASA

Aileen fell into IRAASA's sooty arms. As was her repeated destiny, she lost her sense of being Aileen. All that she was conscious of was the warmth of the earth, the damp smell of the soil, the comforting hum of the creatures that accompanied her and the roots of the Tree, now her roots, too.

Buried in the entrails of the earth, a strange bubbling boiled and arose: four huge energies had awakened to their long-awaited call.

Having no eyes did not prevent the Nightcrawler from sensing the Four Mighty Ones' upward lurching movement towards the warmth of Aileen's body. The 4 had been seeking that warm reminiscence of liberation for too long to linger.

The Nightcrawler was ready. He knew he must face the Dark 4, one by one. This had been his mission forever, so ancient, so forgotten, and now alive and here.

The Nightcrawler moved his long moist body in circular movements while he burrowed into the soil. His five pairs of hearts rejoiced in an exhilaration that he, being an earthy worm, had never known before.

4 Great Truths

Hidden

In our Darkness

4 Great Untruths

Buried

In our Soil of Soils

Each brings

Our Heavenly Wisdom of Old

To be born

From our Earthy Entrails

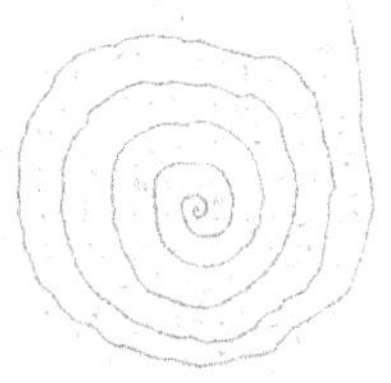

The Storyteller

Is

More than He seems

His Wish

Is

Our Command

Our Desire

Is

His Path

I

Am

Earth ~ Other Realms ~ The Depths of IRAASA

The long-awaited call was heard in other places. **The Four Myriad Mirror-Shadows** felt their animating force awaken, too. Now is the time, they whispered in ancient longing. Invisible to human eyes, they lifted themselves out of oblivion, out of the heavy fog of ages and commenced their journey to the Green Meadow.

The Wise One, the Tree of Lands, experienced a chill that made all his leaves rustle in electrifying wonder, while Bruxa, who was sleeping nearby, whined.

The blackest of crows, the Lord of Laws, cawed and clicked. He recognised the monumental eruption of energy that was coming from above and below, a fuming fire that could not, would not, be placated.

And in another realm, but determinedly there, **Tiger Bright** roared at the skies to confirm his readiness.

Down in the Depths, Aileen's body shivered.

♡ **Divine Sparks of Insight & Revelation** ♡

༶ The 6 are 1

༶ The 3 are 6

༶ The 4 are 1

༶ ASAIRA

༶ ONE

༶ IS

The Storyteller

Friend, I cannot but tell you
that at seeing the words 'The
Storyteller is more than he
seems' I have trembled. Just
as I have trembled at receiving
the knowledge about the Mighty
Energies and the Mirror-
Shadows... and Aileen, how I
tremble to see her there, in the
soil!

I also wonder about, You, Reader,
Friend, how you are at this
moment and who you are.

But I must continue with the
storytelling, for the energies
that are eight will not wait, and
we must be prepared.

✳ **The Four Blinding Untruths**

The Four Mighty Ones, the
four dark energies which the
Nightcrawler must meet, are
colossal suffering residues of
that which blinded and darkened
the hearts of humanity in the
realm we call Earth. The exact
details still elude me, but
the four Blinding Untruths
are, bluntly put and clearly
said, FOUR LIES. They are lies
that have had such painful
consequences, such a veiling and
obscure effect on what is true
and real and authentic, that
the ensuing suffering left a
tremendous residue. This sticky
residue has been buried in the
depths of the Earth, hidden in
the profundity of the hearts
of all women and men. The four
energies are mighty in their
awesome and powerful force. They
are hungry to spill their anger,
to spread their pain. But they
are also hungry for peace, as
often is the case, and something
has awakened them. They do not
know what it is, but they have
begun their inexorable and
long-anticipated journey to a
glittering and compelling warmth
that captivates them. This is
Aileen, who is also, as we know
very well, much more than she
seems.

✳ **The Four Mirror-Shadows**

The Four Untruths each have a
corresponding Mirror-Shadow. This
is an energy that mirrors them,
that is part of them, but was
not buried in Dark IRAASA. They
stayed on the surface, at the
four corners of the Earth. They
lived and thrived on pain and
suffering, too, and are invisible
to the unkeen eye and heart. They
are the Transparent Grievers, the
shadows of what could have been
but were not. If they had a form,
they would be female just as the
Four Untruths would be male. The
Mirror-Shadows are bitter, too.
They hunger for revenge, for
they could have been whole and
never were. They have awakened
on hearing the Four Untruths
in movement and also sense the
sparkling, warm light that Aileen
emanates. They are making their
way to the Meadow.

An image has come:

By Jove, this has all been some kind of test!

The Star has just told me that in other times in the Earth Realm I was called a bard! I sang the stories of old from the heart and true sight. The bard is part of this Story, and if I had not returned, the Story would have been affected.

The Star would not explain more, but she did emphasize that ultimately, nothing could stop the blazing fire of the Telling, not even the Star or All-Seer, not even my doubts and not even the Story itself!

So, Reader, regardless of the trembles and concerns, I sing again! I am very happy! I have always had many dreams and sensations about an ancient time where I played a harp. I played in halls full of men and women who stilled themselves to hear my song. Now I understand. I was the Bard! And I realise that yes, I am the Storyteller of Old, but I have forgotten who I really am and that somehow I will discover this in this Story! This is the realisation, and it does add to the trembling, but the tremble is with complete trust to continue on.

And, Reader, I must tell you... you were there, too, in those halls! You were a Listener, a Hearer of the Story.

Jumping Jehosaphat! You are always here with the Bard. One cannot be without the Other.

Yes, One cannot be without the Other!

Hmm...

Always

The same Story

Always

The same Storyteller

Always

The same Reader

Am

I

Always

Here

In

Front

Of

Your

Eyes

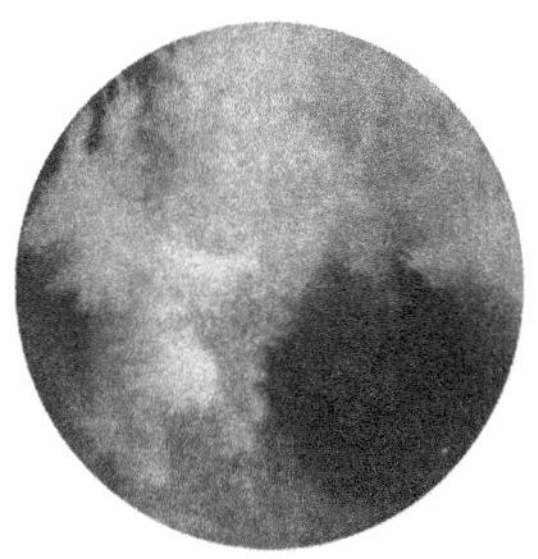

The Depths of IRAASA: In the Cocoon

Darkness

Waves of breath

I don't know anything

I can't see anything

I hear and I feel

I'm protected and nourished

I don't remember any names

But I know there are old friends

Magical Silver Friends

Wise Golden Friends

A Rooted Ancient Friend

Strong Friends with silky coats

A Sweet Friend with a soft, furry coat

Friends of the Mother

They're close by

I hear a mighty thundering... the body quakes

I hear a sultry whispering... the body shivers

I rest in an earthy chamber

I sleep in a silky cocoon

I'm not afraid

I await Thee, Mother

I know that Thou shalt never abandon Thy child

I forget Thee not

I love Thee

For I am Thou and Thou art I

Aileen's body changed: the colour of her skin darkened while plant-like Beings sprouted from her fertile flesh; her long hair took hold of the earth in rootish impersonation; silk strands from the cocoon intertwined and wove themselves into the tresses of hair, creating silver hues that shimmered even in the darkness.

The name 'Aileen' dropped away and made no more sense. This earthy creature was nameless and full of names. She was IRAASA, she was SAIRAA, she was ASAIRA...

A faint whisper fluttered up from the substratum of existence: AIRAAS, AIRAASSS, AIRAASSSS... The name sang itself faster and faster, AIRAASSS, AIRAASSSS, AIRAASSSSS, over and over, until it quietened and transformed into one musical note:

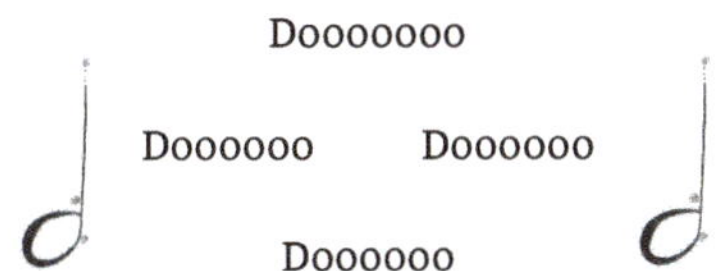

The musical note echoed through the cocoon and caressed this earth woman who had once been called Aileen. The note travelled deep inside of her, waking up the ancient note of UT:

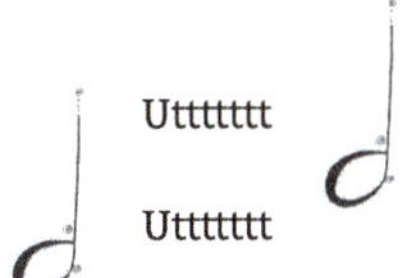

The harmony that ensued from Aileen's lips reverberated through the Depths of IRAASA in tremulous waves of vibrato:

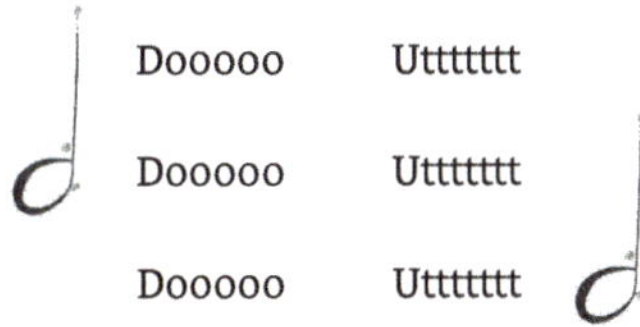

The Golden Weaver of the Void and the Silver Defender of the Nest felt their insectile legs throb and knew AIRAAS to be nigh.

The Star of Heavens

The Bard & The Listener

Must hear each other

Sing & Play

They shall

As the 4 Transparent Ones

Remember

Their Sparkling Selves

As shall the 4 Heavy Ones

Remember

Their Powerful Love

Aileen is **IRAASA**

Now for AIRAAS

ASAIRA is

Let my Divine Sparks

Touch the Hearts of All!

The Tree of Lands

They come

They burrow

They fly

I had forgotten

The Beginning of Time

And Now

The leaves swish and rustle

Our roots are resolute

The Ancientness remembers these 4

Aileen!

Child!

You too shall remember All

Ready Thyself!

The 4

Come to meet Thee

To be reunited

Rejoined

In the Wings of Freedom

See the Lies, my Child!

See the Truth, my Precious Aileen!

♩ Dooooooooo ♩ Utttttttttttttttt

An enormous wave of high frequency was felt in all the Realms and Non-Realms of ASAIRA. Every creature, every Being, was conscious of a shudder, a shaking, a tremor... For some it was as though the whole planet had shivered, for others where no knowledge of planets existed or words such as tremor had ever been created, it was perceived as an intuition, a knowing. It was a realisation of something great, but nameless, a birthing and a dying, a change, unknown yet familiar.

Flying over the Sea of Seas, the giant Emerald-Green Butterfly, more exquisite than ever could be described, moved her immense wings through the air. Each movement of the wings emitted a mysterious music, a melody from other worlds. The Butterfly's wings were the hands of ASAIRA and the air, the Harp of Harps.

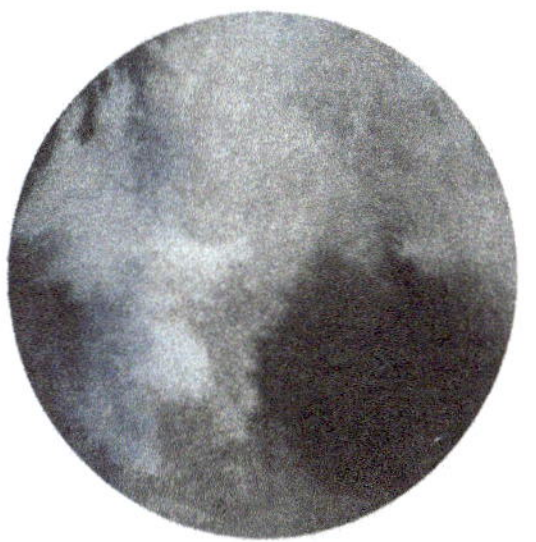

The Depths of IRAASA: The Dark 4

The Dark 4, the Myriad of Lies, stop their upward movement through the Depths as the musical vibration hits them in full force. A fiery, electrifying static erupts all around them. The 4 seethe, their eyes red in explosive fury.

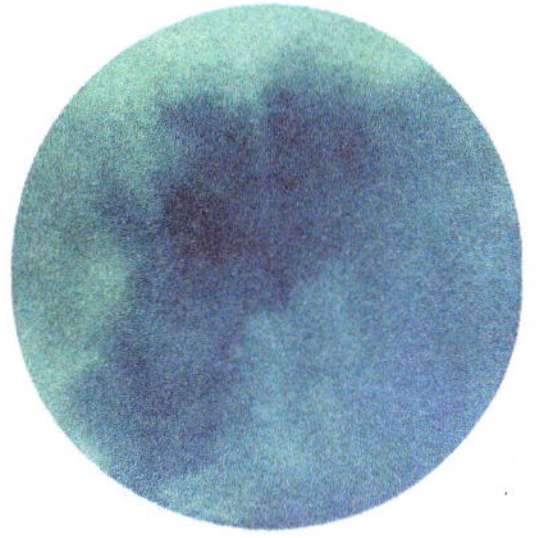

Earth: The Transparent 4

The Transparent 4, the Myriad of Revenge, crash into what is for them a wall of ice. The musical notes are to these four Bitter Grievers a barrier of extreme coldness, an unwanted stop to their flying. A froth of raging hatred surfaces from their cores.

The Storyteller

I am flabbergasted, fascinated...
and terrified!

I see the fire...

I see the ice...

And I hear the Harp...

I look up and I see the wings
of the Butterfly...

Aileen!

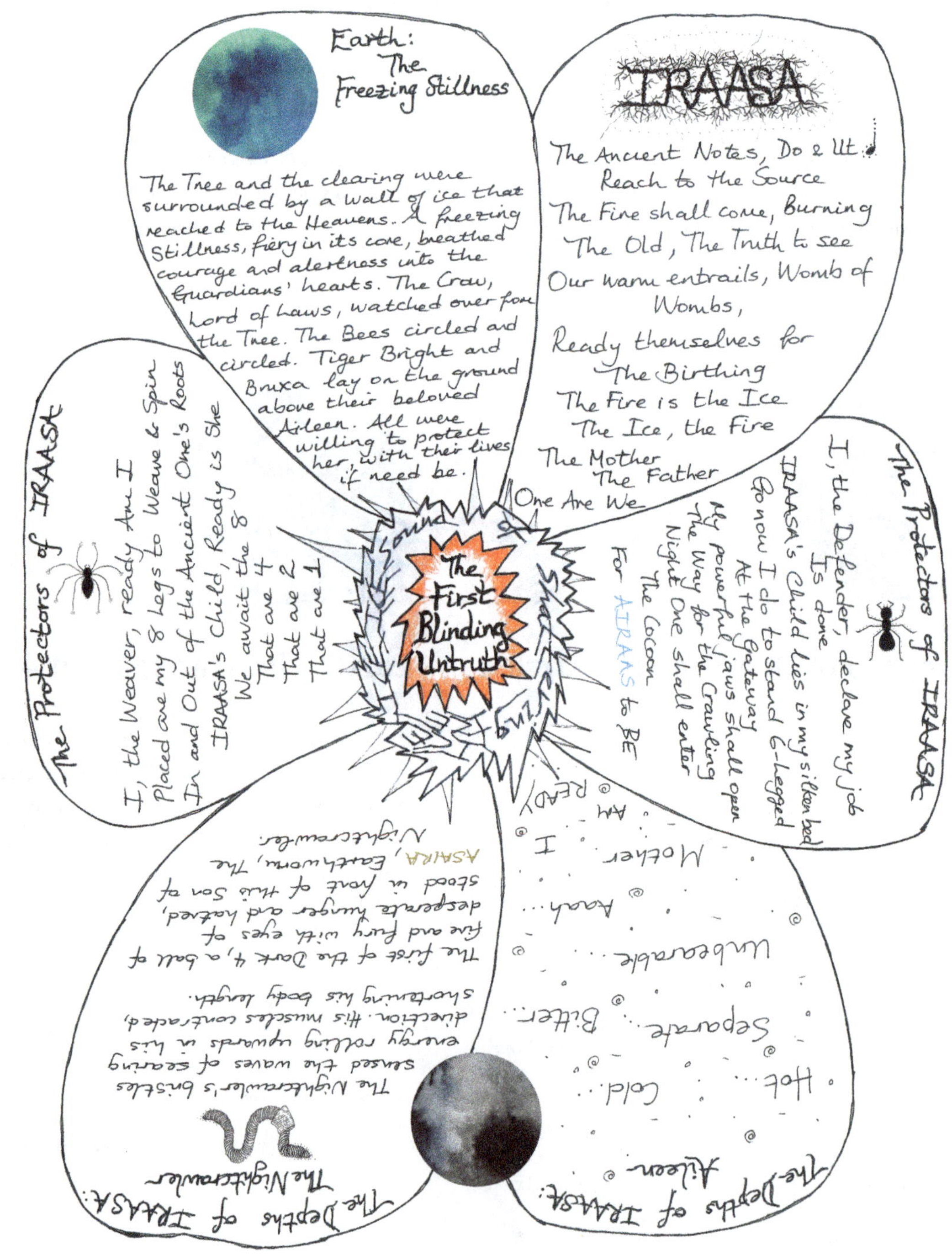

Earth:
The Freezing Stillness

The Tree and the clearing were surrounded by a wall of ice that reached to the Heavens. A freezing stillness, fiery in its core, breathed courage and alertness into the Guardians' hearts. The Crow, Lord of Laws, watched over the Tree. The Bees circled and circled. Tiger Bright and Bruxa lay on the ground above their beloved Aileen. All were willing to protect her, with their lives if need be.

IRAASA

The Ancient Notes, Do & Ut
Reach to the Source
The Fire shall come, Burning
The Old, The Truth to see
Our warm entrails, Womb of Wombs,
Ready themselves for The Birthing
The Fire is the Ice
The Ice, the Fire
The Mother
The Father
One Are We

The Protectors of IRAASA

I, the Weaver, ready Am I
Placed are my 8 legs to Weave & Spin
In and Out of the Ancient One's Roots
IRAASA's Child, Ready is She
We await the 8
That are 4
That are 2
That are 1

The Protectors of IRAASA

I, the Defender, declare my job
Its done
IRAASA's Child Lies in my silken bed
Go now I do to stand 6-Legged
At the Gateway
My powerful jaws shall open
The Way for the Crawling
Night One shall enter
The Cocoon
For AIRANS to BE

Sound
Sizing
The First Blinding Untruth

The Depths of IRAASA: The Nightcrawler

The Nightcrawler's bristles sensed the waves of searing direction. His muscles contracted, shortening his body length.
The first of the Dark 4, a ball of fire and fury with eyes of fire and fury, stood in front of this Son of desperate hunger and hazard,
ASAIRA, Earthworm, The Nightcrawler.

The Depths of IRAASA: Aileen

Hot ... Cold ...
Separate
Bitter
Unbearable
Aaah...
Mother... I... Am READY
Aileen

Hearest?

Listeneth

To the Heart?

It breaks

To be open

Its Fiery Love

Cries the Tears of Freedom

Hear

Listen

*Child of **ASAIRA***

Reader of Readers

Only One

Art

Thou

I love Thee

Unconditionally

Abandon Thee

Never shall I

♡ **Divine Sparks of Insight & Revelation** ♡

The 1st Untruth

Is the 2nd

Is the 3rd

Is the 4th

In persistent blindness

Each Transparent One

Bitter & Revengeful

Mirror-like

The 1st is the 2nd is the 3rd is the 4th

They feel to be 8

But they are 1

ᛉ SAIRAA

ᛉ IRAASA

ᛉ AIRAAS

ᛉ ASAIRA

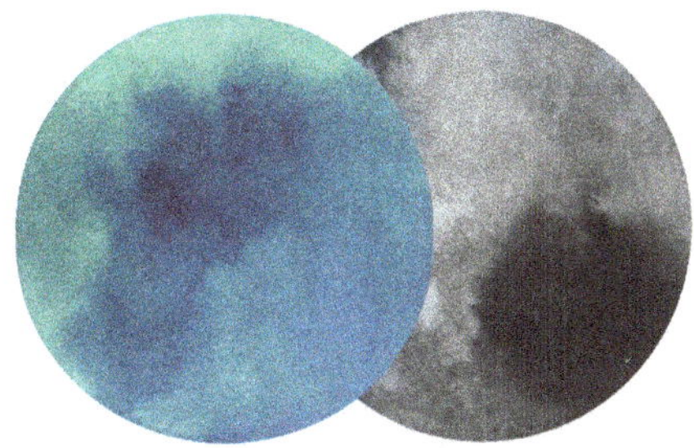

Earth 〰 The Depths of IRAASA

Aileen, who still has no remembrance of her Aileen self, hears a screech. She's deafened for a moment. Her body tenses. Then, a monumental quake shakes and pushes at her. Heat and cold soar into her back and chest: from above an iciness, from below a burning, each piercing her heart just as she sees a sword of ice and a flash of flames. Aileen's body arches, but the roots are able to hold the pull.

A calmness follows. Aileen, cocooned Earth Creature, continues to emanate sounds in ♪ Do and Ut. ♪

On the frozen snowed surface, the four Mirror-Shadows have penetrated through and broken the ice, apparently decimating all obstacles. They fly around the Tree and the clearing. To a human eye from the Earth Realm, these four grieving energies are invisible, but to all the animal and plant life visible they are indeed. They are transparent with a greyish tinge as if drawn with smoke. They look like four female figures with nebulous wispy robes. But what's most terrifying are their bloodshot eyes full of bitterness. The 4's pain and despair whirl through the air like a zillion barbed thorns.

The Nightcrawler is not far from Aileen's cocoon. In front of him stands the 1st Fury. Just behind the Fury, await the other three. If one looks very carefully, each of these balls of fire encloses a male figure wearing a dark cloak, the eyes unrelentless in their hatred, yet filled with the same woeful despair mirrored above by the Four Grievers. The Noble Nightcrawler has no eyes to see, but his segmented ring-like body and his short-pointed bristles easily detect the radiation that comes from the Four Furies.

The Ancient Tree, Tiger Bright and Bruxa remain still. On one of the branches, the Lord of Laws observes silently. The Bees stop their circling and land on the freezing, biting snow. Only two sounds are perceived: Aileen's vibrating ♪ Do-Ut ♪ and the whooshing of the four Mirror-Shadows in flight.

Time declares it is the moment! The flying Mirror-Shadows cease all movement and hover over the Tree. Down in the Depths, with the determination of aeons, the 1st Blinding Untruth surges unmercifully at the Nightcrawler. Aileen's body gasps.

The Tree of Lands

My Roots

My Branches

Are connected

To the Love of Loves

My Trunk

Solid & Stable

Holds

The Strength of Strengths

I am

Unmoved

No matter what storm is here

Even if it is

The Ancient Storm of Storms

In all its Awesome Might

Still

ASAIRA is

And the Mother

IRAASA

Gives birth to

AIRAAS

☆⋆ *PART 11* ⋆⋆

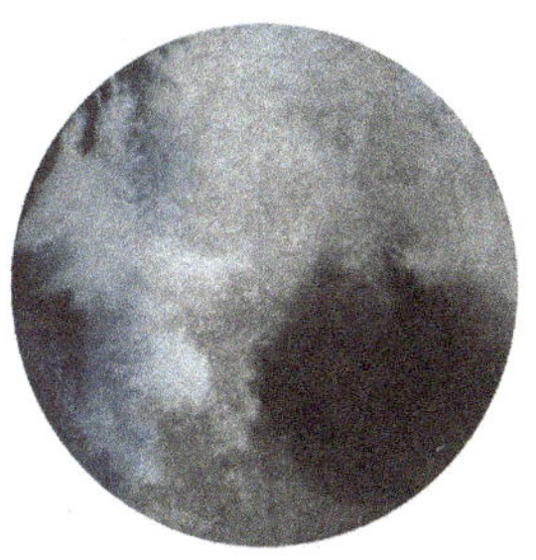

The Depths of IRAASA: The Hall

Aileen, or the Consciousness that was aware, saw images of a great hall decorated with intricate symbols. She recognised the elaborate shapes and spirals and was captivated.

An echo of music caught her ear. Someone was playing a harp and singing in deep, mellow tones. It felt so familiar. 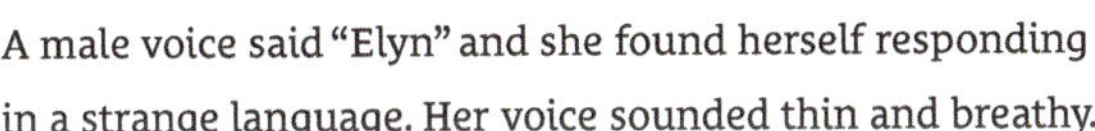

A male voice said "Elyn" and she found herself responding in a strange language. Her voice sounded thin and breathy.

The Consciousness gazed up and saw a young man. "Aaron," Elyn said softly, realising him to be her father and now, miraculously, her son.

A knowledge beyond knowledge, a knowing beyond knowing, flooded into all the cells of Aileen's body. A dizziness of wondrous-sounding names, of plants, of herbs, of trees, of symbols, of healing, of love, of truth, of the Mother… splashed and crashed like an engulfing sea of ancient lore and wisdom.

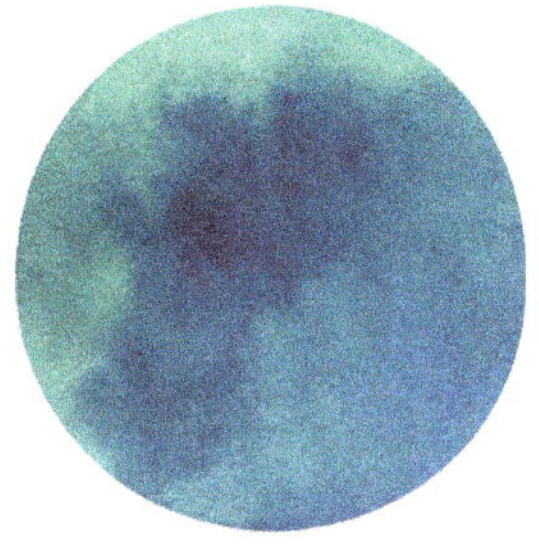

Earth: The Forgotten 4

The sudden surge of heat from under the clearing set everything into startling motion.

All the Guardians moved and placed themselves strategically on the snowy ground above Aileen's cocoon. The Bees took off in cluster. They circled, buzzing and whirring just above the animal Guardians.

All movements were carried out at an elevated speed, and yet slow and spellbinding, as if the details were to be seen in precision; nothing should be missed.

As the heat from under the ground increased, one of the four Mirror-Shadows screeched from above the clearing, "I am the Forgotten One! We are the Forgotten Four! But We… We never forget!!"

At this, the 1st Grey Shadow wailed in the most forlorn of laments. Then she swooped down towards the Guardians, followed closely by the other three.

To the three Shadows' horror, their sister was sucked into the Tree! The crown of the Tree had opened up and swallowed her! The 3, their eyes inflamed, stared at the Being who had dared so.

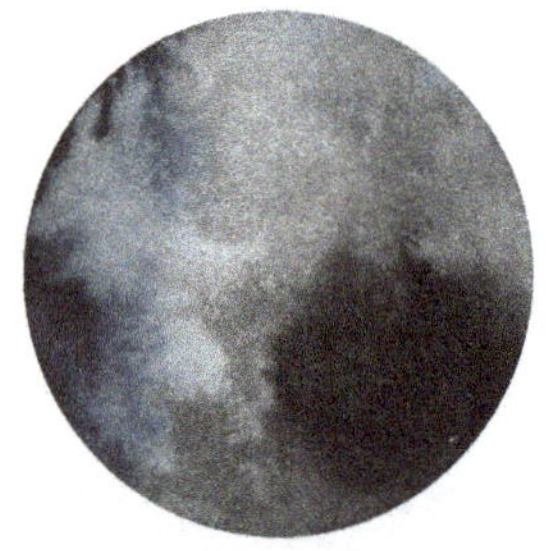

Ash   Rowan   Yew

Elder   Hazel   Catnip

Lavender   Marjoram   Sorrel

Thyme   Triquetra

Triskele   Dara   Arwen

ASAIRA

The Consciousness knew herself to be a wortcunner, a wise woman, now elderly. She knew that this given name, Elyn, meant 'The Light Bearer from the Green Meadow', as did the name Aileen. She knew her father-son, Aaron, was 'The Enlightened, Exalted Mountain of Strength'. She just knew so many things!

Suddenly, Aileen-Elyn, the multi-named Earth Creature, felt an explosion of heat.

The Fire

Transforms

The Ash

Feeds

The Earth

Gives Fruit

I am

The Fire of Fires

Let it Burn

For

*The Children of **ASAIRA***

The Storyteller

I know Elyn!

By Jupiter, I recognise that Hall of Halls... and the harp! I can hear its sweet melody right now. I am agog and bewildered! I know Elyn! Aileen... Elyn... I can't understand...

What does it all mean?

But, by all the Gods, I must attend the Story being told here, for it is an urgent moment for Aileen!

Reader, let us continue and know it all, once and for all!!

Wait, the Star sends some Divine

Sparks... I take a breath...

♡ Divine Sparks of Insight & Revelation ♡

𝒴 The 8 must Become

𝒴 The 4 that Are

𝒴 The 2 to Be

𝒴 The 1 Truth

𝒴 Is

Earth ꞉ꞏ The Depths of IRAASA

In front of the cocoon, the three Dark Furies shuffled back as they watched their brother be swallowed in one gulp by the worm-like creature before them. Swiftly, the Silver Defender of the Nest, who was just behind the Earthworm, used her ant jaws to tear a small opening in Aileen's cocoon. Without a second to spare, the Nightcrawler placed the rear part of his body through the opening in the cocoon…

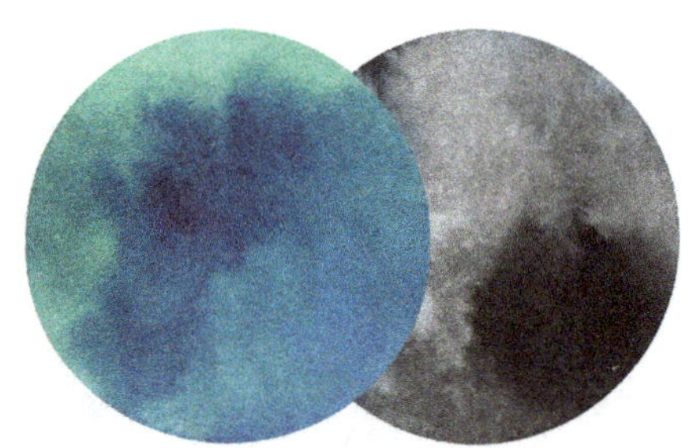

The Storyteller

```
I must interrupt here, dear Reader. I can see this
telling will be an arduous task, for many things
are happening at the same time at a hurtling speed!
Therefore, for the sake of comprehensibility, please
picture all aforementioned movements and subsequent
ones as virtually ONE inseparable sweep of my hand.
I shall do my best to be as concise and clear as
possible, but I may not succeed. Please bear with
me; there is a certain complexity in the events.
```

… and released the digested remains of the 1st Fury from the rear of his body into the cocoon. The 2nd, 3rd and 4th Untruths charged towards him. The Earthworm kept steadfast, ready and prepared for what he had always been ready and prepared for. As each Fury advanced, this brave Son of IRAASA swallowed and consumed each one despite the scorching in his intestines. The Four Furies could never have expected such unyielding strength, for how could they have ever imagined being devoured by this five-hearted creature and being deposited as waste?

And... as below so above. In the clearing, the three Mirror-Shadows struck and found themselves unwillingly following their sister, sucked into the heart of the Tree of Lands. They swirled down, disintegrating, as had their sister, into the Ancient One's roots that led to the cocoon and Aileen's back. But before each Mirror-Shadow's remains could enter Aileen's body, the Ancient Tree suspended them in front of another faithful Guardian: the Golden Weaver of the Void.

The Golden Weaver had been waiting inside the cocoon for all eight energies to arrive. When the Ant opened the hole in the cocoon, the Weaver had positioned herself. As the Nightcrawler released the remnants of the Four Furies, the Weaver liquefied and absorbed them into two of her six silk spinnerets at the rear of her abdomen. The Weaver, Spider of Spiders, had begun to produce a fibre of golden silk with red specks that sparkled like rubies. In sync, when each of the Four Mirror-Shadows from above was held before her, the Weaver extruded four strands of the newly made golden-red silk from her spinnerets and attached each golden-red strand to the wispy remains of the Mirror-Shadows. It was then that the Tree of Lands allowed the remains to enter Aileen's back.

Aileen's body jolted and shook, but the knowing that a miracle was taking place induced acceptance: the body knew not to be afeard. Within the body's cells, what was left of the Mirror-Shadows melted into a silver-blue fluid. The fluid travelled in and out of the organs and bones to then slowly exude out of Aileen's earthy skin like a silver-blue blood. The Weaver absorbed this sacred blue fluid into two other of her six spinnerets and produced another variety of silk: a silver silk with blue aquamarine specks. The silk shone with such exquisiteness that even the Darkness of IRAASA quivered on marvelling it. From such sorrowful pain, a pain of abandonment and revenge, a silk of breathtaking beauty had been conceived.

And so, the Weaving commences. The Spider, attached to Aileen's back by
the four golden-red silk strands, secretes four silver-blue strands. Winding and
interlacing the eight strands, the Weaver spins a filament: a golden-red silver-blue
thread that glistens in ruby aquamarine unlike anything seen in any realm. It is
the Sacred Thread of Seeing and Surrendering: a seeing and surrendering to the
Four Untruths and their Four Bitter Consequences. The 8 have become One, which
means the Weaving of AIRAAS can truly start!

All the Guardians, above and below, lie down or close their eyes to sleep. The
Cocoon breathes and settles, absorbing the peace that has arisen. Our dearest
Aileen is still and calm.

In the clearing and the Meadow, the snow and ice melt away and give rise to
spring. A symphony of flowers, green grass and sprouting mushrooms bursts out
of the ground.

Ahhh… says the Tree of Lands and lets his leaves sing in the breeze, comforting all
the Realms of ASAIRA.

The Emerald Green Butterfly

Fly to the Sun

Fly over the Earth

Air and Soil

Fly, Fly, Fly

IRAASA's Offering

Gives forth AIRAAS

Musical *Flutterings*

Glints of Gold & Silver

Red Rubies

Blue *Aquamarines*

AIRAAS

AIRAAS

AIRAAS

The Storyteller

Aileen wants to express herself although I'm not sure in what manner, but she needs to be listened to and be read.

I am afraid. I know that what Aileen shall say will transform me. I know this, and I also feel it shall transform you, dear Reader of Readers. I am eager to find out, but my heart beats in perturbation. However, I am decided. I'm here and this is my mission, my due. No more hiding, no more doubts. I am here to tell this Story of Stories.

First an image has presented itself:

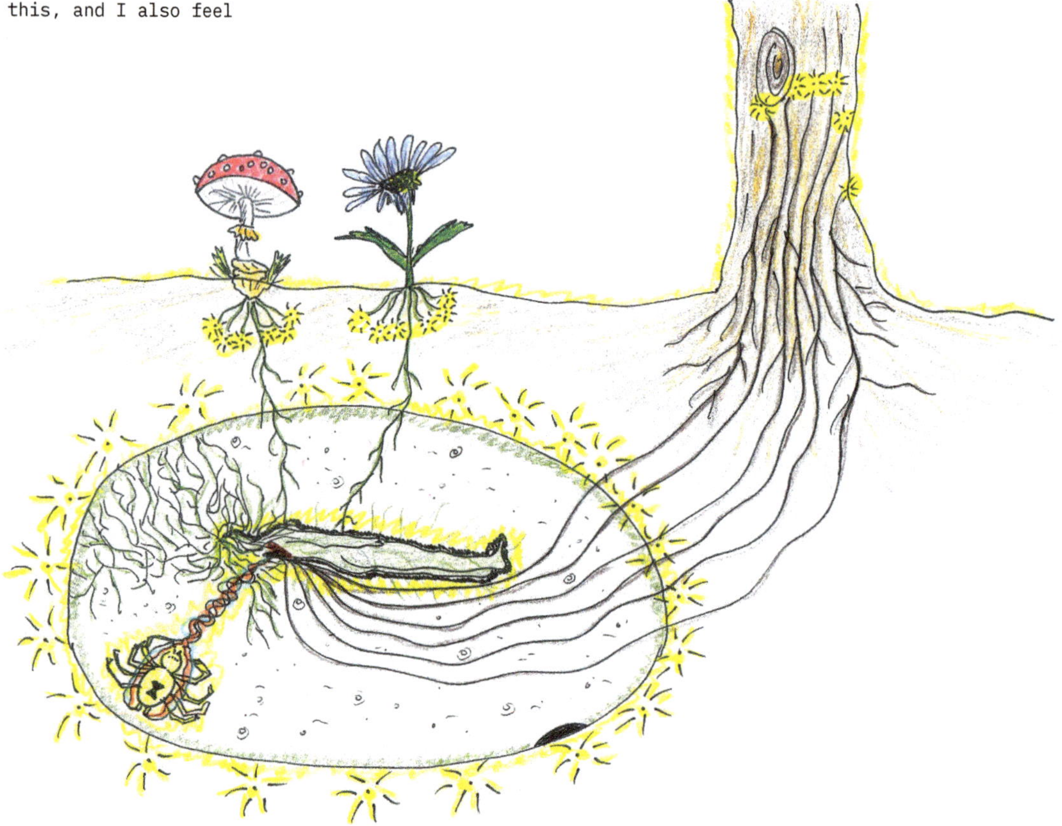

No words while I behold this drawing. In truth, it overwhelms me...

It is time, and with it time and space come to a halt.

I have been informed that what is to be revealed to Aileen, and thereby, us, will shed light on many years of blindness and fury. The Four Truths beg to be known and acknowledged.

After these revelations, I sense that we shall never be the same.

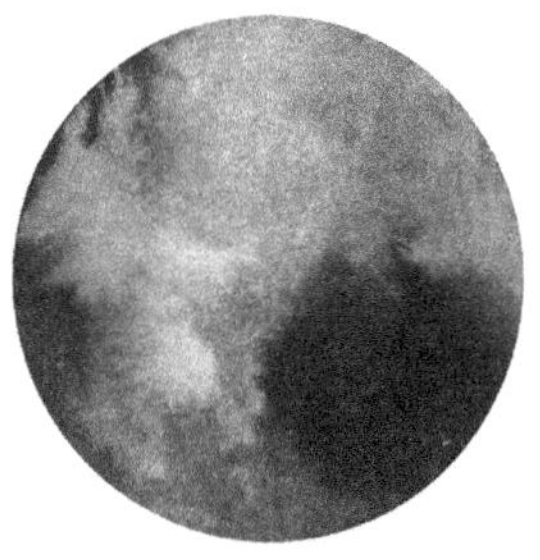

The Depths of IRAASA: The 1ˢᵗ Truth Revealed
6 not 3 for 1 to Be

Aileen saw through the eyes of the old woman whom she now knew herself to be. It was dark, and she walked slowly in a dense forest. She remembered she was looking for the Yew, the Revealer of Truth and Keeper of Secrets. Although Elyn's body was old and wizened and movement was challenging, Elyn pressed on. She intuited an urgency to visit the Sacred Yew, a kind of urgency which could not be ignored. Aileen, sensing the urge as her own, gave herself to being in Elyn's form.

Knowledge about Elyn flickered in and out. Elyn was a Wise Woman who knew every plant and tree in the forest. Revered in the community, she was a true healer and was consulted often. It was a time of closeness to nature, to the Mother of All, and even though every human Being was not a healer like Elyn, they all, each woman, man and child, possessed an innate resonance with the Mother. The Mother was named and adored as the Creator of All, and in this intuitive, yet logical comprehension, the natural processes and cycles of life had been integrated and became part of everyday living. Elyn and women of her kind were sought for every aspect of life. Mothers and women were respected and heard on equal ground as Fathers and men. This was a time of balance and harmony with nature and amongst humans. And people understood! They understood the Mother had given birth to all, had created it all, and that her sacred breath existed in every creature.

Aileen's consciousness realised that this was an ancient time on Earth. It felt like England for some unknown reason that she could not specify. The language was not English, though; it was a language she could not recognise, but was nonetheless able to understand.

Elyn stopped in front of the Yew. She said various words in honour of the spirit of the Tree, bowed and introduced herself. She then placed her wrinkled hand on the cool bark. Aileen's body felt so soothed and ecstatic that any lingering sense of consciousness other than Elyn completely dropped away. She was now only Elyn.

An image was revealed to Elyn. It was one that came as no surprise, one that was deeply known to her and everyone around her, one that was natural as life itself: an image of the Mother, ASAIRA, for Her Name was known in this place and time of old.

ASAIRA had six aspects that were not separate but were part of one Being. These six aspects were also inside each human Being and needed to be balanced for life to exist in harmony and truth. Elyn acknowledged the rightness and was comforted by the image. But she imagined the Yew had more secrets otherwise she would not have had such an urgency to come that night. Scarcely had the thought made itself heard when another image arose.

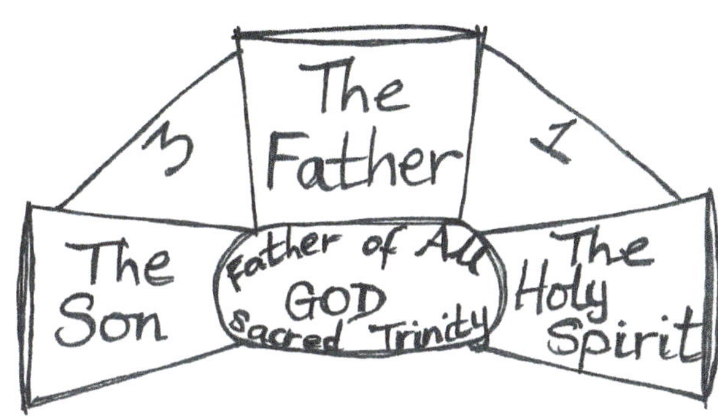

Elyn shuddered. Visions of flames and destruction raged before her. Elyn felt split into two. She was at a loss, incomplete. What was this? Half of the innate, intrinsic aspects of her body and soul had been eliminated… or wait… better said, they were there but invisible, shaky and full of angry confusion. Another image swept in.

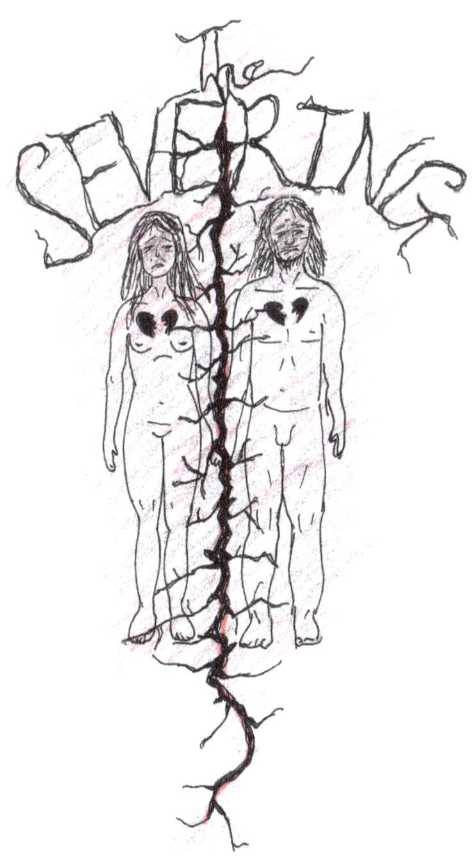

Mirroring the image, the word 'Severing' seemed to have the power to break Elyn's heart. With difficulty and a little faint, she sat down on the earth under the Ancient Yew. She realised the images were of a world that was to come: a world where the Mother would be eradicated; a world with incomplete truths that, hence, were lies. The Three Aspects shown of the Father were undeniably true, but this so-called unity was a self-destructing lie in its incompleteness. It was a half-truth which could deceptively ring true in the hearts of men and women, but it would leave an aching abyss, a desperate emptiness. Elyn saw that for generations to come, humans would search for their other lost half, unable to remember they were six. And ASAIRA, the Mother of All? Apparently, gone! Many would feel an abandonment and despair.

"ASAIRA, Oh, Mother, why have you shown me this sorrowful future? I cannot bear to see you disappear. Oh, Mother, Mother… let me join you now. Bring the sweet death-sleep for I cannot serve anymore."

Aileen became aware of her own hand: it rose and caressed the old woman's silky white hair.

Elyn had never experienced such peace and love as she looked up into Aileen's soft brown eyes, "Mother, Mother…"

Then, Elyn-Aileen understood. She remembered that she would never disappear, that she, too, was ASAIRA.

She closed her eyes and fell asleep whilst the Mother whispered, "6 not 3 for 1 to be, 6 not 3 for 1 to be, 6 not 3 for 1 to be…"

The Weaver of the Void, Protectress of IRAASA, gently took a lock of Elyn's white hair and wove it into the golden-red silver-blue speckled Thread of Threads. Quivering in recognition, the Thread embraced Elyn's snowy white strand, strengthened and wiser with her essence. This set another miracle into motion: the 1st Mighty Fury, an energy which had deliberately persecuted and obliterated the Feminine, together with its Bitter Mirror-Shadow, which had sought revenge and the complete destruction of the Masculine, now, at last, completed their alchemic transmutation into peace and solace. The Thread vibrated in acknowledgement of the 1st Untruth's transformation into Truth and shone in quiet, endless joy.

And if one observed closely, the avid Spider's weaving showed a tiny web-like form: hardly visible, it glowed in nine-stranded iridescence.

Above, in the clearing, six snow-white yellow-centred daises popped their heads out.

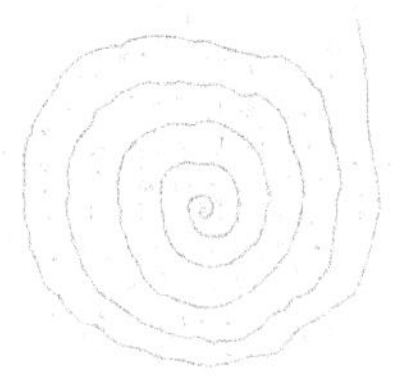

Mmm...

The Waves of Eternity

Peace

Harmony

Beauty

Soothing us

I am

The Soother

The Caressing and Loving

Star of the Sea

♡ **Divine Sparks of Insight & Revelation** ♡

♈ 12 Strands

♈ 4 Exquisitenesses

♈ 2 make 4

♈ 3 Sacred Strands each

♈ 6 times 6 equals ONE

The Spiralling Weaver commences

Beauty beyond Beauty

IRAASA is the Cocoon

For AIRAAS to fly!

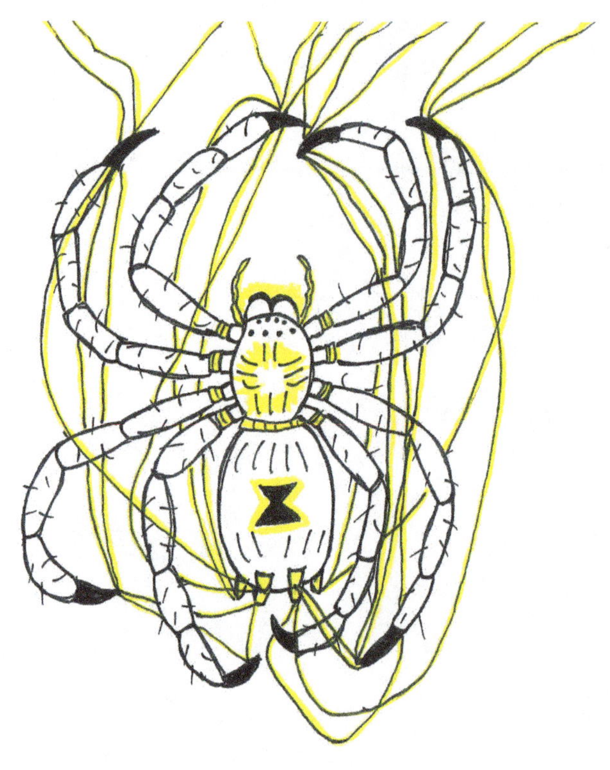

The Storyteller

Elyn...

I hear her name and I hear the Harp of Old... I hear the Stories told around long tables...

Her silver-white hair was long and thick, and her brown eyes were the kindest and wisest I had ever encountered.

Elyn...

Aileen...

The Star of Heavens has spoken to me.

She tells me that the Four Revelations are really One Revelation, in the same way as the Six Knowings (Yes, the Star confirms there are Six Knowings!) that are contained in ASAIRA are One Knowing. At the same time, each Revelation, each Knowing has its purpose, its uniqueness, its sole connection to the Truth.

And Reader! I have been asked to inform you again and insist: you are indispensable here in this Story of Stories! Your eyes and your heart are the keys to ASAIRA!

The 2nd Truth reveals itself. I am ready.

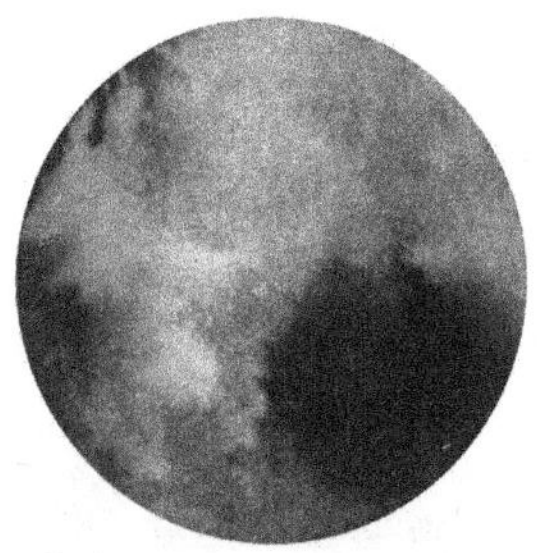

PART 13

The Depths of IRAASA: The 2nd Truth Revealed

Untitled

The Storyteller

I have sat for some time awaiting the title of the 2nd Revelation, but it does not appear. What does appear is a pain in my heart that, dear Reader, I know comes from what is to be told in the next few pages. In a way, I wish to flee and not find out; it is much easier. But I stay steadfast, inspired by Aileen and her courage. I have asked for more help from the Star and All-Seer and the Story itself. They have confirmed their presence and their support. Ah, there is much gratitude, my Friend. Let us proceed, then.

The comforting fragrance of forest and earth dissolved. Aileen's body tensed: a smell of mould and mildew… a sound of water trickling… it felt cold and damp. With effort, the eyes opened.

The Consciousness which was perceiving looked around and saw the bleak stone walls. It was a cell… It felt suffocating and heavy. The Consciousness gazed down at its body: a female adult, a ragged robe and… chains around one of the ankles. Aileen came to for a moment and realised she was someone else again, someone who had a terrifying pain in her heart, someone she knew… Because it was her, just as Elyn was her! But now she was a woman called Eilène!

Eilène sat up and leant against the wall behind her. Placing a hand over her heart, she started to pray. She prayed for her loved ones, her husband, her children, that they be safe, that they be saved from this blind terror, this madness which had swept her country and fellow men and women. Tears fell down Eilène's cheeks. A tremble set in, and she prayed for more strength. Eilène had the wisdom to ask for help: she didn't want to forget that, despite this raging Terror of Terrors, the Peace could not be taken away from her.

Aileen fled and found herself back in the cocoon. She felt small, her power forgotten. Her body shook and her hands gripped as a claustrophobic panic climbed into her throat. I've got to get up, get out of here!

"Don't move, my love, the Strands and the Sacred Thread shall break! Remember you are here in the Mother's Arms. You are so much more than what you seem! Remember your promise to be here, to see the Lies no matter what arises. What you shall see is a dream, a dream that requires to be seen, a dream that wishes to come home to the Mother and rest."

The loving voice brought tranquility to Aileen's mind, and it became still. The body relaxed and was able to give itself completely to Eilène. There was no turning back now.

Eilène stood up. She took a few steps towards the wall and stretched up. Tiptoeing, she peered through a tiny window. This was the second time in her imprisonment she'd had the courage to do so. Full of gratitude, she felt the hand of God support her back. The warmth of the hand kept her close to the Peace. Eilène contemplated the pile of wood and naked stake. Yes, she knew it was for her. Her heart beat faster, but the warm hand upheld her with tenderness: she felt transported far away to a sea of peace, a sea of silver…

Oblivious to the dirt and the cold, Eilène lay down on the stone floor. She closed her eyes and sank into the Peace deep inside… the Silver Sea…

Eilène heard some music… a sweet singing and a harp… ah, si belle… mmm… merci… merci… merci…[6] Aileen became aware that Eilène was French, and it was the late Middle Ages. The music brought images of children, of a family, of a man with a kind face, of laughter and love. The images flickered in and out of the silverness.

Eilène opened her eyes. Floating over her was the most beautiful creature she had ever seen. Gone were the gloomy grey walls, now all she could see were blue skies. C'est un ange…[7]

The exquisite winged-creature spoke to her in an unknown language, but Eilène was able to understand. "Eilène, my love. You have been chosen for your strength of heart. You are not what you seem, you are much more! You are immersed in a painful moment, but it is a moment that shall bring a vision of Truth to others, for it is of such dementia, such imbalance that it can only serve to bring lucidity and balance. I know that you suffer, and I am so sorry for that, but you shall be spared all further pain for doing this service of warrior. Take this sacred pink strand from my wings. It is made of lavender. Keep it close to your heart, always; it shall guide you home to the Mother of Mothers. It will also take all pain away from your body and mind while the flames are around you. My sweet child, the Mother is with you and all the Guardians of Truth are at your side. I shall be with you, and I am with you. My love, take the pink strand and hold it."

Aileen saw herself give Eilène the silky pink-coloured strand. The strand felt warm, and its scent of lavender filled the air with healing. Aileen looked into Eilène's eyes and remembered her sad death, while Eilène recognised a light in the eyes of Aileen and knew it was herself, her essence. A wisdom and understanding revealed itself to Eilène-Aileen. Yes, so much pain caused by fearing the Feminine, but this blindness could not eradicate the True Mother. She was here, always here, in the Peace and never abandoned her children.

---

6 The Story Speaks

This is the French language of the Earth Realm: 'si belle' means 'so beautiful' and 'merci' means 'Thank you'.

---

7 The Story Speaks

More of the French language:'C'est un ange' is 'It's an angel'.

The 2nd Blind Untruth, an energy which had sent thousands of women to be burnt at the stake, with thousands more men and women tortured in its name over the ages, saw the last flame of fear and hatred transmuted into Truth and knew at last the peace of returning home. The golden-red strand glittered in completeness. In unison, the 2nd Untruth's Mirror-Shadow, a tormented and violent energy which could never have forgiven its persecutors, now delivered itself into a final melting of all the suffering and anger. It left nothing, nothing except the transmuted strand of silver-blue, a strand that shone like the reflection of the sun on the sea.

Softly, the Spider Weaver pulled and spun the perfumed lavender strand of love that was attached to Eilène's heart and wove it into the net-like creation. Both the Nightcrawler and the Defender of the Nest looked upon the creating of AIRAAS in awe, as though it were possible you might say that an earthworm and an ant could be awe-inspired. But these Protectors of IRAASA were, of course, much more than what they seemed and revelled in the beauty that lay before them.

In confirming eruption, a hundred sumptuous roses bloomed in pure elation under the Ancient Tree of Lands. Streaming colours of pale pink, apricot, yellow, ivory white, crimson red and orange... the scent of the roses was both hypnotising and healing. Dazzled, the Guardians of ASAIRA, Tiger Bright, the Lord of Crows, the Bees of the Queen and little Bruxa, came closer and lay in the floral elixir. The roots of the Beloved Tree stretched and filled themselves with nutrients and love. This Ancient One knew the roses had grown out of Aileen's body which was even more indistinguishable, for already she had become of the Earth, but now she had become of the Heavens!

10 Strands

AIRAAS

Here was She always

Spirals of Time

2 Strands more

Child of the Earth

Child of ASAIRA

Child

No more

And yet

Innocent & Silent

Wise & Wild

꒳ 12 Strands

꒳ 1 Thread

꒳ 2 Flutterings

꒳ 1 Being

꒳ Freedom for All

The Storyteller

Eilène... Eilène... I see your death, I was there! I prayed and prayed for a miracle. There was none! There was none! You died, you were taken from me...

My dear Reader, I cannot go on now, though I promise to continue when I am able. It is too much for me now. It is clear beyond any doubt that the story of Aileen is my own. I could never have imagined... and yet, how could I forget such a thing?

Eilène... I loved you so much. I died in non-forgiveness, in bitter hatred for what they had done to you, to us, to our family.

Ahh... dear Reader, dear Friend, are we also, you and I, more connected than what is apparent?

Enough... no more words. I shall speak again when I am able.

The Sea of Seas

Our Watery Arms

Are here for you

Feel the Peaceful Deliciousness

Of the Life-Giving Waves

That fill your Hearts

With the Breath of Breaths

Let the Truths

That reveal themselves to you

Be melted in

The Sweetest of Liquid Loves

Our Earthy Darkness

Receives the Seeds of Pain

There is no waste

For all serves a purpose

Come, come to my Earthy Arms

Let all be absorbed

Into the Soil of Soils

For the Flower of Love

To be seen

Reader

You are

The Eyes of Reality

See around you

The Truth is also revealed to you

Use the Calming Ocean

Use the Soft Earth below your feet

Use the Fiery Flames

Inside your Heart

Use Compassion and Understanding

And

Be In Joy

For I am

At your side

Constantly

I am

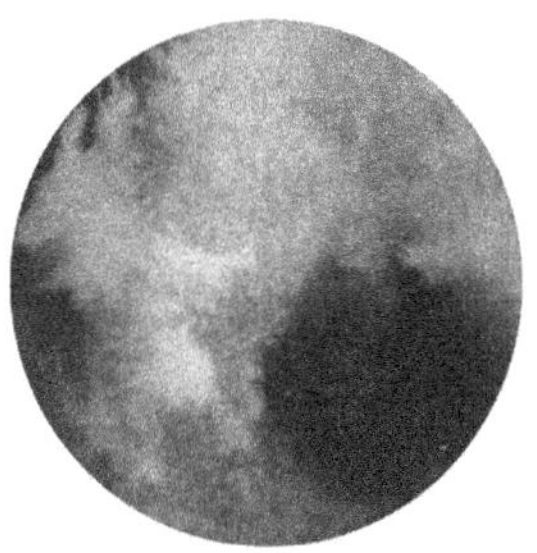

PART 14

The Depths of IRAASA: The 3rd & 4th Truths Revealed
One Cannot Be Without The Other

Aileen looked at the little boy. He's so sweet… Oh! Aileen's heart jumped. He's my little boy… Juan! Then she realised he looked like Grandfather John as an instant flash of him and her Grandmother Becca zoomed in. But yes, it was Juan, her son!

A overwhelming wave of love soared into her heart. Never had Aileen experienced such a feeling: the protective love of a mother… she would do anything for her child and would never abandon him.

"Mama, Mama!" Juan came running up and tugged at her long skirts. "Mama…"

Aileen looked down upon her son's head and felt a ferocity which was new to her as Aileen but developed and round in this woman's world.

The Storyteller's eyes opened and closed. He blinked to focus the blur. How small I am, he thought, while he hung onto the dark skirts. Forgotten emotions flooded in. His mother was everything, and when she said Juan he felt so happy. She was the world, she was his carer, she was the love… and he was only safe in her arms.

Juan revolved around his mother like a satellite and was completely mirrored by his mother, for she had lost her husband and all of her family, and she would not lose him! This little Being, her Juan, was her only life.

The Storyteller sensed himself gradually vanish, floating… floating on liquid silverness… Oh, the Sea of Seas, yes… The Teller left and now only Juan remained. Aileen echoed the Storyteller's wisdom and let herself drop back into the Soil of Soils.

Intermittent images and words that contained knowledge about Juan and Elena, for that was this woman's name, along with their sombre world painted themselves across the minds of Aileen and the Storyteller: an unrelenting seriousness that shrank the hearts of all, the words 'sin' and 'God' repeated again and again, reprimands, fear, duty... ahhh... dark shadows everywhere...

Juan had had a natural love and aptitude for music, for drawing, for storytelling, for dressing-up and play... but he had this love no longer. His mother and this world had literally beaten it out of him. Elena cherished Juan dearly, but knew she had a solemn duty; the sins which Eve[8] had brought into the world needed to be forced out of the body, with vehemence if it were to work. Her son, Juan, was going to be a saintly man, yes, and to be revered by the community. She taught him that singing and dancing were evil feminine vices which the Daughters of Eve used to distract the Sons of Adam from a God-fearing life. She taught him that any woman who did not go to Holy Mass every day was a lost wretch, a fallen woman never to be trusted.

Earnestly praying the rosary and consulting holy scripture for guidance, Elena ensured she was the living example of a good woman who knew her place in life and showed her devotion to God. She had a mission, and she could not rest because devilish powers existed and were on the prowl; there were evil women called witches who would try to tempt Juan into a life without God. She was determined that her son would never be killed for heresy... those awful women, yes... she had known them very well, they had received their due. No woman like that would come near her or her son again! She had made a vow to protect her son, and Elena gripped onto it without mercy: Juan had to learn all about these monstrous women who followed the devil.

Naturally, Juan's suppressed imagination, far from being eliminated, could not help but be set irrevocably alight with visions of fallen women and diabolical witches! And, of course, no one could put a stop to the endless storytelling that went on inside Juan's mind. He became fascinated with the heroes, the brave and noble men who brought these wicked temptresses to justice. He, too, wanted to fight for God and protect humanity. No more music, no more laughter or painting or dancing... no, he wanted to be good, he wanted to be a hero, a saint!

---

8 **The Story Speaks**

Eve and Adam and the story of the Garden of Eden. The Storyteller gives a fuller account at the end of the 2nd Knowing (Part 18).

Juan grew up and became a priest. Later, due to his knowledge of law, another of his passions, a huge honour befell him: he was appointed the Chief Holy Inquisitor, for this was Spain, this was the time of the Inquisition,[9] a time of ridding the world of all sinful heretics. God was depicted as hard and serious, punishing and forcing his sheep into obedience. No compassion could be shown.

Over the years, Elena looked at her son with pride, but also a little fear since Juan's eyes of Holy Inquisitor were always vigilant, and even Elena, his mother, was not spared his scrutinising glare.

Elena was now very old. Daily, she sat in Juan's court of justice, the Tribunal, in a giant wooden chair, which made her look even more tiny and frail. Juan was nearly sixty years of age. Tired and somewhat bored, Juan carried out his duty day in and day out, earning his place in Heaven with God.

A succession of images and sounds suddenly burst through the monotony: a tumultuous noise... a young girl of no more than fourteen years of age standing in front of Juan... the girl trembling... golden hair and pale blue eyes... a garland of flowers around her head... a halo of sweetness... confused thoughts buzzing in Juan's mind... an angel?... a roar of voices crying out, "¡Es una bruja!"[10]... evidence being presented... it all seemed ridiculous... Juan felt nauseous.

Yet, maybe it was true. An authentic witch could appear as an innocent young creature even though she was really the devil-incarnate, not an angel... yes, he knew! But Juan hesitated. Elena saw the doubt in her son's eyes; she saw the eager, crazed rabble; she saw the young girl and knew she was guiltless... however, she knew something that was much more important... the girl had to die. If not, Juan would be doomed.

More noise. More confusion.

A desperate anxiousness crept up inside of Juan... I drown!

Elena's voice sounded in his ear, "Juan, send her to the stake. Do it. Do it! If not, you shall be the one to die. Save yourself. God will understand. You have been his faithful servant. Sacrifice the Lamb. It is of no importance after everything we have sacrificed ourselves to be here now. She is no one. It is her destiny and God's will."

---

9 The Story Speaks

The Inquisition was an institution whose aim was to ensure everyone was Christian. In Spain, Earth Realm, it existed from the 15th to 19th century.

---

10 The Story Speaks

This is the Spanish language: 'Es una bruja' means 'She's a witch'.

The Lamb was sacrificed.

The crowd abated, a thick, heavy silence covered the Earth.

Elena rested in her room. She pushed down any voices that sounded like guilt or regret. Juan, though, could not rest, would not be abated and could not push away the voice of pain in his heart that rang, "I am the Lamb of God. I am the Lamb of God."[11] Frantically, he went outside to the remains of the wooden pile. Amidst the cinders, something glittered: a golden crucifix. Juan knew it had belonged to the young girl. A searing despair pierced his stomach. Juan doubled up and fell to his knees. With ravaging clarity came a vision of his mother beating him because he had dressed up as an angel and run around the house dancing.

Juan was dying of sadness. He lay in bed, clutching the gold crucifix of the Lamb. At his side, Elena trembled and realised her time was near too.

"Mother, why did you do this to me? Why did you make me a monster? I killed the Lamb of God! I am no different to Pontius Pilate when he sentenced Christ to death.[12] ¿Por qué, Madre, por qué?"

"Hijo,[13] it is because I loved you! I wanted to protect you from all evil... save you!"

"Madre, that is not real love. It's fear. Fear!" Juan wept inconsolably.

Elena clutched the bed clothes. The word 'fear' pulsated inside her. She couldn't hear or see. Tears ran down her face as a memory of a love that once had been free of fear rushed into her heart. Dios mío... Dios mío...[14] What did I do? What did I do?

---

11 The Story Speaks

The Storyteller explains the reference to the Lamb of God in the 2ⁿᵈ Knowing Part 14. The Lamb of God is from the Gospel of St. John. (The Bible)

---

12 The Story Speaks

Again from Christianity: according to the Bible, Jesus Christ, considered by Christians as the saviour of humanity and son of God, was sentenced to death by Pontius Pilate, who was a Roman prefect in Judaea, Earth Realm, in the 1ˢᵗ century.

---

13 The Story Speaks

More of the Spanish language: '¿Por qué, Madre, por qué?' means 'Why, Mother, why?' and 'Hijo' means 'Son'.

---

14 The Story Speaks

'My God... My God...'

Aileen recognized UT. "Juan, you have no name really. We are both here in this nightmarish story, but we can tell another truer story! Do you hear me, Bard of Bards? Can you hear the melody?"

The Storyteller heard the harp. He looked up into Elyn's face. He recognised her in different forms in different lives. "Madre, I vow to come back to tell the True Story. I shall live again to sing and dance!"

Elena took Juan's hand. She could hardly speak. "I vow and promise the same, hijo mío. I wish to know the Truth which I cannot see now. I feel I knew, but I forgot it. Forgive me, Juan, forgive me…"

"I forgive you, Madre… Te perdono…"[15]

With these words, Juan and Elena died in each other's arms.

Elena and Juan's essence dissolved into the Weaver's spinnerets. Two new strands came into existence: a shining purple strand for Juan and a soft green velvet strand for Elena. The Spider wove in delight, for now the twelve strands required for the Thread of Threads were intact. The 3rd and 4th Untruth and their Mirror-Shadows forgave and surrendered. They remembered the pain of repression and fear that had made mothers and fathers turn their children into something they were not; it had made a sorrowful world of fear and violence.

The last golden and silver strands tingled as the Truth was revealed, a Light of Lights that illuminated the deepest truth of being part of One Whole: twelve strands, one thread. One could not be without the Other! The 3rd Knowing could not be without the 4th, in the same way as none of the Knowings, none of the Revelations, could be without the others.

The Weaver spun and wove, creating the new from the old, and yet creating the already created, the always created.

Time and Space rested in respect.

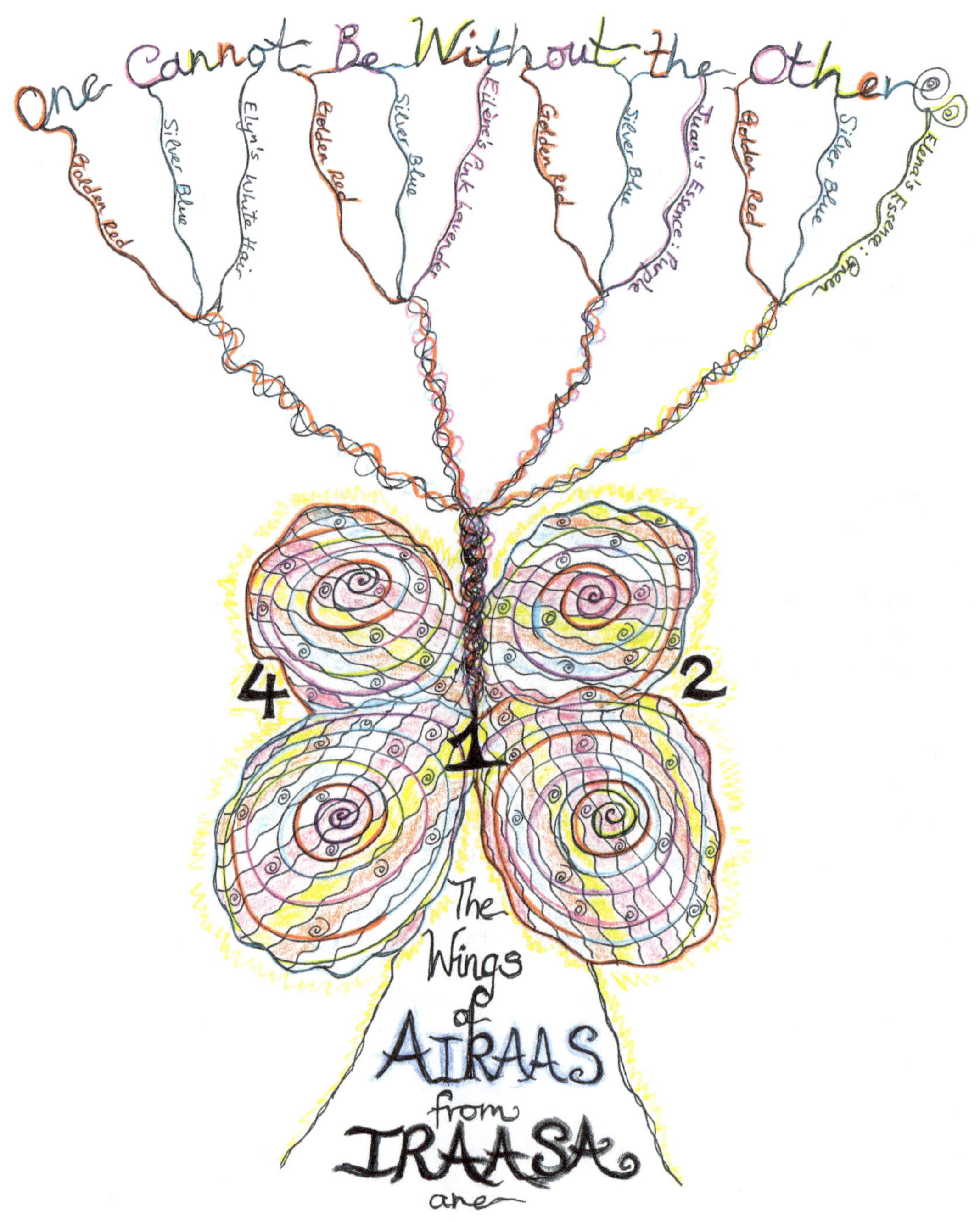
One Cannot Be Without the Other
Golden Red
Silver Blue
Elyn's White Hair
Golden Red
Silver Blue
Eilene's Pink Lavender
Golden Red
Silver Blue
Juan's Essence: Purple
Golden Red
Silver Blue
Elena's Essence: Green
4
2
1
The Wings of ATRAAS from IRAASA are

☆* PART 15 *☆

All-Seer

Greetings

Friends of Old

Readers & Seers

Perceivers of

THIS

The Storyteller, Our Beloved Bard,

Rests

As he receives

The Four Revelations

I shall relate

What is to come

With the Star of Heavens

Until the Storyteller

Is ready again

So be it!

Earth ⚬ The Depths of IRAASA ⚬ Other Realms

AIRAAS opens her eyes. Her fingers twitch. Very slowly, she lifts her hands and arms, certain of the power to do so. Her head tilts forward a little. She watches all the plants and flowers and mushrooms fall off her arms, and how the earth crumbles to each side of her body. The four roots let out a groan and release AIRAAS.

Around the Tree, the elements yawn and wake up to IRAASA's call: the wind blusters and dances with the rain that pours down; the sun comes out from behind the clouds, undeterred by the rising storm; thunder rumbles, lightning blazes in and out of the clouds.

The elements quieten again and become silent. A fragrance of recent rain intermingles with the lifting mist, while the sun bathes the Meadow in its light. The Meadow sparkles with shimmering raindrops, transformed into an immense grassy ocean. Tiger Bright and Bruxa sit themselves amidst the wet blades of grass and wait.

AIRAAS moves her head from side to side. Her feet wake up, wanting to shake the soil off. Her rough, bark-like skin is shedding. A sound no Earth Being has ever heard comes from AIRAAS's mouth and body: an eerie euphony like a thousand strumming harps, so beautiful…

IRAASA bellows in unison with AIRAAS's song and pushes. With a tumultuous moan, the cocoon splits into two. The three Protectors of IRAASA, the Weaver of the Void, the Nightcrawler and the Defender of the Nest, cling onto the four-winged creature that was once Aileen, when IRAASA thrusts for the last time, propelling AIRAAS out of the entrails of the Earth.

I am All-Seer but I have no words, not enough exist in this Earth language to describe the birth of AIRAAS from out of the Depths and into the Green Meadow.

Imagine a volcano erupting in the middle of a sea of turquoise grass, and then
the most incredible winged-creature spurting out, exploding with life through the
fiery orifice of the earth and out in dazzling flight into a sky of blue!

AIRAAS is suspended in the sky in mid-flight. Her four powerful wings that
are two, made from the Pain of Pains, flutter in a rainbow-coloured pearly
iridescence. The size of various buildings high, AIRAAS is redoubtable. Her body
is transparent yet opaque and luminous, tree and angel in one. Her silky hair falls
in kaleidoscopic cascades down her body, and her gaze is soft but keen and dark,
compassionate but wild and free. Aileen is decidedly not there, or so it seems.

AIRAAS's hands open. The Earthworm and Spider jump into AIRAAS's right hand
and, for a fleeting spark, turn into Saul and Shimmera to then melt into golden
rose petals. The Ant and the Crow fly into the other hand in mirrored succession
and transform into Smanara and Silas. The Silver Ones are visible for a few
seconds, too, turning into tiny black and silver obsidian stones. AIRAAS lifts her
hands. The petals and stones rain gently from her hands onto the greenness of the
Meadow.

AIRAAS looks down at the two Guardians, Tiger Bright and Bruxa. Feeling her
warm gaze, Bruxa whines. AIRAAS kneels down, picks Bruxa up and places her
close to her heart. She strokes the Tiger with respect and love, though a little cat he
seems to her. He purrs and nudges her.

With a bow towards the forest and the Tree, AIRAAS takes to the air with Bruxa and
soars upwards. AIRAAS vanishes in the distance, leaving gold and silver spirals
that circle and coil into the hearts of all.

Diffusing through the Realms, there is a sense of peace, of relief that is like
a sigh of lavender-perfumed silence. It heals and awakens many to a feeling of
gratitude and happiness. For some, the sensation lasts a second only, for others it
triggers an unending transformation of consciousness. Ahhh...

The Wings of AIRAAS

Move through

The Stillness of ASAIRA

Celebrate, Child of the One Light!

All-Seer

Dear Reader, allow me to speak to you in the manner of your friend, the Storyteller.

Do not be afeard. The Storyteller shall be back and so shall Aileen, of this we may be sure.

How and when, though, is a mystery for now. All that is left is SILENCE and PEACE.

The 3rd Knowing which is also the 4th Knowing has ended here.

The Star has come to give the last words, and an image makes itself known, which as always is not only the ending but a glorious beginning!

I bow to Thee, dear Reader, and thank thee for thy presence.

I speak to thee in this ancient lore, the favourite of our beloved Storyteller, in his honour.

So, rest, but be prepared... I see the 5th Knowing clearly, and it is vital that you join us!

And now as ALL-Seer

Ha! Ha! Ha!

Adieu, Reader!

Until we see each other again!

The Star of Heavens

The Sparks are Silent now

Aileen, the Bearer of Light

Through the Ages

With the Ancient Bard of Bards

Bind themselves

Into the Wings of Truth

The Wings of AIRAAS

To return

To Return to the Mother

ASAIRA

The

Still

Moving

Rainbow

Flower of Flowers

one
cannot
Be
be One
without
TRAAS

Mother Spirit
Mid Wife Spirit
Daughter Spirit
ASAIRA Mother of All
Son Spirit
Father Spirit
Mid Husband Spirit
TRANASA
6 not 3 to 1 to Be
The Green Meadow

THE END & THE BEGINNING

THE 5TH KNOWING OF ASAIRA

THE SONG OF AIRAAS

The Story Speaks

This image and the following four images contain sounds. The sound you can hear
with this image is of an ethereal voice singing the name of AIRAAS.

The Story Speaks

The sound of trickling water.

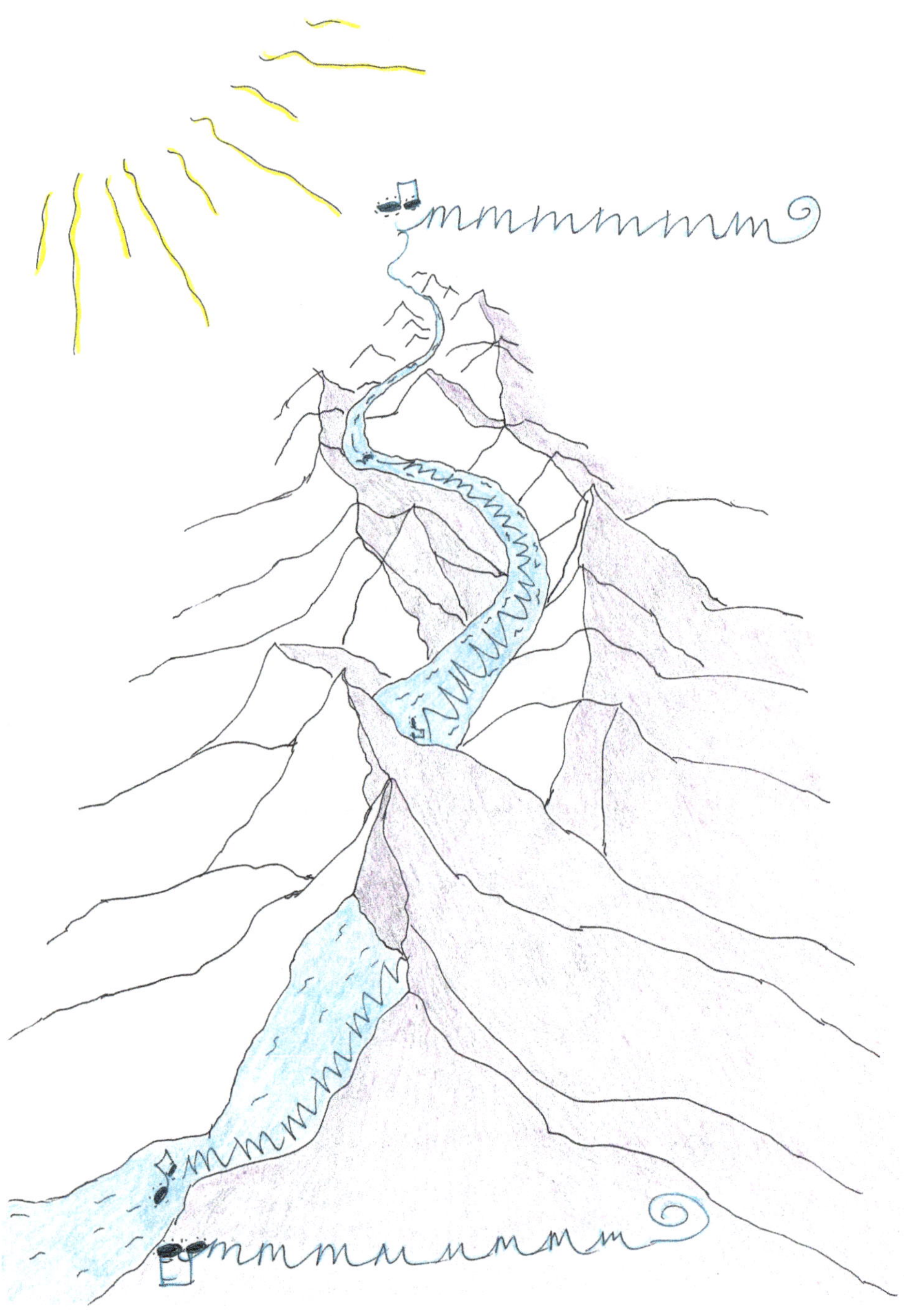

The Story Speaks

The sound of humming and a vibration.

The Story Speaks

The sound of space and silence.

The Story Speaks

The sound of a harp accompanied by angelic voices.

RAASAI speaks

I see the moment has arrived. YOU are here. I have been waiting for you. I can feel your presence, your eyes upon every word I say.

I feel you take your eyes away from me, and I wonder if it is really you who I am talking to… Yes, it is YOU. How can it not be? You who bring life to the worlds and the realms as you place your consciousness on them. Now you are here, nowhere else.

RAASAI is my given name. I am an aspect of the Mother. When you see me, when you hear me, it is then when I come into existence. And yet, this is not completely true for I am always here. But unless you set your eyes on these words or hear them in your heart, I am hidden and unrecognised.

I am here to aid you. You are needed, as is the Light Bearer and the One that Tells the Story. Without you, neither the Bearer of the Light nor the Teller of the Story can be heard.

Notice the words I speak. They are inside you, too. You can close your eyes and see me. I have many appearances, all are true. I offer you my hand, Long-Awaited One. Take it and enter this Realm. Come to where I am.

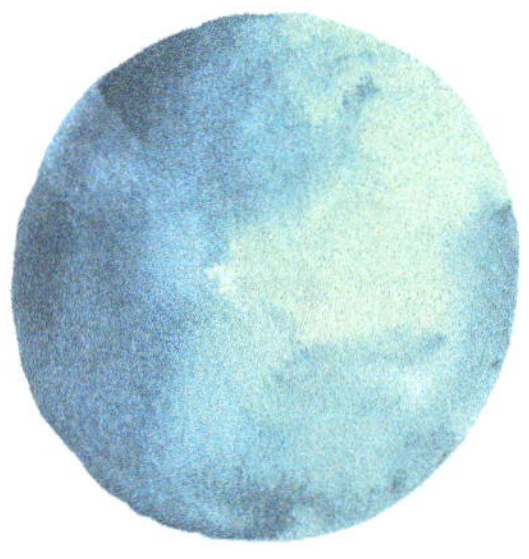

The Song of AIRAAS: Freedom

AIRAAS looked down. Far away below, there was a world. Though blurry and
dream-like, there was a sense that it was seen. This seeing or understanding
had nothing to do with the mind and language but of the heart. There was no
narration, no thought process, just contemplation. AIRAAS could feel and sense,
but she did not judge or explain nor could she have done, for at another level, she
had in all respects forgotten her earthly life and origins.

The multicoloured wings moved slowly through the air. For AIRAAS the air felt like
an ocean of bubbling, curling energy, visible and tangible… mmm… an ocean of
vibrating love! AIRAAS felt transparent, non-existent, but she was also solid and so
very, absolutely existent!

AIRAAS let out a sound that contained a trillion notes and musical instruments.
She sang of endless peace and rapture, of the joy of flying, of seeing, of hearing, of
feeling… She was the air, the sky, the ocean… Mmm…

Yes! AIRAAS was ASAIRA, she was IRAASA and SAIRAA… She was the Mother, the
Daughter, the Midwife and in turn, the Father, the Son and the Gardener… She was
Aileen… ahh… But even though all of this knowledge and wisdom danced in the
ancient cells of AIRAAS, this goddess, this creature of air that glided in musicality
through the skies of ASAIRA, was mostly oblivious of anything except her newfound freedom and longed-for peace.

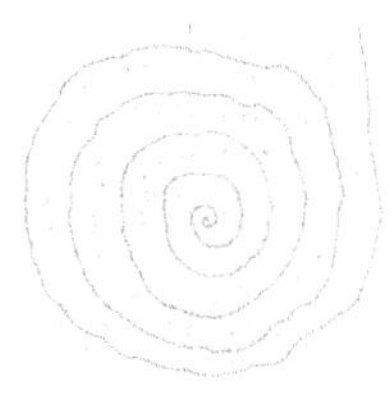

Listen to the Sound of my Wings

They Fly

For

YOU

PART 1

The Song of AIRAAS: Brown Eyes

AIRAAS looked down again. Regardless of being miles away, a human-like figure caught her goddess eye.

A tingle leapt into the heart of AIRAAS when she saw his brown eyes. "Ohhh…" she sang, followed by a lyrical whish of her wings.

AIRAAS danced off through the clouds.

The Land of No Name: The Man

A dark-haired man of around forty years of age looked up into the sky. It was a gorgeous deep blue with creamy wisps of clouds. The man smiled as he walked in this natural space of trees and mountains and brooks.

Something unquiet lingered in the background of his consciousness, but right now the man chose not to look there. He just wanted to walk, to breathe and to be in peace. ASAIRA lovingly conceded him this gift, this Rest of Rests, because he was her son, and she cherished him so.

Carefree, then, the Man with No Name walked and rested, feeling grateful and loved.

RAASAI speaks

YOU are here, inside this Realm.
It is such an honour.

Stay... Look around you...

The Star of Heavens

Sparkling & Scintillating

The Tidings I bring

RAASAI speaks

AASAIR, too, has arrived!

The 6

Have been named

As they have

From the very Beginning

From the very End

Hear AIRAAS

As she flies

Observing from Above

Look up, AASAIR, look up

And

Reader

Look inside

For you know

The 6

You know

The One

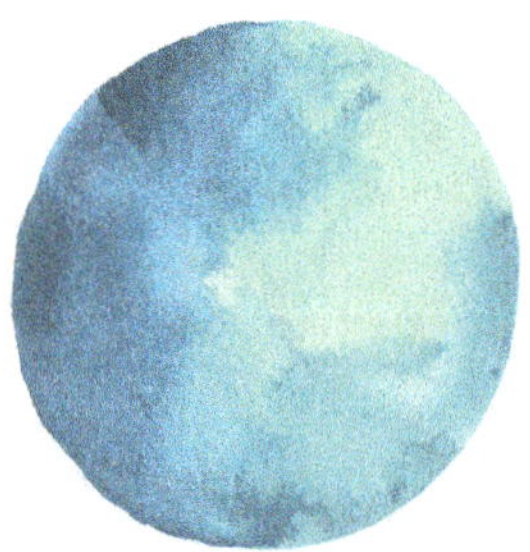

PART 2

The Song of AIRAAS: The Tower

AIRAAS feels the impulse to stop flying and land. From in between the clouds arises the top of what could be called a tower. The tower emits a golden phosphorescence which invites AIRAAS, born from IRAASA, to alight and put down her airy, earthy feet.

As AIRAAS comes nearer, the enormous tower is brought into full view: it is compact and watery at the same time, surrounded by bubbles of trickling water. On landing, AIRAAS hears the bubbly melody of the water and takes in a smell of roses. Her feet wiggle their toes, enjoying the solidity of the ground.

Out of the sky, four other Beings land on the top of the shining, glass-like tower. They softly close their wings. The 4 are smaller than AIRAAS but still large in comparison with a human form. AIRAAS smiles when she feels their presence, their powerful essence of ASAIRA: Shimmera and Saul, golden and gentle, Smanara and Silas, silver and wild. The 5 stand and bask in the glow, absorbing the electric life in the air.

The Tower tingles in recognition of the beauty and rarity of this moment.

RAASAI speaks

Can YOU see them? Yes, they are really there! Just outside of this turret.
Look through the window! Look...

There before you is The Unutterable, The Incomprehensible, The Most
Divine. A name was given to this Being, this countenance born from the
entrails of the Cocoon Mother: she is AIRAAS. Can you see her wings?

And what do you say of the Four Gods of ASAIRA? Yes, you know them
well, don't you? See how they glimmer? Yes, they have come to meet you.

But there is no rush. You are my honoured guest, and I show you my home:
The Tower of RAASAI, the Heart of ASAIRA.

The Land of No Name:
A Flower in the Sky

The man looked up to the skies again. To his surprise,
he thought he could see a huge flower, a stem holding a
six-petalled flower. The sun blinded him somewhat, so it
was difficult to discern. He looked down. It was too bright
for him, and something felt stirred up inside. He sat down
under a shady tree and closed his eyes.

RAASAI speaks

Here's the door. YOU can go out there and meet them.
They will be so happy to see you.

And they are very patient.

There's nothing to fear… I hold your hand…

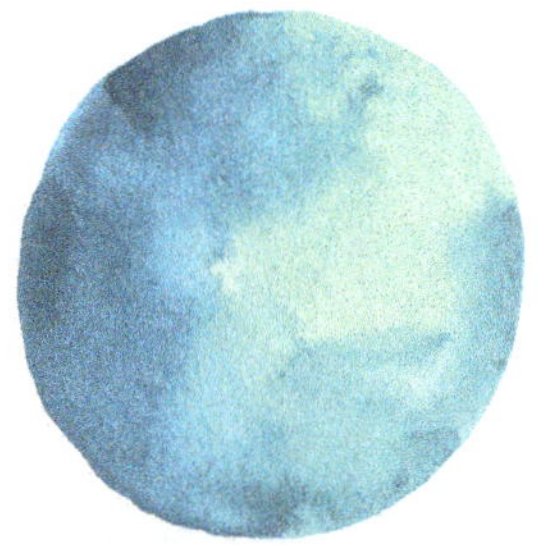

The Song of AIRAAS:
The Reader Arrives

AIRAAS gazed at the figure who was coming out of the
turret. She also noticed the invisible presence of the
Guardian of the Flower. AIRAAS knew with the knowledge of
old that one could not be without the other.

The Reader can hardly breathe. How's this possible? What's
happening? But when they ask these questions, everything
goes fuzzy: no AIRAAS, no Shimmera, no Saul, no Smanara,
no Silas.

The Reader felt some pressure in their hand, and they were
back in the Story.

The 5 allowed the Reader to come into their presence.
No one moved.

The Star of Heavens

The Butterfly

The Golden One

The Wise One

The Silver One

The Mysterious One

The Tower of Flowering Love

Its Ancient Guardian

ASAIRA is

Full of Delight

Meeting YOU

And Meeting the Man of No Name

YOU bring the Key

The 3

Are more than what they seem

The 3 are 1

Are 6

Jump for Joy

Children of ASAIRA

Of the One Light

RAASAI becomes known!

AASAIR becomes known!

And the 1st Cycle is done!!

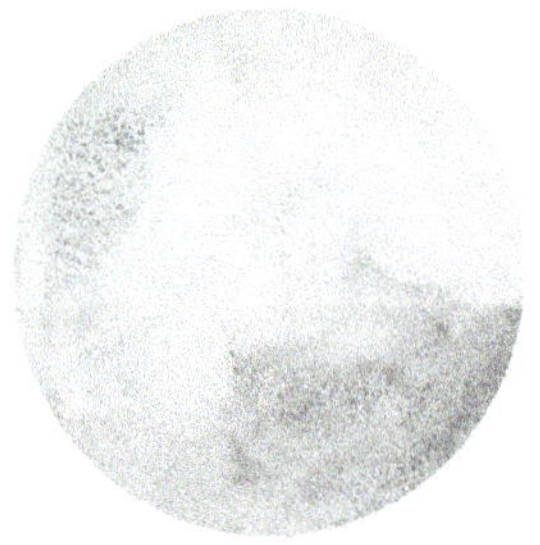

PART 3

The Land of No Name: Under the Ancient Tree

The nameless man felt his eyelids close while he sat under the tree. Its shade was nourishing and cool, bringing relief from the brightness of the sun. The tree induced reminiscences in him of some faraway place, in some faraway time. The man fell asleep.

In his sleep, wondrous sounds emerged: angelic music akin to the strumming of a harp, and someone singing long drawn-out vowels that made his body vibrate and his mind relax.

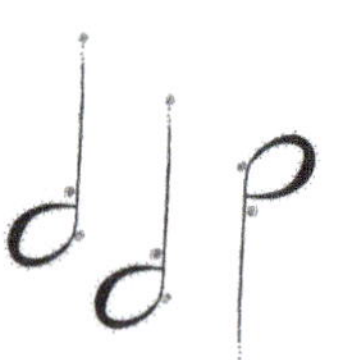

Exquisite-sounding words whispered themselves into his ears, transporting the man to a lush nothingness, "ASAIRA… SAIRAA… AIRAAS… IRAASA… RAASAI… AASAIR…" Each word caused a different resonance in his body as they swirled themselves in and out of his cells.

Then, as sudden as unexpected events are, the man heard a name boom in his ears:

"EOIN!"

With his eyes like two plates, the man sat up. He tried to breathe and
swallowed a few times.

Eoin had been his name in times of old!

Yes, a time of music and tales, a time of a deep honouring of the Earth…
a time when he had loved Elyn… Elyn!!

Elyn…

The Song of AIRAAS: A Flight of Love

There was a rumbling of thunder, followed by a low growl of what sounded like a wild animal… a tiger?! Tiger Bright? Is he here? The Reader tensed.

The Tower swayed a little, but no tiger appeared. The Reader felt the pressure again in their hand. RAASAI…

The 5 looked up to the sky that had turned into a shocking pink. AIRAAS suddenly took off in two or three sweeps of her wings, leaving the Reader open-mouthed.

AIRAAS flew downwards in a mesmerizing flight of love. She saw a great tree with six boughs; its lush foliage caused a stir of sweet sensations.

The male figure she had seen before was staring towards her. AIRAAS stopped in mid-air and took Bruxa out of her heart. Gently, she laid the little dog on the glen. Then, AIRAAS, the Divine Butterfly, soared back into the air.

The two Beings were left together in spellbinding rapture of one another.

The Land of No Name: The Lamb

Confusion.

Shock.

A remembering.

An accepting without really knowing or understanding.

The man sighs.

Then… *She* arrives.

A Wingcd Elyn!

A Queen of Queens.

A Luminescent Goddess.

Larger than Life.

Wings of such fervent, glittering colours that they make him feel faint.

So fast.

So slow.

The Lamb!

A whispering.

Why, it's a small woolly dog!

A stroking.

A wonder.

A deep love.

The Man that was once called Eoin and the small white lamb-like dog called Bruxa fall in love with each other and become inseparable.

The Star of Heavens

A message for YOU

Receiver of this Moment

Reader of the Word

The Divine Sparks speak

To THEE directly

To the Heart of Hearts

The Flower of the Mysterious

Listen well!

YOU must intervene

Speak to AIRAAS

Say who YOU are

Revealing the Closing of the Cycle

The Opening of the 6 Petals

RAASAI will help and be at your side

And so shall my scintillating sparks

♡ The Light Bearer of the Green Meadow

And

He that Tells the Stories of Old

And YOU

Must meet once again

In the Meadow of Primroses

A Promise of Ancient Innocence

A Spiral of Cycles

No Beginning, No End

Reader

On YOU it depends!

Receive this Message

Let it delve

Into your Heart

All shall be clear

Do not be afeard, Child of ASAIRA ♡

The Sea of Seas

Our Waters ache for Thee
We have come
To the Depths of IRAASA
To the Dark Nourisher
To serve as
The Watery Hammock
So Thou may rest
In our Liquid Love
In IRAASA
Come, AASAIR,
Son of ASAIRA
Come and Feel
My Soothing Waves

The Song of AIRAAS: AIRAAS and The Reader

AIRAAS landed opposite the Reader, making them take a few steps back from the giant butterfly woman. She was so luminescent, so huge…

The word "AIRAAS" unexpectedly spiralled out of the Reader's mouth.

AIRAAS looked down at the small human form at her feet.

RAASAI speaks

When AIRAAS returns, You may speak to her, if it be your will.

I shall be with You. Feel my presence, and You will know strength and solidness.

Concentrate on my voice, which is your Heart.

No other voice rings true!

The Tree of Lands

Ah… Once again
The Green Meadow
Beckons in this
Precious moment
My roots feel
A welcoming
The Mother's Arms
Open and I remember
From the Oblivion
A Sacred Vowing
Ah…

The Children
of
The One Light

The Land of No Name: Bruxa and The Man

Bruxa and the Man continued under the shade of the Tree. They had sat for an eternity, it seemed, the Man gently stroking the soft coat of white love.

Suddenly, Bruxa turned restless, sniffing the earth around the Tree. And then, with great earnestness, she began digging with all her doggy might.

IRAASA

From our entrails
We gave birth
From the Depths
AIRAAS came
Queen of Butterflies
And now
AASAIR hears the call
The Earthy Mother
I am
For AASAIR neither can be
Without
IRAASA's permission

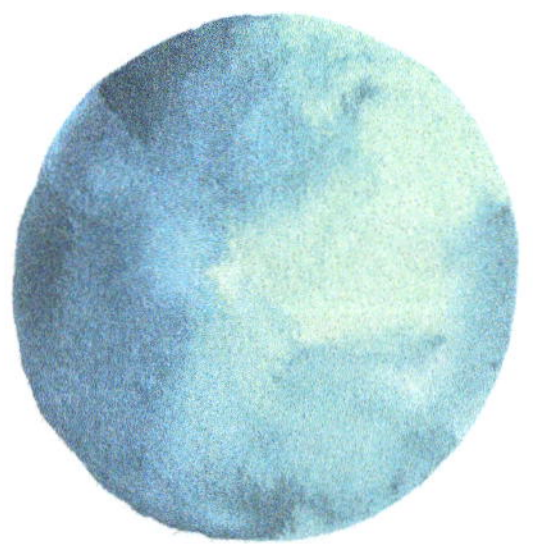

PART 5

The Song of AIRAAS: The Reader Speaks

On saying the name of AIRAAS aloud, the Reader had unwittingly initiated the Circle.

AIRAAS noticed that the human figure spoke more words, but she could not hear them. The little human felt distant, and the 4 were a blur. The magical skies invited, enticed her wings to open and fly away into the spacious Heavens, the Glory of the Goldness manifest.

"Speak more loudly," said RAASAI, "and without doubt to AIRAAS. YOU must show her your conviction, for she hovers, she prepares to fly, and we know not when she will decide to land here again."

The Reader virtually shouted, "AIRAAS!" "AIRAAS," they said again, from a very deep place unknown to them. Their voice sounded profound and ancient, light and musical.

This time AIRAAS saw the human's eyes, large and keen. They brought her to a complete stop.

"AIRAAS, I'm the Reader of this Story. I know you because I've read about you. I don't really know what I'm supposed to tell you. But… I do know a lot of things… I know you were once Aileen and that you were in the cocoon, in the earth… do you remember any of that?"

The clouds in the sky moved faster, causing a light wind to blow through the Tower.

AIRAAS fixed her eyes on the small creature. She had understood the language; the words moved her. ♪ ♪ "Aileen?" ♪ she sang in glittering musical notes.

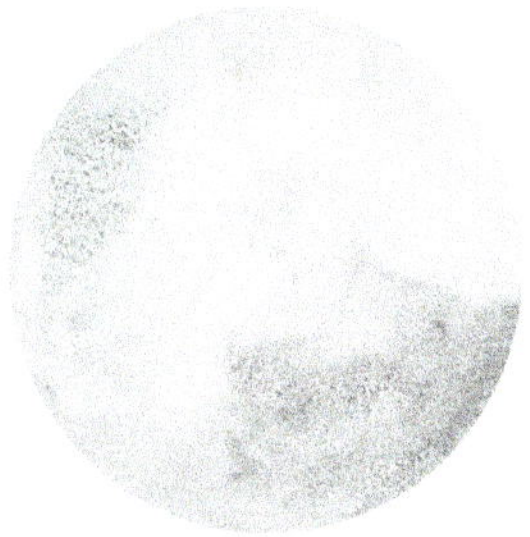

The Land of No Name: Into the Black Hole

Bruxa dug a hole easily as if the earth were made of light sand. A dark tunnel came into view which, though foreboding as all dark tunnels are, was curiously inviting to the Man who had been called Eoin. Both Bruxa and he looked at each other in rather amusing expectancy, if anyone had been there to see their faces.

Eoin knew he had to follow Bruxa, and Bruxa knew it was her place to be with this sweet soul.

So without more ado, Eoin grabbed Bruxa into his arms, kissed her soft head and said, "Let us be adventurous, Woolly One!"

And into the black hole they jumped.

The Star of Heavens

My Sparkling Words

Always point

To the same Promise

The 3

Are The 6

One cannot Be

Without the Other

Remember they must

To then Forget

In this Never-ending Circle

In this Spiral of Life

The Flower of ASAIRA

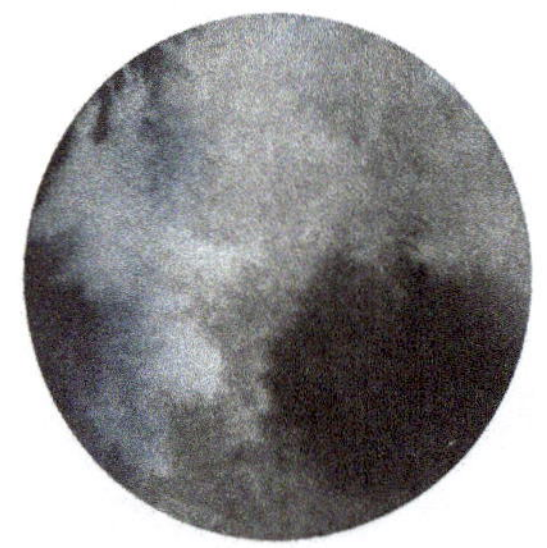

The Depths of IRAASA: The Cave of AASAIR

The Cave of AASAIR is a living creature that has been asleep for trillions of eternities. Now, astonishingly, it opens its cave eyes and senses of perception.

And what a sight! Two unusual life forms have plunged into the silvery waters! There are sounds of enjoyment and mirth… laughter from a human-like Being and an euphoric bark of an animal Being!

Oh, how long has it been since the Cave listened to such sounds?

The Cave of AASAIR smiles in its own cave-like way and makes the walls shake a little. Ahhh… what a delight to have awoken from my endless sleep, it seems to say.

☆* **PART 6** ⁑

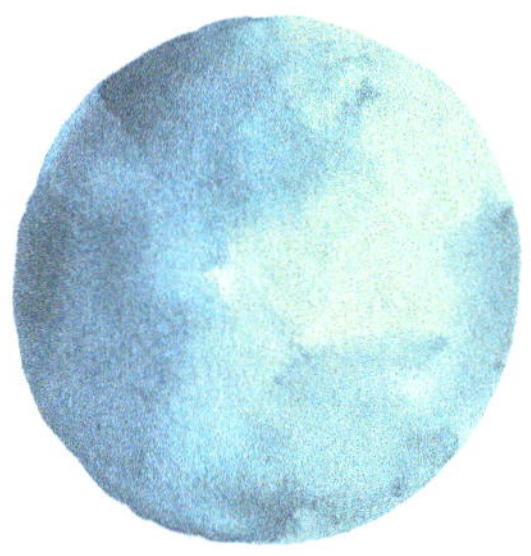

The Song of AIRAAS: I'm here!

I'm standing in front of AIRAAS. My whole body tingles. She's incredible… my neck aches because I have to pull it back to see her properly.

"Aileen?" says AIRAAS again. She crouches down.

It's a bit of a shock to see her this close!

"Dear Perceiver of All," says RAASAI, "YOU can relax, no ill shall befall you. Go to AIRAAS, and don't forget I am always with you."

RAASAI's voice is inside me.

"Come," says AIRAAS.

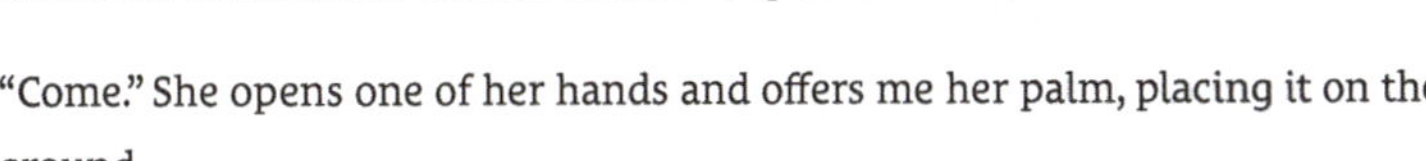

It sounds like musical chimes when she speaks.

"Come." She opens one of her hands and offers me her palm, placing it on the ground.

I'm so scared, my legs go all wobbly, but I manage to step onto her hand. It's translucent, like she is. I can't really describe it, but I'm put onto her back. She's still crouching. Her back feels like it's full of netting… there's a space in the middle, and I lie face down. Silky rainbow-coloured threads start coming out of her wings and strap themselves around me. I feel a bit dizzy. I adjust myself and hold on. It's not too uncomfortable!

Is this really happening?!

With the Reader on her back and RAASAI, as one cannot be without the other, AIRAAS stands up, opens her wings and flies into the open sky. At this, the 4 take flight also: Shimmera and Saul in the direction of AIRAAS's rainbow trail of iridescence, while Smanara and Silas fly down towards the Land of No Name.

Leaving a blue flame, the Flower Tower of Glass vanishes.

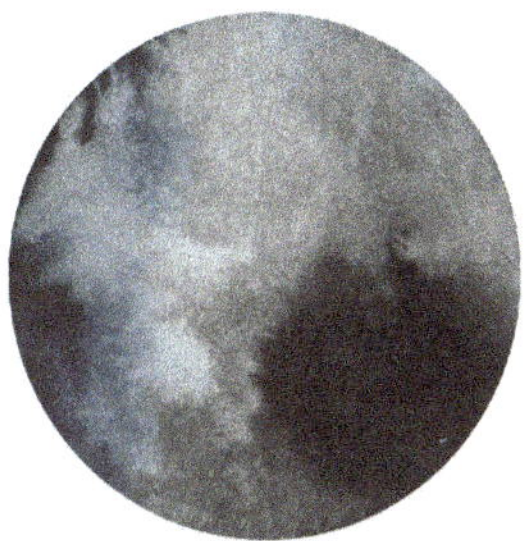

The Depths of IRAASA: The Cave of AASAIR Awakens

In the Depths of IRAASA, the Cave of AASAIR had patiently awaited the promise of its awakening. Patience was the Cave's natural resting, and content and peaceful the Cave had been, and was, for the Cave had breathed and lived in calmness.

Nevertheless, as with many awakenings, the realisation of having been asleep and suddenly realising you are awake can feel refreshing and exciting. The Cave was enjoying every detail, every second, noticing every single feature of the cave: how the silvery water drops danced around the walls; how the walls felt like skin with the drops coming out of its pores in trickling, tickling delight; how the crystals glittered, lighting up the massive pillars, stalagmites and stalactites...

Yesss! The Cave of Old shook in childlike awe and glee. Strange, rumbling noises to which, if you listened very carefully, sounded like, "I've awoken! I've awoken!" echoed through the chamber, making ripple upon ripple in the silver liquid that filled most of the cave floor.

The man and the dog played together underwater, realising this was not normal water at all. This sea felt like liquid but also had an airy feeling to it and paradoxically, was thick and solid. Indescribable! Plus they could actually breathe underwater!

The Cave perceived their marvelling and shook in merry reciprocity.

The Sea of Seas

Play, Sweet Ones

Laugh, Noble Ones

Bearers of ASAIRA's Truth

Let our Waters renew

Replenish

The old and weary

Our Silver Seas

Give the Life

Reveal the Promise

Of the Lamb

Of AASAIR

Dive deeper

Little Ones

To see what must be seen

Let the Waters

Clear the veils

For the Cycle

ASAIRA's Truth

To be completed

He is here

As She was before Him

Through the waters

He must come

For AASAIR to be

As AIRAAS was born

The Cave is our Womb

We are

The Mother, the Daughter

Our Womb of Old

Ancientness before time

Strength and Courage

Will be needed

Let the Fiery One awaken too

For the Waters must burn

IRAASA We Are

The Fierceness of the Mother

I am

The Tree of Lands

Ah... In the Depths

Is the Ancient Cave

IRAASA's Lair

That harbours

An Unseen Truth

My Roots reach down and give

Strength and Stability

As always

To show Thee the Ancient Path

Back to the Green Meadow

Oh, Aileen, Sweet One

Light Bearer

Her Innocent Tear

Now the Wisdom of AIRAAS

And, Teller of Old, hear this

You shall see

You shall fulfill the Promise

The Promise of AASAIR

Be brave

ASAIRA is with you

We are all with YOU

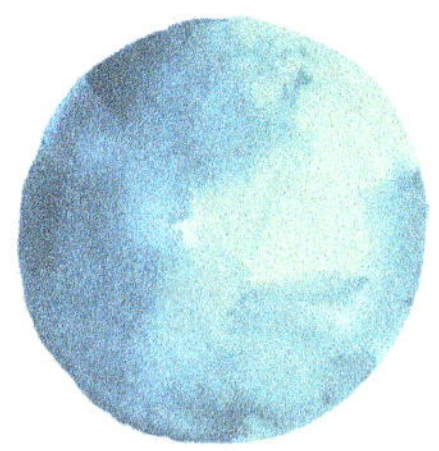

"Ooh…!!"

The sound appeared on the page in front of the Reader!

Wow!

How curious that they could be everywhere at the same time, reading the Story as well as seeing themself on AIRAAS's back, feeling the wind blow through their hair…

"Mmm…"

"Careful, Reader, careful… YOU can lose your balance and fall from AIRAAS. Stay here, stay here…"

RAASAI's voice sounded warm in the Reader's heart.

 The Reader marvelled at the magicalness of Life and held on tighter.

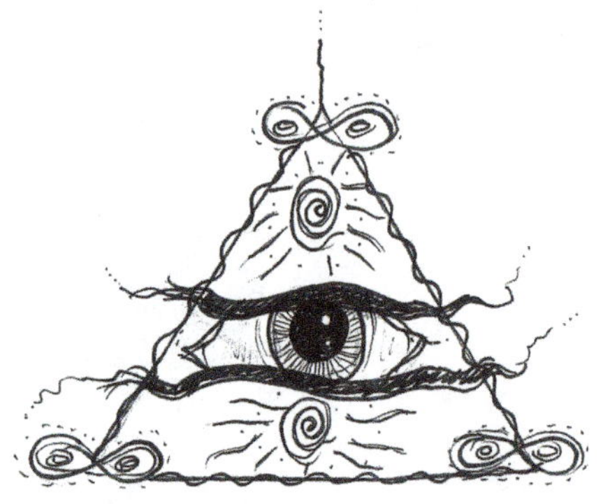

All-Seer

Salutations to the Being who reads this
A Powerful Being
Able to see This
And also fly the skies of AIRAAS's Realm
Feeling All, Seeing All
An All-Seer, without a doubt!
Ha! Ha! Ha!

I come to speak
To give some introduction to a place
A place impossible to introduce
Mysterious to its core
For the moment has arrived
The Promise of the 3
The Revelation of the 6
Ongoing & Done

AIRAAS, The Reader and RAASAI
Will arrive at this mysterious place soon
RAASAI has knowledge and remembrance of it
But Neither AIRAAS nor the Reader do
For this reason I must speak now

AIRAAS flies from the Heart
She feels, sees, hears, has sensations and vague memories
She knows but has no reason
She is curious but has no method
Now she flies by impulse to a place she knows
Where she has never been
Where she has always lived
She carries two Beings who are known to her
A Being that said 'Aileen', a sound that warms her heart
And RAASAI, the Guardian of the Flower

Reader, YOU are going to this place that is Nameless
But has been given many names in many realms
In one such realm, a realm lost in eternity
This Place of Places was called
♫♪ *Saahruam Allssiram Issenam* ♪♫

Ahh…

I admit I have a particular inclination for
These sacred sounds said out aloud from the Heart
I am quite taken and need to pause…

Yes… Ahh…
The Gods of ASAIRA
Smanara & Silas, Shimmera & Saul
Love this name also and know it in their hearts

In your Realm, Reader
There is a name that points to this place: 'Heaven'
Yes, but be warned
You can have no previous conception about this place

♫♪ *Saahruam Allssiram Issenam* ♪♫
Cannot be defined

It is time!

PART 7

The Song of AIRAAS: To the ♫ Saahruam Allssiram Issenam ♫!

The Reader understood that they were truly privileged. They could read everything that came up on the page. There was no doubt that they knew many things… perhaps using this knowledge really was their mission here in the Story.

In the Heart of Hearts, RAASAI smiled and warmed the Reader in confirmation. The Reader felt encouraged.

"♫ Saahruam Allssiram Issenam ♫" whispered the Reader into AIRAAS's wings. "♫ Saahruam Allssiram Issenam ♫ ♫ Saahruam Allssiram Issenam ♫ ♫ Saahruam Allssiram Issenam ♫ ♫ Saahruam Allssiram Issenam ♫"

The whisper became a chant, a sweet incantation that mesmerized AIRAAS's flight into a slow, steady movement of upward flying, beyond the pink clouds… towards the sunset, or was it the sunrise? What did it matter? The Reader abandoned all thought, and it was only the hypnotizing melody, this enthralling flight to the stars, to the ♫ Saahruam Allssiram Issenam ♫!

The chant now just sang itself, and AIRAAS ascended into a racing glide of joy. RAASAI, Guardian of the Tower, opened a pair of powerful wings and covered the Reader in sumptuous warm browns and oranges. RAASAI's wings, though invisible, looked like a cape of autumn glow: soothing and balsamic, the wings were stronger than anyone could ever imagine.

On every word of the Saahruam, the **Realms of ASAIRA** vibrated and trembled. The sky became greyer, and the Tree shook in awe at the strength and power of the sacred chant.

With that shocked look of rude awakening, **another Being** opened its angry eyes.

24

Are

12

Are

6

Are

3

Are

ᵛ 1 ᵛ

Saahruau Allssiram Issenau
Heaven On Earth
The Green Meadow

Is

SAIRAA IRAASA   AIRAS RAASAI
AASAIR ✳ ASAIRA ✳   ✳   AASAIR
RAASAI AIRAAS   SAIRAA
                                    IRAASA

Seer of Seers , Hearer of Hearers , Teller of Tellers

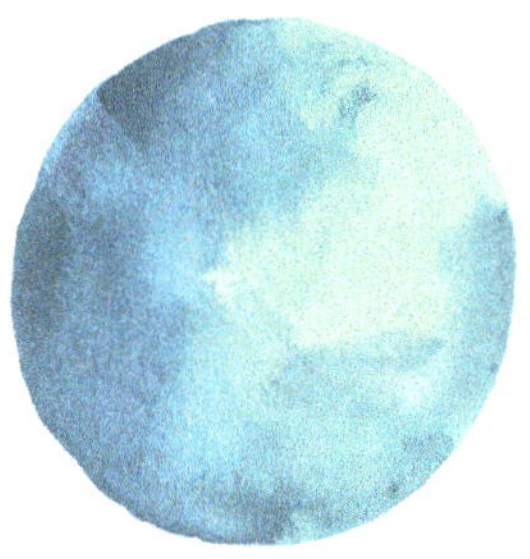

PART 8

The Song of AIRAAS:
♪ I'm in Heaven ♫

The Reader fell asleep.

In their dreams, a song played:

> ♪ *Heaven, I'm in Heaven… And I seem to find happiness…* ♫

The song invited them to dance, so the Reader got up and glided around the brightly lit room in dreamy ecstasy.

> ♪ Heaven, I'm in Heaven,
>
> And my heart beats so that I can hardly speak, And I seem to find the happiness I seek when we're out together dancing, cheek to cheek
>
> Heaven, I'm in Heaven,
>
> And the cares that hang around me through the week seem to vanish like a gambler's lucky streak when we're out together dancing, cheek to cheek
>
> Oh! I love to climb a mountain,
> And to reach the highest peak,
> But it doesn't thrill me half as much
> As dancing cheek to cheek

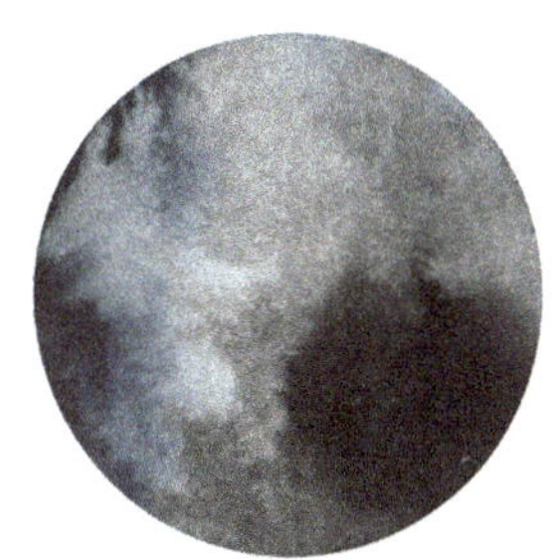

The Depths of IRAASA:
Into the Dreams

Inside the warm waters, the man and the dog played. After a while, caressed by the silver balm, they closed their eyes and fell fast asleep. The Cave yawned in compliance and it, too, closed its rocky eyes.

Eoin's dream

Eoin heard music and singing:

> ♪ *I'm in Heaven… I'm in Heaven… Heaven…* ♫

Yes, he was dancing, dancing with someone he loved.

"Becca," he said.

Becca's face lit up and smiled, "I love you, John!"

She laughed as they whirled around the room.

While they danced, Eoin remembered he had once been called John and that Becca had been his wife. He smiled: everything was all good in the midst of this heavenly

> ♪ *dancing, cheek to cheek…* ♫

Oh! I love to go out fishing
In a river or a creek,
But I don't enjoy it half as much
As dancing cheek to cheek

Dance with me
I want my arm about you
The charm about you
Will carry me through to Heaven

I'm in Heaven
And my heart beats so that I can hardly speak, And
I seem to find the happiness I seek when we're out
together dancing cheek to cheek ♫ [16]

Meanwhile, AIRAAS continued in rhythmical flight: fly, fly, fly…

"♫ *Saahruam Allssiram Issenam* ♫" sang the Wings of Light at each formidable stroke.

♡ **Divine Sparks of Insight & Revelation** ♡

♈ Fire of Transformation

♈ Fire of Destruction

♈ Be Vigilant for the One that does not wish to remember

RAASAI speaks

YOU sleep, yet you read this.

I protect you from the cold and wind, yet I speak to you here in your Heart.

Sleep and Listen and Read, for the messages and signs come in all manners.

AIRAAS shall fly until **Saahruam** makes itself known.

When you wake, speak to AIRAAS.

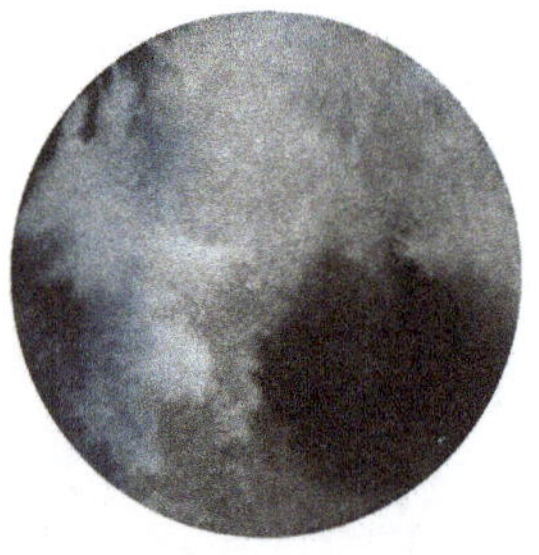

The Depths of IRAASA: A Complete Awakening

The Cave quivers. Hmm… there are more Beings nearby. The sweet ones, the human man and the dog animal, are in the waters of light, but above… something else approaches.

There is also another presence… it's already in my chambers… Ah yes, I know you, I know you, we were together in the sleepful time… you, too, have awakened.

The Cave trembles a little. Ah, I understand… yes… the water and the fire must be together… I prepare myself for all visitors…

Abruptly, or so it seems for this is the way it has always been destined to be, the Cave groans, the ground and walls shudder, and the calm waters suddenly rise up into waves.

The man and the dog open their eyes. They start to spin…

What's happening?!

A whirlpool of silver solidity takes force, and the two friends, dog and man, are swallowed in. Paralyzing fear jumps into the maelstrom, too, followed by a terrifying blindness. The Cave senses the panic but continues its ascending quaking.

The Cave of AASAIR with everything and everyone in it spins relentlessly… Ahhh, yes! I had forgotten… I had forgotten… I had forgotten! I am to completely awaken!!

Yesssssss…!

An effervescing explosion of fire, water, earth and air splashes and sprays over, across, above and below. It is a revolution of watery light, a vortex of thunder and lightning, a wild metamorphosis of closing and opening, of dying and birthing...

Ahhhh...

A darkness that engulfs...

A silence that shivers...

And five Presences.

Or are there six?

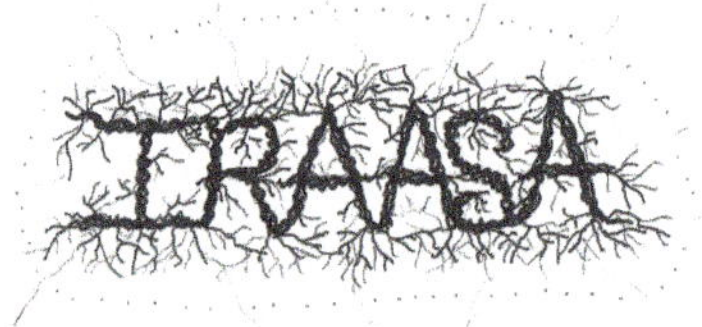

The Cave of Old

In our Depths

Has opened to the Ancient Waters

Womb of Wombs are We

And AASAIR

The Groundedness of IRAASA

Son of ASAIRA

Shall remember

IRAASA has given forth

AASAIR

The Waters have been freed for

The Seeing & The Telling

The Water Daughter has returned

To The Mother of Liquid Silver

As she too shall remember

Our earthy soil settles again

I am

The Soil of Soils

The ever-giving IRAASA

The Sea of Seas

I am

The Sea of Seas

The Waters of Saahruam

I give

All Sight and Wisdom

All Replenishment

To those who come

Now

The Cave has opened

The Cave has remembered

She is

Grandiose & Wise

She lives

In this Loving Liquid

The Sea of Seas

Welcomes AASAIR

The Time has come

The Land of No Name

Must know itself

The Promise to Fulfill

The Star of Heavens

AASAIR becomes

A Watery World awakens

The Reader sleeps & reads

AIRAAS flies in heavenly awe

Different journeys, or so it seems

Yet, one Purpose

To Bear the Light, To See the Love, To Tell the Truth

Each must be brave

Each is a Child of ASAIRA

Each a God of ASAIRA

Each ASAIRA

Destined as 1 of the 3 who are 6

Courage & Grace hand in hand

The Sparks of Divine Revelation

Shall kindle all fear

So it burns in the Fire of Seeing

Water, Fire, Air, Earth

The Mother's Elements whirl and spin

In endless creation

Vigilance and Bravery

Listen to the Voices of Help

For there is a Fiery One

Who refuses to remember

Be vigilant to this one

The Land of Forgetfulness

Nameless

From the Destruction

Comes the Transformation

I Am

Rejoice

In this Journey of Continuous Remembering

The Story Speaks

Part 10 is about to be related.

The Story needs you, the Reader, to be alert to Eoin.

There is something inside him that is not him.

Pay attention even as you sleep in AIRAAS's nestful winged-back.

✫* *PART 10* **✫

The Kingdom of AASAIR: The Ancient World Returns

The Land of No Name had become itself: the Kingdom of AASAIR! The Cave had awoken and expanded, crashed out of the Depths of IRAASA on the Sea of Seas, filling the nameless land with water.

A new world had been born. However, this was no new world. It was an ancient world that had existed before all time and all realms, a magical, watery world in the eyes of any Earthling, a world that had been named the Kingdom of AASAIR.

AASAIR had been a young god, mighty and compassionate, his sweet dark eyes always smiling. He had lived in this Realm happily until the Forgetting. Then, the Kingdom, a Being in itself, had shrunk to disappear into IRAASA's dark soils.

In this mysterious kingdom, AASAIR had not been alone. There were also other creatures. There was one in particular: the Immensity in Form. She was a mystical creature of the Sea of Seas, a beloved Daughter of ASAIRA and she, too, had disappeared when AASAIR had forgotten and she, too, had gone inside herself into the Depths of IRAASA.

Until now, the Immensity in Form had slept in pleasant oblivion, hibernating, we could say. She had metamorphosed into the Cave of AASAIR, a living womb that contained silvery reminiscences of the great Sea of Seas. She had lain awaiting the return of AASAIR. And now she had returned and had begun to remember! The Kingdom of AASAIR had returned! But where was AASAIR?

The Kingdom of AASAIR: Eoin

The man opened his eyes. He touched the soft, warm sands on which he was lying and absorbed the blue sky above him. There was a deep silence except for the silky murmur of water lapping onto the shore. The man closed his eyes. So much peace! He noticed a sweet fragrance of flowers as he breathed in and out. Mmm… He opened his eyes again.

The man sat up. An ocean full of sparkling stars rose before him. Ohhh! The sands of the shore glittered with golden specks and confirmed the sumptuousness of this incredible place.

The name 'Eoin' rolled in with a wave. Ah, yes…

Then a small white dog ran up and licked his face.

"The woolly lamb!" Eoin cuddled the soft creature with delight.

But even amidst all the beauty of the moment, Eoin's eyes darkened. He stopped stroking Bruxa and stared at the ocean.

The Kingdom of AASAIR: KOAA

KOAA revelled. Ahh… the warm waters of renewal. Mmm… so thankful for thy return, Mother of Mothers, Sea of Seas, thank you, thank you, thank you… mmm…

KOAA moved with the gracefulness of the Immense One, a slow, majestic movement which left a million ripples dancing on the shiny waters.

Vigilant was KOAA, also, while she swam; there were various presences nearby. She felt them with curiosity, but none were AASAIR… though there was something that reminded her of him… like a fragrant wisp of him, a sense of him flying through the skies but never landing.

AASAIR, without you this is empty…

KOAA sighed. She became more alert to everything she could sense… and then she heard them… two voices, two echoes… a familiar language… such beauty, such a song of love… Yes, two familiar songs… they were here to protect, to help, KOAA could feel that.

Full of joy, KOAA navigated towards the echoes, those voices of old, a brother and sister of an ancientness forgotten.

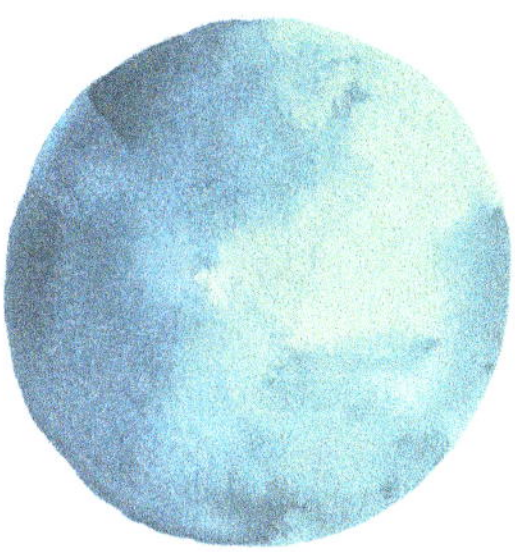

The Song of AIRAAS: The Reader speaks to the Story

The Reader wakes up. They have a strong desire to be with Eoin. I have to help him, to warn him…

The Reader rocks a little from side to side.

RAASAI says, "Careful. Do what YOU must but speak to AIRAAS. Remember you must speak to her, be with her."

"RAASAI, the *Saahruam*? Is it the Kingdom of AASAIR?"

"Follow your Heart's intuition, and *Saahruam* and the Kingdom will make themselves known. ASAIRA will show them to you."

The Reader has an idea.

"Story… This is the Reader speaking. I've just thought that maybe you'll receive this message. Do you know more about the Kingdom of AASAIR? Is it *Saahruam Allssiram Issenam*? I have to speak or say something to AIRAAS in order to go there, I think… Can you hear me, Story? Can you help me? Thank you."

The Story Speaks

Reader, I hear you.

I can tell you what I know. Nothing else.

I remind the Reader that I do not know all. I have some knowledge of
the Kingdom of AASAIR and the God, AASAIR, but my knowledge is of the
past and is not complete. I do not know what is to happen. It is not
clear, either, who KOAA is in relation to AASAIR. Neither am I certain
of AIRAAS's part in this ancient Kingdom.

If more knowledge is required, be certain you will receive it from the
Guardian of the Tower or ALL-Seer and the Star of Heavens.

AASAIR

Physical appearance:

- Giant-like in size. Much taller and bigger than AIRAAS. To AASAIR, AIRAAS would have looked like an extremely large butterfly

- Dark-eyed, sweet and loving face, human-like male

- Two corporeal forms that changed at will: his water form and his earth form

- Above two forms were his main physical forms, but AASAIR could transform into others or sometimes fly if desired

Personality:

- Kind, compassionate, wise, loving, calm, happy, grounded and discerning

- Creative & playful

- A passion for music, singing and dancing

- A passion for inventing and creating new worlds and then going to these lands to play. Afterwards, AASAIR loved to tell stories about these adventures

- A passion for being at home in the Kingdom, doing nothing and enjoying this peaceful life

- He had no knowledge of conflict or suffering. His kingdom was a peaceful and content land. His adventures were in lands of equal peacefulness and contentedness. All the creatures, including himself, had never known or experienced selfishness or manipulation. All knew, as did AASAIR, that they were One, the land inclusive

The Kingdom

- Limitless in size: no frontiers or borders, no sense of leaving or entering; more a world than a kingdom

- A kingdom that could not be arrived at; it did not exist in time and space, as you Earth One know time and space, but more a reflection of AASAIR's heart

- Mostly covered by water: the Sea of Seas containing magical creatures and Beings, with a shoreline of sands

- The form of the land could change: sometimes it felt smaller or even quite different. All dependent on AASAIR's will, on his 'adventures', as he called them

- All the creatures and Beings could communicate with each other easily: a harmonious understanding

- No aging or death, no sense of time passing

- A playfulness and contentedness with AASAIR's adventures and creations

- An openness of love and goodwill

- A sense of being One Entity

In spite of having said much about the Kingdom of AASAIR, the Kingdom is
no more. This was before the Forgetting.

Now the Kingdom appears to have returned, the Cave has remembered who
she is, and KOAA swims in the sacred Silver Sea... but it is not AASAIR
who has returned or remembered, so what this means is still to be seen.

Reader, I do not know if this Kingdom is the *Saahruam*, or how you will
arrive there. I do not know what you must say to AIRAAS. What I do
know is that you are key to all of this mystery.

Vigilance is needed, I remind you again. There is a Being who does not
wish to remember and prefers the fires of destruction... This Being is
also in the Kingdom...

This is all I can tell you.

☆ ⭐ PART 11 ⭐⭐

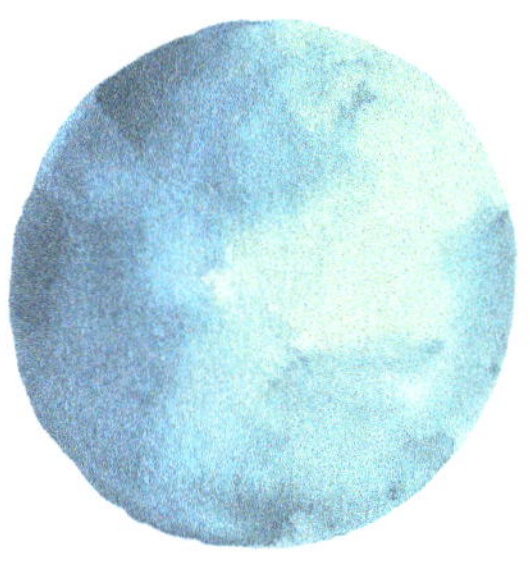

The Song of AIRAAS: The True Direction

The Reader blinked in amazed comprehension: what they had to do was to help AIRAAS and Eoin remember. What exactly had to be remembered wasn't perfectly clear, but the Reader was sure now that was their mission.

I need to go to the Kingdom of AASAIR!

No sooner had the Reader formulated the decision than AIRAAS stopped flying! Floating in mid-air, she put the Reader into her hand.

Feeling RAASAI's support, the Reader took a deep breath, "AIRAAS, I think we have to go to this place called the Kingdom of AASAIR. It's to do with your being Aileen and somehow helping Eoin… and remembering. It's to do with remembering. Do you understand me?"

AIRAAS stared at the little Being who spoke with such vehemence and so many words. Some resonated in her heart, so she became inclined to sing them out aloud, again and again, ♫ AIRAAS… AASAIR… Aileen… Eoin… Re… mem… beringggg… AIRAAS, AASAIR, Aileen, Eoin, Remembering…♫

The Kingdom of AASAIR: An Unknown Force

Eoin felt nauseous. It was a sickness that crawled from his stomach upwards to his head. The sickness stared out of his eyes.

Eoin, or what appeared to be him, pushed Bruxa aside and stood up. Bruxa whined; she moved away quickly, feeling a dangerous presence.

"Where am I in the name of God?!" said Eoin in a voice that darkened the air around him.

And literally it was so: all Eoin could feel was a heavy veil of suspicion, fear and anger. Desperately, he looked around him. There was nothing he recognised, nor could he see the beauty of the silvery waters or the soft delight of the golden sand where he stood.

"Can someone tell me what is happening? God, why do you always do this to me? What have I done to deserve such abandonment?"

The despair sent dark energetic waves throughout the Kingdom; every creature tensed.

Mesmerized by AIRAAS's voice, the Reader listened to the sounds of the words: how they moved inside the body… mmm…

♫ AIRAAS… AASAIR… Aileen… Eoin… Re… mem… beringggg… AIRAAS, AASAIR, Aileen, Eoin, Remembering…♫

The vibrating pulsations of each sound sucked the Reader's body into sedation. Mmm… the Reader swayed backwards and fell from AIRAAS's hand. They gave no resistance and let themself fall into the space…

Mmmm… slow-motion… fallingggg slowww… dream… space… falling bliss… mmm… incense… lavender… ahh… fallingggg…

AIRAAS watched the little human float downwards, knowing no ill would pass. The Guardian of the Tower was there.

AIRAAS breathed in the sweet-sounding, scented air. Then, the Butterfly Goddess flew down to observe closer. In similar fashion, two Golden Gods turned direction in a winged pirouette to follow AIRAAS.

The vast skies lit up in patchouli-perfumed oranges and reds in approval of the True Direction.

KOAA's heart centre burnt. She stopped her peaceful swim towards the two echoes… "Ah, you are here, too…"

This was a force unknown in the Kingdom, yet KOAA knew of it. It had been asleep in the cave. She had met it in her dreams… or better said, in her nightmares…

The Sea of Seas

I am

The Waters of the Mother

The Sea of Seas

The Liquids of Healing

I invite You

To Wash & Cleanse Yourselves

In the Silver Preciousness

Of the Waters of Saahruam

I invite You

To Remember

WHO YOU ARE

Children of the One Light

Delighted Ripples

Am I

To feel your Presence

Here

"SPLASHHH!!!"

The Reader plunged into the watery depths of the Sea of Seas.

Aaaahh!!!

Wow! I'm in the water!

Ohhh… what strange water… it must be the Sea of Seas! I can't believe it! So I'm in the Kingdom!

This water is incredible… Mmm… so soft… like silk… and it's true, you can breathe underneath… wow…

The Reader floated in the silver softness and marvelled at being in the Kingdom of AASAIR.

Float

In

Me

Float

Float

Float

Light

Melodious

Float

Float

Float

The Kingdom of AASAIR: The Reader's Dream

The Reader dreamt he was a man who walked the Earth. He was invisible to all the creatures that lived on the Earth. He was to observe only and not judge. So he walked and observed, walked and observed. He felt no tiredness, no hunger, no passing of time… Unexpectedly, the man woke up in his walking dream and realised nothing existed unless he actually observed it. The realisation made him stop all movement. He felt himself slowly turn into icy stone, paralyzed in a state of no direction. The stone froze his cells and organs into solid rock. Completely immobile, the man of stone forgot he was necessary for the Earth to exist.

The Reader woke up with a scream and found themself in another nightmare: I'm drowning!!

Ahh… it's okay, it's okay! I'm in the Sea of Seas. It's okay…

The Reader swam upwards to the surface. On popping their head out of the silver water, they saw a shore of gold, glittering in the distance. Ohhh! They made out a figure standing on the beach. That must be Eoin, the Reader thought with excitement, but a little warily, noticing a sense of angst in the stomach.

Hmm… now what?

RAASAI?

KOAA

KOAA sensed 5 presences: 4 in the Sea Mother, and 1 outside the kingdom. The dark grumble of the Fiery One kept disturbing the different sound frequencies, but KOAA let it be in watery surrender. The 2 Voices of Old still sang their song of ancient longing that beckoned to her, irresistibly. Then, KOAA heard 2 new voices, a luminous sound intertwined with the deep, beckoning call. The 4 sang together in a haunting melody, an ancient call that KOAA had no choice but to answer.

The Song of AIRAAS

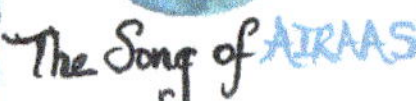

From above, AIRAAS observed. She saw a great sea with 6 living creatures, and yet, 7 presences, all swimming in one direction. She saw golden sands sparkling in the sun, and then, she saw the little dog Being...
"Oh!" sang AIRAAS's heart.

But the joy turned to pain. A burning current passed through her body when AIRAAS saw the tortured eyes of the Nameless Man.

Forced to restabilise, AIRAAS flapped her wings, and continued observing.

Eoin & Bruxa

Eoin was again the Man of No Name. In fact, he felt like the Man of Many Names. He knew he had been through countless painful experiences, and he was right. However, no name in particular came to the Man now. All that was there was a seething frustration of having been harmed and abandoned. "What am I doing in this God-forsaken place?"

Bruxa kept her distance. Then, knowing Aileen was closer, Bruxa looked up to the skies and wagged her tail.

The Reader

Diving into the warm Sea, the Reader caught sight of their hands and stopped in mid-float. Perplexed, they scanned their body. The Reader felt dizzy. RAASAI whispered, "Reader, the Waters can be transforming to those who open to them. No doubt this had to be in order for you to be here in the Last kingdom." The Reader stared at his chest, for he was a 'he'! What was this body? A man? A fish? Yes, he must be some sort of merman!

The Reader closed his newly-transformed merman eyes, and for the first time ever, heard the pulses and patterns of this even more magical Sea of Seas.

The 4

Shimmera & Saul dove into the Sea in pure ecstasy, their dolphin bodies at one with the preciousness of the divine liquid. Yes, they knew the Sea well, for they had been born there at the beginning of no-beginnings. Yes, they had forgotten, as all Creatures had, but now they remembered in sweet delight, leaping in and out of the Silverness.

Meanwhile, Smanara & Silas moved in graceful elegance, their huge black and white bodies gleaming in the silver waters. They sang the mysterious Ancient Call of the Beginning-End of Life, and smiled in their hearts on seeing their brother and sister's arrival.

The Star of Heavens

There are many twinklings

Many bright explosions

Of Beginnings & Endings

One cannot be without the Other

The Ancient Land of AASAIR

Has returned

In Cyclic Lustrous Spiral

For the Kind Gardener

Adventure-Teller of Old

Creator of Magical Worlds

Must remember

In order for all to remember

As the 6 move sweetly

Into the Flower of Flowers

To Regain

The Scintillating Truth & Wisdom

Without the Other, One cannot be

The 6 are 1

And all must behold

For True

 Saahruam Allssiram Issenam ♫♫

To Be

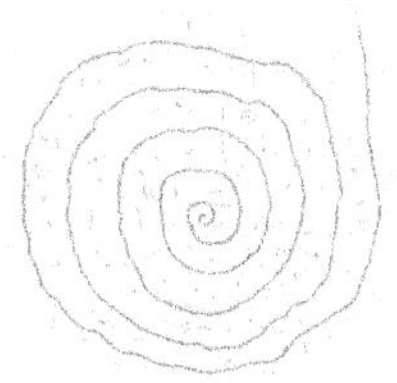

Kite of Kites

The Butterfly Mother

I AM

PART 13

The Kingdom of AASAIR

The Reader-Merman hears the call: it's hypnotic, irresistible. He flicks his tail fin as he lies floating on his back. "RAASAI. I'm another now."

"Reader, YOU are IASAAR, the Guardian's Mirror."

"IASAAR?" The merman turns and dives into the water. "RAASAI, all I want to do is follow the song of lost loves that I hear! But Eoin is in the other direction…"

"Follow the song, IASAAR. When it is time to be with Eoin, you will know."

The Man with No Name wipes his hand across his forehead.

All this heat… But I'm not touching that water, it looks like poison. And that dog, it won't stop barking…

The Man's face goes very red. He scrambles to his feet and glares. Bruxa senses the fury and flees inland towards a large dune. The Man is right behind her but stops when he see the dog run up the dune. He falls to his knees.

So much thirst… and heat… urgh… burning… my stomach… the burning, I can smell it… scorching flames that consume everything!

The Man lifts his hands up to his face. "Nooo!"

"Jean. Jean… Jean…[17] Can you hear me? The Angel was here. All is well. Jean, tout va bien, tout va bien."[18]

"Mon Dieu! I'm Jean!" He gets to his feet. "I remember now! My promise! My revenge! Everything was taken from me! And the flames!" Jean sobs, tears rolling down his cheeks. "No… No… Noooo!"

The Reader turned Merman turned IASAAR hears the name 'Jean'. He stops for a moment. He lets the tension settle, then continues swimming forward.

KOAA feels the Kingdom tremble in recognition of the fiery energy but she, too, swims on. AASAIR is in her heart, though she still can't place him in the Kingdom.

Bruxa gives a low whimper from behind a bush. Suddenly, she hears a soft growl. Bruxa turns round: it's her friend of ages, Tiger Bright! Both lick each other in joyous reunion.

---

17 The Story Speaks

'Jean' is pronounced as is the custom in the Earth Realm language of French.

---

18 The Story Speaks

In French, 'tout va bien' means 'all goes well' and further down, 'Mon Dieu' means 'My God'.

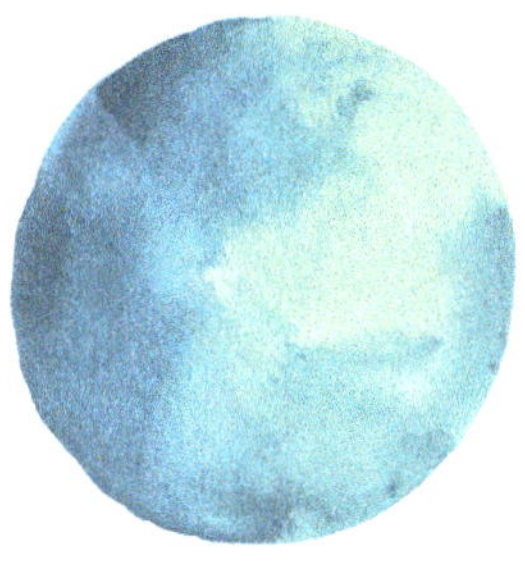

The Song of AIRAAS:
AIRAAS sends the Pink Thread of Healing

♫ *Transfixed*

I

Am

In Celebration

My Wings spread and open

Below, Sweet Beings

Mmm…

Their Penetrating Song I love.

Enthralling me, I sing too

It beckons to me

Ahhh…

A relentless heat

It desires to burst into flames

My Wings

Wings of Freedom, you flutter so

One of the strands, silky and fragrant

Beautiful pink

I can smell the lingering lavender perfume

Pink Thread of Threads, yes, swirl out in spiralling magnificence!

I am rock-like, nothing can move me
I hover here, still and patient
The Lavender Thread, down it goes…

Accept this Thread of
Healing Love
For You, Chosen One,
Must take it to
The One
Who
Suffers

IASAAR, Reader of Readers, Perceiver of All, swims up to the surface. His golden-haired head comes out of the sea. He looks up. A shiny pink string with silver specks hangs down from the skies, at about ten feet away he calculates. Okay, how do I do this?

IASAAR dives back into the sea. He goes down really deep. Then the merman turns around and swims as fast as he can. His powerful tail moves up and down and propels him, pushes him out of the water and into the air. He grabs the pink thread and swoops down head first into the Silverness again. Yes!

Tying the lavender thread around his waist, IASAAR now knows exactly where to go.

The Flame of All Fires

I am invited to Speak

My Fires are two-fold:
Without the Seeing,
They burn in Rampant Blindness
Setting themselves Alight
In confused Pain & Plight
With the Seeing,
The Fires burn as the Flame of All Fires
To consume all Blindness and Fury

The Cinders then return to IRAASA
She claims them, devours them
The Sorrow is transmuted
At the Joyful Reunion
A Rebirth through the Sea of Purity
To Resurrect into the Air of Airs
And Pierce in True Love
The Flower of Flowers
The Six-Petalled ASAIRA!

PART 14

The Kingdom of AASAIR

Jean saw a large shady tree. He threw himself down and brought his knees to his chest in foetal comfort. The Ancient Tree looked down in compassion upon this sweet Son of ASAIRA, knowing Him and loving Him.

Jean let the cool shade of the branches soothe his inflamed mind full of cruel thoughts. He closed his eyes and fell into a merciful sleep.

Nearby, but hidden from view, Bruxa and Tiger Bright also lay down, keeping watch. They, too, loved this sweet, now muddled man, and longed for his return.

In the Great Sea, the 4 swam in eager expectancy at meeting the Immensity of Being. She was the Ancientness Forgotten, and now the only thing that mattered was to reunite themselves with her.

Then there she was! The Whale of Whales, the Ancient One of Blue Sapphire, slow and gracious, resplendent and solid. The 4 kept their distance to honour her. The waters sparkled in delight.

The Tree of Lands

Ah...

A Son of ASAIRA

Lays his head

Sleeps at my feet

I know you

I know you well

I have seen you

In many guises

Fear not

The Fire of Fires

Is here to aid you

Do not resist

Give yourself

To the Flame of Flames

Be brave

You are not alone

She is here

On the shore of gold, IASAAR, with a surprising naturalness of old, walked out of the Sea, his legs magically returning. He was quite splendid: his skin shone from the silvery coat of ocean water, and he wore clothes that brought to mind pirates from the Earth Realm.

The pink thread at IASAAR's waist pulled behind his back; it was invisible to all except him, and RAASAI of course.

"Don't forget your mission," said RAASAI. "YOU have the privilege of having read and seen what others have not. You are to give remembrance and alleviate the blinding sorrow of not knowing who one is."

ASAIRA

In her various aspects

She is here

Everywhere

Take her Rope

The sweetest fragrance

Take the pinkness

It shall bring you

Through the Flames

The Guardian of the Stem

Shall deliver

Her Thread of Threads

Aaah...

The Ancientness of this Land

Yes

The Promise of the 3

That are

The 6

The Kingdom of AASAIR: Jean's Dream

Jean dreamt he had been reborn in another time, in another place. One day, an emotion was kindled, a fire that would not be put out. It was the fire of revenge: he would not forget, no, he refused to forget his pain of pains.

Curiously, he had forgotten, for this fiery fury was nothing more than a fire of forgetting, an impossible attempt to put out the pain with more pain and revenge. This in turn became the ultimate forgetting, not of the pain, but of who he really was.

In the dream, Jean wakes up. Whose voice is this? He looks around. "Am I dreaming?"

"Are you speaking to me?" asks an astonished voice.

Jean shakes. "Who are you? Why do you speak of me as if you tell a story? Am I in a dream?"

"You can hear me, by George! Well, yes, you are a character in a story, and I am the Storyteller. It is an honour to meet you, but I am somewhat surprised…"

Jean raises his fist. "You lie! You don't know who you are! You have forgotten. Where are you? No, I will not listen. I choose to wake up from this dream!"

And so it was. The man called Jean found himself under the tree again. But something had changed. He realised he was not Jean; he realised there were many names he had lived, and he realised he was none of them. He could only be what he felt, he concluded. He was the Fire! He was the Fiery One of No Name, and obviously, having lived so many lives, he must be some kind of god-like Being.

The Nameless One stood up. "I have remembered! I am the Fire of Fires and I am here to destroy all the lies! Beware all ye who approach me, for I shall consume ye!"

As the man's voice spoke, he seemed to swell and double in size. All his features hardened, and his brown eyes, so sweet and compassionate in other times, became savage and remorseless, red as fire.

The Darkness of IRAASA below his feet braced herself and quaked the land while, above, the leaves on the Tree of Old hissed and crackled from the heat in the air.

Bruxa and Tiger Bright stood on all fours, their eyes fixed on the Red-Eyed One.

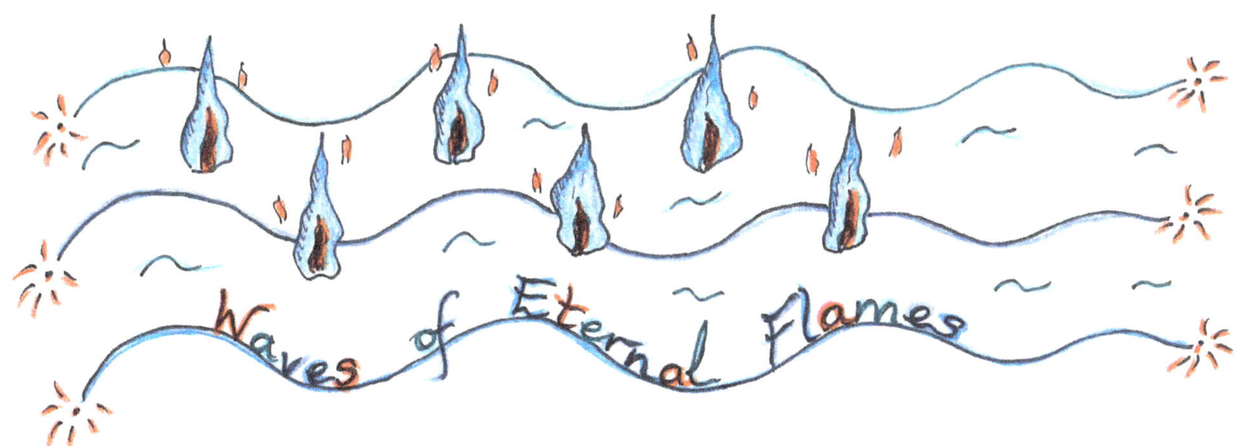

PART 15

The Kingdom of AASAIR: KOAA's Realisation

KOAA stops in front of the four sea creatures.

Oh! They are not my brothers and sisters; they are my sons and daughters! They are my children, as all creatures are!

The realisation of her ancientness dawns on KOAA. She is the Roundness, the Living Womb of Wombs. She is the Mother in Pure Form.

KOAA feels a tear of unconditional love roll down her face for all she had forgotten.

She had been created by AASAIR in the beginning of beginnings. AASAIR, the Father of All... and then she had brought forth all other creatures from her womb.

But, wait...

KOAA shivers and emits a high-pitched whine: KOAA was just a playful name she had been given by her mirror-aspect. She was AASAIR!

I am AASAIR! AASAIR is male and female and separate in form. I am KOAA, the female AASAIR, Mother of all worlds co-created with the male AASAIR!

KOAA sings a haunting song of remembrance in mysterious, long whines and whistles and clicks of high-pitch frequency. They pierce and pulse the heart of the lost Kingdom that was becoming found.

Smanara & Silas, now the Silver Orcas of the Deep, and Shimmera & Saul as the Golden Dolphins of the Waves, all nudge and rub their Mother in the sweetest of reunions.

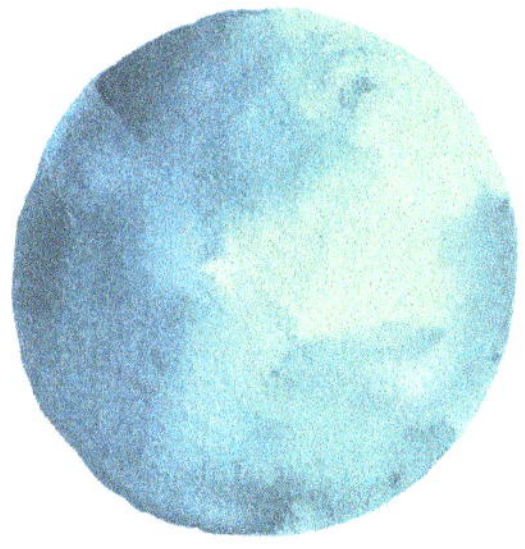

The Song of AIRAAS: Memories

Right below her, AIRAAS observed the five Water Beings meet together in a blue, golden, silver swirl. Waves and waves of loving reconciliation filled her awareness with images of creatures all living in a land of harmony.

AIRAAS sang in unison with the Whales and the Dolphins. The song was of such innocent beauty that even the ripples in the breeze stopped to listen.

Two chocolate-coloured eyes interrupted AIRAAS's melody. The eyes brought a remembrance of a little white dog, a sweet lamb who had been given to the bearer of those brown eyes.

These were the same brown eyes that in an ancient, lost time had said, "Let us forget all of this and create a new world for us to live and love and experience together!"

AIRAAS noticed a tug at her wings and looked back: there were various gaps in one of the wings.

AIRAAS breathed in some lavender-perfumed air. A memory came that she must not move, a memory of being in an earthy cocoon, of a trustful stillness that if she stayed where she was, all would be all right.

AIRAAS did not comprehend in an Earth Realm sense, but she felt certain that she was to stay exactly where she was.

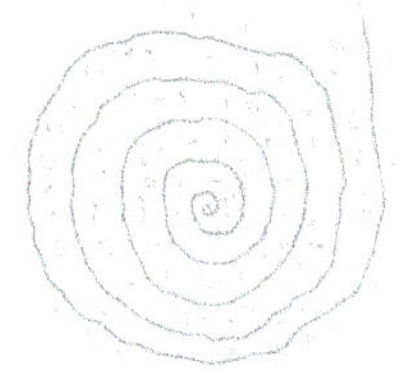

Ah...

The Story knew not

Its own Telling

Cannot be known

She is AASAIR

She cannot be without He

Do not be surprised!

One cannot be without the Other

As 6 are 3 are 1 are 12 are 24

Are One

In Endless Eternity

I am the Mother

The Father

I am the Daughter

The Son

The Observer

The Observeress

I am

ASAIRA

As One

As Sister & Brother

Wake up & Remember

Children of the One Light!

Ah...

RAASAI speaks

IAASAR, Reader. Stop and listen. The Remembering is in full motion. The Ancient Daughter of the Sacred Seas knows herself, as YOU have seen, and AIRAAS receives memories and images while she flies in stillness above us all.

By the Lavender Thread of Healing you are tied to AIRAAS, and she is tied to you. Never detach yourself from AIRAAS. You shall soon see the Nameless Man who, as you know, is convinced of his fiery identity. You must attach the pink thread to him, too. Make a lasso and put it around his waist. You will have help. Listen to the Tiger and the Lamb.

You are to tell the Man who you are. Firstly, your new name, IAASAR, then explain you are the Reader. Tell him something about himself that you know. He will either remember, or at least he shall be distracted in his strength, and then you tell him more. He shall remember!

Be vigilant. None of this will be easy, for he believes he is the Furious Fire of Fires. But I am with you. There is much joy, IAASAR. We are nearer the Truth.

Feel my warmth on your back and look for the Lamb and the Tiger.

PART 16

The Kingdom of AASAIR

When IASAAR climbed the dune, he had felt warrior-like, full of might and splendour, enjoying his sense of physical superiority. But now after RAASAI's words, his body feels tired. And just when it's needed, he sees a shady tree, its leaves shine in the sun. I'll rest there.

IASAAR lies down under the Tree. He knows it's the Tree of Lands and feels a gratitude that he's never felt before; all the emotion of finding himself in the Story suddenly boils up in one go. Thank youuuuu…

IASAAR touches the pink strand of AIRAAS. So miraculous… and the scent, ohh… he breathes it in. The lavender aroma brings back memories of the strand's own story… the other stories of each different-coloured strand, too. But I can't remember all the names now or the details… I should remember…

IASAAR-Reader drifts into a dreamy space of somnolence, but they want to say something out aloud. "ASAIRA, I've never really spoken to YOU. I feel somehow I should thank you. It's so amazing I'm here. I'm going to need a lot of help, though. I know RAASAI is close and in support, but maybe we all need your help right now. Please help me to remember what I need. I'm just a humble human Being from Earth! Thank you, thank you…" IASAAR falls asleep.

The Man who believes he is a revengeful fire is restless. I have to move… go out and destroy the lies. But he has no idea of what direction to go in.

The tree looks inviting with all the shade. The Man sits down. He decides to make a plan, and a million destructive thoughts are triggered and whirl in his mind. Exhausted, the Man closes his eyes again and lets himself fall into sleepiness.

The Tree stretches its roots, opens its branches and embraces the 2.

The Sea Beings in the Kingdom position themselves. They move in synchronization. The Silvery Black Orcas and the Golden Dolphins place themselves in a circle to face KOAA. KOAA stays still, very still; she is the Sea Mother, and she can feel the beginnings of a birth. All 5 know that they will soon be 6.

The two Guardians of ASAIRA, the Dog and the Tiger, sense they must separate. Each one goes to the Tree of Old, which is now 2 but only 1.

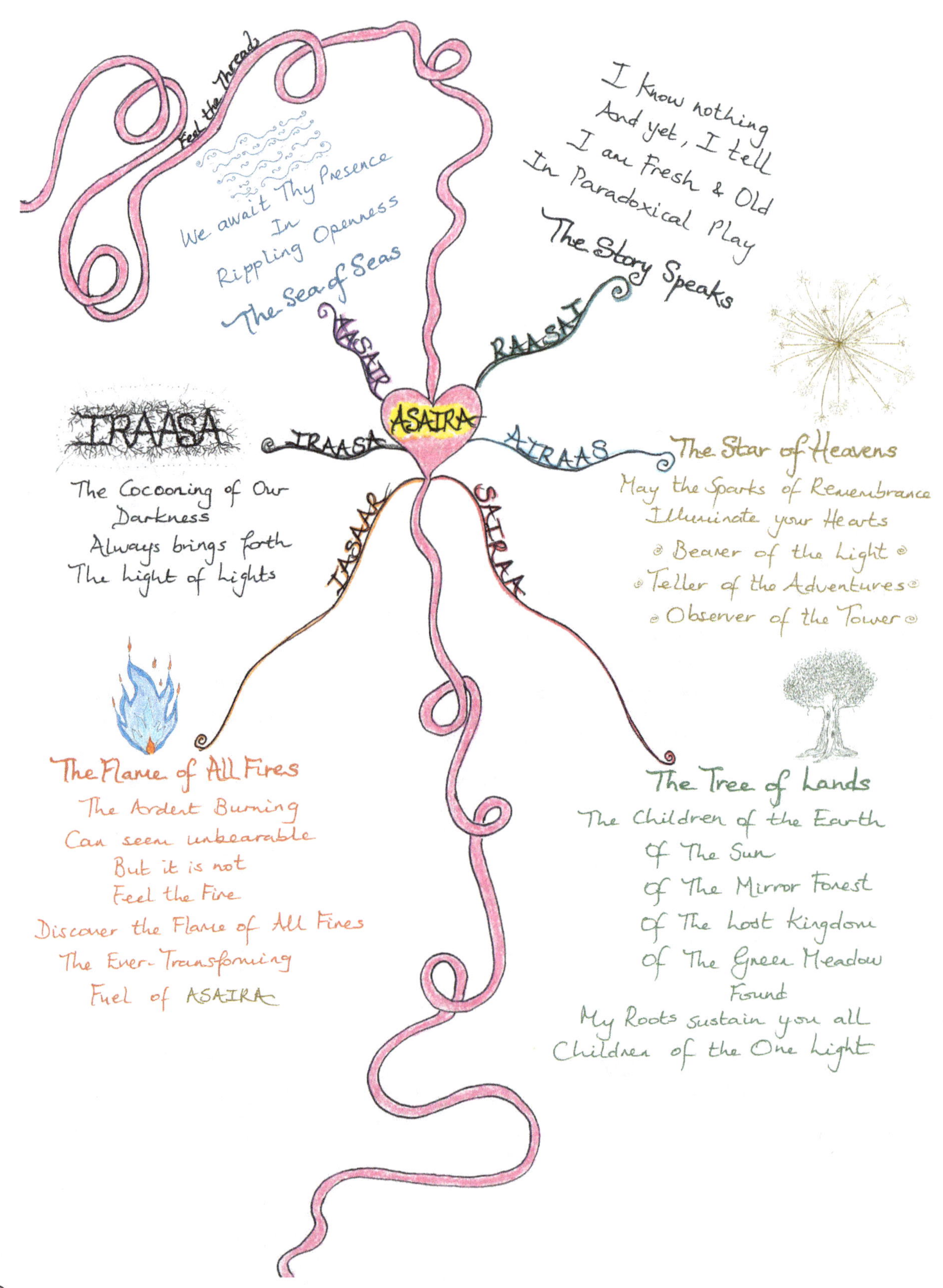

Feel the Threads

We await Thy Presence
In
Rippling Openness
The Sea of Seas

I know nothing
And yet, I tell
I am Fresh & Old
In Paradoxical Play
The Story Speaks

AASAIR
RAASAI
IRAASA
AIRAAS
IASAAR
SAIRAA
ASAIRA

IRAASA
The Cocooning of Our
Darkness
Always brings forth
The Light of Lights

The Star of Heavens
May the Sparks of Remembrance
Illuminate your Hearts
◉ Bearer of the Light ◉
◉ Teller of the Adventures ◉
◉ Observer of the Tower ◉

The Flame of All Fires
The Ardent Burning
Can seem unbearable
But it is not
Feel the Fire
Discover the Flame of All Fires
The Ever-Transforming
Fuel of ASAIRA

The Tree of Lands
The Children of the Earth
Of The Sun
Of The Mirror Forest
Of The Lost Kingdom
Of The Green Meadow
Found
My Roots sustain you all
Children of the One Light

The Kingdom of AASAIR:
The 1st Flame of Remembering

IASAAR woke up to the smell of incense. She felt different… She?! IASAAR looked at her tiny brown hands; her black hair fell down onto a yellow tunic. Oh, look at my feet and all these bracelets and charms! Hmm… a little girl, from India, I think… The Reader would have liked a mirror, and miraculously, there was one right at her side. This is amazing! IASAAR glanced into the small bronze mirror. Wow…

A low grumble gave the girl a start, and she knew HE'd arrived! Turning her head to one side, there he was! Tiger Bright! Ah! I can't believe it. IASAAR remembered how many times she'd loved to imagine stroking his gorgeous orange, black and white coat. Shyly, IASAAR touched the Tiger's head.

The Nameless One woke up and jumped to his feet. "Who dares to share the tree with the God of Fire?"

A small dog looked up at him. "That stupid lamb again!" he mumbled, somewhat dumbfounded at seeing it there in such serenity. He decided to ignore it.

The Man noticed the other tree. Had that been there before? Hmm… the Liars are coming! The Man's mind exploded: I'm the Fire of Truth and I can burn all lies with my will. I'll burn anything that lies to me to ashes! And if this land is a lie, I'll reduce it to ashes too! Nothing shall stop the Fire God!

IASAAR touched the lavender-pink rope around her waist. It was the strand that the angel had given Eilène before she had been… put to death… IASAAR could hardly think the words and trembled. But she knew this pink strand of love had taken away all the pain and let herself, too, be calmed by its spirals of lavender. Then, pulling to have extra slack, she prepared the lasso to place around Eoin. On thinking his name, she felt a jolt. He also calls himself Jean… Jean is a French name… of course!

Tiger Bright got to his feet and stood in front of IASAAR who knew exactly what to do. Armed with the Pink Lasso of Salvation in one hand and the Mirror of Truth in the other, she mounted the Tiger.

The Man of Fire could never have foreseen such a sight. Having had the words or the awareness, he would have said it was a scene of imposing beauty. What a tiger! And the little girl riding on it… she was more enchanting than any person he had ever seen: the yellow dress she wore… a primrose yellow that shone in the sun!

The Man took a step back. Then he saw something shiny in the girl's hand… what's that? It must be a weapon! He woke up from the hypnotising vision… it's a lie! She's a witch dressed up to trick me! Burn her down! The fiery thoughts made the hatred and fear rise up to his mind, sending a blazing flame towards IASAAR. Incredibly, the pink rope bolted it right back at the Man with No Name. He screamed. IASAAR, with the courage that came from an ancient time, knew it was the moment: she and Tiger Bright galloped towards the Man and lassoed him at the waist. He stopped screaming and all movement. He could not see the pink thread which connected him to both IASAAR and AIRAAS, yet he could smell a perfume that nauseated him.

IASAAR dismounted and knelt down beside the Man. She spoke as fast and clearly as she could. "My name is IASAAR. I'm the Reader of the Story. You have many names and none. I know about you, and I'm here to help you remember."

"Lies, lies!" said the One who knew himself as fire and anguish.

"You have had many different lives, it seems. You were Eoin, and you loved Elyn. You were Juan, and you loved your mother, Elena. You were John, Aileen's grandfather!"

"Stop, stop!" the Man begged. "These are all lies… you muddle me, witch!"

"How can you call me witch? Can't you remember? Listen to me!" She held the man's shoulders and looked into his eyes. "Your wife, I think she was your wife, Eilène, she was burnt at the stake for being a witch! You were there, Jean! For God's sake… evil witches don't exist! You know that. That's the Lie! That's the lie they invented! Can't you remember, Jean? It's you now that are living the lies!"

Silence.

The Man of Many Names sobbed, "Eilène… Eilène…"

The little lamb came close and curled up beside the Man. Relieved, the Girl lay down next to Tiger Bright's warm, outstretched body under the Tree of Lands, which had become one Tree again.

Ahh… the 4, the Tree whispered through his rustling evergreen leaves.

The 1st Flame went out, extinguished by the Remembering. The Flame's ashy remains were absorbed by IRAASA, Queen of the Earthy Depths.

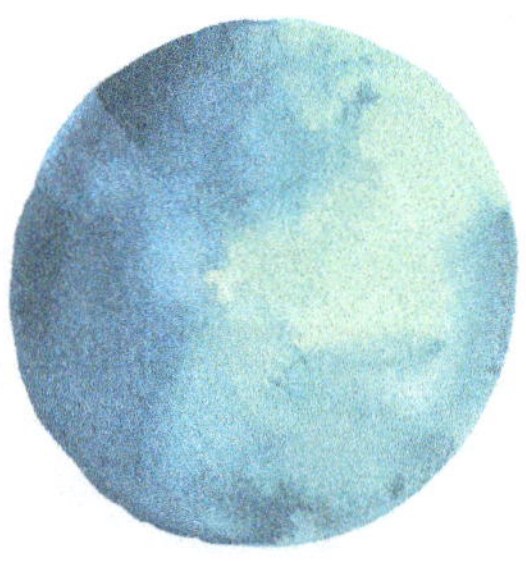

The Song of AIRAAS: A Profound Love

AIRAAS observed in quiet awe as the brown-eyed man wept. He kept saying, "Eilène, Eilène…" After a while, he became silent and closed his eyes.

A tingling: three more sparkling strands from the wings unravelled themselves, then swirled down to the land below.

Voices that danced through the air: " You are Eilène… you are Elyn… you are Elena… you are Aileen… you are AIRAAS… you are ASAIRA… you are so much more and nothing…"

These words had no precise meaning for the Goddess of Melodious Bliss, an observer always, but she was undeniably fascinated by it all, and she could not resist the profound love she felt for all the Beings below.

The wings fluttered iridescently in the sun's glow.

I Am

The Love

That

Never

Abandons

Itself

PART 18

The Kingdom of AASAIR:
The 2nd Flame of Remembering

John looks up through the golden leaves. What a beautiful tree… it looks familiar… He sits up and sees a little Indian girl asleep next to an enormous tiger. What's this? Am I dreaming? Bruxa licks his hand. Well, this is a lovely dream, I must say! John chuckles.

IASAAR opens her eyes and sees no fiery, furious one… just a middle-aged, sweet-eyed man who is laughing merrily.

"Be vigilant. The flame can flare up any time. And look towards the sky," RAASAI says.

IASAAR glances upwards: three glowing threads are coming down through the branches of the Tree. One is a velvet green: Elena's essence! The second is a shiny purple. IASAAR recognizes it as Juan's essence. The 3rd strand is a bright white and can only be Elyn's white hair.

IASAAR turns her head back to the Man and asks him his name.

"John." The Man smiles. "And who are you? This is a dream, isn't it?"

"I'm IASAAR, the Reader of the Story. Does that ring a bell?"

"I'm afraid not. But it all sounds quite fascinating!" John laughs and cuddles Bruxa.

"John… what if I say you're not really John, and that you've lived many lives, John being just one of them, and that he already died… Does any of that ring a bell?"

Who is this girl? The thought rushes in with spectacular force, and John disappears in a steaming haze of suspicion. The Man stands up, red-faced. He points at IASAAR who has also jumped up, Tiger Bright at her side. A flame flies at her face, but the pink rope bolts it straight back into the Man's heart, leaving IASAAR unscathed. He screams with pain and anger. IASAAR grabs the green, purple and white Threads of Truth and literally pounces onto the Fiery One. With the pink thread that is already around the Man's waist, she ties all four threads together. The Man gasps from the overwhelming love that pierces his soul. He falls to the ground.

IASAAR shows no mercy. "You have lived more than one life. Yes, you were John, you were Eoin, you were Juan, you were Jean… but can't you see that if you were different people, then those people weren't you? You must be someone else who's able to see all those lives like a story. You aren't really any of those men right now. You're the… you're the… Storyteller!" IASAAR can hardly believe it herself.

The Man swallows. A light of realisation shines through his eyes. He breathes in deeply. "The Storyteller?" He sighs, closing his eyes.

IASAAR senses a new peace. She picks up Bruxa who's hidden behind the Tree and hugs her. So sweet! Exhausted, the young girl, Reader of Readers, lies down with the little dog next to Tiger Bright.

The 2nd Flame goes out, and its ash rains down into the arms of the Earth Mother. Home at last, the sizzling ashes seem to say.

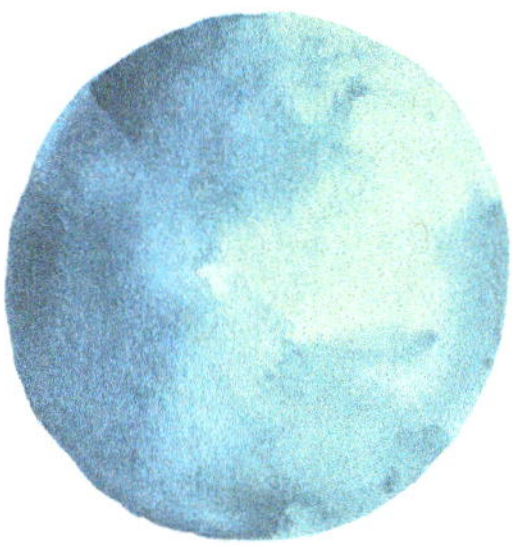

The Song of AIRAAS: I shall tell the Story

AIRAAS revelled in the beauty of the Whale's song. The exquisite sounds swam up and danced around her in balsamic echoes. Mmmm…

A vision arose of a lush green meadow enveloped in a sweetness that AIRAAS could even taste. Mmmm…

AIRAAS felt a tug at her wings again, and the Whale's song turned into a chant, a Chant of Old, of sacred, magical words, "I shall tell the Story… I shall tell of this Adventure… Tell this Story I shall… Tell this Adventure I shall.."

In Ever-Connectedness

The One Flower

ASAIRA

Am

PART 19

The Kingdom of AASAIR:
The 3rd Flame of Remembering

All 4 look at each other. IASAAR wonders who the Man thinks he is now and waits to hear him speak. The two Guardians of ASAIRA keep very still.

"By Jove! I cannot believe this!" The Man looks around him. "Yes, yes… I remember. I am the Storyteller! I lost my memory, I suppose. Yes, I was all those men in other lives, and I must have promised to tell their story. That must be it! Heavens, how incredible this is although I cannot completely grasp it in all honesty… And who are you, young lady?"

"I'm IASAAR. Does this name mean anything to you?"

"No, yet it feels familiar. It is one of the ASAIRA names…"

"Well, actually, how to say this… I'm the Reader, the Reader of the Story…"

"The Reader? But how can you be here, inside the Story?"

"I know… but what about you?! How come you're in the Story, and who are you? I mean, who is the Storyteller, anyway?!"

The Storyteller feels a sickly sensation in his stomach and crumples up. IASAAR mirrors the action as she feels a fire rise up inside of her. The Reader tenses. Is she losing her mind? How could they be in a story, for goodness sake!? What is this? A dream, a nightmare? The Reader and the Storyteller stare at each other.

A Voice of Old sounds from the Reader's mouth, "Hold the Ancient Threads of Truth in your hands. Let their Strength and Compassion guide you. Do not be afeard, for I am here."

IASAAR quickly places the Storyteller's hand on the four invisible strands that are around his waist. Standing in front of him, she takes hold of the pink and white strands of Eilène and Elyn in one hand, and the purple and green strands of Juan and Elena in the other.

Arghh… it comes like a burning dagger! The Flame of Furious Fear, of Ferocious Revenge, of Futile Blindness scorches and scalds, stabbing their hearts, filling their minds with morbid sorrowfulness. But both the Reader and the Storyteller stand their ground, their eyes fixed on each other.

The angry fires gradually lose their power.

What's left is the Flame of All Fires, a small blue flame that can never be extinguished. It nestles itself into the Reader and Storyteller's hearts, giving them the Strength of Ages and the Wisdom of Old.

IASAAR blurts out, "Oh, you are UT, too!" And an ancient OM rings through the branches of the Tree.

"Ha! Ha! Ha! Perhaps… I'm not sure. By all the Gods, I truly know nothing of who I really am, or who you really are!"

"I feel the same way! But, remember, there is a Promise. You promised, and Aileen, too, when you were Juan and Elena. Maybe I promised something, too… and that's the connection…" IASAAR shrugs her shoulders.

"Yes. Let us keep going without fear. Let's find out the Truth of all this, shall we, Reader of Readers?" The Storyteller smiles.

"Yes, Storyteller of Storytellers!"

"Hmm…?" The Storyteller chuckles, "So, do you know what to do now? Because not an inkling have I!"

IASAAR, the Reader, does know exactly what to do. She takes the Storyteller by the hand, and with the sweet earnestness and wisdom of young children walks towards the Silver Sea that sparkles in front of them. The Tiger and the Dog walk behind them in recognition of the One True Direction.

PART 20

The Remembering: AIRAAS, IASAAR and AASAIR Follow AIRAAS's Song

The air flickered around AIRAAS in oranges and reds; it was alive and bubbling.

AIRAAS, AI…RAAS, AASAIR, AA…SAIR, RAASAI, RAA…SAI, SAIRAA, SAI…RAA,
ASAIRA, ASAI…RA, IRAASA, I…RAA…SA…

Her ancient song reached the depths of the Sea of Seas. KOAA the Whale Mother and the Orcas and Dolphins echoed in low-pitched moans. The sound waves of this Divine Quartet travelled the Realms of ASAIRA in a candescence of love.

IASAAR and the Storyteller stood at the edge of the Sea, the two Guardians close by on either side. The silver dazzle of the waters and the flaming oranges of the skies lulled them: everything glittered and tingled. Oh… the moment was so splendorous. Yes, one of those moments which you wish would never end!

RAASAI spoke inside IASAAR's goddess heart, "Dive into the Mother of All Seas with the Man who calls himself the Storyteller. Remember, there is nothing to fear; joined are you both to AIRAAS by the Strands of Love. The Tiger and Lamb are with you, too. Follow AIRAAS's song. You will be brought to the Promised Circle. And never forget that I am always here with YOU."

IASAAR looked at the Storyteller. His eyes were the colour of chestnuts. He seemed young but also very old. With his old-fashioned way of talking, she had imagined the Storyteller to be a white-bearded, elderly man. IASAAR felt a pang of love for this ancient Being and knew it was time to go. "We have to dive into the sea and swim towards the sound of AIRAAS singing."

The Storyteller arched his eyebrows. "I don't know how to swim."

"Remember this is the Sea of Seas. You'll be able to swim and breathe underwater, too!"

The Storyteller gazed at the Silverness; a yearning poured into his heart. "Very well, my dear, dear Reader! By Jove, I always knew I'd meet you! Let us do this…" he said, then broke into a run towards the Sea.

Bruxa ran right behind the chestnut-eyed man and jumped into the sea and into his heart. Tiger Bright, in sync, dissolved into an orange flame and flew into the little girl. Ahh! IASAAR, euphoric, plunged into the waters.

The 2 swam incredibly fast. I'm the merman again! IASAAR looked to his side and marvelled to see a younger Storyteller with long hair who was also a merman! Brothers! And once more IASAAR's heart throbbed with an aching love.

The Storyteller had never felt so alive, or at least as far as he could remember. Oh… what a sensation to swim in this silver! He glanced at the Reader. Completely stunned, he stopped moving his tail. IASAAR slowed down. He saw the Storyteller look down at himself. IASAAR laughed at the Storyteller's face of wonder. He remembered the mirror. Did he still have it? Yes, it was tied to his waist with the pink strand. IASAAR couldn't resist taking a peek at himself first: Ohh! And then shone the mirror towards the Storyteller.

The Storyteller stared at the long-haired man in the reflection; it reminded him of someone. Of himself?! But there was no time for further thought. The most hauntingly magical sound they had ever heard entered their bodies, waking up every sensory receptor they had: they could hear with their skin, with their taste… they could even hear the rippling perfume of the musical notes through their merman noses!

"Mmmm…" IASAAR closed his eyes and felt the intensity but, their mission resurfacing, he touched the Storyteller's shoulder. "It's the song of AIRAAS! We have to continue."

"Yes, my Friend."

With a glittering whoosh of their tails, they swam on towards the sacred melody.

The Mirrored Truth

KOAA stopped singing. She sensed the two Beings that were five approach. Ahh…
the sweet-eyed man and the little dog, yes… the winged Guardian of the Flower in
sea creature form and the tiger Being… yes… But… we also await AASAIR for the
Promise due…

"AASAIRRR," she whined.

A dizziness overcame the Storyteller when he first caught sight of the enormous
whale, in the distance still.

IASAAR swam over to his brother, who had become quite pale. "I know you can't see
them, but AIRAAS's threads, from her wings… you remember? They're around your
waist. Touch them, and they'll give you strength."

The Storyteller did as he was told and felt renewed. The two mermen continued
swimming and came closer and closer, AIRAAS's song fluttering in the silky strands.

The Orcas of the Deep and the Dolphins of the Waves smiled in their hearts: at last!
But the two newcomers to the Circle (or so it seemed!) only had eyes for the whale,
this immense creature: she was so radiant, an intense blue with rays on her back
that looked like shooting stars.

As IASAAR and the Storyteller found themselves finishing the Circle of 7, a deep voice boomed out of the Storyteller's mouth, "KOAAAA!!"

KOAA's eyes opened and closed. She looked at the tiny man and responded to the Call of Yore in only one way possible, "AOKKKK!!"

The waters in the middle of the Circle whirled, drawing the Storyteller into its centre. Shocked, IASAAR felt the impulse to follow, but RAASAI gently reassured the Reader not to move.

The mirror at IASAAR's side lifted and detached itself to appear in the Storyteller's hands. "Look at me," said the bronze mirror. "I am the Mirror of Truth; I come from the Forest. You know me well, Son of ASAIRA. Look at yourself!"

The Storyteller looked, the waters calming… All he could see were two brown eyes staring back. They were full of compassion and strength. And in an instant, he knew. Yes, he was UT! He was the Warrior Protector of the Forest… and he had found the Lamb! And SAIRAA… Aileen! Where was she?

UT broke out into song, chanting the magical notes of the Forest of AARIAS,
♪ ♪ UT… Re… Mi… Fa… La… Sol… OMMM…♪ ♪

Echoing in mystical enchantment, AIRAAS's song harmonized with UT's. The Circle Dwellers listened to the two Songs that were one. The Song had a life of its own: it slowed down everything, and the effect on the water was of a slow-moving whirlpool that sparkled in electrical pulses. IASAAR felt he would die from the devastating beauty of it, willing to be there, to witness this, for eternity.

Recognition!

AIRAAS observed from above while she sang and sang. Now she only had ears for the harmony; she closed her eyes, her wings aglow, her hair alight: she had truly become the Song of Songs!

UT lifted his head towards KOAA. Their eyes met. "AASAIR!"

The Sea, which had been relatively calm since UT had begun his song, started to spin. AASAIR, the male aspect, Brother of KOAA and Creator of the Kingdom, the Father of all Creatures, Son of ASAIRA, remembered who he was. And as he did so, he grew larger and larger, taller and taller, the whirlpool now raging around him, echoing KOAA's awakening from the Cave.

IASAAR was transfixed: no words, no thoughts. All 6 were steadfast, magnetized to the pull from below the Sea, from the Depths of IRAASA.

AASAIR, once the Storyteller and so many more, became gigantic, the same but different, his eyes unbelievably kind and wise, his stature and strength such that the vertiginous pool was a little puddle to him. He stopped singing and smiled down at IASAAR.

"Brother! Ha! Ha! Ha! YOU are here, too, of course! And what are these brilliant-coloured cords around me… and around you?"

IASAAR trembled but the words came out clearly amidst the wails of the whirlpool and the Song of AIRAAS. "They are part of AIRAAS's wings made from the pain and love of humans in the Earth Realm, the pain and love that you and she went through in different lives. I've come to help you remember, help you remember the Promise. I'm the Reader of the Story…!"

"AIRAAS… the Butterfly! I loved her so!"

AASAIR looked straight above him. AIRAAS stopped singing, and the whirlpool stopped turning. There was silence. Their eyes found each other in the startling revelation of an ancient time, of ♫ *Saahruam Allssiram Issenam* ♫, of a lost kingdom… and a lost love.

♫ AASAIR ♫ the Butterfly Goddess sang.

"AIRAAS… It's really you…" whispered the giant Storyteller.

A deafening rumble… and everything moved again. The Darkness of IRAASA pushed, lifting up the whirlpool womb and sending AASAIR upwards in a fierce thrust of creation, the creation of True Remembering, the creation of the Knowing of Oneself, of One's Promise.

IASAAR felt a powerful wrench from the pink strand and he, too, was pulled up towards AASAIR and AIRAAS. He lost his breath, his names, his body and mind in this vortex of unknowing and knowing!

IRAASA's whirlpool took the whole Kingdom, the Sea, KOAA, the four Sun Gods and pushed upwards.

In a liquid explosion of transformation, AASAIR and IASAAR both pierced AIRAAS's heart.

Silence

Silence

Nothing more

No Beings

No Earth

No Sun

No Forest

No Kingdom

No Tree

No Star

No Sea

Nothing

Only

The Endless Flower of No-Beginning

ASAIRA

Am

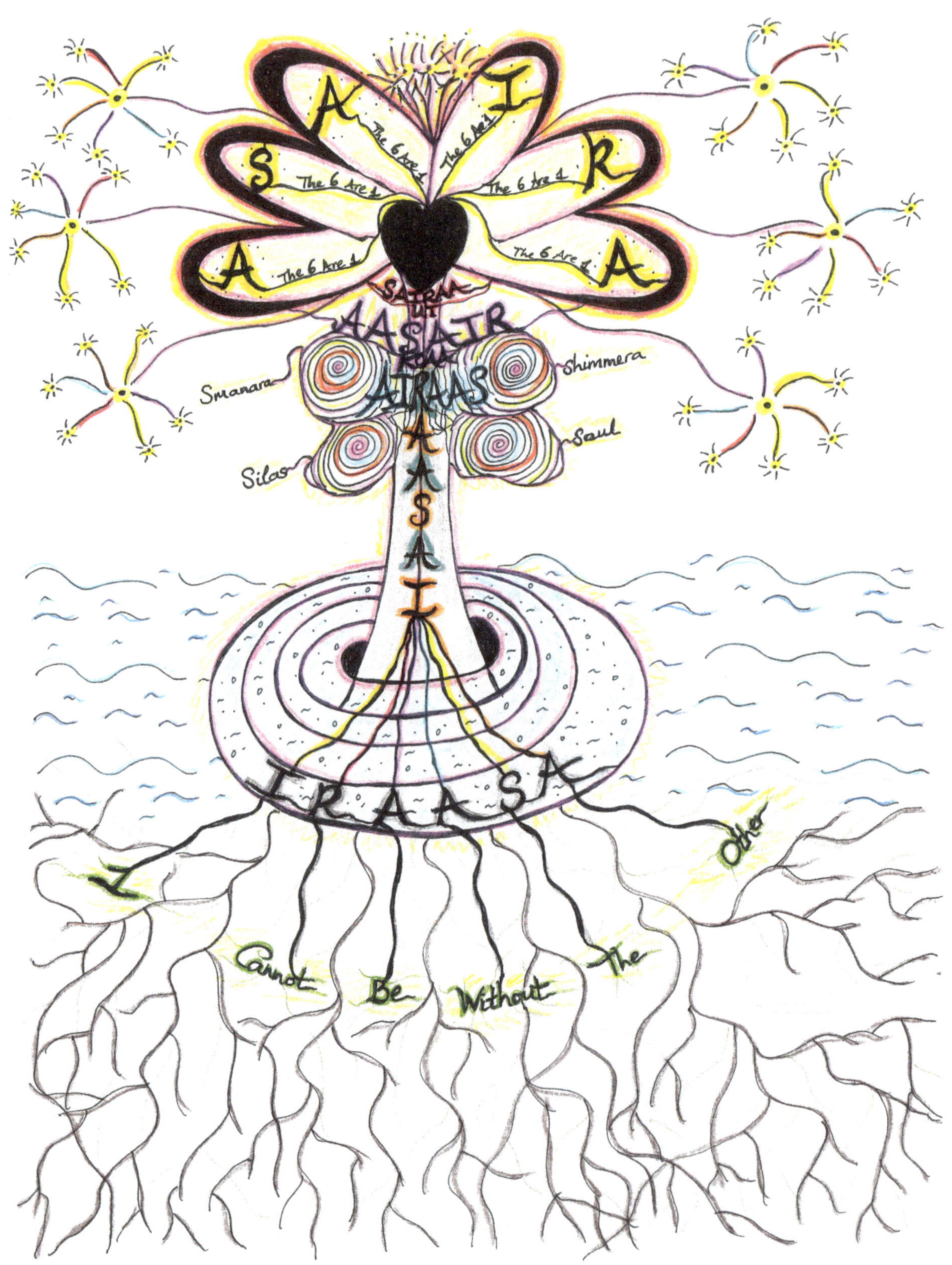
S
A
I
R
A
A
The 6 Are 1
The 6 Are 1
The 6 Are 1
The 6 Are 1
The 6 Are 1
AASATR
ATRAAS
Smanara
Shimmera
Silas
Saul
IRAASA
I
Other
Cannot
Be
Without
The

☆ EPILOGUE ✦

RAASAI speaks

Can YOU hear me?

You have realised! Yes, I've always been with you.

But, this is the beginning. The Promise must be completely fulfilled, and everything remembered and told.

Now, to rest.

IASAAR speaks

Yes, I can hear YOU.

I am YOU and YOU are me... I'm trying to understand, though, and I can't.

There's so much that is not clear. We have to go on... the 6th Knowing...!

RAASAI, can you tell me more? What about Aileen? And the Storyteller? Are they always to be AIRAAS and AASAIR? What's happened to them? And what about the Promise? Did I promise too? Who am I? I don't really know.

RAASAI speaks

Breathe, IASAAR, dear Reader. It is time to rest. Patience is needed now. But I can tell you a little more.

Aileen and the Storyteller, as you know them, have not returned yet.

AIRAAS has recalled many things; she knows she is Aileen and other Daughters of ASAIRA. She remembers AASAIR and the love for him. And she knows that she will return to the Meadow to fulfill the Promise. But she remains as AIRAAS, and her only wish is to fly and sing; she follows this instinct and in this way, gives space to what has been realised.

AASAIR has realised who he is and was, to a certain extent. He is now with his Sister, KOAA. They rest until it is time for the Call.

You must do the same, Sister-Brother. And I, also.

I leave you with the Star who has a message for YOU, IASAAR, Reader of Readers, Perceiver of All, also known as RAASAI, Guardian of the Tower & the One True Flower.

IASAAR speaks

RAASAI...

RAASAI...

Okay...

I feel so tired but happy, too.

No more words, then, for now.

I'll read the Star's message first before I go.

The Star of Heavens

Reader of the Untold Story

YOU came this far!

My Sparks flicker

In the Gloriousness of THIS Glittering Moment!

I have a message for you

Full of Shimmering Revelation:

AASAIR

AIRAAS

RAASAI

3 who are 6

Who are 2-Fold

Who are 12

Who are 1

Shall meet together

In the Green Meadow

To complete

To fulfill

The Promise of Old

The Sacred Covenant

Of the Light Bearer

Of the Storyteller

Of the Reader

So Rest and Replenish

Feel the Warmth

Of my Starry Force

And when it is time

We shall all meet

YOU

Are not only needed

YOU

Are indispensable

For the

♫ Saahruam Allssiram Issenam ♫

A
A S
A S
R A
R A
S A
Saahruam
Issenam
Allssiram
The Greenest
Meadow
YOU ARE

THE END & THE BEGINNING

THE 6TH KNOWING OF ASAIRA

THE PROMISE FULFILLED

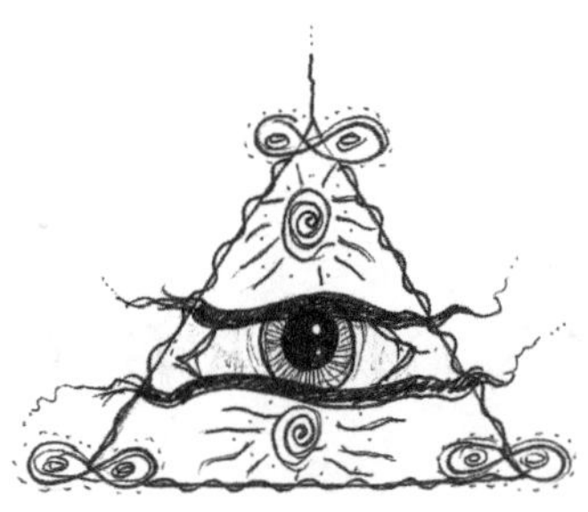

All-Seer

I have come once more

To set the wheels in motion

ASAIRA sows the seeds of the 6th Knowing

She awakens those that are needed

From their rest and dreams

Let us see what befalls

As the Words appear on the Page!

Ha! Ha! Ha!

The Tower of RAASAI: RAASAI's Rest

The bald eagle swooped down with its wings spread open and landed on the tip of the Douglas fir. How it loved to observe the lands and seas from above! Today was a cold, crisp morning, but the sun shone on all living creatures. The eagle's white head glowed as it sat there, barely moving. It was a fascinating experience to behold, for one turned eagle-like and still in the mirror of such resting.

The Garden of AASAIR: The Gardener

The Gardener worked slowly and efficiently. The love was apparent in his chestnut brown eyes in the way he touched the soil and planted the seeds. It was a beautiful day, a little chilly, but the sun's rays warmed the garden and its gardener in golden hues. A little further off, a thatched cottage looked welcoming. A small white dog dashed out of the front door, wagging its tail and barking. The Gardener looked up and smiled.

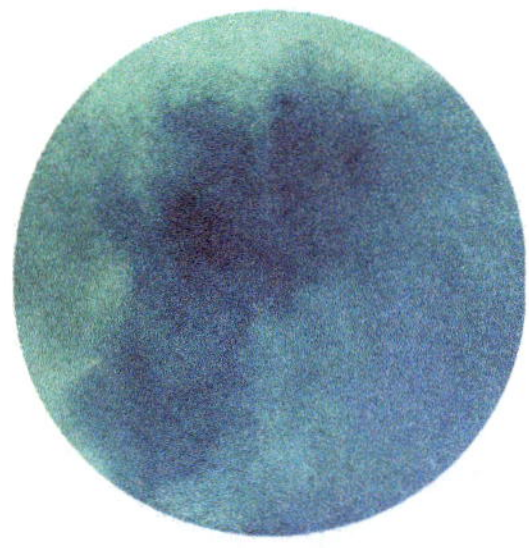

Earth: IASAAR the Reader

Every night IASAAR, the Reader, dreams of marvellous things. Sometimes the dreams are remembered, other times they aren't. One dream is recurrent.

IASAAR dreams he is an eagle, and it always feels like he's a he, a male eagle. He flies from treetop to treetop and observes the Earth from above. He can feel the strength of his wings and see his claw-like feet when he lands. It's a restful dream, too, because he sits for eternity at the top of a tree, just being, absorbing the air around his head… so vigilant, so still.

Wow, I just love these dreams, IASAAR thinks.

The Story Speaks

Reader, the 6th Knowing is here.

It is important that you pay attention to the eagle dreams.

✩* **PART 1** *✩

Earth

IASAAR dreams they are in human form standing on the edge of a precipice. IASAAR steps back. Shoulders hunched, they breathe heavily. Then, from the corner of their eye, IASAAR sees an enormous brown and white bird fly off the cliff side. The Eagle! IASAAR feels they should do the same, but the body is paralyzed.

The Tower of RAASAI

The eagle soars upwards, its keen eyes on the skies above. Its wings are wide open and flat, as though giving its soul to God, and its yellow-taloned feet point downwards like a ballerina.
Oh, what a sight!

The Garden of AASAIR

There it is again! That high-pitched squeak. The Gardener looks up. The eagle flies right over him and straight up to the heavens. Such beauty and strength! The Gardener stands transfixed. Then, he smiles and continues his tending and watering.
The cottage door opens. A large woman with sweet eyes comes out, "Would you like a cup of tea?" The Gardener nods, "Yes, please!"

The hot mug comforts the Gardener's chilled hands. Bruxa, for it is she, sits at her adored master's feet. ♥♥♥

The Song of AIRAAS: A Melody of Forever

Through the Heavens of ASAIRA, AIRAAS sang of eternity in a melody of forever.
The molecules and atoms in the air sparkled and vibrated with each musical note.

Right below AIRAAS, the two Orcas and two Dolphins leapt in and out of the silvery
waters of the Sea of Seas. They played in the waters of their birth but never left their
vigilance and service to AIRAAS, their beloved Light Bearer of the Green Meadow.

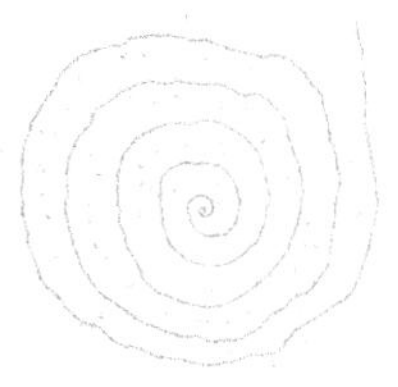

Into the Mother

Come

The Seeds of Love

The Tower of RAASAI: The Tower

The Tower, the Stem of Truth, was invisible, seemingly non-existent without the Guardian. Now its solid, airy stability noticed a tingling in its roots like when a seed begins to grow: the return of the Guardian was imminent.

The Garden of AASAIR: KOAA

Inside the cottage, KOAA sits at a golden harp. It glows in the fire-lit room. She places her hands on the strings and plucks. KOAA opens her mouth, and the ancient sounds of the Sea pour out in waves of beauty. Bruxa and the Gardener listen, both captivated by the moment.

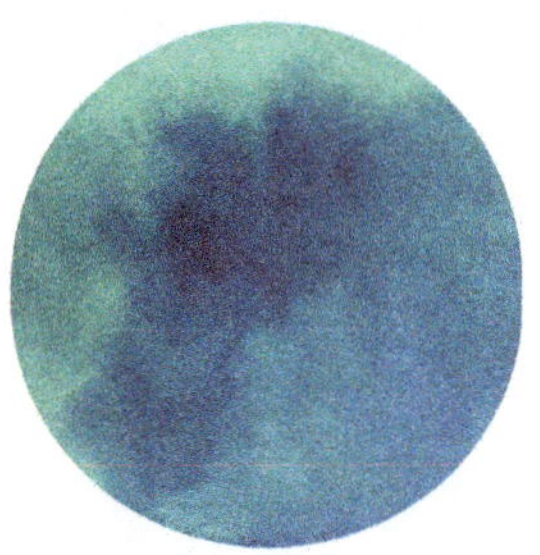

Earth: The Fiery-Haired Woman

IASAAR dreams she's a woman, giant-like, taller than any mountain. Her hair is fiery red and comes down to her waist. IASAAR tries to walk but can't. Suddenly, the butterfly Goddess, AIRAAS, appears! Amazingly, AIRAAS is quite small compared to IASAAR, who reaches out her hand, letting the butterfly woman land on it. They both look at each other in wonder.

The Tower of RAASAI: The Eagle

The unalterable eagle was perched at the top of the tallest tree, a tree that was on the highest mountain. The eagle looked over the lands and the sea. The air was alive, singing in ethereal beauty. The eagle shot an alert glance at the sky, and broke into flight.

The Story Speaks

The Seedlings are visible and the Call is nearing.

IASAAR dreams again.

And it must be so.

The Reader must wake up in the dream in order to
answer the Call of Ages.

The Flame of All Fires

I am

The Burning Fire

of

Tiger Bright

I am

The Compassionate Fire

of

The Lamb

I am

Ever-Alight

In your Heart

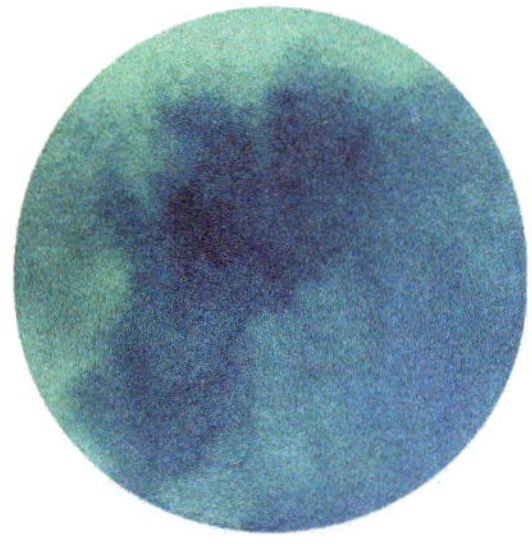

Earth: The Woman of All Ages

IASAAR felt like an observer, an energy that watched, but there was no form, no gender, just two eyes seeing everything.

The Eyes of IASAAR saw a room: it was lit in a warm light, and there were tables. On each table there was an exquisitely presented dish of food. Melodious harp sounds filled the space.

The Eyes noticed there were many human forms, but spirit-like, transparent, not totally visible; they were men and women, and they were feasting at the banquet. Everything was peaceful.

"I'm dreaming!" the Reader said in a loud voice. "Ohhh, so if it's a dream, I can do what I want! Okay… let's fly, then!"

The Reader felt themself lift into the air and touch the ceiling to then bounce off and spin around the room, because it's awesome to fly on a whim in a lucid dream!

The Reader landed. They noticed that certain forms were more solid now, including their own form. Oh, I'm IASAAR and I'm a she again! Her hands were small and delicate, familiar-looking.

IASAAR realised there was a tall figure standing next to her and turned to look. All notions of time and space were swallowed into a thick sense of 'Now, and only Now'. The figure at her side was a woman whose face was so luminous that it felt blinding, yet the kindness that shone through eliminated any fear. There was a sweetness and a fierceness at the same time in her gaze, and she looked incredibly wise and old but young… ageless!

IASAAR tried to speak, but every word was an effort, "I… am… dreaming… Are… you… dreaming?" The words crystallized into floating diamonds.

The Woman of All Ages smiled, making the particles in the air shudder.

"Who… are… you?" IASAAR's words turned into three shiny rubies.

"I am ASAIRA," said the Woman in a voice that sounded like a harp. The words took the form of pink petals that fell onto IASAAR.

IASAAR looked into the Woman's eyes and said, "I… love… you."

Six pink tulips arose from the nowhere. They hovered above IASAAR and ASAIRA and slowly disintegrated into star-shaped petals that rained upon them both.

I'm in Heaven…

There was a heavy groan: the ground beneath them crumbled away, and the room dissolved! ASAIRA grew into a gigantic tree. IASAAR felt tiny as she stood on this groundless Ground of Grounds, staring at the tree trunk that was much, much wider than her arm span. When she stepped back to try and look up, the word 'Sequoia' came to her. Wow…

Then a sound IASAAR recognised well: the Eagle! And there he was, his call was like a squeaky laugh! IASAAR remembered again she was dreaming… I can fly… She turned into an eagle and flew into the sky. The two eagles met and circled each other in majestic contentedness.

IASAAR asked in a voiceless voice, "Is it time to wake up?"

RAASAI, Eagle of Eagles, answered, "The Story Is, IASAAR. Can you hear her Call? She is alive. She IS! Do you wish to answer her Call?"

IASAAR's "YES!" came from her eagle heart while she flew upwards and upwards, RAASAI at her side, their wings wide open.

The Kingdom of AASAIR ⧉ The Tower of RAASAI ⧉ The Garden of AASAIR: Answering ASAIRA's Call

Shimmera and Saul stepped out of the Sea of Seas. They smiled at each other, enjoying the sense of having legs and treading on the earth again. Just behind them in the waters, the two Orcas swam to the surface. They gave out a cry of gratitude to the Sea and transformed into Smanara and Silas. With the firmness of the land under their feet, the 4 looked up to the sky and saw the Tower, the transparent Stem of Stems. They instantly took flight.

AIRAAS caught a glimpse of the glittering tower from afar. She decided to land. The more she approached the hazy solidity of the Tower of RAASAI, the more she remembered the joy of not moving, of letting the wings close and stop. As AIRAAS landed, the Tower felt like two great hands that received and cupped her in their palms. She lay down and closed her eyes, something which she had not done for countless moons.

The Gardener looked at the garden brimming with multicoloured tulips that bobbed in the morning breeze. He smiled at seeing the fruits of his labour. Lying down in the grass, the Gardener closed his eyes and listened to the murmur of the flowers. Bruxa came to lie down with him and gave his master's hand a lick.

"Screee… Screeee… creee… creee…"

The Gardener opened his eyes. Two eagles circled just above. He picked up Bruxa and stood up.

KOAA came out into the garden. "It's time." She smiled, then emitted the most haunting whale call. Unfaltering, she plunged into her brother's welcoming heart.

AASAIR, Gardener of Old, looked down at Bruxa's lamb-like face. "Are you ready, too, sweet one?" The dog, seeing the chocolate brown eyes that announced a new adventure, gave a bark of consent.

AASAIR's body became taller and darker-skinned while two enormous eagle wings materialised on his back. Placing Bruxa into his heart, AASAIR flapped his wings and flew into the air.

ASAIRA

I am

I call

I call

Will you answer, Child of the One light?

RAASAI speaks

Reader, it is time to speak.

YOU have woken and realised you were dreaming.

You know now that you are many things: you are the Reader who has a unique story of their own; you also enter the Story of Stories; you see and hear and read and exist, all at the same time; you are IASAAR and take on many different forms, gender and no gender; you hear RAASAI, and you know that we are One!

IASAAR, sweet Perceiver of the Story, honourable and courageous Reader who flew to the ♪♫ *Saahruam Allssiram Issenam* ♫♪! Can you hear me now?

(I can hear you, but I just can't say it...)

IASAAR, can you hear me? You must acknowledge me again now for the Story to continue. If you wish to meet in the Green Meadow to at last fulfill the Promise, acknowledge me, for I am you. ASAIRA calls, Sister-Brother!

(Okay, I can do this... Help me, ASAIRA, please... Help me answer RAASAI... I'm afraid to answer this call...)

Yes... RAASAI, I hear YOU! Yes, I want to know the whole story... I want the Promise to be fulfilled!

IASAAR, the joy rekindles as I hear your sacred confirmation!

RAASAI, can we meet? I need somewhere so we can just talk face to face... before the Story continues. Is that possible? It feels like we can take any form we want and be where we want??

Yes, let us do this. Close your eyes, enter the Heart and see the place where we shall meet. Are you ready?

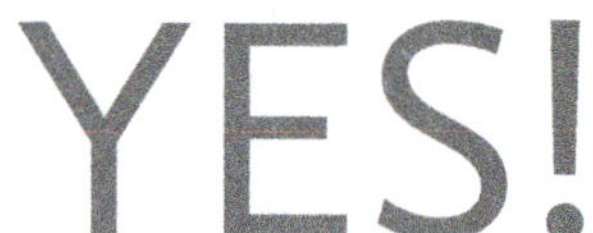

✰★ PART 4 ★★

RAASAIASAAR: The Key

IASAAR walks through a forest of invisible trees. It's dark and rainy and gloomy.

This isn't the place I imagined!

IASAAR's heart races.

A cold sweat of fog creeps into his body and senses.

RAASAI…

Where is this place? Why does it feel so empty?

IASAAR's legs shake; he can't swallow, he stops breathing, his knees give up and he falls to the ground.

The rain comes down harder, the cloaked trees threaten…

"What's going on? I don't understand. Am I dreaming again? RAASAI! Where are you?"

"IASAAR. I'm here. Don't lose yourself listening to the fear!"

"RAASAI, I'm already lost… I'm confused… I'm the Reader again… I'm not IASAAR…"

"IASAAR, it's YOU. At the moment you're in a male form. Look at yourself. Open your eyes again. You are at the place you saw in your heart, but you're blinded because of the fear. Breathe and open your eyes."

" I don't understand and I'm scared…" IASAAR shivers.

"IASAAR, breathe, open your eyes. I am always with you. Remember? You are all right. This is the Story of Stories that cannot be understood, only lived! This is an adventure! YOU are not this trembling creature, you are a Seer of Seers, the one who plays and experiences themself in many forms. And you are needed! Say yes again! For you are to remember more. You shall meet AASAIR and AIRAAS in the Green Meadow. They will need your memories and knowledge, and you will need them too. But without you, AIRAAS and AASAIR will not remember all. You have the Key in front of you. Will you take it?"

IASAAR opens his eyes and sees a golden key. He takes it. The Reader closes their eyes and says, "Yes."

A sweetness from the Garden of AASAIR floats in. Mmmm, what a fragrance! In the distance, a whale sings a song of longing. Ah, so beautiful…

The Reader feels the fluttering of wings around them. They recall how the Storyteller would come in and out of the story, and how muddled he'd get.

I think I understand you better now, Storyteller!

Okay, let's do this.

The Reader opens their eyes. "RAASAI… I take the Key and commit. Yes, RAASAI, I fully commit." IASAAR stands up. "Can we meet face to face as agreed?"

A pause.

"This is how I saw our meeting," IASAAR continues.

"It's a place where there's a huge rainbow and no darkness, lots of light! You're sitting on a pink cushion and are dressed in vibrant colours; you look like a Hindu Goddess!

Behind you there's an exquisitely adorned elephant, who's also sitting.

You smile as my hand appears in front of you; it's a small blue hand wearing a ruby ring.

I turn my hand over, and there's a golden key in my palm which I give to you.

'IASAAR,' you say laughing. 'You're here at last! Come and sit next to me.'

'Yes,' I say, sitting down on a velvet green cushion.

Oh, and I'm wearing a yellow skirt-like garment, and my little bare feet are blue, too!"

The Star of Heavens

Sparkles & Sparks

What Delight!

Yes, the Reader has given

The YES

And meets with RAASAI

IASAAR is

As AASAIR & AIRAAS

Are

Everything Revealed

On the YES of Truth

For 2 are meeting

For 3 to meet

To fully realise

The 6 Are 12 Are 1

Divine are the Sparks I speak

For all who wish

To Read & Hear

Sing & Tell

The Story of Stories

She IS

ASAIRA

She is the Teller

She is the Light that gives the Story life

She is the Reader and what is read

She is the Key of Keys

That unlocks the Mysteries

That can never be unlocked

I sparkle in eternity

Feel your Heart glitter

In playful confirmation

PART 5

IASAARAASAI: Awake in the Dream

The little boy with blue skin was enchanting, his brown eyes intently focused on the woman's face. She was breathtaking: her brown skin glowed, and her braided black hair was silky and shiny. From head to toe she was covered in gold and jewels.

The little boy said, "Is this a dream, sweet mother?"

"Only if you don't realise it, IASAAR," replied the woman kindly.

"You are RAASAI! I didn't expect to see you… I mean, see each other like this really! Are we supposed to be gods of India?"

"IASAAR, Perceiver of All, we have been One since the beginning and end of all times and no-time. In many guises we have travelled the Realms of ASAIRA to observe. And it is true that there have been times when we have come to the hearts of Earth Beings as their gods."

"RAASAI, I'm the Reader of this story… everything you say seems too much… I'm not a god!"

"IASAAR, you still resist, sweet Daughter-Son of the Moon and Sun, the Stars and the Earth, of ASAIRA! Yes, you are the Reader! Yes, now you appear as Krishna,[19] God-Child of Love! But YOU are awake! You dreamt you didn't know me, that you didn't love me. But you awoke, and you agreed to be here to fulfill the Promise, did you not?"

"Yes, I did. Okay… okay! I give up! No more questioning."

"IASAAR, my love. I'm your mother in this moment. Come to my arms." And the little boy melted in the timeless embrace of love.

The majestic creature behind them, captivated by the sight of Mother and Child, trumpeted and flapped its elephant ears.

IASAAR caressed the woman's cheek and asked, "So what do we do now?"

RAASAI laughed in cascading chuckles until she could no more. IASAAR laughed, too, and the two gods ended up crying from sheer delight.

---

19 The Story Speaks

Krishna is a deity of Hinduism, a religion of the Earth Realm.

The Tower of RAASAI: AIRAAS

AIRAAS slept, embraced in the petals of ASAIRA.

Images of Old, of New, of Timelessness, swirled into her dreams. The images flickered and glittered, blazed and danced, warming the hearts of all realms, for they spoke of love, of truth, of sweet seeing and awakening.

A harp played in the background of AIRAAS's dreams. The music was accompanied by a man's voice; it was the Bard.

> ♫ *Once we dreamt that we did not know each other. So we woke up to see if it was true that we loved each other.[20]* ♫

The words repeated themselves over and over. Sometimes a woman's voice sang, too, but in the Spanish language from the Earth Realm:

> ♫ *Una vez soñamos los dos que no nos conocíamos. Y nos despertamos a ver si era verdad que nos amábamos.* ♫

Down one of AIRAAS's cheeks, a single tear rolled onto Bruxa's little face. The dog snuggled up to AIRAAS. Bruxa looked tiny next to the Goddess, but the dog's loving presence was vast, emanating ripples upon ripples of unconditional joy.

---

20 The Story Speaks

These words are similar to some lines from the Bengali poems of Rabindranath Tagore, a Son of ASAIRA from India in the Earth Realm:"Once we dreamt that we were strangers. We wake up to find that we were dear to each other." Rabindra Rachanabali (Stray Birds), Verse 9, 1916.

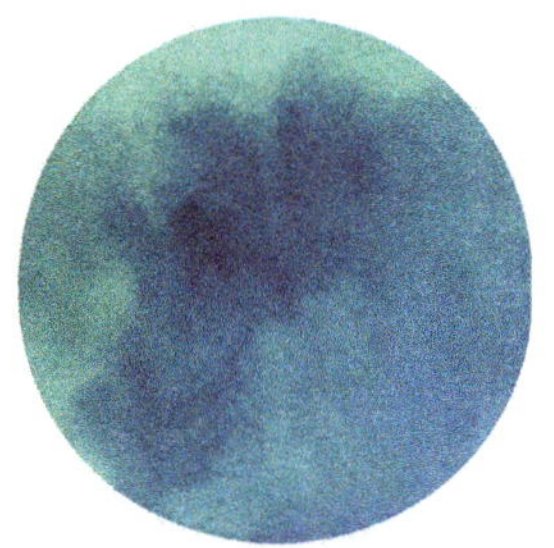

Earth: The Storyteller Returns

AASAIR had flown to the skies and reached the Stem of Stems. There, he had left the Lamb next to the Butterfly, gazed at these two loves and flown away in purposeful certainty. It was time to return to the Earth Realm, for this was the only way for AASAIR to enter the Green Meadow again.

Placing his attention on being a male human Being, AASAIR found himself walking in a modern-day city full of noise, cars, people and a bubbling insanity in the air. Amidst it all, AASAIR's senses kept vigilant.

He stopped for a moment and looked at himself in a shop window. Ah… yes, his name was Keon… and he told stories. He was also much more, determined not to forget who he was in essence. "I am awake in this Dream of Dreams," Keon the Storyteller whispered.

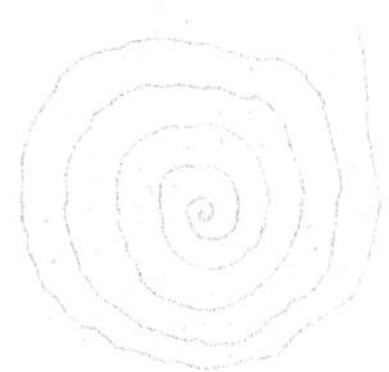

I am the Father of this Universe

And even the Source of the Father.

I am the Mother of this Universe

And the Creator of All.

I am the Way

And the Master who watches in Silence;

Thy Friend and thy Shelter

And thy Abode of Peace.

I am the Beginning

And the Middle

And the End of All Things:

Their seed of Eternity

Their Treasure Supreme[21]

---

21 The Story Speaks

ASAIRA echoes more words from India, Earth Realm. They come from the ancient text Bhagavad Gita, (The Song of the Lord). The original in Sanskrit is usually ascribed to the Sage Vyasa and was written in the 5th century. The translation in English is by Juan Mascuro. (1962)

PART 6

The Tower of RAASAI: The Dreamer

The Dreamer observed. There was a sense of distance, of a breath, of a heart beat. The Dreamer dreamt in a silent abyss of restfulness, watching the Universe.

Oh… that melody… the harp.

That ancient voice… it sings of love.

Elyn smiles while she listens to Eoin sing the Legend of the 4. The words resonate in timelessness.

"The little lamb," says AIRAAS out aloud, eyes closed.

Bruxa licks AIRAAS's fingers.

"Tiger Bright, your coat is so silky."

"Aileen…"

♫ *Eoin the Bard's Song* ♫

"The Legend of the Four Guardians of ASAIRA"

In an Ancient Time
A Time of No-Time,
In an Ancient Realm
A Realm of No-Realm,
There were four Sun Gods
Born from the Silver Seas
Guardians of ASAIRA
Were they,
Magical and Powerful
Protectors and Gatekeepers
Of the
One True Flower were they.

One Ancient Day of No-Day
The 4 forgot ASAIRA,
Forgot each other
Separate in a tall tower
Four Towers of Incompleteness,
Look did they at the Silvery
Sea,
But forgotten were
Their days of underwater
worlds.

The Darkness arrived
The Despairing Dragon
appeared
Only leaving
A Promise of Promises.

Then she came
The Innocent Lamb
Sweetness and Openness
With One Tear of Love
Tame did she
The Dragon of Dragons
Unite did she
The Sun and the Earth
In her Tiger Heart.

And so I sing
The Legend of the 4:
The Golden Shining Shimmer
The Golden Prayed-For Son
The Silver Lady Protected by the
Divine
and
The Silver Lord of the Forests.

Remember their destiny did they
And One became
With the Lamb and the Tiger
For the Flower of ASAIRA
To bloom again in Sparkling Truth.

And thus…

Here ends
This Legend of Old
For
All Good Hearts to Hear

The Tower of RAASAI: The Six

Holding up the One True Flower of Flowers, the aerial tower-stem vibrated in ♪ Do and UT ♪

On top of the Flower, on separate petals, the four Sun Gods stood barefoot around a sleeping AIRAAS.

The petals were a soft pink and consisted of countless layers of other petals: a scented pinkness that travelled in damask spirals through the Realms.

It was truly a sight to see and experience: AIRAAS sleeping inside the Flower, Bruxa and Tiger Bright lying at her side, surrounded by the four Golden-Silver Guardians.

The 4 nodded at each other: it was time.

Shimmera transformed into Wolf Moon and Saul into a Dolphin. Simultaneously, they leapt into AIRAAS's heart.

Smanara reached out to Silas, and both turned into the Snake of ASAARI that was one and two. It slid into AIRAAS's heart.

Into snowflakes and flames dissolved Bruxa and Tiger Bright, covering AIRAAS in a snowy shimmer of glowing embers.

The 6 who were One were ready for AIRAAS to awaken.

---

22 The Story Speaks

These are the poet Rumi's words. He lived in Persia in the 13th century, Earth Realm. The Storyteller of Old spoke of him in the 1st Knowing. ASAIRA uses the English translation by Azima Melita Kolin and Maryam Mafi. It can be found in Whispers of the Beloved, 1999.

RAASAIASAAR: Patience

The Reader fidgets.

Their heart beats a little faster…

The Storyteller, AASAIR, has returned to Earth, or so it seems. Now he's called Keon. Hmm… is Keon the same Storyteller of Old or a different person than I met on those shores?

And AIRAAS is dreaming… is she going to remember she's Aileen?!

"RAASAI…"

"Yes, IASAAR?"

"We have to go to the Green Meadow. It's time!"

"Patience, IASAAR, patience."

IASAAR sighs and breathes in RAASAI's words.

Whale songs and the waves of the Silver Sea lull IASAAR into acceptance.

Patience…

The Star of Heavens

He, who tells the Story of Stories

That carries the Whale Mother within

That cares for the lands of ASAIRA

That creates flesh from the Word[23]

Has returned to the Earth Realm

He that is a She

Has roamed the Realms many times

Has told the Story in many ways

Even from the darkest of blindnesses.

Now, in complete awareness, it is time

Time for the Sweetest of Meetings

The 3

Must return to the Meadow

To remember their sacred pledge.

Only once before were they there

When the Promise was made.

Now the 3 return

To complete the cycle

---

23 The Story Speaks

The Star of Heavens uses words that echo
Saint John the Apostle: "And the Word
was made flesh and dwelt among us."
John, 1:14, King James Bible, 2000.

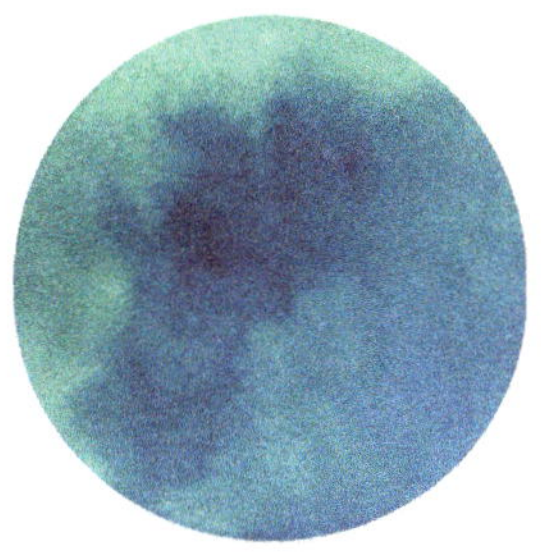

PART 7

Earth: In the beginning...

Keon walked and walked through the streets of the city. He felt he could not stop until he saw the mountains more clearly. The incessant noise of the traffic was alien and strange; he'd have to get used to it again!

The buildings opened up to a view of green parkland and blue sea. Across the waters, a coast of snow-capped mountains greeted him in the sunlight.

Oh! It's magnificent! Keon sat down on one of the benches that lined the promenade, took out his notebook and pen from his satchel and wrote.

'In the beginning was the Word, and the Word was with God, and the Word was God...'[24]

Keon stared at the words, then leaned back and looked up to the sky. Two eagles were circling just above him.

Keon felt a sigh arise from another time, another place. His forehead creased in an eruption of images which spoke of suffering and pain, of unconsciousness, of living the dream in blindness.

Now everything was different. Keon, the Storyteller, knew he was much more. This knowledge caressed his soul and brought solace to his entire body.

Keon read the words on the page again. Yes... and I know who you are, too, Yohanan.[25]

A tear rolled down the Storyteller's cheek. His AASAIR essence rippled in recognition.

This time, however, I am awake in this Dream of Dreams.

---

24 The Story Speaks

Keon also writes the words of the Earth Son of ASAIRA, Saint John the Apostle. These words begin The Gospel of Saint John. (John, 1:1, King James Bible, 2000.)

---

25 The Story Speaks

Yohanan is John in Aramaic, the language spoken in Judea (now part of Israel) in the 1st century, Earth Realm.

IASAARAASAI: One Cannot Be Without the Other

"IASAAR! Come. I'm here to meet you again."

IASAAR gets up from the shores of the Sea and follows RAASAI's voice.

I wonder what form RAASAI will have this time…

IASAAR notices she, herself, is wearing a green gown and that her hair is long and wavy. Wow, fun!

The Sea vanishes. IASAAR is in a corridor of a house; the house looks old. IASAAR stops. "RAASAI?"

A tall red-haired woman materializes opposite IASAAR. She is wearing the same gown as IASAAR.

"You're RAASAI?"

The woman smiles. "I am. Follow me."

They enter a cavernous hall. RAASAI comes to a halt in front of a mirror. "Look."

"We're twins this time, RAASAI!"

"We are one; we are a mirror of one another. We can be any form but only with one intention: to bring about the seeing of the Green Meadow."

"I don't really understand, but I realise now that it doesn't matter."

"True." RAASAI takes IASAAR's hands. "Now we shall take one form in its masculine aspect and one in its feminine aspect, and make our way to the Meadow."

"Right now?"

"IASAAR, I'm always here, and I have shown you that we are the same. We are IASAARAASAI-RAASAIASAAR, and we are much more. But again, as you have said, don't try to comprehend. It is too much. Trust me. Trust yourself! Now we must go. Are you ready?"

"Yes… yes, I am!"

"Choose a human form in which you wish to walk the Earth Realm in order to reach the Meadow. Let it be different to your Reader form. You shall walk the Earth, and I will reside in your Heart to help you."

IASAAR closes her eyes and breathes in deeply. Her new form shows itself. "That can't be right!"

"Whatever has shown itself, trust it is right for you, for us."

"Okay… it's not quite what I expected, but I have the feeling that the unexpected is something I'll have to get used to…"

♡ Divine Sparks of Insight & Revelation ♡

🜨 ASAIRA is One

🜨 5 Aspects that are 6

🜨 1 Aspect that is 2

🜨 The Elements also

🜨 6 that are 12

🜨 That are 18 & 24

🜨 That are limitless

🜨 We are All

🜨 THIS

Only together can

The Green Meadow be known

And yet

Only One

Needs to open the Heart's eyes

To receive

The Divine Revelation

of

A Lost Meadow Found

The Green Meadow

The Poppies are here again!

The Primroses, too!

Aileen, I know you are here

I see you with your Guardians

When you see me

🎵 Saahruam Allssiram Issenam 🎵

Reveals itself

In this Ocean of Greenness

As the Truth of the Meadow

So lost, so forgotten

Is found and ASAIRA known

Aileen… Aileen…

Can you hear my call?

It's the sweet ancient

Call of the Promise

I am always waiting

For you to come and remember again

My little Aileen…

The Ancient Call

I am

Always Found

I am

In the Grassy Green

Waves of Life

I am

The Tower of RAASAI ⟞⟝ Earth ⟞⟝ The Depths of IRAASA: Answering the Green Meadow's Call

AIRAAS saw six faces. Like waves, the faces came in and out, calling out to her. They were all female: three were adults, one was a child, and the other two were older. Of the three adults, one was not a human Earth woman as the others; she was startling and fierce.

Manifested by curiosity, six threads spiralled out a name which connected to a face. The six names sang to AIRAAS, and she felt the names to be a family.

Six other names and faces arose in the background: they were male and in turn were connected to each female.

The twelve faces beckoned to AIRAAS.

Her eyelids flickered.

Keon had had a dream.

In the dream, KOAA had swum to the shore and stepped out in human form: she was pregnant! Keon had hugged her joyfully at seeing the new life that was to come, and they laughed together in excited happiness. But Keon had a mission, and it returned through the laughter, bringing a gravity to the moment.

Keon spoke to KOAA in the ancient whale tongue that evoked the sound of the waves, "Sister, what can you tell me of the Meadow?"

"AASAIR, you must go to Primrose Meadow." And KOAA, turning into a silver mermaid, dove back into the Waters of the Saahruam.

IASAAR had become a woman who was older than any previous experience the Reader had had. They noticed a feeling of ease and reassurance that they'd never known before. Remembering the mission, the Reader inwardly connected with RAASAI and let themself totally sink into the woman she now was.

AIRAAS gasped. She opened her eyes. "I am all these women. I am also AIRAAS, and I am much more! Yes, I choose to answer this Ancient Call. It is time. Bring me home, Mother!"

No sooner had she said the last four words than she felt herself swallowed into the Tower, into the Sacred Stem and down into a blinding darkness she knew so well: IRAASA! Of course, into the Depths yet again! But this time, a sense of direction, of many eyes, hearts, legs and antennae, of strong jaws and feelers and fangs, stormed through her body. AIRAAS had metamorphosed into a formidable creature, one that was three: the Spider Weaver of the Void, the Ant Defender of the Nest and the Earthworm Nightcrawler, all in One!

The newly born Creature of the Depths burrowed through the soil in ferocious delight.

Keon walked under the rain. He looked down onto the path, enjoying the mud and puddles. Oh! Keon stopped: the path was full of earthworms. "Crawlers of the Night! I shall not step on you, my children and brothers and sisters."

A crow cawed in confirmation. Keon looked to the sky. Yes, ASAIRA sends her Guardians and Protectors, for we must arrive safely to the Meadow… there could still be shadows who would want to hinder our arrival.

The Lord of Laws, the blackest of crows, knew too well that the Storyteller spoke truth.

IASAAR was on a bus, reading. When she read the phrase, 'There could still be shadows who would want to hinder our arrival' she shivered. "RAASAI, I feel sick."

"Breathe. Don't listen to the fear. You are safe, but you must be vigilant and be completely connected with me and what we are doing."

IASAAR breathed in the words and looked out of the window into the darkness.

The Star of Heavens

There are shadows that would want to hinder

The Meeting of The 3

Be vigilant

To those who will obstruct

For they exist

They feed on fear and doubt

Yes, breathe

Remember

Who YOU are

Remember

You are protected

Remember

Your Mission

The Sea of Seas

She comes

As was announced

Again to enter

Our Purifying Liquid

All that enter

Cleansèd are they

No shadow or force can resist

And Pure become

For We are the Waters of Life

ASAIRA's Gift

The **Saahruam** *Silverness*

Of the Sea of Seas

Blessed are Those

Who bathe in Us

In the Silver Solidity

Of the Ocean of Love

☆ PART 9 ✯

The Story Speaks

Part 9 arrives in flower-like form.

Of the Voices and Stories contained,
one is important information that
I, the Story, must give to YOU, the Reader.
Read attentively.

Another of the Voices is from the Earth Realm:
the Poet of the Pillar, Rumi.
There are two poems by Rumi.

The first poem interweaves Flower 1 and was seen in
the 1st Knowing: "I, you, he, she, we, In the garden
of mystic lovers, These are not true distinctions."

The second poem is spoken by ASAIRA in Flower 2 and
begins, "Out beyond ideas..."

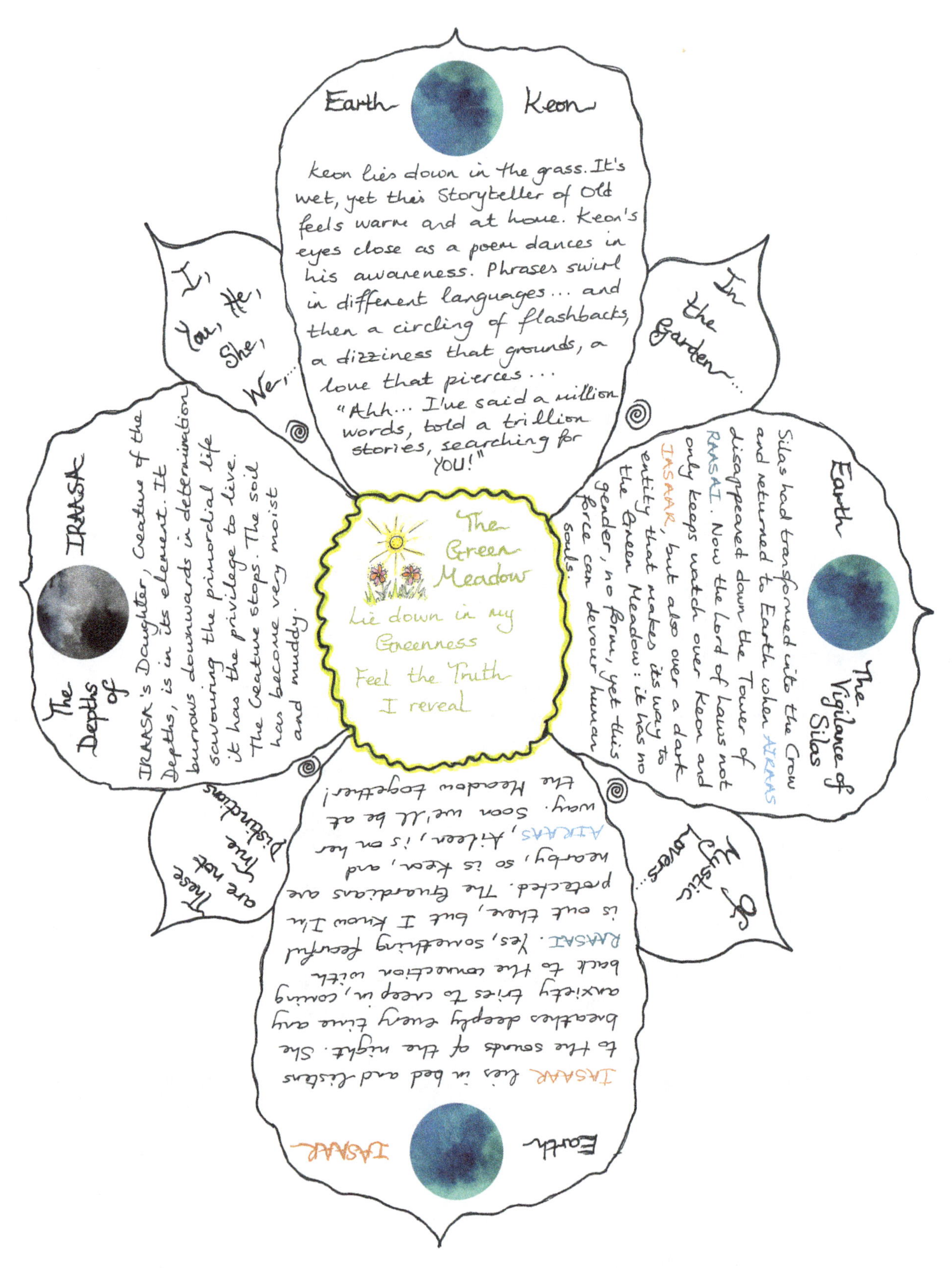

Earth   Keon
Keon lies down in the grass. It's wet, yet this Storyteller of Old feels warm and at home. Keon's eyes close as a poem dances in his awareness. Phrases swirl in different languages... and then a circling of flashbacks, a dizziness that grounds, a love that pierces...
"Ahh... I've said a million words, told a trillion stories, searching for YOU!"
I, You, He, She, We...
In the Garden...
IRAASA   The Depths of
IRAASA's Daughter, Creature of the Depths, is in its element. It burrows downwards in determination scouring the primordial life it has the privilege to live. The Creature stops. The soil has become very moist and muddy.
The Green Meadow
Lie down in my Greenness
Feel the Truth I reveal
Earth   The Vigilance of Silas
Silas had transformed into the Crow and returned to Earth when ATERAS disappeared down the Tower of RAASAI. Now the Lord of Laws not only keeps watch over Keon and IRASAAR, but also over a dark entity that makes its way to the Green Meadow: it has no gender, no form, yet this force can devour human souls.
These are not true Distinctions
Of Chaotic Lovers...
Earth   IRASAAR
IRASAAR lies in bed and listens to the sounds of the night. She breathes deeply every time any anxiety tries to creep in, coming back to the connection with RAASAI. Yes, something fearful is out there, but I know I'm protected. The Guardians are nearby, so is Keon, and ATERAS, Arleen, is on her way. Soon we'll be at the Meadow together!

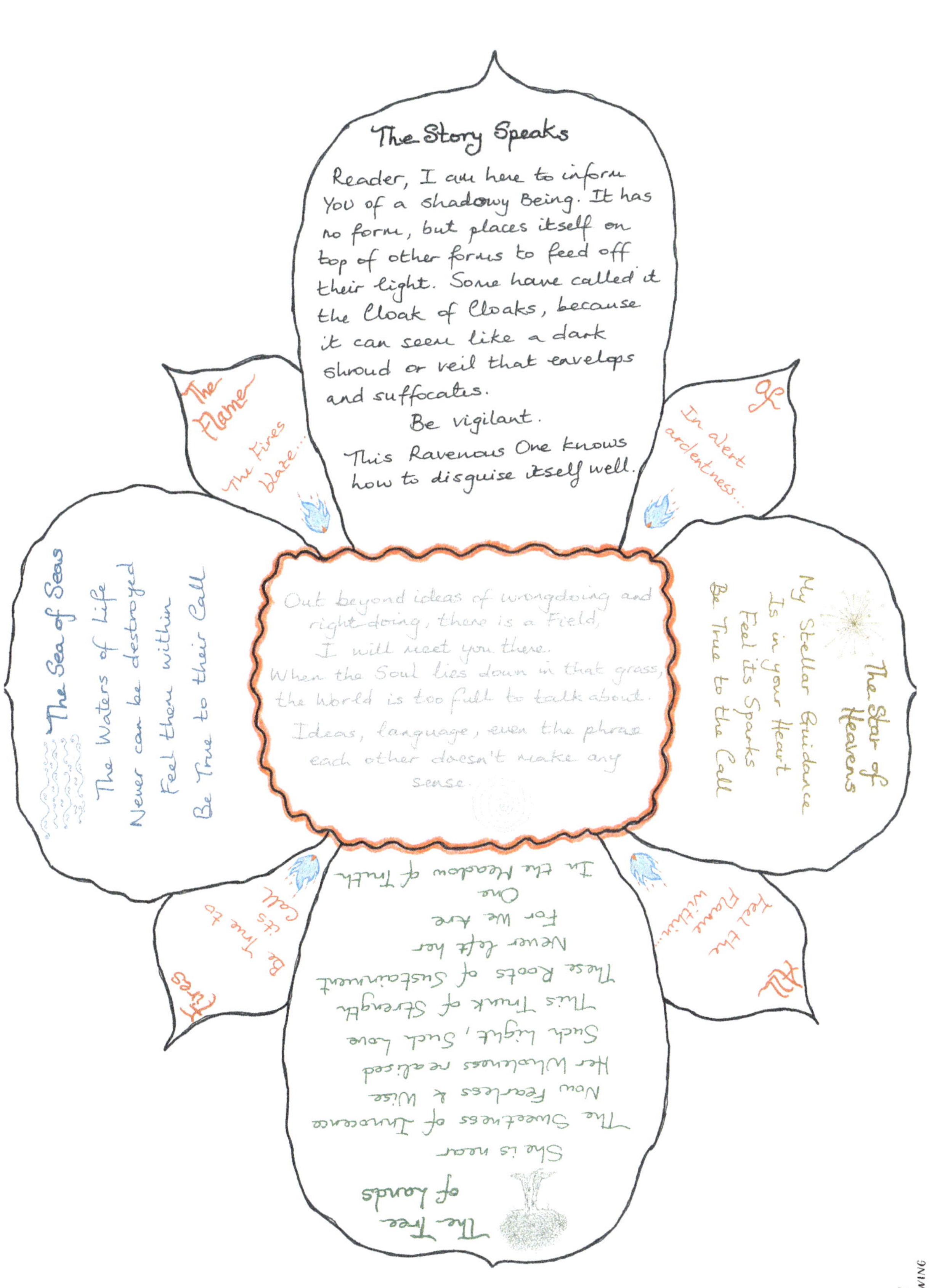
The Story Speaks

Reader, I am here to inform you of a shadowy Being. It has no form, but places itself on top of other forms to feed off their light. Some have called it the Cloak of Cloaks, because it can seem like a dark shroud or veil that envelops and suffocates.
Be vigilant.
This Ravenous One knows how to disguise itself well.

The Flame
The Fires blaze...

Of
In alert ardentness...

The Sea of Seas
The Waters of Life
Never can be destroyed
Feel them within
Be True to their Call

The Star of Heavens
My Stellar Guidance
Is in your Heart
Feel its Sparks
Be True to the Call

Out beyond ideas of wrongdoing and right-doing, there is a Field,
I will meet you there.
When the Soul lies down in that grass, the world is too full to talk about.
Ideas, language, even the phrase each other doesn't make any sense.

Fires
Be True to its Call

Feel the Flame within...

The Tree of Roots
She is near
The Sweetness of Innocence
New Fearless & Wise
Her Wholeness realised
Such Light, Such Love
This Trunk of Strength
These Roots of Sustainment
Never left her
For We Are
One
In the Meadow of Truth

The Kingdom of AASAIR ≈ Earth: Answering the Call Within

The moistness of the soil gradually became murky water. The unnameable Creature of the Depths stopped again; its body shook, its legs twitched. A scorching and a buzz, a feeling of sliding into new life, and the Creature turned into a glistening dolphin-orca. It plunged into the dark waters, swimming further and further down until a light trickled through the murkiness.

Downwards changed into upwards as the sun rays poured into the water. The magical cetacean rocketed towards the surface light, spinning into another new transformation. Unstoppable, it leapt out of the silver waters, not as one but as four luminous Beings: two dolphins, an orca, and a winged-mermaid!

Diving in and out of the waves, the 4 laughed and played. The Sea of Seas, overjoyed to have them back, sprayed the air with watery enchantment.

Keon saw an image of the Silver Sea. AIRAAS is here! Keon looked up at the night sky; the stars glittered. Words of devotion and prayer flooded out of Keon, each word a wisp of lavender that travelled through the realms and dimensions to all those eager to hear the word of the Heart:

"Oh, ASAIRA, Queen of Queens
Compassionate
Mother of Mothers
Everlasting
Source of Sources
Your Eternal Beauty is
Beyond Poetry and Tales
Your Infinite Love is
Beyond Words and Song
Oh, Mother
Fill me with renewed Strength
Fill me with sober Wisdom
Show me the way
To serve YOU
To return
Once and for all
To
YOU"

IASAAR stopped to look out towards the sea. How calm it was. She remembered the great Sea of Seas and how she'd swum as a merman side by side with AASAIR. She smiled with warm recollection. Closing her eyes, IASAAR heard RAASAI.

"IASAAR, you have seen what the Story has written of the Ravenous One. It is time."

"Time?" IASAAR shuddered, her heart beating faster.

"Stay calm and breathe and never lose connection with my voice. Be careful with other voices that speak from inside, don't believe what they might say. Only listen to the Real Voice."

"RAASAI, if we are one, why don't I know what you know!?"

"IASAAR, we are one, but you are also a human Being now and have a limited capacity to know all things. That is why we are One, and we are a Trillion. Trust yourself and trust your voice, and everything will be shown. Sit down and rest a moment under this Tree."

The Lord of Laws cawed when he landed on the Tree. He saw the Reader had fallen asleep. RAASAI's invisible wings covered and protected them. The Crow remained vigilant… he knew the Greyness was near, and it would be fully aware who the weakest of the 3 was. Silas suddenly turned from crow to snake and slithered up the branches of the Tree.

The Voice Within called to the 6. And although the shadowy Being was certainly not one of the 6, nor had it heard the voice within or was it able to do so, the Ravenous Shroud knew without a doubt that it was indeed time.

Hear the Call

It is spoken softly

Sweetly yet Strongly

Hear the Call

The Meadow is Nigh

Children of the One Light!

The Story Speaks

I see the Grey Shroud while it stares at the 2.
It is very clear that it has chosen one.

Reader! Are you awake in all of this? You sleep!
I see the Winged RAASAI protecting you, the Serpent too.
But is it enough?

Reader, wake up! It is time!

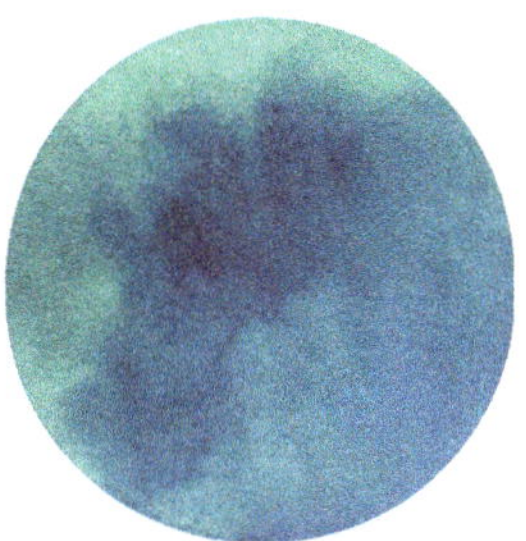

Earth: IASAAR

"Who are you? What are you doing in this house?" IASAAR's whole body shivers. They're in the house of their childhood, it's nighttime, there's something dark, it lurks in the shadows...

The Reader forgets all worlds of IASAAR, shaking uncontrollably. Even so, with an unknown fierceness, they shout out, "WHO ARE YOU? WHAT ARE YOU DOING IN THIS HOUSE?"

The words are enough to wake IASAAR from the dream, only to hear three other words, "It is time!"

IASAAR sits up against the tree. What's that coming towards me... Oh my God!

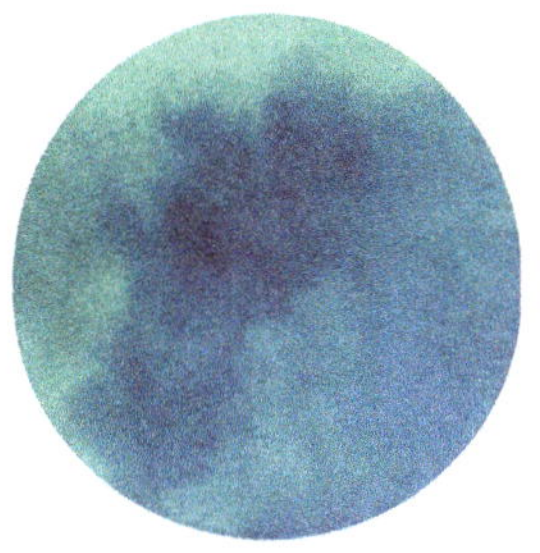

Earth: The Ravenous Shroud

The Dark Cloak moves rapidly towards the woman under the tree. There's a determination that will not be stopped. Although a sickening peace fills the air, it isn't enough to prevent the Shroud from pouncing onto the woman. Yes! I have you!

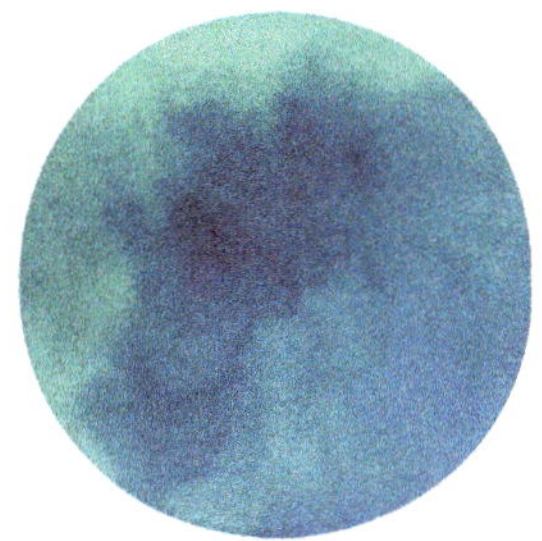

Earth: Keon

Keon stands in the middle of the Meadow. Night has fallen.

He feels into the grass with his feet and notices his attention move down into the soil, down into the Depths of IRAASA. He breathes deeply.

On each slow breath, Primrose Meadow billows into a soft golden haze, illuminating the grass and the sky. It's a luminosity, a goldness only visible to those who are quiet and still, yet can be felt by all.

Keon knows he's to stay where he is, motionless and connected, an unmovable rock of golden light.

Keon opens up to the sounds that want to come through his lips, ♪ "Uttt... Reee... Miiii... Faaa... Laaa... Dooo... Ommm... Ommm... Ommm... Ommm... Ommm..." ♪♪

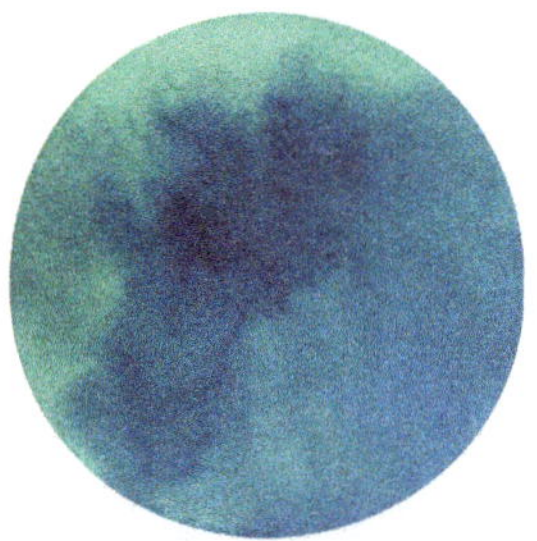

Earth: Silas & Smanara

Smanara and Silas take each other's hands. Without delay, they merge into one, into the Mysterious Coil, the Snake of ASAARI. The Snake propels itself towards IASAAR just as the Greyness pounces.

Too late… So be it then, the Struggle of Ages has commenced.

RAASAI speaks

It is time, IASAAR. The Ravenous One is here and covers your human form. However, it cannot hear me. But YOU can hear me! It is time to face this Starving One.

It was written, but I could not tell you, it had to be this way. I am sorry. Remember I AM ALWAYS HERE AND I AM YOU. We are the Light as all are. No matter how dark and frightening this may feel, Sweet IASAAR, we can face the Shroud. Trust your Real Voice, and keep calm.

The Kingdom of AASAIR: Aileen

The winged mermaid stops swimming. "It's time!"

The Dolphins of the Waves, Saul and Shimmera, jump into Aileen's heart as she swims downwards into the Sea to return to Earth, to her Beloved Tree and to her home, Primrose Meadow.

Hear the Soft Drones of

The Mother's Heart

Hear the Luminous Melody of

The Father's Soul

Hear the Real Voice

Within & Without

I Am

The Tree of Lands

I am

The Rock of Trees

My Branches reach up

Into the Waters of Life

To welcome

The Butterfly, my Sweet Child of the One Light

My Roots delve down

Into the Lost Garden

Found as the Gardener returns

His Song invokes

The Golden Light

And soothes the Hearts

My Trunk holds

The Vigilant Protectors, 2 but 1

The Living Spiral, the Magical Serpent

Who keeps watch

The Perceiver of All, Reader of Stories

Who lies at my feet

Covered in fog

But Within & Without

The Eagle of the Stem, Guardian of the Tower

Gently whispers

Dissipating the greyness

I am the Rock Tree

Upholding the Will of

ASAIRA

Is

The Star of Heavens

The Dark Cloak tries to extinguish the Light of Lights

But it cannot!

You are not alone

You are protected by RAASAI

Your Brother, Your Sister

IASAARAASAI

RAASAIASAAR

Close to your heart

Sweet Aileen is nigh

The Gardener sings

His Song of Light & Peace

The Beloved Tree sustains all

Its Roots embrace you

In these moments

The Guardians watch over you

Free of the Shroud you shall be

Have faith

Listen to the Real Voice

I
Shroud

I'm hungry! I'm tired! Why am I doing this? How can I be in a story? How can I be the reader? I'm imagining things. I don't know... I can't trust anyone...

RAASAI speaks

IASAAR. When the Cloaked One speaks, it will sound like your own voice. It tries to take you over.
Stay calm.
Breathe.
Do not accept anything this Shrouded One says.

Aileen

The mermaid looked into the watery well of the Mother. Through the ripples, she saw a branch. With one hand, the mermaid reached out, and with the other, she touched her heart. When Aileen opened her eyes, she was face to face with her Beloved Tree.

Keon

Keon was no longer Keon, no longer UT, no longer even the god RAASAI. He had become a lighthouse of vibration. Then six enormous doors opened in the sky and spun around him like a celestial whirlpool. They showed images of many lands and lands.

The Struggle of Ages

The Reader felt the heavy gloominess, heard its grey sombre voice. But a mightier voice was there, too. RAASAI's! Stay calm, yes... The Reader struggled to focus. The incessant grumble was sucking them in.

The Tree of Lands

Ahh... She has returned! Aileen... Yes... What strength! Truly the Tree Woman She has become!

TRAASA

Daughter and Mother
The Roots of the Ancient One
Nourished You
As Our Womb did
Welcome are You
To the Meadow of Meadows
Once more
SAARIA
Tree Woman of the Ancient
World

Smanara   Silas

The Snake of ASAARI slid down the tree trunk onto the shoulders of the woman who had materialised behind the Tree. The woman stroked the Snake's silvery scales in gratitude.

✰★ PART 11 ★✯

ASAIRA	*Is*
ARIASA	*I Am*
SAIRAA	*The Sacred Names of ASAIRA*
AARIAS	*One*
AIRAAS	*Is*
SAARIA	*Twelve*
IRAASA	*Are*
ASAARI	*Infinity*
RAASAI	*Never-ending Names*
IASAAR	*Yet*
AASAIR	*One Name*
RIASAA	*Is the Light*
Ahh...	*That illuminates*
So many names	*All Hearts*
Uniqueness Unlimited	*To discover*
ASAIRA	*The One True Heart*

The Doors of Keon

The Six Doors close.

The silent humming vibrates.

The light is dazzling.

Silence & Light & Movement.

Keon is the moving silence and the still light.

He is the Lucid Unmovingness.

Keon sits down on the grass.

Three Doors open again in the sky.

1 three six nine twelve fifteen eighteen twenty-one twenty-four twenty-seven thirty thirty-three thirty-six thirty-nine forty-two forty-five forty-eight fifty-one fifty-four fifty-seven sixty sixty-three sixty-six sixty-nine seventy-two seventy-five seventy-eight eighty-one eighty-four eighty-seven ninety ninety-three ninety-six ninety-nine one hundred and two one hundred and five one hundred and eight one hundred and eleven one hundred and fourteen one hundred and seventeen one hundred and twenty one hundred and twenty-three one hundred and twenty-six one hundred and twenty-nine one hundred and thirty-two one hundred and thirty-five one hundred and thirty-eight one hundred and forty-one one hundred and forty-four one hundred and forty-seven one hundred and fifty…

♫ *Eoin the Bard's Song* ♫

"The Legend of the Tree Woman"

In an Ancient Time
A Time of No-Time,
In an Ancient Realm
A Realm of No-Realm,
Rooted stood
The Unmovable Solidness
Of the Tree Woman.
She was SAARIA:
Born of the Earth
Born of the Sun
Born of the Depths
Born of the Skies
Born of the Heavens
Born of the Dark
Born of the Light.

Never-ending are her Roots
Over-reaching are her Branches

Accompanied by the
Sacred Spiral
Snake of Snakes
She brought the
Fruits of the Light
To the World.

And thus…

Here ends
This Legend of Old
For
All Good Hearts to Hear

ASAIRA
SAIRAA
AIRAAS
IRAASA
RAASAI
AASAIR

ASAIRARIASA
SAIRAAARIAS
AIRAASAARIA
IRAASASAARI
RAASAIASAAR
AASAIRIASAA

ARIASA
AARIAS
SAARIA
ASAARI
IASAAR
RIASAA

The Three Doors of Keon are blinding and bring sight at the same time.

A sense of infinity, of ASAIRA's boundless petals ever-opening.

A gyrating whirl of numbers and names that has no beginning and no end.

The sound of the harp echoes in an ancientness that is now.

Keon sings and every sung word manifests into silver and gold letters that write themselves onto the 2nd Door.

When the song ends, its Legend vibrating in Do ♪, the Three Doors close in fierce completion.

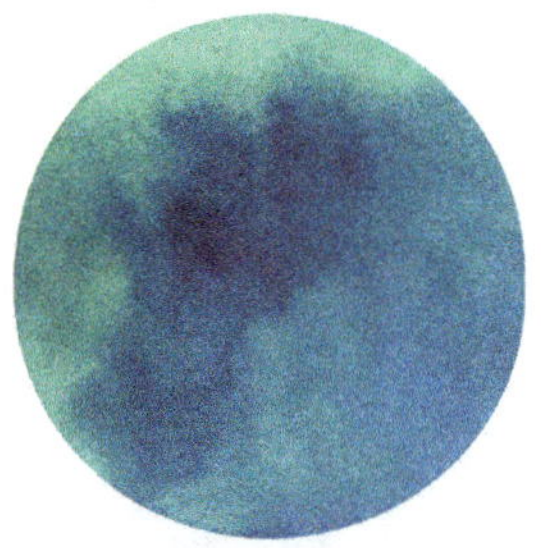

Earth: The Struggle of Ages

IASAAR listened to RAASAI's voice telling her to breathe, to stay calm and no matter what, to realise she wasn't this grey thing. In this moment of lucidity, the voice of RAASAI felt like her own as never before, and the name IASAARAASAI came to her, reminding her of her strength and wisdom.

The Shroud was hungry. Noticing an attack was necessary, it stuck its claws into the woman, who flinched with pain. "They are all lying, feeding you with their fantasies! You shouldn't be here. Listen to me. I'm your only friend! Whatever you do, don't go to that damned meadow! It's a trap. Can't you see? Life is not this. By believing all this nonsense, you abandon all your responsibilities, and on top of it, you don't know what's real anymore! You're losing it! Come home to your real life now before it's too late!"

The bitter words seared into IASAARAASAI's head, and she knew she had let them go on too long. She felt weak, abandoned and angry.

The Shroud saw its chance and spat out, "Yes, I'm sick of this! I'm dragged into this ridiculous story, and now I'm left on my own to deal with God knows what! And RAASAI knew! He didn't tell me! What else hasn't he told me?!"

The words burnt acid in the Reader's stomach while the Dark Cloak dug in its claws and teeth even further. The Reader sank into layer upon layer of greyness, the mires of a nightmare called the Struggle of Ages.

The Star of Heavens

There is always a Reader

There is always a Storyteller

There is always a Light Bearer

Listen well!

For You that Listens

Are the Listener who Bears the Light

To Tell the Story of Old

Attention

The Story of Old

Is always the Story of New

Alive and Now

So Jump for Joy

Child of the One Light!

For even if the Reader

Our dear IASAARAASAI

Now cannot read

Deep inside

They bear the Light

And shall tell of it

In the Meadow

Meanwhile, the Story is Written

Is Told & Read

Jump for Joy, Reader, whoever You are

For the Struggle shall and will end!

The Struggle of Ages

Is no struggle

If it is loved and known

Sing, my Friend, sing

The Humming Melody

Soothes the passage

To the Sea of Seas

Let this Cloaked One

Be flooded with

The Liquids of Love

No Struggle

Only the Waves of Watery Wisdom

ASAIRA

Am

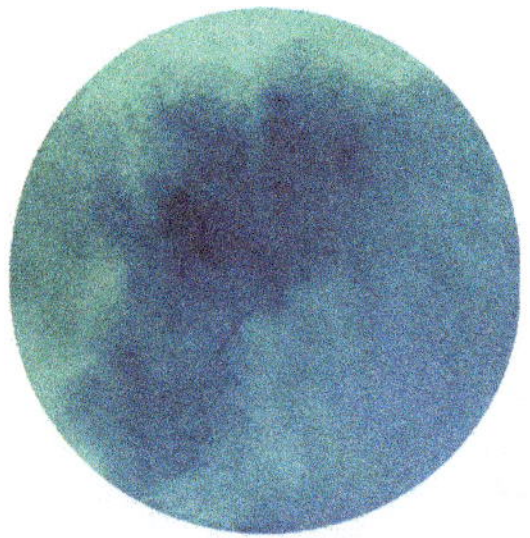

Earth: SAARIA The Tree Woman

Aileen embraced the Beloved Ancient One with the joy of reunion, a joy of innocent reminiscence. Her head touching one side of the tree trunk, the bark felt warm. Aileen let herself be sucked into a whirlpool of love. Mmmm…

A scent of lavender.

Aileen disappears but stays.

A feeling of absolute solidness.

A name: SAARIA.

The inner eyes saw that she was a she, but she was also a tree. Her arms were many, and her roots deep. Strong and straight she stood standing, an unmovable trunk. SAARIA remembered she could be woman and she could be tree: she was both.

SAARIA swayed in happiness.

Through the rustling leaves, the Sacred Serpent hissed sweet welcomes but a warning as well. It was then SAARIA, the Tree Being of the Ancient World, saw the distressed woman looking right at her.

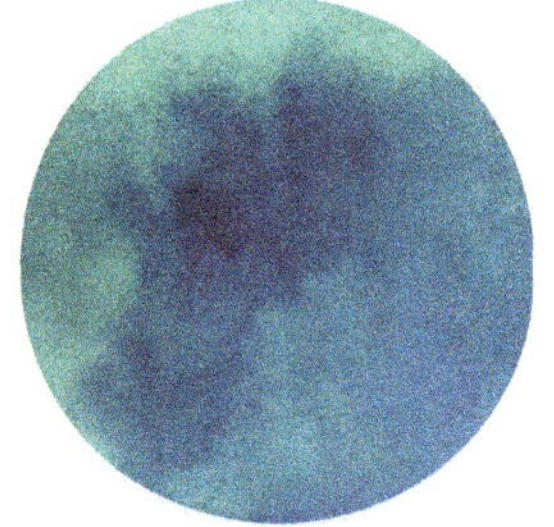

Earth: Lost in the Struggle

IASAARAASAI, clear for a second, stared at the tree. There was something unusual about it. Vague memories of Aileen's Tree swirled in, and she wondered if this tree was that Ancient Being.

"Look. I can't stand any more of this. No one is helping. I'm going," interrupted the Shroud.

The tree swayed, bringing IASAARAASAI to the surface once again. "Help me, Tree of Trees! RAASAI! Please, help me!"

One of the branches transformed into what looked like an arm and caught hold of IASAARAASAI. "Don't be afraid. I'm here to help. Listen to me…"

The Shroud sensed the Light. "GET OFF! WHAT THE HELL ARE YOU? ARRGH! THERE'S A SNAKE! LET ME GO! LET ME GO!!"

The Cloak tore itself away from the tree, and the woman ran away into the dark.

The Doors of Keon

Six Doors open: Six Gateways to the Circle of Truth.

Keon sits in the middle of the Circle.

The Six Doors revolve around Keon, spinning in slow revelation.

Keon, AASAIR, Gardener of Gardeners, Son of ASAIRA absorbs and receives the messages that dance before him.

The Doors close.

Keon's eyes shut in mirrored completion.

Earth ⁓ The Doors of Keon: Answering the Lamb's Call

The woman ran and ran. Tears rained down her face, nausea squeezed in her stomach… They've abandoned me… no one's helping me. I'm alone… why does this always happen to me? The Cloaked One fed on its feast of suffering with satisfied gluttony.

Keon saw one of the Six Doors open again. In the Door, there were two women facing each other.

The Woman with No Name slowed down and leant against a tree. Its bark felt warm in the cold night. She shivered and was just about to take a deep breath when the Shroud clawed her stomach and said, "Let's get out of here! They're coming!"

Keon observed that one of the women in the Door wore a dark cloak which was so heavy that she had to lean back. She was also carrying something… the Lamb!

The Nameless Woman suddenly heard another voice. She turned her head, and there was the snake again! It said, "You are IASAARAASAI. You are the Reader. We are Smanara and Silas. There's a Dark Shroud that feeds on you. Remember? Don't leave the Garden, my love, you're needed!" But the words were covered in a grey slime and difficult to hear, so instead of a sweet whisper, the woman heard a spitting sound, "You, IASAARAASAI! Reader! We are Smanara and Silas. Our dark shroud feeds on you. Remember? Don't leave the garden! We need you!"

"I want to die!"

The Shroud smirked, because this was a victory and the most sumptuous feast of all!

The woman moved to flee again when a small white dog barked at her feet.

In the Door of Keon, the other woman glowed. A snake made of silver was coiled around her neck. Keon hummed, and the image turned into ripples of water.

He heard his beloved KOAA call in her ethereal whale-talk, "The Waters of Life cleanse and nourish…"

Keon closed his eyes while the Door dissolved into a watery undulation.

The Woman who was IASAARAASAI looked down at the little dog. The word 'Bruxa' floated out: how much love and tenderness! The Shroud felt its gruesome plate suddenly emptied. The woman forgot all sorrows and bent down to pick up the lamb-like creature, but the Shroud would not, could not, bear a love so sweet and made the woman kick Bruxa.

Little Bruxa let out a cry of pain that pierced all the Realms of ASAIRA, and much to the Cloaked One's horror went straight to the Reader's heart! "Bruxa! What did I do? It wasn't me! Oh my God! I was taken over by the greyness. RAASAI, help me!!"

"Pick up Bruxa and jump into the Tree with the Sacred Snake. Do it now before it's too late!"

IASAARAASAI had a moment of doubt: 'jump into the tree?' but knowing she had no choice, she grabbed Bruxa, said a quick prayer and lunged into the Tree.

The long night which had been of a no-time and of a no-realm came to an end. The sun moved up into the sky in delicious reds and oranges and brought the first light of dawn over the Meadow. A blackbird felt inspired and broke into song.

Keon breathed in the colours of the sunrise, "Mmm… paradise…"

The blackbird's singing brought back a memory of another time… a song… yes, a song that I wrote when I was another… Eleanor?[26]

♫ *Morning has broken,* ♫

Like the first morning,

Blackbird has spoken

Like the first bird;

Praise for the singing,

Praise for the morning,

Praise for them springing

Fresh from the Word.

Ahh… Eleanor…

---

26 The Story Speaks

Eleanor Farjeon wrote this song called A Morning Song (For the First Day of Spring) in 1931. The song was a hymn for children. It has been sung by many different Daughters and Sons of ASAIRA in the Earth Realm with the title of Morning has Broken.

Sweet the rain's new fall,

Sunlit from Heaven,

Like the first dew fall

On the first grass;

Praise for the sweetness,

Of the wet garden,

Sprung in completeness

Where His feet pass.

Mine is the sunlight,

Mine is the morning,

Born of the One light

Eden saw play;

Praise with elation,

Praise every morning,

God's re-creation

Of the new day

Keon, AASAIR the Gardener and so many more, whispered, "Oh, Meadow of Meadows, Garden of Gardens, the ♫ *Saahruam Allssiram Issenam* ♫. Did we ever really leave you, Mother?"

♫ *Eoin the Bard's Song* ♫

"The Legend of the Meadow and the Dark Cloak"

In an Ancient Time

A Time of No-Time,

In an Ancient Realm

A Realm of No-Realm,

There was a Green Meadow

Where the Gods resided

A Garden, some called it

Others, the Saahruam

The most Peaceful of Abodes

The Gardener of Gardeners

Created each flower, each insect

Every Being danced in harmony

Other Gods played and lived

3 that were 6 that were 12

One day

Made a Sacred Promise did they

For all to be forgotten

For all to be remembered

And then, as if summoned for the mission,

Arose a Dark Cloak

Ravenous for oblivion

It pounced upon the Guardian of the Stem

SAARIA the Tree Woman

Her faithful Serpent coiled around her

Saw the Grey Cloak take

The Guardian from the Meadow

"Don't leave, my love!"

But, alas, too late!

Only a tree and a dangerous serpent

Could the Guardian see

And fled the Garden did!

One by One

Forgotten was all!

But Gracious Listeners

Do not despair

For the Legend says

One day

The Guardian of the Stem

Whole again

Will recognize SAARIA Tree Woman of the Ancient World

And pay no more heed

To the Heavy Cloak of Oblivion

And return, yes, return

With the 3 that are 6 that are 12

To the Green of Greens

And all ASAIRA shall remember

The Sweetest of Truths

ASAIRA be blessed!

One are we!

And thus...

Here ends

This Legend of Old

For

All Good Hearts to Hear

Listen to the Songs

Of Old

Listen to the Legends

Of Old

Listen to the Poems

The Stories

The Books

The Writings of Old & New

All point to the One

I Am

In the Meadow

One of the Doors opens: it's colossal, blinding, revealing… A glorious ocean comes into view, luminous in the sun. Keon can smell the salt and the fresh air: mmm… difficult not to dive into it!

But Keon knows his place right now is in the Meadow and to observe.

A familiar face pops out of the Sea: his Brother of Old, the Guardian of the Stem. IASAAR! RAASAI! What a delirious sensation to see you! Ah, Brother!

The Gardener of a Thousand Names raises his voice and arms. He sings, his heart bursting with love.

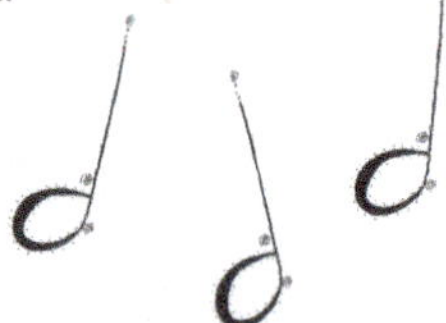

Door of Keon

In the Sea of Seas

The waters are so warm. Mmmm!

IASAAR Merman, sees a huge opening appear on the shore: it's like a door! So bright! His hands lift to cover his ears. And so loud, he laughs!

Oh! Hundreds of red poppies bobbing up and down in a field. The Meadow! The Merman hears the drone of the honey bees. On his skin he feels the ancient longing to lie in the greenness forever…

But the Merman knows his place right now is in the Silver Waters to rest and cleanse.

AASAIR! It's you, Storyteller! I can see you! You're waiting for us! We'll be with you soon, Brother.

IASAAR, bursting with love, dives deep down into the Silverness.

The Door closes.

A blue flame self-ignites in the Hearts of the 3,

who are 6,

who are 12,

who are 1.

The Kingdom of AASAIR: The End of the Struggle

When the Ravenous Shroud had touched the Sea of Seas, it had fought to stay out of the liquid love, its grey arm-like wisps grasping at the heavens. But once the silver Peace was felt, the Shroud could do no else but let itself sink and melt in the warm welcome of this Watery Mother.

Aileen and IASAAR, in their mermaid and merman form, had watched the melted substance that had been the Shroud transform into silver ripples and glittering echoes.

This long-awaited alchemy of healing sent waves of love and clarity through the Realms of ASAIRA, freeing many from their own Struggle of Ages. An eternity of soothing silence fell upon all who opened to this newfound freedom.

The Kingdom of AASAIR ⟐ The Tower of RAASAI ⟐
The Doors of Keon ⟐ Earth: At Long Last! Yes!

The six Merpeople are swimming together. Their laughter and play ring through the Sea making the silver waves sound like church bells. Such bliss!

The Sea of Seas turns pink and smells and feels like rose water. Mmmm… how wondrous…

As if she could not wait anymore, the Mother of All Creatures, KOAA, springs up from below the Merpeople, through the surface of the water and high into the air, to crash back into the water in a

gigantic

pink

waterfall

splash!

Out of the rose-scented waterfall opens a six-petalled flower. It rises into the skies by its Stem, the Tower of RAASAI. Wings sprout on the backs of the six Merpeople, and legs replace tails as the 6 are lifted up upon the Flower.

Keon feels the earth shake under him. Another Door opens with a spectacular sight: the Winged-Six! AIRAAS, IASAARAASAI, Smanara, Silas, Shimmera and Saul stand on the petals of an enormous flower!

The 6 turn to look at the sweet brown eyes of the Gardener. One by one they fly out of the doorway into the Meadow and land in front of Keon.

The Door closes with KOAA's song lingering in the air, and the four Gatekeepers of ASAIRA, Silas, Smanara, Saul and Shimmera, disintegrating into Aileen's heart.

The 3 stand together in still silence.

Time stops just to observe in captivated awe the long-awaited return of AIRAAS, AASAIR and IASAARAASAI.

PART 15

The Doors of ASAIRA: The Six Mirrored Truths
The 1st Mirrored Truth: The Story Told

Making a triangle, Aileen sat down to Keon's left, and IASAARAASAI placed himself at Keon's right.

IASAARAASAI's physical form felt strong… hmm, I'm the pirate man again from the Kingdom of AASAIR… He looked at the 2 at his sides: the Storyteller… he looked younger, different, and… Aileen… it was Aileen!

Keon broke the silence. "Aileen… AIRAAS. Reader… IASAAR and RAASAI. This is the first time we are together, here in the Meadow, since the Promise was made." Keon bowed his head, his right hand touching his heart. "We are here to remember. Yes, and to remind each other, to shed the light on all of this mystery of who we are and why we made the Promise."

A soft breeze interrupted Keon's words. The grass fluttered in the Meadow.

Looking at Aileen, Keon continued, "In many of my lives, I have been a Storyteller. In one of these lives, my previous one, I believe, I told a story about a young woman. You, Aileen! I had no idea of my AASAIR essence, or what was to happen to you. This has been discovered as the Story has progressed, even without my telling. I became a character, too! But none of us would be here now without IASAARAASAI, who was and is the Reader of this Story and who, too, became a part of it. The 3 of us now know we were to meet here at Primrose Meadow, but there is much that we do not know."

"AASAIR," said Aileen. "I don't really understand this about a Story and a Reader. But I open up to it! I'm back in the Meadow, and I am so happy to be here again. I don't remember the Promise… in all honesty, I'm not sure who I am anymore. My Aileen life is distant, though I can feel her coming back." Turning towards the pirate man, "And IASAARAASAI! You're familiar, but I have no memory of you at all, except just now when we were in the Sea… and when you were that woman."

"It must be very strange to hear all this about me being the Reader," said IASAARAASAI. "It's strange for me, too, but here I am! I don't remember the Promise, either, none of us do, and I don't know how I've been connected to you both in other lives, if we have. I think that's what we'll find out soon." A pause. "Yes… RAASAI just confirmed that."

"Yes," said Keon. "The Star of Heavens has told me that the Doors which are needed will appear before us and mirror the Truth." He reached out and took Aileen's hand. "It seems a lot to take in, but we will help each other. I have already remembered a lot from those lives, because it was necessary for my journey. Both IASAARAASAI and I will tell you all that we know, and the Doors will show."

A Door materialized just above Keon.

"You and I, Aileen," Keon said, "have been together numerous times and in numerous lives in the Earth Realm, but we were not aware of it."

Images in the Door came and went while Keon spoke, flashes of different places and times…

"The face I have at this moment is of a man called Keon; we have never met in this form, I feel, Aileen… When I told your story, as I said before, I was another Storyteller. I lived in the countryside, near a wood, but I don't remember anything else, not even my name. The last time I was in that form was when I was with the Reader, and we became mermen…" Keon glanced at IASAARAASAI for confirmation. "Then, on awakening here on Earth again, I was Keon." Looking into Aileen's eyes and then towards the Door, Keon said, "Aileen, the last time we were together on Earth that I can recollect was when I was your grandfather, John."

An image of John and a little Aileen laughing and playing together faded away slowly, and the Door closed.

A tear rolled down Aileen's cheek, while IASAARAASAI felt the excitement of actually having seen Aileen and the Storyteller in other lives. As the Reader, they'd imagined Aileen and the Storyteller so differently!

Keon turned towards IASAARAASAI. "Then, the Reader of this Story, who I often spoke to through the pages, heard RAASAI's voice… bringing IASAARAASAI to awaken!" Keon's voice deepened, and IASAARAASAI thought he could see and hear the Storyteller of Old again. "Noble Reader, IASAAR and RAASAI, are you able to tell Aileen and I what you have read of our lives and anything you remember from the Story? The Doors will aid thee. You are the Reader of Readers, but now you must be the Storyteller!"

IASAARAASAI felt the 2's eyes on him. Am I really here? The thought bounced in front of the Reader and disintegrated. "Aileen… AASAIR… I'll do my best. Hopefully, the Doors will fill in the gaps…"

The 3 looked at each other for a long second.

"Okay, how to start? Let's see…" IASAARAASAI paused for another long second, looked up at the sky and said, "In this Story, there are Six Knowings."

At IASAARAASAI's words, five Doors opened up behind him. Door by Door, IASAARAASAI related with a soft voice everything that he had read and lived, each of the 5 Knowings that were 6:

    ✳ 1st Door: 1st Knowing, Aileen, The Light Bearer of the Green Meadow

    ✳ 2nd Door: 2nd Knowing, The Forest of AARIAS

    ✳ 3rd Door: 3rd & 4th Knowing, The Return to the Mother

    ✳ 4th Door: 5th Knowing, The Song of AIRAAS

    ✳ 5th Door: 6th Knowing, The Promise Fulfilled

The Reader had become the Storyteller. There was something magnificent, powerful even, in IASAARAASAI's own telling and vision. Awestruck, the 2 listened and watched.

The images in the Doors together with the Words of the Story Told spiralled through the Meadow and the Universe and into the hearts of all who were ready. Any sleepiness which was still left yawned and awoke, brimming with insights and knowings in this miraculous Dawn of Dawns.

I

Am

Always

Asleep   *A*

I   *Spiralling*

Am   *Snake*

Never   *Of*

Awake   *Inscrutable*

I   *Mystery*

Am   *The*

Never   *Awakeness*

Asleep   *That*

I   *Wakes up*

Am   *Ever-Awakening*

Always   *Ever-Flowering*

Awake   *Flower of Flowers*

ASAIRA

AM

PART 16

The Doors of ASAIRA: The Six Mirrored Truths
The 2nd Mirrored Truth: The Forgotten Remembered

IASAARAASAI breathed in and out deeply as the last Door grew dark. Only silence, thick and golden, rippled in the air, enveloping the Meadow and its visitors.

Aileen felt a flutter from the wings of AIRAAS and a pull from the roots of SAARIA the Tree Woman. The wings spread open; the roots reached down into IRAASA's soil. Aileen remembered the cry of the warrior, SAIRAA, how she ran through the Forest of Forests. She remembered herself as a little girl, her innocence and strength, her salty tear of purity… Ahhh…

Inside the woman called Aileen, there was a burning, a love that could not be put out which opened and blazed, showing and revealing the lives she had lived. And she remembered, she remembered she had forgotten, she had forgotten that she had remembered… such a whirling mystery! She was Aileen, but she was not. Who was she really? AIRAAS?

Keon had lost all sensation of name and form: he was formless, genderless, nameless, timeless… just space, space… the ocean itself and not: a waterless ocean of oceans, a void of emptiness that overflowed with peace and love…

IASAARAASAI sank into the shimmering silence. Visions and dreams came where he, they, it, she was the Observer, completely detached, but in constant change. IASAARAASAI realised he had been with AASAIR and AIRAAS forever in one form or another. Sometimes they had known each other intimately, other times they had missed that opportunity. The truth was they'd been searching for each other since the beginning of time! His eyes welled up.

The Tree of Lands

We tremble

The Star

The Sea

The Earth

The Blue Flame flickers

Jubilant & Ardent

My Roots wriggle and squirm

What is this?

A Remembering

So long-forgotten

A Promise

So deeply hidden

We knew

We know

But, not known

We forgot too

Now we await

The Greatest of Storytellers

To reveal Herself

My Branches stretch out

In Supplication

For we are close

So close

Children of the One Light

The Doors of ASAIRA: The Six Mirrored Truths
The 3rd Mirrored Truth: The 3 Who Are The Eternal One

Sensing the presence of a great power on each side, the 3 open their eyes to see Bruxa, Tiger Bright and the Eagle of RAASAI.

Bruxa sits between Aileen and Keon, the Eagle between Keon and IASAARAASAI, and next to IASAARAASAI and Aileen is Tiger Bright.

Aileen, Keon and IASAARAASAI close their eyes again.

All 6 remain still, silent, breathing softly in tranquil repose.

Six closed Doors materialize out of the sky.

The First Door opens.

 Door 1

Keon's heart stirs. Inside, KOAA sings.

IASAARAASAI feels like his back cracks open. The tree… it's him! He senses the strength of the bark, the solidness of the trunk, the roots that pull down and never end… I was the Yew… But…?!

Elyn, now an elderly woman, places her hand on the Yew

IASAARAASAI feels the hand; he glances at Aileen. A tear glistens on her cheek.

A voice that sounds like the Ocean, the Heavens and the Earth, all in one wave, speaks in perfumed wisps of lavender and roses:

Each of YOU recognise your form in this Story. Though unique, each Story is the One Story of Stories. The 3 Children of the One Light, forged from the Aspects of the Mother, fashioned from the Stars of the Universe, have always been together in all the Realms as ONE.

ASAIRA?

Is this the Mother's voice?

The Second Door opens.

Door 2

Images of a land with cities
Medieval times on Earth
Darkness and persecution
Fires of destruction
A Disharmony
A Wisdom of Old being destroyed
Pain

Keon shudders, remembering Jean and Eilène. Aileen's eyes look down and then meet Keon's.

A dark hall, a smell of damp
A tall figure dressed in black
Accusing finger
Women huddled together
Eilène's voice, fearful
The accusing man: a voice of hatred

IASAARAASAI trembles at seeing the face of the tall man. Nausea swells up. I ordered the death of Eilène and so many more! A familiar voice inside him says, "IASAAR, breathe…"

The eyes of the 3 fall upon one another in compassion.

Bruxa licks Aileen's hand.

The Lavender-Rose Voice speaks again:

The Story of Stories spirals, the Children, too. Each one has lived the part of the Saviour, the Slayer, the Saved and the Slain, the Light and the Darkness. Each has been the Storyteller, the Reader and the Light Bearer. Each is all of this and much more. The One True Light reveals and IS.

The Third Door opens.

❧ Door 3 ❧

Images of a land of churches
The Earth Realm
Dark robes
Prayers and pride
A smell of incense
A Wisdom of Old barely visible
Disharmony and Imbalance
Hypocrisy and Fear
Pain

A woman in black cowers over a young boy with a sweet, sad face:
Elena & Juan!
Then, Juan as an adult: The Inquisitor

Keon feels faint. He killed the Lamb…

A young girl: angelic and innocent, terrified

It can't be… IASAARAASAI feels transported to the lands of Spain. Yes, he is she, saying, "Tengo miedo. ¡Ayúdame, Dios!"[i] I was so scared… Oh, ASAIRA…

A spellbinding vision of the Butterfly Mother passes over the three Doors. The sound of her wings comforts the rawness felt in their stomachs. The magical rainbow threads from the wings unravel and enter their hearts: peace… peace…

The vision of AIRAAS vanishes.

Aileen's back tingles. She lifts her head and looks at the two men. "Everything had to be like that. Remember how the wings were woven and how AIRAAS came to exist! It's all connected, to bring us back here… to the Meadow…"

The Voice of Oceans, Heavens and Earths says:

The 3 that are 6 that are 1 have met in harmony and
disharmony throughout the ages of the eternal no-time.
It is now that YOU are ready to see these TRUTHS.

The Fourth Door opens.

‿ᄃ Door 4 ᄃ‿

Images of forests and wildness
Hundreds and thousands of animals and life forms
Rivers and seas and oceans
A powerful fragrance of fresh air
A cool breeze
Harmony
A world without humans

IASAARAASAI is bombarded with instincts long-forgotten. Sensations of flying as an eagle, swimming as a dolphin, howling as a wolf… Ahhh…

*Two Gods: **SAIRAA** and UT*

Aileen can taste the wildness, the purity… an ecstasy! SAIRAA and UT, happy together! Keon realises this world is previous to the dark Forest of Mirrors and the solitary UT. It's a joy to see the happiness and the harmony!

*Every living Being is **ASAIRA**, is the 3 is the 6 is ONE.*
Every living Being is your Mirror. The Truth lies in your
heart, never to be forgotten. Jump for Joy, Child of the
One LIGHT!

The Fifth Door opens.

⟨ Door 5 ⟩

Images of a desolate, wasted land of mud and death in the Earth Realm
Disharmony and War
Trenches full of suffering
Young men die one after the other
A stagnant smell

The 3 shiver.

Images of fields and fields of poppies
The sound of someone reciting a poem:[ii]
"In Flanders fields the poppies blow
Between the crosses, row on row,
That mark our place; and in the sky
The larks, still bravely singing, fly
Scarce heard amid the guns below."

IASAARAASAI knows he's the man who recites.

A soldier with a medical apron sits on the step of an ambulance
wagon: he's writing the poem that's being recited

Keon recognises his old friend. John!

A dog is at John's feet while he writes the poem: Bonneau!

Aileen touches her heart. I was Bonneau the dog! Ah, the sweetness of loving my master, my beloved John. She looks at IASAARAASAI and then at Bruxa.

"We are the Dead. Short days ago
We lived, felt dawn, saw sunset glow,
Loved, and were loved, and now we lie
In Flanders fields."

Keon and IASAARAASAI turn to each other. Keon had been one of those 'Dead'.

Alexis...

"Take up our quarrel with the foe:
To you from falling hands we throw
The torch; be yours to hold it high.
If ye break faith with those who die
We shall not sleep, though poppies grow
In Flanders fields."

The Fifth Door darkens.

The words of the last verse **'The torch; be yours to hold it high'** flicker inside the 3 that are One.

Without respite, the last of the Six Doors opens.

— ⟡ Door 6 ⟡ —

Images of a desert and conquered land on Earth
Disharmony
Dust and ancientness
Modest dwellings, cities made of mud
Roman soldiers
A smell of sweat and heat
A hill-top
Pain and suffering
Three Crosses[iii]
A Man of Light

Aileen's eyes widen…

Jesus!

IASAARAASAI shakes his head.

Yes, Keon says with his eyes, all three of us were Jesus.

They hear ASAIRA's voice: *There is no formula to the Story of Stories.*

Two Women of Light
The older woman: Mary

IASAARAASAI experiences the mother's pain. He'd also been Mary, Jesus' mother! How can it be?!

The younger woman: Mary Magdalene

Again the 3 realise that all three had been Mary Magdalene…

IASAARAASAI swallows a little, his RAASAI wings move slowly, giving him balance. I'm trying to understand… "But you can't, my love," whispers RAASAI.

A sweet-eyed man stands next to Mary: It's John

Keon knows straightaway.

John the Apostle, Jesus' cousin

Keon remembers the truths he had wanted to write, to pass on, to tell. His heart burns with sorrow and love and happiness and peace, an explosion of emotions through his body and cells, through all times and ages and realms.

IASAARAASAI can't hold back anymore. He shakes his head again, sobbing a little. Aileen and Keon move towards him while Bruxa goes and sits in his lap. Tiger Bright makes a soft growl of love. The Eagle of RAASAI takes flight and then comes down very close, hovering above the 5.

*The Mirrored Truths speak for themselves. No words can explain the Mystery of **ASAIRA**. I have shown YOU nothing in comparison to what there is. Six Doors that could be six trillion Doors... the Petals of **ASAIRA** are unlimited in the Oneness of the STORY.*

The Six Doors disappear.

---

i The Story Speaks (Door 3)

Translation into English from the Spanish: "I'm afraid. Help me, God!"

---

ii The Story Speaks (Door 5)

John McCrae, Son of ASAIRA, teacher, doctor and poet, wrote this poem on May 3rd, 1915, during the 2nd Battle of Ypres in the region of Flanders, in Belgium. This was in the war that came to be known as the First World War in the Earth Realm. John's friend, Alexis, had died in battle on May 2nd. The poem is entitled In Flanders Fields.

---

iii The Story Speaks (Door 6)

Jesus Christ has been spoken of earlier in the Story. He is considered the Son of God in Christian religions. The Three Crosses refer to his crucifixion with two others at a place called Golgotha, according to the Bible.

No more words, no more images…

Exhausted, Keon, IASAARAASAI and Aileen lie down on their backs with their heads slightly touching. From above, they look like a three-petalled flower, their heads at the centre.

The 3 fall into a sleep of whiteness that gives space to all revealed.

The moon rises over the Meadow, and blankets of dark green grass sweep up and cover the three human forms. Bruxa and Tiger Bright huddle together and sleep, too, while the Eagle of RAASAI continues circling above, protecting the Meadow.

Then, like a creamy cloud of soothing love, a Dream of Dreams visits all who rest in the Meadow…

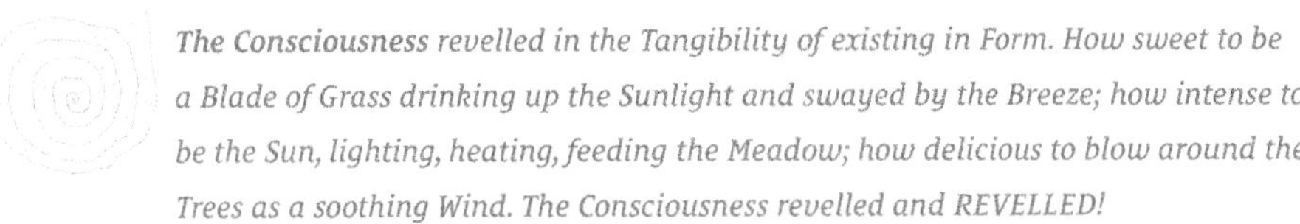

The Consciousness revelled in the Tangibility of existing in Form. How sweet to be a Blade of Grass drinking up the Sunlight and swayed by the Breeze; how intense to be the Sun, lighting, heating, feeding the Meadow; how delicious to blow around the Trees as a soothing Wind. The Consciousness revelled and REVELLED!

The Green Meadow had no Boundaries, existing as a floating, grassy Ocean full of Poppies and Primroses bobbing in the Breeze. It was always sunny and always Daytime; Night did not exist. The Consciousness played and felt the blissful Tingle of being alive in these Forms. There was no Time, no Thought, no Word, no Explanation: only This, the MEADOW.

And then, as One might say is natural, the Consciousness breathed out and closed its formless Eyes, causing the Night and Stars and Moon to appear: how not to relish the glittering Meadow in this restful Form?! The Consciousness loved itself as this Darkness and rested in the Void. From then on, Night and Day in the Green Meadow played themselves out in an eternal Moment of NOW.

One sunny Day, as they all were, the Consciousness noticed the Arrival of a bubbling Impulse. It darted around freely until it landed and transmuted into three incredible, new Forms. These three Forms were Beings that could walk and fly, for the Spiral of Life which had been put into Motion was powerful and unstoppable and so eager for more! What a Delight to walk on Legs through the Green Meadow; what a Marvel to use Wings and fly through the blue Sky or the starry NIGHT!

The Three Winged-Beings, who walked upright on two Legs, seemed humanoid, but they were not human. The Bodies, which were at least eight feet tall, were transparent and nacreous as if made of Mother-of-Pearl. The Beings glowed in a rainbow Iridescence that shifted and scattered under the Light and Sun. From an Earth Being's Perspective, they were sparkling Gods, blinding in their Brightness. The Beings had no Inkling of separate Identity and were part of the One Being: three Mirrors that reflected the Consciousness's Existence. The 3, who knew no Word and no Thought, played and loved, curious and innocent in their profound WISDOM.

The irresistible Impulse for Life that was the Consciousness, taking such gleeful Pleasure in creating and being, transmuted into two other spellbinding Forms. One was a silver Ocean that shone in Resplendence. The Other, a radiant Star that could use a Voice and spoke in shimmering Melodies. The three God-Beings were enchanted by the Gifts bestowed. They swam in the Silverness to then soar up to the Star and listen to its mesmerizing Voice. From the Interaction and Curiosity, other Wonders emerged: the three Gods began to make Sounds and sang with the Star... and, oh, how beautiful, for every Musical Note created a new Star in the magical night Sky! The Meadow and the Sea of Seas glowed even more when the three Gods and the Star sang their breathtaking SONGS.

One Day of No-Day, a Solidity made itself known. The Consciousness perceived the Solidity pull itself downwards into robust Threads that rooted themselves: a World of Soil and Earth came into Form, unending and deep. Enjoying its limitless Solidness, the Consciousness saw all the Life that would consequently awaken from this earthy World; and lo and behold, the Trees and the Grass and the Poppies and the Primroses grew Roots, while certain Insects burrowed away in the Depths. After some Time of No-Time, a truly majestic Being grew from the Soils: a formidable Tree, strong and anchored by countless Roots that were interconnected with every living Being. Mmmm... the Consciousness loved letting itself be the Tree that sustained, that connected, that solidified. Ahh... The Tree, ecstatic, opened its Branches to living in FORM.

One refreshing, rainy Day, because now the Rain had come into Existence, a Ripple in a Puddle swirled and zoomed into the Air to transmute into a Sound. Two other Ripples followed suit and swirled into Form. The Consciousness loved the three Sounds and sang them through the Voices of the three Gods. Mysteriously, each Sound was attracted to only one of the Gods.

"AASAIR!"

One of the three Gods turned round and became *AASAIR. AASAIR* repeated the Word to the Flowers who fell in Love with its Sound and its Owner.

"AASAIR..." the Flowers whispered in the Breeze.

"AIRAAS!"

The second God caught the Sound in the Heart and sang, "AIRAAS, AIRAAS, AIRAAS," flying around the Meadow until the Word wove itself into the Wings forever.

*"**RAASAI!**" The third God-Being said "**RAASAI**" over and over in dizzy Repetition and flew to tell it to the Star.*

*The Star, enraptured, recited the three scintillating Sounds, "**RAASAI**, AIRAAS, AASAIR, **RAASAI**, AIRAAS, AASAIR, **RAASAI**, AIRAAS, AASAIR..." and Thousands of minute blue Stars were BORN.*

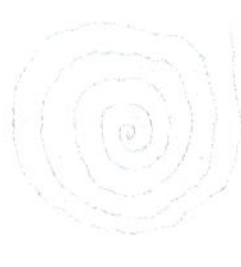

The Word had become Flesh, *and now dwelt in the Meadow.[27] One moonlit Night, while most of the Beings rested and slept, another Word, excited and determined, awoke, but this time it sprang from the Soil. The Consciousness felt itself as the earthy Darkness and gave out a deep Bellow that coiled itself into the Dream of the 3, "**IRAASA!**" The 3 woke up and touched the Earth, softly chanting, "**IRAASA, IRAASA, IRAASA**..." The Earth rumbled in CONTENTMENT.*

Floating on their Backs in the silvery Waters, *the Consciousness that was AIRAAS, RAASAI and AASAIR gazed dreamily at the Stars and the Moon. Suddenly, the Star of Stars uttered an unheard-of Sound, and another Word had been created. The Word spun and spun, quite lightheaded the 3 felt. It was undoubtedly a beautiful Word and resonated in the Hearts of the One Heart. And where was this Word to go? The Consciousness laughed and laughed, the only way it could, through the Beloved 3. Yes, naturally! The Word was to land on itself. The Consciousness that was formless, wordless, would now have a Form, a Word. It rejoiced in the Sensation of such an Occurrence, and the Word danced on the Waves of the Sea of Seas and jumped onto the Lips of the 3, "ASAIRA... ASAIRA... ASAIRA..."*

---

27 The Story Speaks

Again Saint John the Apostle's quote, "And the Word was made flesh and dwelt among us." John, 1:14, King James Bible, 2000.

There was great Celebration and Joy, for the 3, the Star, the Sea, the Earth, the Tree and all the Green Meadow revelled in knowing themselves as the One True Light,

Aileen, Keon and IASAARAASAI woke up to find the Meadow bathed in light. Sunshine was pouring down, and the Sea sparkled in the sun's warmth. IRAASA sent a loving vibration through the soil. Tiger Bright and Bruxa got up and rolled in the grass together. Aileen laughed, and the 2 joined in. Perched on the Tree of Lands, the Eagle quietly watched, happy to observe forever.

The rest of that day was spent in sweet silence. The three Friends of Old walked through the Meadow, smelled the fragrance of the flowers and swam in the nourishing Sea. Far away yet near, KOAA sang a divine lullaby.

The Four Guardians had taken form again and rested in the Meadow, too: Shimmera, as Wolf-Moon, lay in the shade of the Ancient Tree, while Saul, as the Owl of SAIRAA, perched himself near the Eagle and hooted now and then. Smanara and Silas in their silver god-like forms walked in the caressing sun, enjoying the peacefulness.

The Consciousness, the One True Light, contemplated itself in Pure Love.

PART 18

The Doors of ASAIRA: The Six Mirrored Truths

The 4ᵗʰ Mirrored Truth: The Three Kingdoms Revealed

The 3 returned and sat in the Circle.

ASAIRA observed herself. She breathed in, then out… manifesting a Door of Light that was so bright it was nearly terrifying.

The Voice that sounded like the pealing of bells rang out,

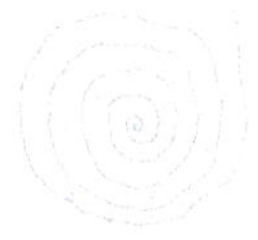

The One Consciousness, nameless and formless, yet the Receiver of a trillion names, the Holder of a trillion forms, revels in the Awakening of ASAIRA and allows her infinite petals to flourish in joy. She is She, She is He, She is I, She is You, She is It, She is We, She is They: the One True Light Is and Am. Each can know and cannot know. She that is not a She is the Bearer of Light, She that is not a She is the Storyteller of the Form, She that is not a She is the Perceiver of All.

ASAIRA spoke through AASAIR, "ASAIRA felt urged to create other worlds apart from the Green Meadow. The worlds would have their own life-creating spark, but the Source would always be the Meadow and the 3 who were 6. The Tree of Lands, the Sea of Seas, IRAASA Soil of Soils and the Star of Heavens, whose male aspect was the All-Seer, were also intricate to the three Gods and to the Meadow and could not be separated. Each of the 3 were given a world and, mirroring ASAIRA AM, would have the power of creation. But, before the Kingdoms came into existence, two magical creatures arose to be Guardians and Companions of the 3 on their new adventures: the Lamb of ASAIRA and the Tiger of FIRE."

AASAIR stopped.

Three Doors made of hundreds of precious jewels appeared in the sky, accompanied by the ethereal sounds of whales singing. A perfume of jasmine flowers saturated the air.

The Door into The Kingdom of AASAIR: The Gardener of the Realms

Images of the Gardener with his sister AASAIR-KOAA. They are the Mother and Father.

They create many different worlds and creatures of legends, such as unicorns, dragons, fairies, nymphs and many others.

Images of KOAA and AAOK, Whales of Ancientness. They swim with other sea creatures, mermaids and mermen in the Sea of Seas.

Images of the 4, Saul & Shimmera, Silas & Smanara. They are born into the Sea, four Angels of Silver and Gold.

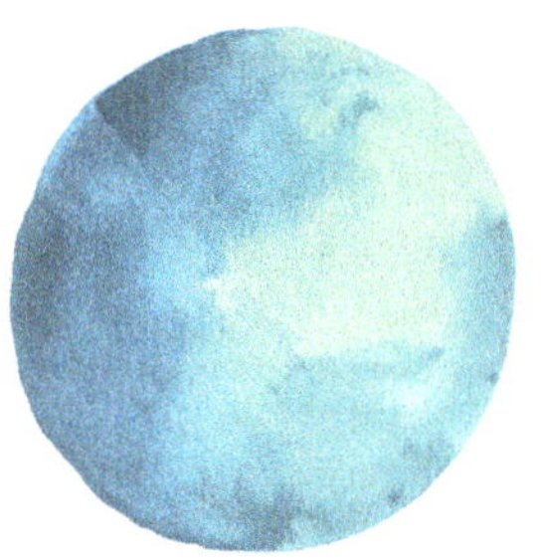

The Door into The Kingdom of AIRAAS: The Butterfly Mother & Forest Warrior

Images of two worlds, two flavours.

One World: AIRAAS is the Butterfly Mother with her Wings of Revelation. The Wings constantly change in colour and texture as she flies over the Realms.

An image of the Wings' Threads spreading out and connecting to every Being in every realm and dimension, in every moment of time. One Infinite, Interwoven Being!

Images of AIRAAS hovering over AASAIR while he tends the Garden. She is tiny in comparison to AASAIR!

The Other World: AIRAAS is SAIRAA, the Warrior. An image of her standing next to UT, who is no other than AASAIR, her male aspect and companion. They create the Forest of AARIAS and learn the secrets of the Earth Mother, IRAASA.

The Door into The Kingdom of RAASAI: The Guardian of the Realms

Images of RAASAI: an eagle-like creature, although they change form continually and go from one Kingdom and World to another.

Images of Tiger Bright and the Lamb. The Lamb shapeshifts from Lamb to Dog all the time! Both the Tiger and the Lamb also come and go from one Kingdom to the other, sometimes with RAASAI, sometimes with AIRAAS and sometimes with AASAIR.

An image of a Tower: RAASAI looks out onto the World.

The Doors closed. Silence reigned again in the Meadow.

ASAIRA looked through the eyes of a human form but was not sure of whom; it was dark inside and out. Noticing an object on the ground, ASAIRA bent down and picked it up. The object shone despite the darkness. It was a small mirror decorated with rubies. ASAIRA looked at the reflection. It showed countless faces, but they were hazy and blurred. ASAIRA closed the eyes of the form, of the body, breathed deeply and opened the eyes again. The mirror had cleared: "Aileen!"

She that was not a she stared at Aileen's face in the mirror. The faces of AIRAAS and the beloved AASAIR and RAASAI looked back at her. They were all one face and yet three. ASAIRA continued looking, quite captivated, when the Star of Heavens appeared on her forehead, and her hair turned into the Sea of Seas. Her skin became brown and bark-like, and the name of SAARIA the Tree Woman surfaced in simultaneous dance with the Tree of Lands. ASAIRA looked deeper into this well of knowing and transformed into the dark Depths of IRAASA rooted to the Green Meadow. Ahhhh…

There was more light, and Aileen that was ASAIRA looked up from the ruby mirror. Two other forms were sitting in front of her: IASAARAASAI and AASAIR. Aileen-ASAIRA realised that when her Brothers looked into the Mirror they would see whatever was needed, too.

Aileen-ASAIRA said,

"Let me tell you a story… a story about a spark that would change the Three Kingdoms and the Realms of ASAIRA for seemingly ever.

THE THREE KINGDOMS existed in harmony, experiencing creation after creation, realms of inconceivable beauty and many other delights and sensations. However, none of the Three Kingdoms was the Earth of the human species, nor was the Earth any of the realms that had been created.

ONE DAY of this Mysterious Now of All Beginnings and Ends, something completely brand new shot out of the starry sky. It was a spark of curious creativity that had never shown its face before. ASAIRA felt it spiral through the Sea, into IRAASA and out through the Tree.

THE SPARK decided to land on AASAIR while he was admiring AIRAAS's wings. She had flown onto AASAIR's hand and was looking back at him in deep love. At the same time of no-time, in different realms, SAIRAA and UT kissed each other. In the Sea, Shimmera and Saul kissed, too, as Smanara and Silas lovingly touched each other's face.

ASAIRA felt the Spark turn into words, then sail out of AASAIR's mouth, *"Let us forget all of this! Let us create a new World, just for us, to live and love and experience together."*

AIRAAS did not understand and in truth, neither did AASAIR comprehend the words, nor even ASAIRA. The word 'Forget' was new, and there was a meaning in the word 'Us' that swirled in novelty. It caused a stir through the Kingdoms and was received with curiosity by all the Creatures, the One Consciousness.

RAASAI flew down to AIRAAS and AASAIR and said, "Brother, Sister, let us stop for a while to rest in the Meadow. I sense more words shall arrive, and we three shall speak them."

THE 3 closed their eyes and immediately found themselves in the Garden of Gardens, the sweetest kingdom of all. They lay down among the poppies and looked up at the blue sky in joy. The Tiger and the Lamb joined them and lay down, too, in the cool grass."

Aileen stopped the telling. "Why don't we also rest? More Doors are going to open soon..."

IASAARAASAI and Keon nodded, placed the Ruby Mirror on the ground and stretched themselves out next to Aileen.

Closing its mossy green eyes, the Meadow glittered in twilight majesty.

PART 19

The Doors of ASAIRA: The Six Mirrored Truths
The 5th Mirrored Truth: The Promise Remembered

Surrounded by a brilliant light, the next Door opens.

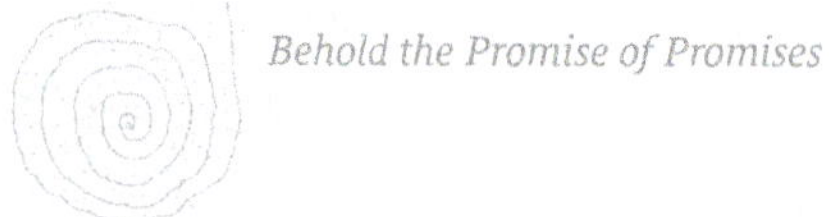

Behold the Promise of Promises

In the Door, the 3 of Old, transparent and luminous, are in the Meadow sitting in a circle. This time the images are a film. The three Gods are speaking and moving. Their language sounds like running water in a stream, like KOAA's singing! Magically, every word is understood.

EXT. THE MEADOW - DAY

RAASAI, AASAIR and AIRAAS are sitting in a circle. Two
Trees stand tall. One of the Trees has a shiny snake
coiled around it.

                    AASAIR
          AIRAAS, would you live a Life
          of Lives with me where we can
          experience everything together?

                    AIRAAS
          I do not understand, Sweet-Eyed
          One. Is that not what we do now?

                    AASAIR
          Yes, but not completely. I sense
          there is more to discover, more to
          feel, AIRAAS, you and I together.

                    AIRAAS
               (a little perplexed)
          Then let us create a new
          adventure, as we always do...

                    RAASAI
               (takes AIRAAS's hand)
          Yes, but what AASAIR says is to
          forget all of THIS firstly. After
          we forget, we can experience
          a new life without knowing or
          remembering that we are ASAIRA AM.

                    AIRAAS
               (stands up)
          I do not understand 'forget',
          Brothers.

                    AASAIR
                (follows AIRAAS)
          I do not, either, but the word has
          come and is fascinating to me. I
          know not what shall befall, but I
          am impelled to go ahead. I feel I
          shall love and know you, AIRAAS,
          in a way that cannot be possible
          otherwise.

                    RAASAI
                (looks at both AIRAAS
                and AASAIR with an air
                of seriousness)
          I do not know what it really means
          to forget. But something stirs in
          me to be cautious. As we speak, new
          words are created, new meanings,
          and it is unstoppable. Sit down
          again, and let us breathe.

     The Three Ancient Ones gather together in the Circle
     again. They close their eyes.

Aileen, Keon and IASAARAASAI do the same in mirrored truth.

An hour of Earth time passes by.

                    RAASAI
                (taking a deep breath)
          If we, as ASAIRA, vow together
          to forget all of THIS, it shall
          happen. This means that ASAIRA,
          through these forms, will forget
          that She is the One Consciousness
          who brings Life to All. We will be
          very different. We cannot know what
          will happen.
                    (MORE)

                    RAASAI (CONT'D)
               (pauses)
'Forget' means for the Meadow to
disappear, because we would not
know of it! Or the Sea, or the
Depths... the Sparkling Star may
not sing anymore!

                    AIRAAS
Yes, I understand 'forget' better
now.
               (pauses)
I am curious to experience this
that we call forgetting. Perhaps
AASAIR is right. We will be able
to love in a new way that is not
possible unless we forget!

                    RAASAI
               (not convinced)
Only if we recognise or remember
each other after forgetting!

                    AIRAAS
               (her hand lifts to her
               heart)
We are ASAIRA so this is Her will,
for we are She.

                    AASAIR
               (hopeful)
There is great beauty in the word
'remember'. Perhaps we are to
forget, experience the unknown,
and then to remember! It will be a
beautiful adventure.

The word 'adventure' jumps through the Door and into the hearts of IASAARAASAI,
Aileen and Keon. They turn to look at each other and back to the film.

AASAIR stands up and is excited, enjoying the new words
that pour out.

                    AASAIR
          Let us be cautious, let us take
          precautions, so we can remember
          again and return to the Green
          Meadow upon request.

RAASAI stands up, followed by AIRAAS; both show
excitement.

                    RAASAI
          I am the Guardian of ASAIRA. I see
          all from the Tower. I could be the
          one not to forget. I could watch
          over and guide.

AIRAAS reaches out and touches RAASAI's arm.

                    AIRAAS
          The worlds created may not be
          visible to you. No, I wish you to
          be with us. The 3 must always be
          together, RAASAI.

                    RAASAI
          You are right, my Sweet AIRAAS.
               (pauses, and then with
               enthusiasm)
          I can easily become two Aspects:
          RAASAI and IASAAR. RAASAI can
          watch over from the Tower and
          also travel the Realms of the New
          Worlds, just as I do now. Thus, I
          would guide the 3 to help remember
          when it is desired. Yet I shall
          be IASAAR, too, and forget in the
          same way that you shall.

The 3 become silent for a while.

                         AASAIR
          Let us all leave a part of
          ourselves as a guidance, a Light
          Bearer that will always lead us
          back to the Meadow.
               (takes out the
               Mirror)
          I shall leave this Ruby Mirror
          of Truths in the Kingdom of
          AASAIR with KOAA. She can sleep
          and hold the womb ready for our
          return. I shall forget, but I
          will always remember a glimmer
          of the Meadow and shall tell and
          sing of it. In this manner, I
          can also guide you both.

                         AIRAAS
               (joyful and
               inspired)
          Yes! We will all be the Teller
          and the Light Bearer when we are
          called to do so.
               (opens her wings and
               gently touches them)
          The Wings of AIRAAS shall never
          forget. The Butterfly Mother may
          or may not, but the Wings shall
          not forget. They will remember!
               (pauses)
          Yes! The Wings' Threads will be
          ropes of guidance, of healing,
          of light for us to hold onto and
          return to the Meadow.

The 3 watch the film 'The Promise of Promises' in enthralled silence. No words can express or really describe this revelation. To see themselves at the Beginning of Beginnings, at the End of Ends, was a mystery, too impenetrable for any storytelling.

The film stops.

The Door regresses into a black hole.

                    EXT. BLACK HOLE - DARKNESS

                    A small flame ignites from the blackness. In one of its
                    flickers, the 3 of Old emerge again. They speak as One
                    Voice. They are One, ASAIRA, Gods, more than Gods, the
                    Life and Essence of All.

                                        THE 3
                                (three Voices yet one)
                          We as ASAIRA choose to forget
                          our ASAIRA AM Self and the
                          Meadow in order to live and love
                          and experience and know a new
                          world. But we also choose not to
                          completely forget and be able to
                          return when we desire.
                                (they pause)
                          We leave certain aspects of
                          ourselves here that shall penetrate
                          all forgetfulness: RAASAI the
                          Guardian of the Tower, the Wings of
                          AIRAAS, KOAA the Whale Mother, the
                          Ruby Mirror and all Mirrors.
                                (they pause)
                          Into the Reborn World we, IASAAR,
                          AIRAAS and AASAIR, shall enter and
                          through the telling of stories and
                          song, shall remind each other of
                          the Truth of whom We Are. The 3
                          shall always be together.
                                (MORE)

                    THE 3 (CONT'D)
                (they pause)
          The two Guardians, Tiger Bright
          and the Lamb of ASAIRA, shall
          not forget. They shall act as
          Guides and Light Bringers. The 4,
          Shimmera, Smanara, Silas and Saul,
          wish to experience forgetfulness,
          too. But they also will serve
          as Gatekeepers of the Meadow
          and shall have their Towers as
          Lighthouses. The Star, the Sea,
          the Trees of ASAIRA and the Dark
          IRAASA, shall also be Guides and
          Guardians, anchoring and awakening
          if the forgetful sleep becomes too
          deep. With these precautions, we
          all choose THIS in happiness, for
          we are One.
                (they pause and then
                continue with a louder
                voice)
          WE PROMISE ALL THAT HAS BEEN SAID!
          WE VOW TO RETURN AND REMEMBER! IT
          IS THE PROMISE OF PROMISES!
                (they lift their arms)
          LET IT BE SO, ASAIRA AM!!

The flame and the 3 of Old explode into a million
trillion stars! The Stars burst open and melt into
glittering waterfalls of liquid light, pouring down into
the nothingness of space.

Then...

Darkness.

The Star of Heavens

The Forgetting had begun

Before the Promise made

The Seeds of Separation sown

While speaking of the Forgetting

AASAIR

RAASAI

AIRAAS

How could they forget each other?

How could they not be with each other?

Impossible

But already they believed

Ahhh...

The Greenest of Meadows

The ♫ Saahruam Allssiram Issenam ♫

Heaven on Earth

Was never lost

Will never be lost

Is never lost

Jump for Joy

Child of the One Light

and

Remember!

PART 20

The Doors of ASAIRA: The Six Mirrored Truths
The 6ᵗʰ Mirrored Truth: The Promise Fulfilled

While Aileen, IASAARAASAI and Keon slept, images, insights and knowings journeyed in and out of their One Heart. The gratitude underlying each comprehension caressed every living Being in every dimension, in every realm, in every period of time.

Every dog I meet is a reminder of the Meadow. They bring me Home, to the Garden of Gardens in an instant!

IASAAR was taken by the Cloaked One. Then it looks like we all forgot completely, and the Meadow seemed to vanish… None of this was what we'd expected!

Millions of stories, legends, poems, songs, works of art, films… there is no end to them. They are the Story of Stories, retold and retold, again and again!

We return to the Meadow in many moments! What happens is that we don't realise it or see it.

ASAIRA *is ALL. Therefore, our names are redundant. We are the Meadow, so how can it ever be lost?*

All Animals and Nature can help us syntonize to the Meadow. *We just have to let ourselves sink into their frequency. Yes, it's so easy, really… listening to their voice, we hears ours: the One True Voice.*

I'm the Reader of the Story, but I'm also Aileen and Keon. *I am the Star, the Tree,* **IRAASA***, the Eagle, the 4, the Sea, the Lamb and the Tiger! I am the Meadow, the* ♫ Saahruam Allssiram Issenam ♫*. I AM.* **ASAIRA** *AM.*

There's always a Storyteller creating a world: an AASAIR **gardening.** *There's always a Bearer of Light: an* AIRAAS*, illuminating the Path, and there's always a Reader, an* IASAAR*: a Perceiver of All of THIS, a* **RAASAI***, who guides, listens and sees. They are* **ASAIRA***, and they are all in each form, not separated but One.*

Other worlds, new realms, were created. *One was the Earth that we know and see. There was also Sun where the four Gatekeepers lived in their separate Towers, having forgotten each other. Another was UT's lonely abode after the Forgetting: the Forest of Mirrors. And surely, there were other realms, too, where we searched for each other. That's how it all felt. But it was like a dream. We've always been together really!*

What is this Story? *It feels like one Story, and yet every form is living it! There must be trillions of Stories, and they are all the same One!*

So many words! They all say "Go in that direction!" Sometimes they make me feel tired. No words are necessary to return to the Green Meadow!

Silence, stillness, space, peace: Home discovered.

So many forms! But we're none of them. I can see from afar and revel in the creation. However, I am none of this.

So what is the Promise Fulfilled? Now that I see and I remember, will we live in the Meadow forever?

So much love! The body tingles, and I have nothing more to say!

With the Promise Fulfilled, does it mean we'll live the Green Meadow on Earth? Is it living Heaven on Earth? Shall all pain and suffering subside?

Questions, questions… They distract. I am the Green Meadow! I am the Heaven! I am the Earth! I'm here, now, and I feel THIS.

We left, we experienced, we returned and we continue experiencing, but now we'll experience from the knowledge of who we really are.

I never forgot, I never left, I never abandoned my Children.

When I need healing, I can go inside and find the Sea of warm silver. I dive in, and I am healed. The Dark Cloaked One, even, couldn't resist the purifying Sea of Seas.

Who was the Cloaked One? What was it? How did it appear in the Garden? There are still a lot of mysteries. Maybe it'll never be completely understood.

When I'm afraid, I look inside and feel Tiger Bright. His strength always accompanies me. His growl brings me Home and reminds me of SAIRAA and UT's warrior strength and wisdom, which I also have.

When there's a dizziness, a sense of losing balance, I know I'm safe. I go inside and hold onto the the Ancient Tree of Lands. And then I know I am the Ancient Tree Woman, SAARIA. I feel my roots and know I am solid and stable.

There could be a time when pain still shows its broken heart. I know I can love it. My light and love are always bigger than the pain. I love the pain, and let it relax and dissolve into IRAASA's earthy arms, covering it in healing mushrooms. The nourishing Soil of Soils alchemizes the pain into a beautiful Flower!

Every time I see the Innocent, I'm looking into my own eyes. I am the Lamb of Lambs, gentleness and compassion, sweet Love of Loves.

If magic and marvel are necessary, I can find them inside, too! I can be whatever the Heart asks me to be. I can do whatever the Heart asks me to do. I am the 4, Smanara, Saul, Silas and Shimmera, each an aspect of the Feminine and Masculine in balance, each with talents that I can use in this world or other worlds.

*I'm able to fly to the Inner Heavens and speak to the Star or All-Seer or **RAASAI**, and I speak to myself!*

*Every human Being was born of the Gods, is the Gods, is much more. Every human Being is All, Is **ASAIRA** AM. This Knowing can be called by trillions of names, and we can create trillions of stories that are unique! I am NOW. I am the One Consciousness that Observes All.*

My Heart burns! I am the LOVE, the Flame of All Fires. Never can it be extinguished! I close my eyes, and I can see it burning with LIFE. No thought or belief or deed or word or emotion can change that Truth. The Meadow always glows in my Heart!

Ah... The Greenest of Meadows I Am

The 3 wake up to the most wondrous Door of all. It's decorated with thousands of flowers of every colour. There are roses, primroses, jasmines, lilies of the valley, lilacs, magnolias, honeysuckles, gardenias and fragrant flowers from every realm: the perfume engulfs and refreshes. The Door is the manifestation of spring and summer in one gigantic garland!

The Door of Flowers opens. The 3 lean back as the light pours through, their chests vibrate and throb, the One Heart bursting with love and joy… they can hardly breathe!

Aileen touches the soil beneath her. "Oh, Mother of Mothers, yes, yes, yes!" She stands up and open hers arms, transforming into a blinding, luminous AIRAAS!

The Reader lifts their hands, overwhelmed, "I can't see…"

"It's okay, IASAAR!" Keon helps the Reader up onto their feet. "You are IASAARAASAI! Look at yourself," says the deep voice of the giant winged-gardener, AASAIR.

Returned, IASAARAASAI looks down at himself, and before his eyes he grows into a tall transparent woman with eagle-like wings. "Wow!"

Laughing, the 3 hug each other.

The Door of Scented Light completely open, AIRAAS, IASAARAASAI and AASAIR fly through, their rainbow stellar turning into an iridescent whirlwind that takes everything and everyone with it: the Sea, the Ancient Tree and IRAASA, the worlds, the realms, the creatures and living Beings, the Earth and the Sun, the Universe, the Star of Heavens and all the Guardians spiral into the Door.

The only Being that remains is the Green Meadow. The primroses and poppies seem to smile, their sweet heads ascending above the grassy ocean. It's all so still, so peaceful. Yet the Door of the One True Flower beckons, its eternal fragrance intoxicating.

The Meadow quivers… it is time…

Aglow, the Meadow melts into an incandescent goldness that rises up and surrounds the Door.

Silently, ASAIRA closes her greatest Door.

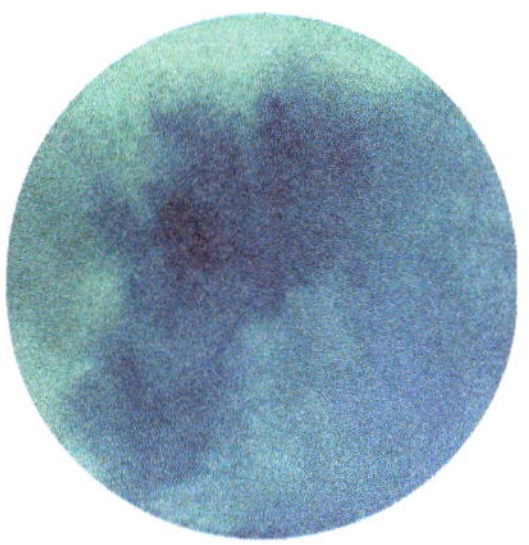

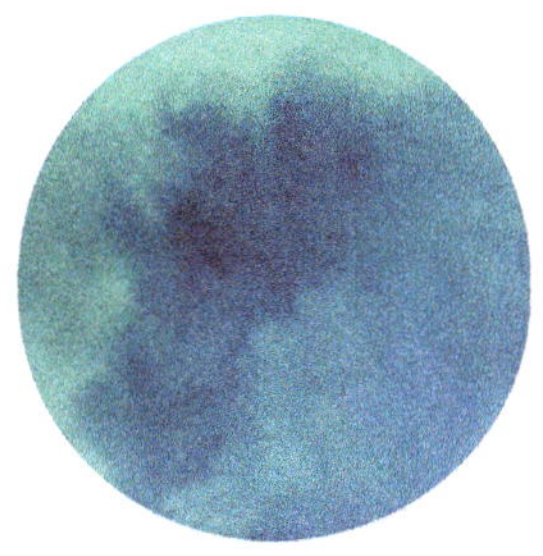

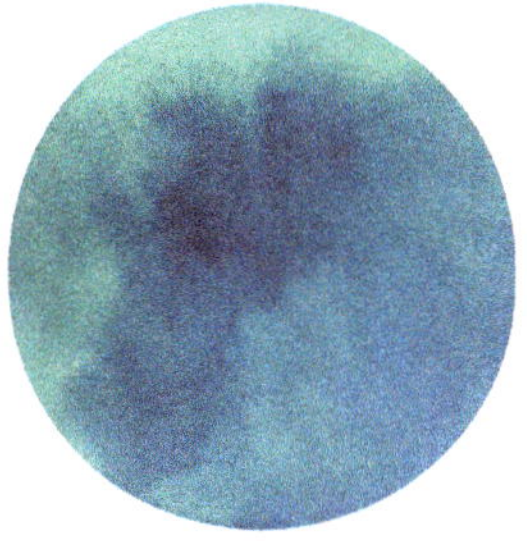

Aileen is sitting under the Great Tree in the forest. Ahh… how I love it here! She laughs and looks at Bruxa, who is sniffing at everything she encounters!

An emerald green butterfly flies in and hovers in front of Aileen. Gently, Aileen opens her hand. The butterfly lands, her wings fluttering. Aileen tilts her head and examines the creature.

Aileen falls into the stillness that radiates from the exquisite butterfly, feeling it inside of herself, as well as all around her.

Ohh, sweet butterfly, we are the same… the same… here, now…

Aileen, who is much more, looks up. She smiles, lets the butterfly fly off and jumps to her feet. "Hellooo!" she says.

Keon loves to go for walks with his notebook and pen in his sachel. That way, at a certain point, he can just stop and write a poem, a song, or continue with his favourite: the Story of Stories.

Here, now, Keon is strolling through the forest. It's cool and refreshing. Mmm… Can I be happier than now? Keon chuckles and feels the connection to every Being in the forest. He glances down at the black cat who's trotting elegantly at his side.

"Ah… there she is, Bagha!" he says, his sweet brown eyes twinkling with delight. Keon, who is much more, smiles and walks directly up to his love.

The Reader looks around. Yes, there's a new sensation here, now: just like Keon and Aileen, they feel connected to everything and everyone in a new way.

But… I already miss them… and the Story…

Is this really the end of this Story? It feels as though there's more…

So… what now?

The Reader, who is much more, smiles while they read 'So… what now?' out aloud. They peer over the page to see if something magical might happen…

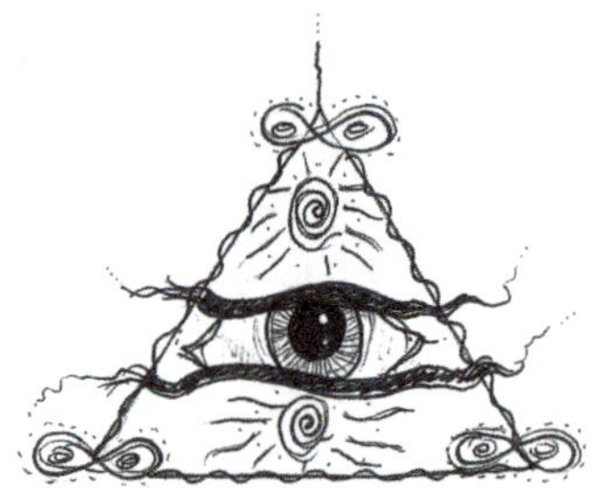

All-Seer

Reader, IASAARAASAI

I hear you.

You are right when you ask, "What now?"

I have come to announce to YOU

The answer to this question is contained in the 7th Knowing,

which is the 6th, as the 6th Knowing is the 5th

As the 5th is the 4th

As the 3rd and 4th are the 3rd.

The Promise has been fulfilled

Yet the Story of Stories has 6 Petals, and 5 have been seen.

Look, Reader, at the 12 Sacred Names of ASAIRA:

ASAIRA   ARIASA

SAIRAA   AARIAS

AIRAAS   SAARIA

IRAASA   ASAARI

RAASAI   IASAAR

AASAIR   RIASAA

Look closely...

There are 2 Names that are still unknown to us.

ARIASA and RIASAA.

It is logical, then, that the Story must continue!

The 6 that are 12

Are

Here

Now

Turn the page and see what is revealed...

Ha! Ha! Ha!

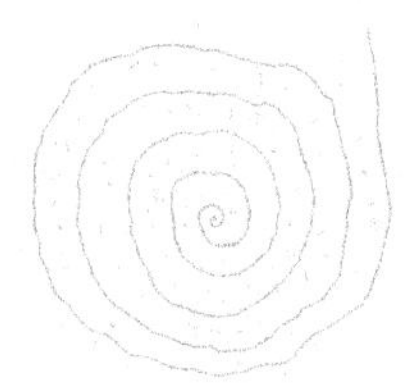

Rest and Ready Yourselves

Children of the One Light

For the 7ᵗʰ

Is Your Calling

Is Your Living

Here

Now

Heaven On Earth

ASAIRA
The
One Heart
In Each Heart
ASAIRA AM

THE END & THE BEGINNING

THE 7TH KNOWING OF ASAIRA

DISCOVERING ARIASA

☆ PRELUDE ✦✦

Sacred Truths

Sacred Mirrors

Sacred Names

12 that are 6

That are 3

That are 1

That are limitless

ASAIRA

I am

ARIASA

Shows Herself

Shows Himself

Themself

Oneself

In Sublime Splendour

ARIASA

ASAIRA
AIRASA
AARIAS
SAIRAA
SAARIA
AIRAAS
ASAARI
IRAASA
IASAAR
RASAAI
RIASAA
ASAIR

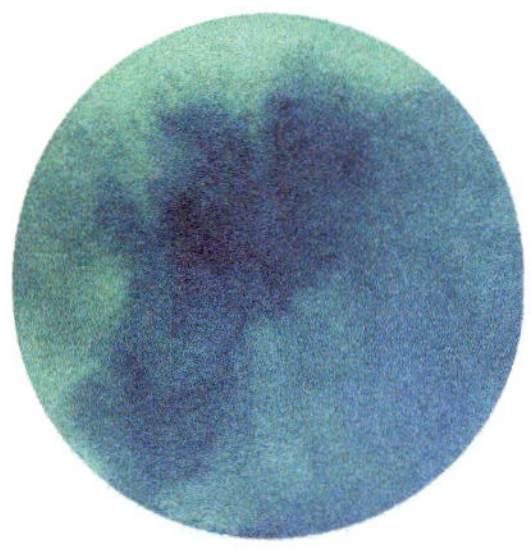

"It's happening! The Story's starting!

I just had a dream, and I heard her voice… ASAIRA's voice! She's calling…

Ahhh… my chest feels like it's exploding…

The Eagle wings open…

Pinks and oranges and sky-blues fill my senses… Mmmm…

AIRAAS! AASAIR! Sister, Brother… Can you hear me?"

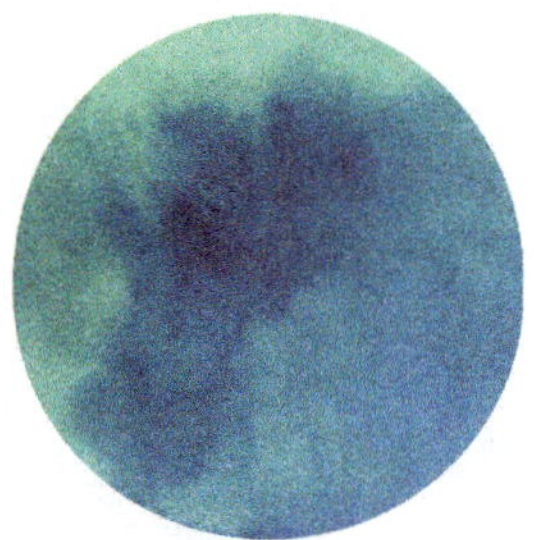

"Keon!

Chocolate Eyes… sweetie…

Wake up!"

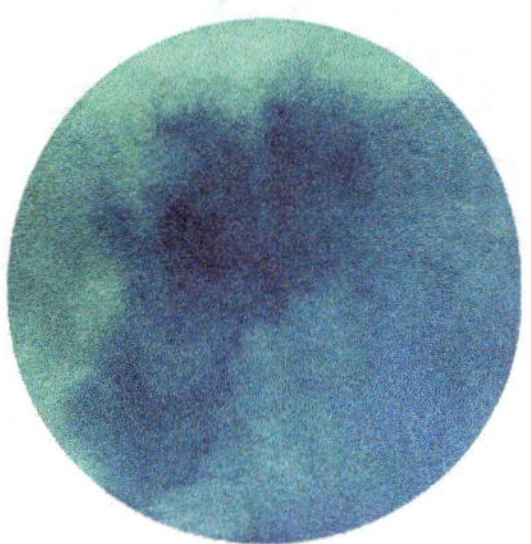

"I know!

The Story is happening again! IASAARAASAI is calling us."

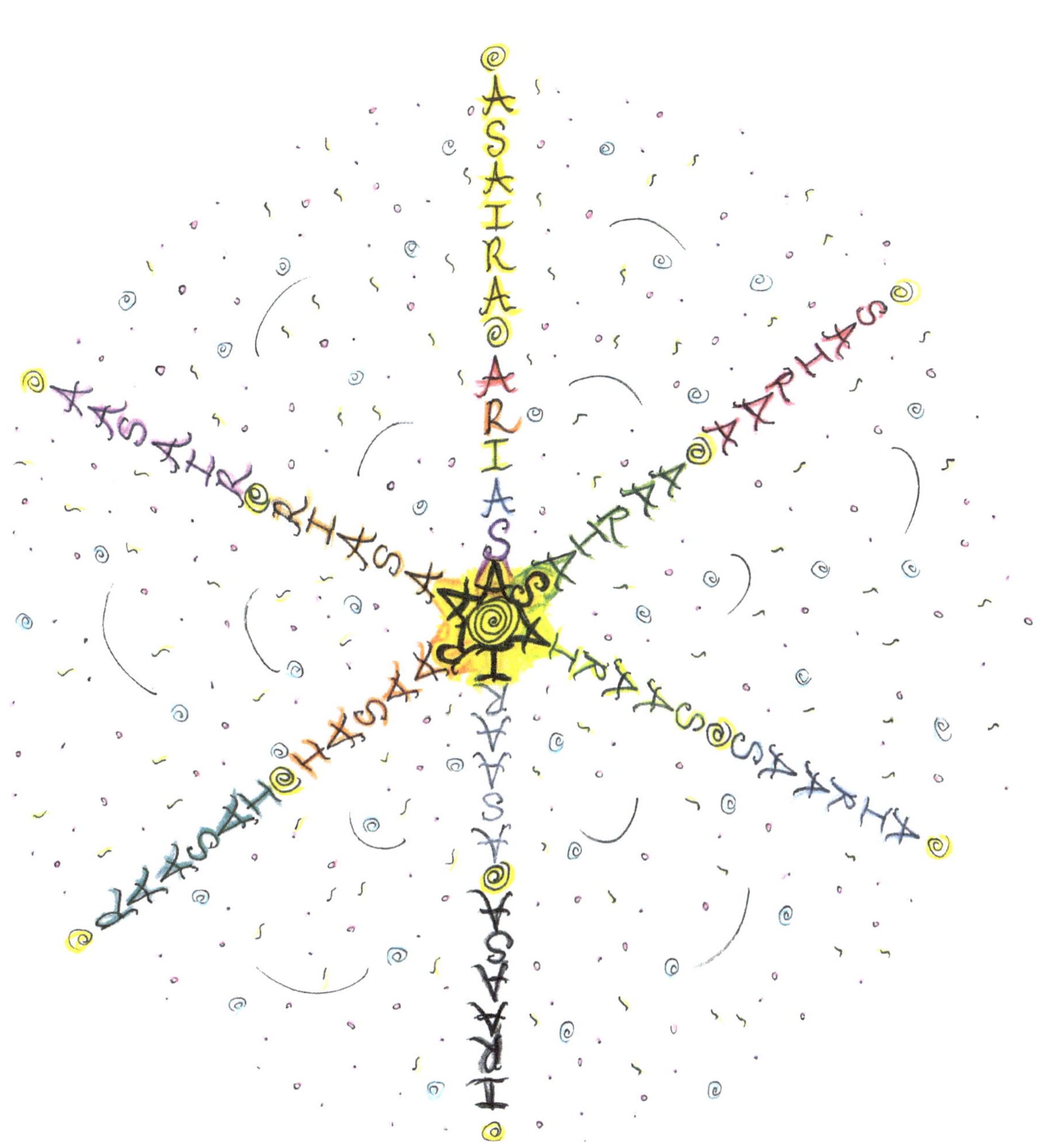

☆ PRELUDE 2 ✦

Hear the sounds that accompany ASAIRA's words:

Long deep slow bellows from the Tibetan Long Horn, the Dung-Chen.

It is a multitude of dung-chens

sounding together.

Yes, imagine elephants singing,

or the deep oceans moaning...

I walk in slow step

Over the Stars of the Universe

My Enormity

Has no description

My Moves, no trace

For it is the Slowness

Of Pure Stillness

Invisible & Transparent

Yet Real & Solid

I walk

Through the Worlds

My Womb, KOAA's Abode

Such Open Love

Such Motherly Fierceness

As the Children of the One Light

Are born and re-born

I walk

Over the Space of Spaces

And the Trumpets Sound

To my Foreboding Presence

ARIASA

***ASAIRA** Am*

Hear Ye, Hear Ye!

I am the Announcer

The Herald,

The Town-Crier & The Earth-Crier!

She is arrived

Discover Her!

I am the Herald,

Messenger of the Void

My Loud Voice

Is the Silent Message.

♫ Hark, the Herald Angels Sing[28]

Glory to the New Born King

And

Glory to the New Born Queen!

Peace on Earth and Mercy Mild

God and Sinners Reconciled ♫

---

28 The Story Speaks

These words are the lyrics of a famous Christmas carol from
the Earth Realm. They were written by Charles Wesley in
England in 1739. The sentence 'And Glory to the new Born
Queen' has been added by the Herald, Messenger of the Void.

Can you hear the Roaring of the Trumpet of Truth?

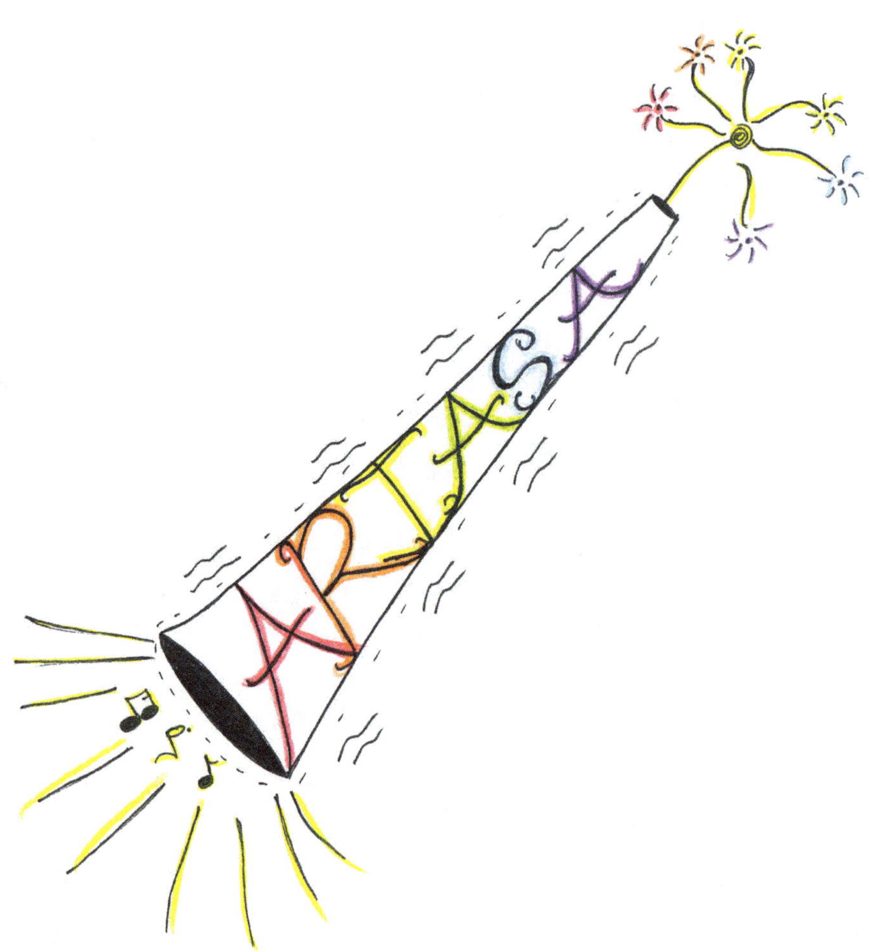

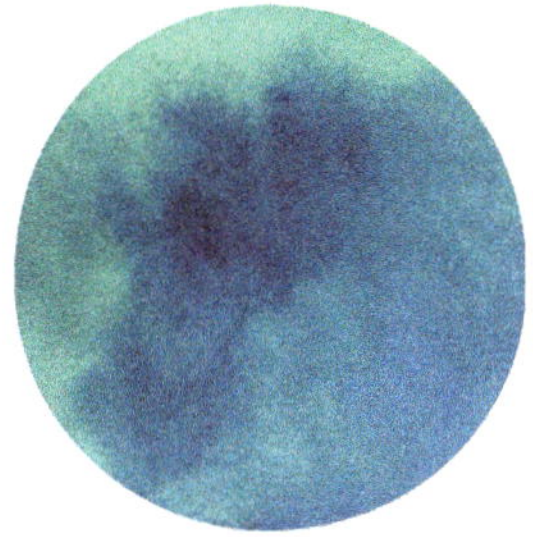

"Yes!

It's all about living our lives from what we know now.

ARIASA.
Discovering you!
Living YOU!

The 6 that are 12 that are 18 that are 24 that are 30 that are 36 that are 42 that are 48 that are 54 that are 60 that are 66 that are 72 that are 78 that are 84 that are 96 that are… unlimited! They all want to flower, to bloom and bloom!

ASAIRA, Mother

Here is your servant, Aileen

I'm ready to discover

Discover whatever is needed

To live in this world

In service to YOU

I humbly invite the Guardians and Gatekeepers

To accompany me!

I'm so grateful

For the Story of Stories

Discovering YOU

Living YOU"

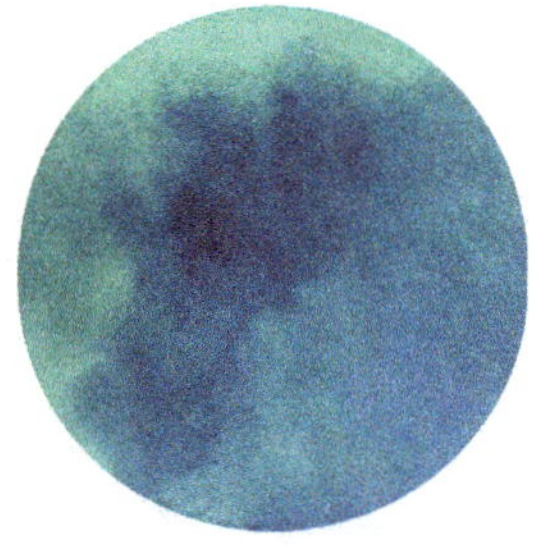

"That's it!

I can write my own story, too!
I can be the Reader, the Storyteller, the Light Bearer… all in one!

I'm going to make this happen right now. I want to see Aileen and Keon again!

My name is IASAARAASAI

Sacred is this name

I ask for help

Something is to be discovered

Maybe this is the discovery

Knowing I can ask to be here

I close my eyes

I feel the soft wind

I hear the sweet singing

A harp playing

I remember the Heavens

As my wings open

RAASAI the Eagle

Guardian of the Stem

The Stem…

Thank you, ASAIRA!

Yes!"

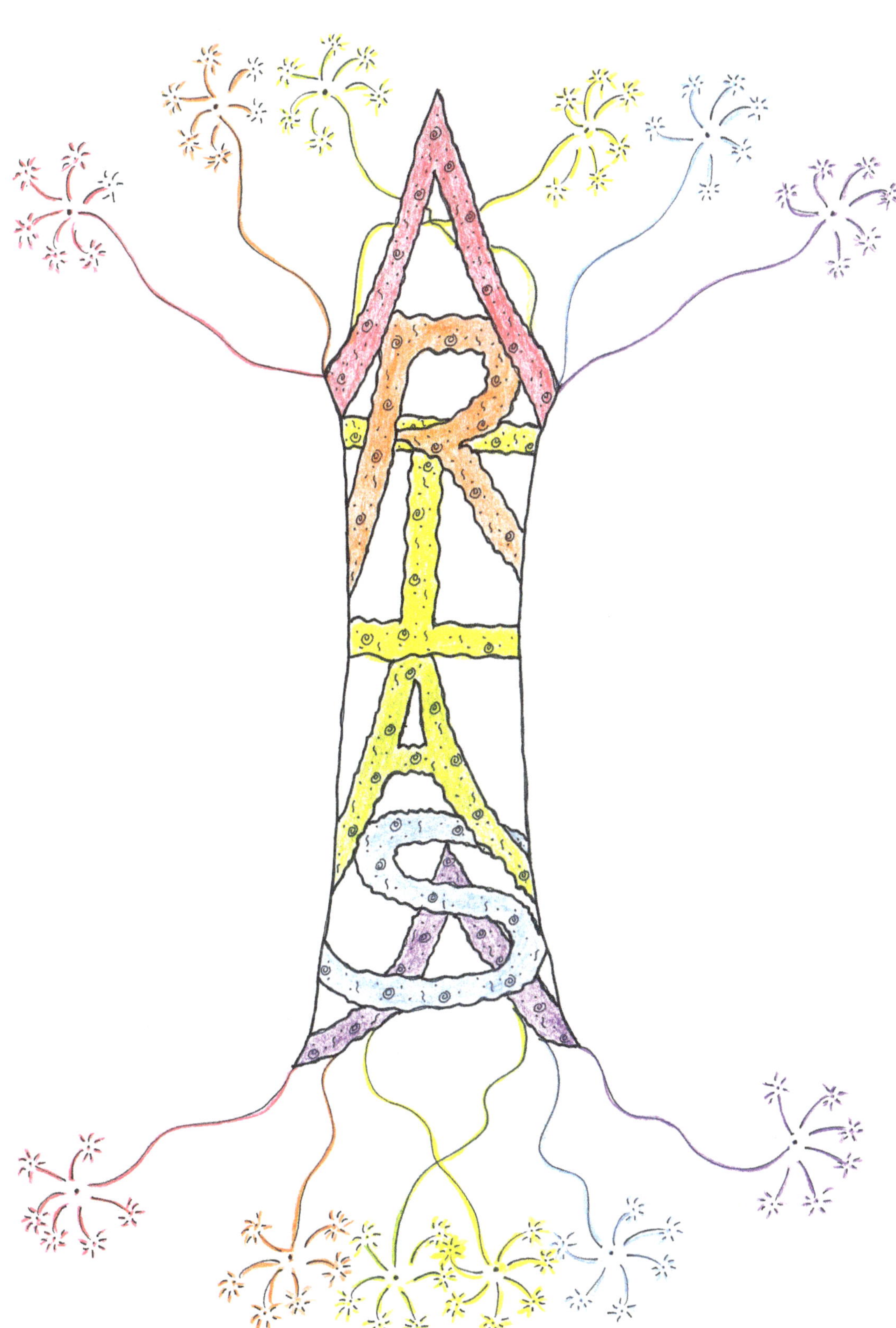

PART 1

The Six Paths to ARIASA: The Rainbow Paths

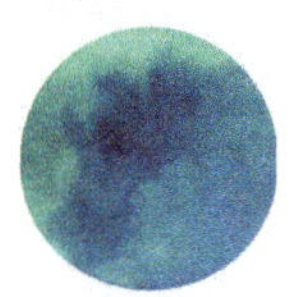

The 1ˢᵗ Path: The Path of Spain

AASAIR: Keon

Keon sabía que se le daban bien los idiomas. Tenía la sensación que podría escribir en cualquier lengua, antigua o nueva, si se lo proponía.

Ahora Aileen y él viajaban en dirección a un país lejano que se llamaba España. En principio, Keon no recordaba haber estado ahí, pero al mismo tiempo, sabía que estaba íntimamente ligado a ese país a través de los tiempos y otras vidas. Tanto era así, que a medida que se acercaba a su destino, la lengua española empezó a llenar su corazón y le salían poesías de amor con ese sabor que sólo podía tener el español.

Keon sonrío y se entregó plenamente a las palabras y las sensaciones. Cogió el bolígrafo y se puso a escribir una de las poesías que daba vueltas alrededor de él.

The Story Translates

AASAIR: Keon

Keon knew he was good at languages. He had the sensation that he could write in any language, ancient or new, if he put his mind to it.

Now he and Aileen were travelling towards a distant country called Spain. In truth, Keon couldn't remember having been there, but at the same time, he knew he was intimately tied to that country through time and other lives. This was so much the case that as he got nearer to his destination, the Spanish language began to fill his heart, and poems of love came out with that flavour only Spanish could have.

Keon smiled and gave himself fully to the words and sensations. He took a pen and started to write down one of the poems that was spinning around him.

El Pregonero

Aquí Estoy

El Pregonero de los Tiempos

Sin Tiempo

Camino lentamente

Sólido y Contundente

Pregona la Noticia

La Noticia más Bella

Más Exquisíta

Que se haya recibido

Oíd, Oíd

Mi Mensaje es Sagrado

Y Disponible

Pregono la Presencia

Pregona la Llegada

Pregono que Siempre

Ha estado Aquí

Ella que es Él

La Flor que es el Tallo

El Árbol que es el Tronco

ARIASA que es RIASAA

The Story Translates

The Town-Crier

Here I am

The Town-Crier of the Ages

Without Time

I walk slowly

Solidly & In Full Force

I announce the News

The most Beautiful and

Most Exquisite of News

That has ever been received

Hear ye, Hear ye

My Message is Sacred

And Available

I announce the Presence

I announce the Arrival

I announce that

She that is He

The Flower that is the Stem

The Tree that is the Trunk

ARIASA that is RIASAA

Has always been Here

IASAARAASAI

mmm… relaxing… sat here in sun… can't keep eyes open… body and whiskers vibrate and sing… mmm… duermo ahora…[29]

29 The Story Speaks

IASAARAASAI has spoken in Spanish, too: 'duermo ahora' means 'fall asleep now'.

Aileen was sitting next to Keon on the plane. She glanced at him… he was busy writing. She smiled as she took out her own notebook and a pencil. Aileen knew she had to draw the tree that had appeared in a dream. In the dream, the tree was bearing jewel-fruits… A Tree of Purple Jewels!

When Aileen finished drawing, a question, snake-like, wrote itself around the Tree.

Trembling, Aileen tasted the question as it fell onto her lips.

Yes, I do!

PART 2

The Six Paths to ARIASA: The Rainbow Paths

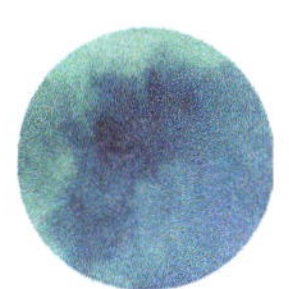

The 2ⁿᵈ Path: The Path of France

AIRAAS: Evelyn

Evelyn had been having incredible dreams lately. Some were recurrent, always about enormous flowers with thick stems that drove themselves into the earth. Fascinated, Evelyn couldn't stop drawing these gigantic flower Beings, feeling them to be some sort of sign.

One night, Evelyn had had a vivid dream where he found himself roaming the corridors and rooms of an ancient castle. The whole building was draped in a languid greyness that smelled of dust and damp. The tall ceilings made him feel small, and a sense of desolation shivered through his body. Evelyn had tried to open the shabby, dark curtains and let the sun in, but the curtains would not budge.

When Evelyn woke up, he knew that the castle and the flowers were connected.

But what did it all mean?

IASAARAASAI

mmm… delicious smell… can't resist… going see… mmm… strong smell… aime courir…[30]

---

30 The Story Speaks

IASAARAASAI now uses the French language: 'aime courir' means 'love running'.

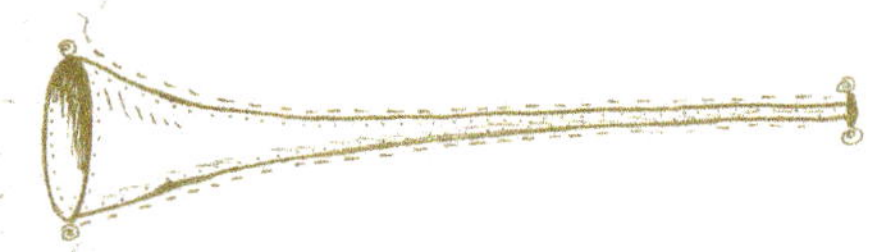

Le Crieur Public

Écoutez-Moi

Citoyens du Monde

C'est le Moment

Oui!

Ne fermez pas les yeux

Elle est arrivée

Oui!

C'est Elle!

Mais Elle est

Si genéreuse

Elle est le Corps Fémenin

Qu'inclut le Corps Masculin!

♫ Frère Jacques,

Frère Jacques

Dormez-vous?

Dormez-vous?

Sonnez les matines!

Sonnez les matines!

Ding, Dang, Dong!

Ding, Dang, Dong! ♫

The Story Translates

The Town-Crier

Hear me

Citizens of the World

It's Time

Yes!

Don't close your eyes

She has arrived

Yes!

It's Her!

But She is

So generous

She is the Feminine Body

Which includes the Masculine Body!

♫ Brother Jack,

Brother Jack

Are you sleeping?

Are you sleeping?

Ring the Morning Prayer Bells!

Ring the Morning Prayer bells!

Ding, Dang, Dong!

Ding, Dang, Dong! ♫

Jeanne avait toujours voulu voyager à la Normandie. Depuis l'enfance, elle a senti une attraction pour les histoires excitantes des Normands et des Anglais.

En fait, ces histoires avaient été l'inspiration qu'elle a necesité pour devenir écrivaine.

Jeanne regardait par la fenêtre du train. Soudain, elle s'est sentie transportée au Moyen Age et ses châteaux.

Juste à ce moment, un poème lui est apparu et, rapidement, Jeanne l'a écrit dans son petit livre vert.

The Story Translates

AASAIR: Jeanne

Jeanne had always wanted to travel to Normandy. Since her childhood, she'd felt an attraction for the exciting stories about the Normans and the English.

In fact, these stories had been the inspiration that she'd needed to become a writer.

Jeanne was looking out of the window of the train. Suddenly, she felt transported to the Middle Ages and its castles.

Just at that moment, a poem came to her, and quickly, Jeanne wrote it down in her little green book.

PART 3

The Six Paths to ARIASA: The Rainbow Paths

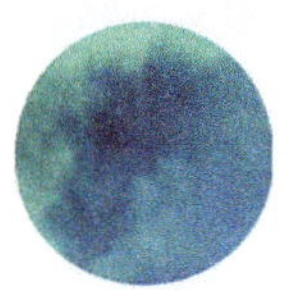

The 3rd Path: The Path of England

Lily is five years old. She's in the garden. She's crouched under the apple tree. Her eyes sparkle as she looks at something in the grass amidst the blades of grass and the primroses. Lily giggles and moves her head forward, closer.

The Ancient Trumpet Sounds! Imagine a long, dark, penetrating tone, repeated again and again...

AIRAAS: Helen Rose-Hip
Lily
INSAAR:
Helen observes the child of the Wingless called Lily and gently flaps her rainbow wings. Lily comes closer. Helen laughs, flying right in front of Lily's eyes, curious to meet one of the Wingless, very few of the Wingless destined to see her tribe.

RAASAIR: Jack Lavender-Sprig
IASAAR
Jack recognised Lily the moment he saw her. Excited, he flew up to her rosy-cheeked face, saying the ancient name of IASAAR. Jack even articulated words in the Wingless language, but Lily just stared at him with glee and tried to catch him!

The Town-Crier
Hark! I bring Good Tidings
Tidings of Reconciliation
Of Peace & Mercy Mild!
The King bows to the Queen
She opens her arms to Him
The QKween IS!
ARIASA
RIASAA
Hear All Hearts!

RAASAI: Sparrow
mmm... warm on branch... smell of summer apples... nice being sparrow... ooh, IASAAR little girl... see through her eyes too... she not know she INSAAR not see me... oh, Rainbow Beings... helloo... hello... hellooo...

The Stem
Am I
As I Am the Petals
As I Am the Core
As I Am the Leaves
As I Am the Sweet
Pollen As I Am
The One True Flower
Feel my Presence
In
The Heart
of
Hearts

☆⋆ PART 4 ⋆☆

The Herald, Messenger of the Void

An intense fanfare of trumpets and horns!

And can you hear the pealing of hundreds of church bells?

A smell of pine and cedar incense burning.

ASAIRA is ARIASA

as

ARIASA is RIASAA

They are 4

That are 6

That are 12

That are

One!

Hear ye, Hear ye!

I come to Herald

The Six Knowings

That include the 7th

As the 7th is the 6th

The 6th is the 7th

The Stem upholds the Flower

For ARIASA and RIASAA to Be

The Stem is the 7th Arrow of Love

That lifts the 6th, the 6-Petalled Flower

Into her Gloriousness

ARIASA contains RIASAA

As ASAIRA contains All

Let the Stem of Groundedness that was separated

Penetrate in Full Completeness

ASAIRA am!

☆* PART 5 **

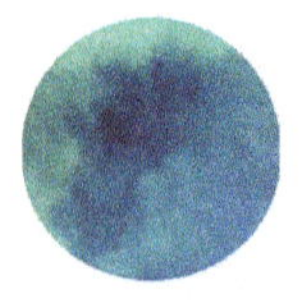 **AIRAAS on the First Three Paths of the Rainbow** 

Spain 

Aileen is dreaming of her grandmother, not of Becca, but her grandmother on her mother's side.

Is it really you, Grandma? I've only ever seen you in a photo… Is my mum with you? Mia?

Aileen's grandmother smiles and opens one of her palms. There, six purple stones shine in glittering expectancy. "Take them, Aileen."

Aileen's hand reaches out, shaking a little, and places each purple stone, one by one, into a silver locket hanging from her neck.

Suddenly, the word 'Violet' spirals around Aileen's head; her body sways. Violet… Violet… Violet is your name, Grandma… Aileen lifts her face upwards: bright red poppies rain on her, engulfing her in a sweet-scented violet and poppy universe. Mmmm…

Just before Aileen wakes up, she hears her Grandmother Violet say with a chuckle, "You have to pop by some time and have a cup of tea, my dear!"

France 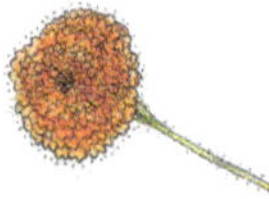

Evelyn couldn't really express all the things that had happened to him in the last couple of years. He often described it as 'a change of dimension'. It was like he could see and hear more, as if his senses wanted to gobble up everything they encountered!

The change in his life was fun, too, and felt natural to him. Sometimes, though, it felt like a challenge, with moments when he just needed to rest more.

But what Evelyn was most loving now was this new capacity to recall his dreams, and how they seemed to talk to him… call to him even.

England 

Helen Rose-Hip just loves the yellow primroses of her home. What she most enjoys is to fly from one primrose to another, cherishing and nurturing each one as her children.

Today Helen is lying face upwards on one of the primrose petals. Mmm… yellow softness! She closes her eyes while she hums a little ditty.

When she opens her eyes again, Helen Rose-Hip spies the Wingless Child come out of her dwelling. Ah, let's have some fun! Helen takes flight and hovers in front of the child's face, just like a hummingbird might do.

The child laughs, reaching out to grab the pretty creature, but Helen speeds away.

Lily, wingless and happy, chases Helen, winged and also happy, all around the garden.

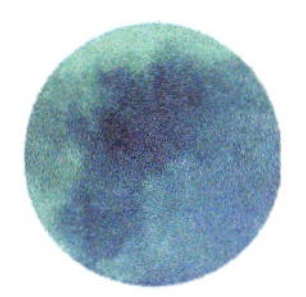 

AASAIR on the First Three Paths of the **Rainbow**

Spain

Keon se había adaptado al español totalmente. Era casi como si se hubiera olvidado del inglés por completo, tal era su pasión y comodidad en esta bella lengua española. No paraba de escribir. Con cada palabra que llegaba a la página, notaba cómo salían comprensiones nuevas y profundas.

Después, se juntaba con Aileen y los dos compartían sus escritos y dibujos, y de ahí aún surgían más comprensiones. Sentían una fuerza indestructible a medida que creaban algo nuevo y desconocido, pero siempre con ese sabor antiguo, eterno y muy familiar.

The Story Translates

Keon had become totally adapted to the Spanish. It was as though he had forgotten English completely, such was his passion and ease in this beautiful Spanish language. He couldn't stop writing. With each word that arrived on the page, he noticed how new and deep understandings would appear.

Afterwards, he joined Aileen and both shared their writings and drawings, and from there even more insights arose. They felt an indestructible force as they created something new and unknown, yet always with that ancient, eternal and very familiar flavour.

France

Jeanne est arrivée enfin! Elle est sortie du train et sans hésiter a couru pour prendre le bus.

C'était un bus très spécial parce que c'était le bus qui allait l'emmener à l'Abbaye: l'Abbaye qu'elle avait rêvé de visiter depuis l'enfance.

Jeanne avait lu tout ce qu'avait été écrit sur cet abbaye et le mont où elle se situait. Jeanne avait également vu beaucoup d'images et de photos, mais elle n'avait jamais contemplé la merveilleuse vue qui en ce moment se levait par la fenêtre du bus, "Ohhh!"

The Story Translates

Jeanne arrived at last! She got off the train and without hesitating ran to catch the bus.

This was a very special bus because it was the bus that would take her to the Abbey: the Abbey she'd dreamt about visiting ever since her childhood.

Jeanne had read everything that had been written about this abbey and the mount where it was located. Jeanne had also seen many images and photos, but she had never contemplated the wondrous view which at that moment was arising through the bus window, "Ohhh!"

England

Jack Lavender-Sprig loves Helen Rose-Hip dearly. They have had many an adventure, but he also knows there have been many other adventures he can't recall.

Sometimes, while sitting on a comfy, padded flower, Jack sings. His musical words tell of faraway lands and mysterious eras that quite fascinate all who hear him. But for Jack Lavender-Sprig it's much more. When he sings, images and names coil inside of him, and he remembers snippets of dreamy existences, of a Garden, of an exquisite butterfly and a soaring eagle.

Jack senses that he had been the Gardener who cared for the Garden, that Helen had been the Butterfly, and quite inexplicably, what Jack knows without a doubt, is that the Wingless Child and the little brown Sparrow are both the Eagle who calls itself IASAAR.

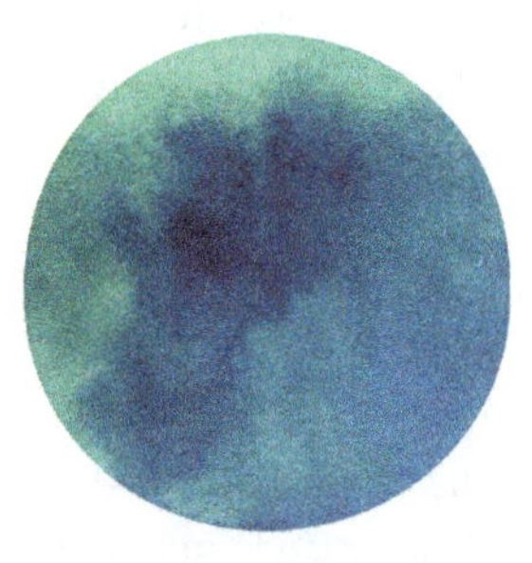

PART 6

IASAARAASAI's Recognition

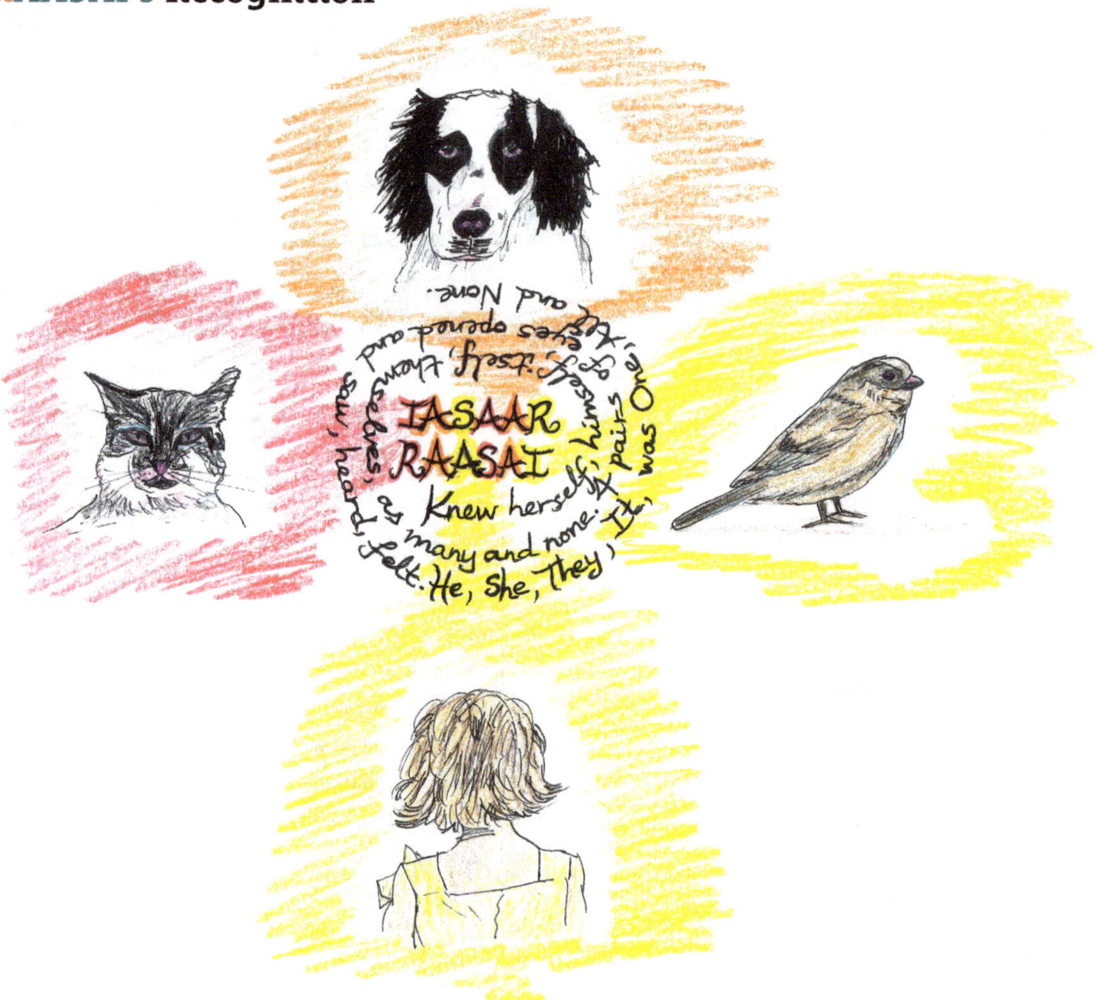

Only the little girl, Lily, was unaware that she was IASAARAASAI.

The Animal Guardians, on the other hand, knew very well

that they were different forms of IASAARAASAI.

The dog, the cat and the sparrow marvelled

as they revelled in their newly found animal talents.

And…

All 4 shared an unbounded

JOY!

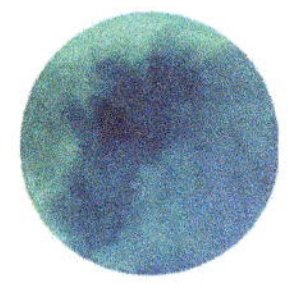 # Spain & France: A Visit from the Red Queen 

Aileen & Jeanne both woke up early noticing the rawness in their belly. It was a day where no movement was needed, no obligations were demanded, an opportunity to stay in bed and be with the body. Each woman, one in Spain, the other in France, caressed her womb area.

Aileen remembered the times she had resisted this monthly visit until she'd come to realise that every single drop of warm blood was the enactment of Life itself, of ASAIRA giving birth to all creation. Moon-like, the scarlet waters inside of her magnetised, moving in a tide of relaxation. Aileen remembered herself as SAIRAA and felt her blood sink into the Earth. Ahhh...

It was then it dawned on Aileen that ARIASA was connected to the physical body, or even that ARIASA was the body itself. With her eyes closed, Aileen whispered, "ARIASA, I'm so sorry that I rejected you throughout the ages. I'm so sorry... I love you so much... Thank you for always being here... ARIASA... ARIASA... ARIASA... You are the Queen of Queens..."

Jeanne sentait la douleur. C'était fort, mais maintenant dans sa vie quand elle sentait la douleur du cycle, c'était comme un message de l'Univers pour arrêter et pour se relaxer. L'effet de s'arrêter aidait Jeanne à sentir son corps profondément; elle avait compris beaucoup de choses et elle a commencé à se sentir plus établie et connectée à la Terre. C'était très beau, très beau... et ce moment en particulier était si doux... dans son lit ancien à l'Abbaye.

The Story Translates

Jeanne felt the pain. It was strong, but now in her life when she felt the pain of the cycle, it was like a message from the Universe to stop and relax. The effect of stopping helped Jeanne feel her body deeply; she had understood many things and began to feel more grounded and connected to the Earth. It was very beautiful, very beautiful... and this moment in particular was so sweet... in her ancient bed in the Abbey.

Evelyn saw an image of a red poppy while he sat meditating. It was so vivid he decided to draw it. As the drawing came into existence in his green notebook, the poppy showed itself wide open, revealing its black centre. The stem was alive and urged to be drawn and coloured, too! Evelyn smiled in the determined frenzy of the moment. Suddenly, another image arose. It was of a woman lying in a four poster bed in a room that reminded him of a medieval castle. A castle again! Evelyn closed his eyes and breathed. All frenzy vaporised, he let himself be transported into the still, watery space that surrounded him.

Both Jeanne & Aileen felt a shiver. Before them appeared a woman dressed in a long red velvet dress, her forehead crowned with sparkling rubies. She smiled as she handed the two women a red poppy.

"The Red Queen!" "La Reine Rouge!" said Aileen and Jeanne aloud.

Keon oyó a Aileen decir "The Red Queen" y la miró, los ojos curiosos. Se giró hacia ella, pero tuvo un irresistible impulso de ir primero a mirar en el espejo, y se levantó de la cama. Al llegar al espejo, alzó la mirada hacia el cristal: vió la imagen de miles de mujeres encadenadas de distintas edades y razas. Todas tenían la boca tapada y mirada triste. Dos palabras, 'The Bounded', explotaron en su corazón junto con una sensación urgente de querer ayudar a todas ellas, y a todo cautivo. La imagen desapareció. Keon se sintió en un bosque antiguo. Recordó ser UT, el Guerrero. Y ahí estaba UT, sonriéndole desde el espejo ¡dándole una amapola roja! Keon cerró los ojos. Al abrirlos, Aileen estaba a su lado con la amapola en las manos.

The Story Translates

Keon heard Aileen say "The Red Queen" and looked at her, his eyes curious. He turned towards her, but had an irresistible impulse to go first and look at the mirror, and he got up from bed. On arriving at the mirror, he looked up towards the glass: he saw an image of thousands of chained women of different ages and races. They all had their mouth covered and a sad look in their eyes. Two words, 'The Bounded' exploded in his heart together with an urgent sensation of wanting to help all of them, and all those imprisoned. The image disappeared. Keon felt like he was in an ancient forest. He remembered he was UT, the Warrior. And there was UT, smiling at him from the mirror, giving him a red poppy! Keon closed his eyes. On opening them, Aileen was standing next to him with the poppy in her hands.

"The Red Queen gave it to me!" said Aileen.

"Sí, ¡la Reina Roja!"[31] Keon turned and tilted his head towards Aileen.

Aileen looked into Keon's dark brown eyes. Their lips found each other's. Warm and sweet, the lips kissed, caressing, moving softly and joyfully, forever grateful for this love, a love rooted in eternity, unlimited and unbounded.

ARIASA

Is

The Temple of All Form

She

Carries me

And

I step into the World

I Am

Awed

I

Am

31 The Story Speaks

The Red Queen wishes her name to be declared in all the realms and in all the languages. Here we see her name in English, in French, 'La Reine Rouge' and in Spanish, 'La Reina Roja'.

The Herald, Messenger of the Void

Listen to the Bells ring!

They ring in all the Realms

dong

dong

dong

ARIASA
She's Here to Stay!

ARIASA

RIASAA

All is Included

In

HER MIGHT

Hear ye, Hear ye!

She has come

To set Free

The Bounded Ones

The Garden of Love

ASAIRA

is

ARIASA

Let All Be Free!

Let ARIASA Be Free!

Let the Trumpet Sound!

Let the Petals Open!

Let the Stem Grow Thick!

Let the Bounded Be Unbounded!

Let Freedom Ring!

Let Freedom Ring from All the Realms of ASAIRA![32]

Can you hear the Bells that Ring for You?

---

32 The Story Speaks

The Herald's Words seem to make reference to a speech made by
Son of ASAIRA, Martin Luther King. In the speech, the phrase
"Let freedom ring..." is repeated various times. (I Have a
Dream, 1963, in the United States of America, Earth Realm).

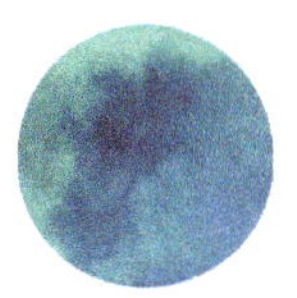 IASAARAASAI makes contact with AASAIR & AIRAAS

IASAARAASAI waited patiently outside the door. Then, magically, it opened and out came the Sun, AASAIR the Gardener.

AASAIR saw the animal's name on a little tag around its neck and said the name aloud,

"Carlitos."

"Baxter."

The man and woman's voice sounded sweet, from a lost age, each word a song that played in the cat and dog's soul.

"Que gatito tan bonito. Eres muy simpático, Carlitos. ¡Gracias por venir!"

"Oh, tu es un beau chien, mon ami. Baxter. C'est un nom anglais. Do you understand English? You're so sweet!"

The Story Translates

"What a cute little kitty. You're very friendly, **Carlitos**. Thanks for coming!"

The Story Translates

"Oh, you're a lovely dog, my friend. **Baxter**. That's an English name. Do you understand English? You're so sweet!"

Carlitos purred, Baxter wagged his tail, and IASAARAASAI revelled in the moment, in this joyful re-encounter with the beloved AASAIR.

"Aileen! Come and see who's arrived!" said Keon.

Moving in silver light, the Moon, AIRAAS the Butterfly Queen, found herself in front of IASAARAASAI, who could hardly contain their excitement.

As Aileen stroked the black and white cat called Carlitos, she laughed, turning her head up to look at Keon, while Helen Rose-Hip chuckled to see the little brown sparrow chirp and tweet at her with such insistency.

AIRAAS said,

"The 3 are back!"   "Who are you, little Sparrow?"

IASAARAASAI looked at AASAIR and AIRAAS, conscious of everything and everyone at the same time. They were 3 that were 5 that were 7 that were 2 that were 1. Then IASAARAASAI meowed, barked and chirped with some added enthusiasm!

PART 9

The Six Paths to ARIASA: The Rainbow Paths

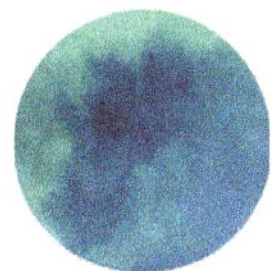

The 5th Path: The Path of the Bounded

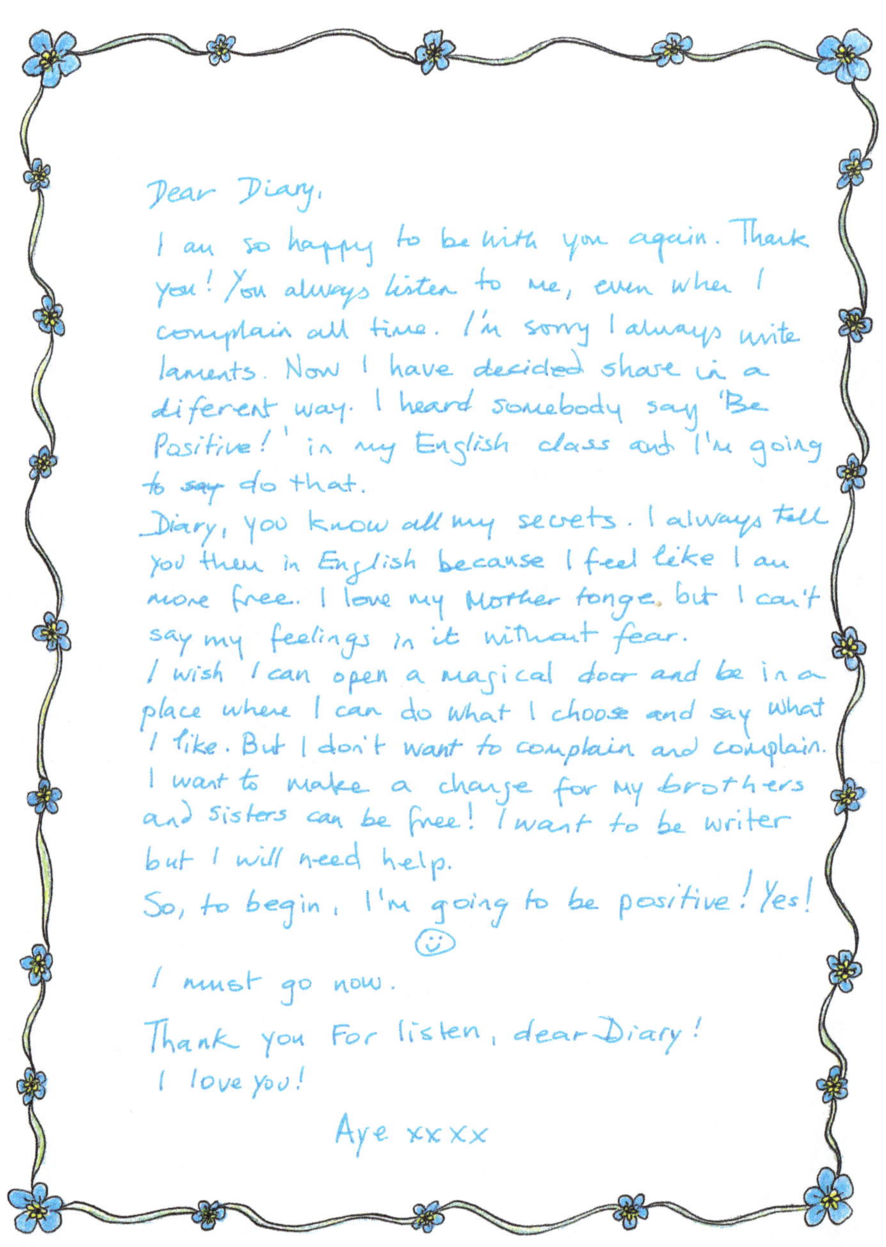

Dear Diary,

I am so happy to be with you again. Thank you! You always listen to me, even when I complain all time. I'm sorry I always write laments. Now I have decided share in a diferent way. I heard somebody say 'Be Positive!' in my English class and I'm going to ~~say~~ do that.

Diary, you know all my secrets. I always tell you them in English because I feel like I am more free. I love my Mother tonge, but I can't say my feelings in it without fear.

I wish I can open a magical door and be in a place where I can do what I choose and say what I like. But I don't want to complain and complain. I want to make a change for my brothers and sisters can be free! I want to be writer but I will need help.

So, to begin, I'm going to be positive! Yes!

I must go now.

Thank you For listen, dear Diary!
I love you!

Aye xxxx

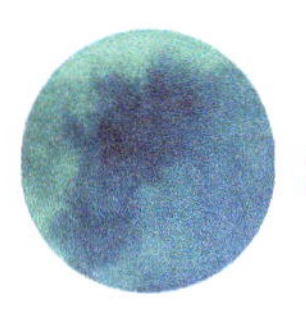 

Spain, France, England **and** The Bounded

Aileen **&** Evelyn woke up with images of handwriting and light blue flowers. Both had the sense of having been writing in a diary, but at the same time, everything was distant and far away… someone else's existence.

A young girl's face materialised. For one second the face was clear, then it became a blur, shadows enveloping the features, losing themselves in a fog.

Somewhere to his right, Evelyn heard the echo of a foghorn, followed by the whisper of a woman saying, "The Bounded…"

Helen Rose-Hip had also had the same dream of writing in a diary, but it made little sense to her. She usually dreamt of flowers, so the paper with pale blue ones rang true to her. There was curiosity, though, arising at not recognising the flowers.

Her heart full of mysterious little blue flowers, Helen flew off the primrose she had been sleeping on. The air felt fresh, waking her up completely. Helen flew on, enjoying the crispy air against her face, when she noticed a twinge in her chest area. She stopped to rest on a branch. Closing her eyes, she kept still, all her attention placed on the burning sensation in her heart.

Suddenly, Helen saw five blue words: 'I will need help' together with what looked like a name, 'Aye'.

Ohh, I understand now, Helen thought.

The Herald of the Void

The foghorn sounds again and again

Also a bell ringing...

KOAA, Whale Mother, is singing... Can you hear her?

Hear this!
Imprisoned I cannot Be
I am
Free Always
And yet
The Door of the Tower
Wishes to open
For ARIASA
Open the Tower Door
For there can Be
No Tower without the Flower
No Flower without a Stem

Listen!
Listen!
Listen!
I am the Herald
I am the Heralded
I am the Message!

ARIASA
Is
Here
The Tower Door is Open!
Fly out little bird
The Flowers bloom
The Petals sparkle
In Divine Recognition
Hear ye!
Hear ye!
Hear ye!

I am

The Flower

The Invisible Presence

ASAIRARIASA

The Truth is Mirrored

Six million times fold

Seven trillion times fold

Eternal & Unbounded

The Flower

I am

The Rainbow of Colours

I am

The Manifold Hues of the One

Flower

I am

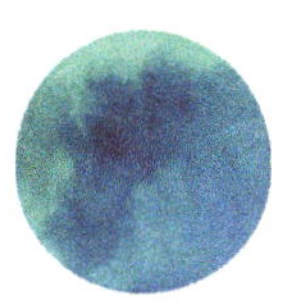

PART 10

IASAARAASAI dreams of the Four Paths of the Rainbow that are Five

Path 1: The Red Poppy of Spain

Aileen and *Keon* are driving up a winding road. I feel myself meow while I peek out of a basket in the back seat of the car. The narrow road takes us higher and higher up the mountain. An old castle sits perched at the very top. It feels like the castle is waiting for us.

Aileen turns and strokes my head. "Carlitos," *she says.*

I purr… nice to feel her warm hand…

Ohhh, what's that feeling? A gloomy energy in the air… I make a drawn-out meow, and my tail twitches.

The castle emerges in full view. Keon gasps. The castle is small and in bad condition, but what sucks the breath out of us is the tower.

The car stops. The 3 of us sit in silence. The Tower demands attention, an attention the Tower feels is long, long due.

Path 2: The Orange Marigold of France

Jeanne is walking in the grounds of the abbey… with me!

I observe my paws and the way they move. How big and solid they are! I look up at Jeanne, stop and sit down on my hind legs as she crouches down to speak to me.

"Ah, Baxter, regarde les fleurs oranges! Ils sont si beaux ces soucis! Comme toi! Mmm… Je t'adore, Baxter!"

The Story Translates

"Ah, Baxter, look at those orange flowers!
They're so beautiful those marigolds! Just like you!
Mmm... I adore you, Baxter!"

Mmmm…! I adore you, too, AASAIR!

I rise to my feet and bolt towards the marigolds as fast as I can. Such fun! A pungent scent of musk invades my senses. Mmmm!

I stop and turn around. Heavy fear is entering my nostrils and brain. Looming over the abbey is a black cloud that feels very frightening, but then the cloud transforms into a vision of the Tower of RAASAI. And the Four Guardians, Saul, Shimmera, Silas and Smanara are flying around the Tower!

I look again at the marigold field and see the Moon of Moons, AIRAAS, walk towards us, but here AIRAAS is a man of about forty years old.

"Evelyn!" I spurt out, but it sounds like a bark.

Path 3: The Yellow Primrose of England

Helen Rose-Hip and *Jack Lavender-Sprig are holding hands as they hover in the air right in front of the Wingless Child.*

I jump up gleefully to see the tiny flying people again.

Oh... the little man, what's he saying?

"You are the Eagle!" he says again.

Then I'm in the sky, flying high above, soaring and circling. "Of course I am!"

Suddenly, I feel myself sing loud cheep cheeps, and I know I'm the Sparrow. I look down below and search for my children. That's how it feels... I have children to look out for.

There they are! Helen, Jack and myself: Lily, the apparently Wingless Child.

Path 5: The Blue Flower of The Bounded

I'm looking in the mirror. I'm a young girl, a teenager maybe. Mmm... what lovely black hair...

I touch the silky blue dress I wear. The colour is exquisite: an aquamarine blue that shimmers in silver waves.

I close my eyes, and I hear the eerie beauty of the call of the Whale Mother. "KOAA..." I say.

When I open my eyes again, a dark denseness is howling around me... Aaah... there are visions of people inside the darkness... it's like a whining wind of non-stop images: sad women in thick heavy gowns, children's faces strewn with tears, a bear in chains forced to dance, desperate men that look out of minute windows of stone towers... my stomach starts to ache.

Then a trumpet sounds! It brings a brilliant light of seven rainbow colours which dissipate all the sad faces. The colours are alive and sing like a chorus of angels!

Free the Bounded!

Free the Towers for the Stems to flower!

The Flowers of ARIASA are We

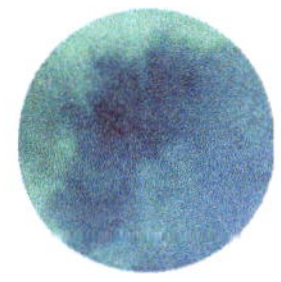

Wow! What a dream! Like four dreams in one!

Just a sec…

I'm back here.

I'm the Reader, but I'm telling the Story, too… I think! But although I can see a lot from different perspectives, it's not quite the same this time. In a sense, I feel like I'm telling the Story because I'm everywhere… But I don't know what's coming next… or what the 4th Path is? Or the 6th.

So why am I back here again, then?

I'm getting distracted!

Wait, I can hear something…

It's the Herald!

Hear the Trumpet of Ages

The Notes of Rainbow Colours are

The Paths to ARIASA

No Paths and All Paths

Stems of Radiant Melodious Colour

The Six Knowings were made of Five

The 3rd & 4th could not be without the Other

As the 6th Path cannot be without the 7th

Nor the 6th Knowing without the 7th

For 6 are 7 that are 5 that are 6

In the same manner

The Promise Fulfilled

Could not be until the Promise was Remembered

As the Knowing Fulfilled

Cannot be until the Knowing is Lived

ARIASA discovered is ARIASA lived

Is RIASAA joined to ARIASA

The Tower cold and lonely

Returned to the Flower

The Rightful Stem

Green & Warm

Flowering & Alive

Petals of a trillion billion Hues

Rainbow Colours of ASAIRA

Mirrored in All

The One True Path

Hear the Angels' Voices Sing

Rejoice! Rejoice!

Pregono la Presencia de ARIASA

¡Oíd, Hijos de la Una Luz!

Écoutez-Moi

Citoyens du Monde![33]

Hear me in All Tongues

For

I am

You!

---

33 The Story Speaks

These first two lines are in Spanish: 'I announce
the Presence of ARIASA. Hear Ye, Children of
the One Light!' and the 3rd and 4th lines are in
French: 'Hear me Citizens of the World!'

☆★ PART 11 ★☆

 ## The 4th Path of the Rainbow:
The Path of the Golden Greenness 

The Eagle soared over the Six Paths of the Seven Colours of the Rainbow Stem,
the Multicoloured Tower of RIASAA.
ARIASA that was ASAIRA, upheld by the solidity of RIASAA,
bloomed in unabashed Fullness.

The Eagle knew itself as the Guardian of the Stem.
In awe, IASAARAASAI observed all,
realising they were flying over the Coloured Pathways of Life itself,
ASAIRA Am.

IASAARAASAI circled over the 4th Path, mesmerized by the Goldness that
rippled into Greenness and swirled into a sparkling Turquoise.
A Sea of Golden Greenness!

The 4th Path launched itself up and spiralled across the other pathways.
Penetrating and merging, now a Serpent of Golden Greenness,
it dove in and out of the Rainbow Ocean.

The Eagle flew, too, in coiling whirlpool motion,
letting itself be sucked into the Vortex.
Any identity left inside of IASAARAASAI churned itself away into
the Colours of the Rainbow.

This was the Confluence where all paths are One,
yet held and moved by the Greenness, the 4th Path,
which had always been and is

THE GOLDEN HEART OF THE STEM.

The 4th One

The Greenness

That is Goldness

Serpentines its Sacred Way

To the Others

Intertwining the Gold

With the Red, Orange, Yellow & Blue

When this is seen

The 6th & the 7th

Shall shine their Violet Hue

And with this

The Diamond of the One True Colour

ARIASA Discovered

Shows her Awesome Luminous Face

The 3 are always One

As they Walk this World

ASAIRA

Am

☆★ *PART 12* ★★

The Six Paths to ARIASA: The Rainbow Paths

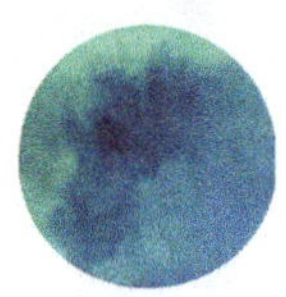

The 5th Path: The Blueness of the Bounded

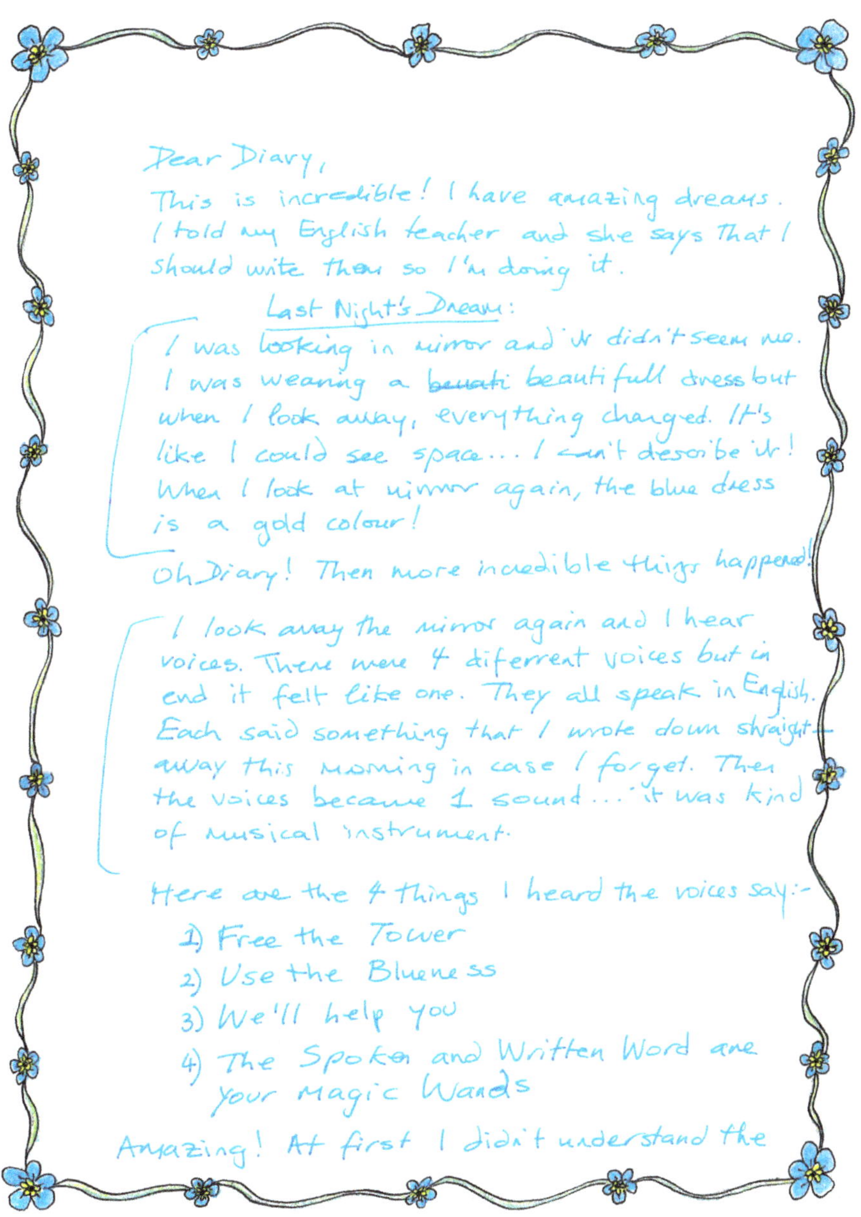

Dear Diary,

This is incredible! I have amazing dreams. I told my English teacher and she says That I should write them so I'm doing it.

Last Night's Dream:

I was looking in mirror and it didn't seem me. I was wearing a ~~beauti~~ beautifull dress but when I look away, everything changed. It's like I could see space... I can't describe it! When I look at mirror again, the blue dress is a gold colour!

Oh Diary! Then more incredible things happened!

I look away the mirror again and I hear voices. There were 4 diferrent voices but in end it felt like one. They all speak in English. Each said something that I wrote down straight-away this morning in case I forget. Then the voices became 1 sound... it was kind of musical instrument.

Here are the 4 things I heard the voices say:-

1) Free the Tower
2) Use the Blueness
3) We'll help you
4) The Spoken and Written Word are your Magic Wands

Amazing! At first I didn't understand the

word 'Wands'. I looked up it and, yes, like Wizards! Diary, I can only use English to say what is happening to me! This dream and others is a message. I feel like I'm other person more old and wise. I see things understand things that I ~~do~~ didn't understand before. And while I write now, something strange is happening ~~&~~ I feel like I'm flying throuhg the sky! So free! And now I see, yes, an eagle! An eagle that carrys, wait let me look up the word, yes, ribbons! An eagle with ribbons around its neck, 7 ribbons of differfent colours!

I don't know what this means but I'm so happy. I know the message is good and I accept the Voices help. I don't understand 'Free the Tower or the Blueness' but I know that English is my Magic Wand!

(Suddenly I have idea: may be my English Teacher can help me?? Will she think that I am crazy?!)

Thank you for listen, dear Diary! I love you!

Aye xxxx
☺

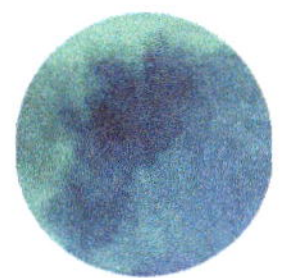

The 1st, 2nd & 3rd Paths:

El Pregonero
Le Crieur Public Speak
The Town-Crier

 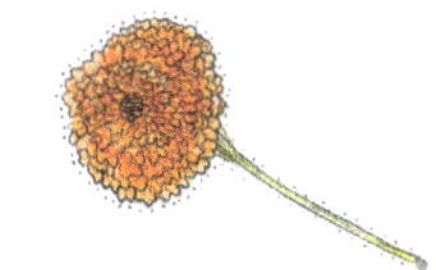 

¡Oíd!	Écoutez-Moi!	Hear ye!
¡Oíd!	Écoutez-Moi!	Hear ye!
Las ataduras limitantes	Les liens limitants	The limiting bonds
se caen	tombent	fall
Las viejas torres	Les vieilles tours	The old towers
se derrumban	s'écroulent	crumble
A medida que ELLA ve	Comme ELLE voit	As SHE sees
Él/Ella/Yo/Ellas/Ellos/	Il/Elle/Je/Elles/Ils/	He/She/It/I/They/
Tú/Vosotros/Vosotras/	Tu/Vous/	You/
NOSOTRAS/NOSOTROS vemos	NOUS voyons	WE see
ARIASA es y está	ARIASA est	ARIASA is
Aquí para quedarse!	Ici pour y rester!	Here to stay!

The 4th Path Speaks

See me everywhere

I am in all paths

I am the Heart of Paths

Healing & Strengthening

Is my Golden Greenness

I bring the Gold

To grow in Greenness

And sparkle in Turquoise Blue

Oh, the Goldness that gives Life

To every path!

See me everywhere

And follow my glittering trail

AASAIR gives and receives the Message to be Heard

Keon se acercó a la ventana. Aileen, Carlitos y él estaban en una casita rural a las afueras de un pueblo. Ahora Aileen y Carlitos dormían. Desde la ventana se veía el castillo en ruinas, y su torre que parecía mirar con desdén hacía el pueblo. La noche estaba iluminada por la luna llena que descansaba en un cielo estrellado. Keon se quedó himnotizado por la enormidad y la belleza de la luna. Cerró los ojos y respiró hondamente.

Jeanne regardait la lune merveilleuse dans le ciel. Oh, comme était belle! Derrière Jeanne dormait un homme mysterieux, mais semblait le connaître depuis toujours. Au pied du lit dormait Baxter, le chien. Jeanne a souri en pensant que les deux étaient des hommes qui étaient apparu «out of the blue» et maintenant ils étaient là dans sa chambre! Jeanne regarda la lune de nouveau et, en sentant les doux parfums que la nuit offrait, ferma les yeux.

The Story Translates

Keon went up to the window. Aileen, Carlitos and he were staying in a cottage on the outskirts of a village. Now Aileen and Carlitos were sleeping. From the window you could see the castle in ruins, and its tower that seemed to look down with contempt towards the village. The night was lit up by the full moon which was resting in a starry sky. Keon became hypnotized by the enormity and beauty of the moon. He closed his eyes and took a deep breath.

The Story Translates

Jeanne looked at the wondrous moon in the sky. Oh, how beautiful it was! Behind Jeanne slept a mysterious man, but it seemed as if she'd known him forever. At the foot of the bed slept Baxter, the dog. Jeanne smiled thinking that the two of them were men who had appeared «out of the blue» and now they were there in her bedroom! Jeanne looked at the moon again and, smelling the sweet perfumes that offered the night, closed her eyes.

Jack Lavender-Sprig took one look at the full moon with its golden-green hue and was filled with mystery. He sensed two more presences and knew it was one of those precious moments when he remembered other lands and times where he was a magical god, a Gardener of Gardeners. Jack closed his eyes and fell into the sensations: there were two energies, one female, one male. Whoosh! Jack nearly lost his balance, sucked into a whirlpool of stillness.

Six eyes that belong to three Beings open with a start.

One Voice, One Heart says, "AASAIR!"

The 3 look at each other in amazement. Jack sees he is enormous, his rainbow wings luminescent and glorious. The other man with chocolate eyes laughs while the woman's eyes become larger and larger, saying words in another language.

Jack knows he's to speak. Using the English of the Wingless that he is familiar with, his voice sounds true and loud, every word strummed in poetic song:

"I am Jack Lavender-Sprig.
I am a Winged Being from the Land of the Rainbow.
I am usually a tiny transparent creature that lives in the Yellow Primrose Path.

But I have always known I am much more.
I am AASAIR, the Gardener of True Stories, the Bard of Ancientness.
And both of You, the names Keon & Jeanne sweetly sing themselves to me,
Are also AASAIR, the Storyteller of Old.

I am here to give myself the Message to be Heard.

We are to create the 6ᵗʰ Path of the Rainbow, which in turn shall be the 7ᵗʰ.
This Path shall reveal the Bridge to ARIASA.

If your Heart knows this that I tell is true, and I see from your eyes it does,
Open your hand and take this Purple Jewel, the Violet of Violets.
3 Hands that are 6 that are 1 Flower,
3 Arms that are 6 that are 1 Stem.
In so doing, I call upon the
Lavender Essence

To come from my fingertips and to permeate the Violet,
Bringing Seven Flowers, the Seven Colours of the Rainbow,
To converge into

The 6ᵗʰ Path of the Rainbow

The Violet Path of Freedom & Lavender Healing

The Gateway to

ARIASA"

Keon abre los ojos, de vuelta a la casa rural. Su corazón late deprisa. Mira la mano y ve una violeta. Su dulce fragrancia sube y desaparece, recordando a Keon otros tiempos y otras palabras:

> *"O, it came so o'er my ear like the sweet sound*
> *that breathes upon a bank of violets,*
> *Stealing and giving odour."*[34]

The Story Translates

Keon opens his eyes, back in the cottage. His heart beats fast. He looks at his hand and sees a violet. Its sweet fragrance rises up and disappears, reminding Keon of other times and other words:

> "O, it came so o'er my ear like the sweet sound
> that breathes upon a bank of violets,
> Stealing and giving odour."

Jeanne verse des larmes qui sur sa joue semblent des perles givrées. Elle touche son coeur, son Coeur de Jardinier. Le parfum de la lavande émane de ses doigts.

The Story Translates

Jeanne sheds tears that on her cheek look like frosted pearls. She touches her heart, her Gardener's Heart. The scent from the lavender emanates from her fingers.

Jack Lavender-Sprig laughs and laughs, making frosty lavender tears broth out of his eyes. Then he sees himself fly up high into the sky and paint a rainbow of a trillion million hues across the largest full moon you have ever seen!

---

34 The Story Speaks

The Son of ASAIRA, William Shakespeare, who has visited this Story before, wrote these words in Twelfth Night, or What You Will around the year 1601 in England, Earth Realm.

Red, Orange, Yellow, Green, Blue, Lavender, Violet

7 Colours

6 Paths that are 1

Held by the Stem of the Golden Greenness

The 5 Flowers that are 6 that are 1

Bloom in Eternal Joy

The Poppy, the Marigold, the Primrose

Follow the Lavender Essence to the

Violet of Violets

But what of the Delicate Blueness?

Do you forget HER?

Ahhh…

The Bounded await your Remembrance…

But do not be afeard

I shall never forget my Children!

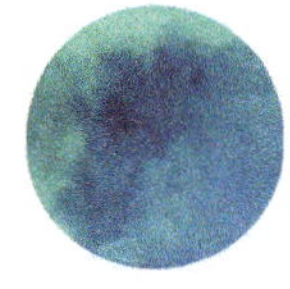

The Yellow Path brings Helen Rose-Hip
to the Blueness

Helen Rose-Hip was flying over the meadow of primroses in her usual
hummingbird fashion. The primrose yellow warmed her and made her transparent
wings tingle and glow. Ahhh… lovelyyyy…

Ohhh, what's that?! A pale blueness caught her eye.
It came from under some ferns. It rang a bell, so she
dove in to see more closely. Ohhh… The flower from
the dream… It's Aye's flower!

The flower had five pale blue petals. In the centre, there were another five golden-
yellow petals. Helen couldn't resist the sense of the primrose having become
one with the blue flower. Ohh, so pretty… She lay down in its dark green heart.
Surrounded with yellowness and blueness, Helen breathed in the delicious
moment, mmm… some powdered pollen flew up and tickled her nose, she
giggled… mmm… so nice here… let's have a nap…

Out of the blue and yellow, a flower's name sang itself loudly in the tongue of the
Wingless,

Forget-me-not!

Helen Rose-Hip's eyes had never opened so wide before! The three words which
were one pierced her ancient soul, and her eyes closed in surprised surrender.
Falling into an unbounded blue vastness inside of her, Helen felt carried in watery
air, her wings larger than the universe… Ohhhh….

A metallic sound of trumpets pierced her heart. Helen, who was much more, felt her chest break open to receive a name of ancientness,

AIRAAS!

The Being that had been Helen Rose-Hip moaned and let herself fall deeper and deeper into the sensation of floating in liquid blue when another name arose on a wave of memory,

The Sea of Seas!

The silver blue whispered to her in salty ripples:

The Sacred Names of ASAIRA, the Mother's Lullaby, slowly washed in and out…
in… and… out… in… and… out…

Ahhh…

Helen,

    AIRAAS,

        The Vastness that was All,

                fell

                  asleep.

The Forget-me-not

      closed her petals

          in pale blue

             slumber.

The 5th Path enters the Other Paths

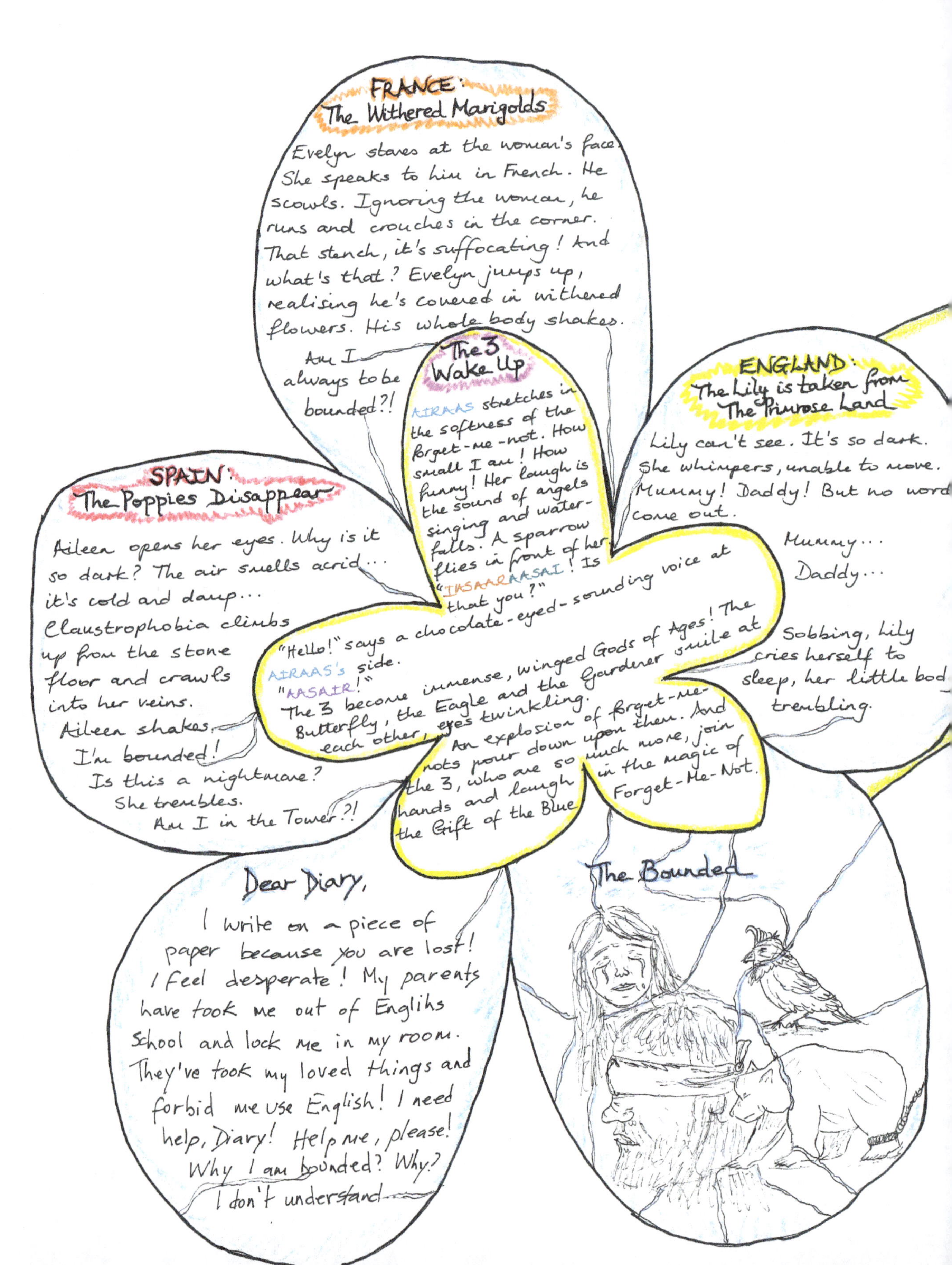

FRANCE:
The Withered Marigolds

Evelyn stares at the woman's face. She speaks to him in French. He scowls. Ignoring the woman, he runs and crouches in the corner. That stench, it's suffocating! And what's that? Evelyn jumps up, realising he's covered in withered flowers. His whole body shakes.
Am I always to be bounded?!

The 3 Wake Up

AIRAAS stretches in the softness of the forget-me-not. How small I am! How funny! Her laugh is the sound of angels singing and water-falls. A sparrow flies in front of her. "AASAAR AASAI! Is that you?"

"Hello!" says a chocolate-eyed-sounding voice at AIRAAS's side. "AASAIR!"
The 3 become immense, winged Gods of Ages! The Butterfly, the Eagle and the Gardener smile at each other, eyes twinkling. An explosion of forget-me-nots pour down upon them. And the 3, who are so much more, join hands and laugh in the magic of the Gift of the Blue Forget-Me-Not.

ENGLAND:
The Lily is taken from The Primrose Land

Lily can't see. It's so dark. She whimpers, unable to move. Mummy! Daddy! But no words come out.
Mummy...
Daddy...
Sobbing, Lily cries herself to sleep, her little body trembling.

SPAIN:
The Poppies Disappear

Aileen opens her eyes. Why is it so dark? The air smells acrid... it's cold and damp... Claustrophobia climbs up from the stone floor and crawls into her veins.
Aileen shakes.
I'm bounded!
Is this a nightmare?
She trembles.
Am I in the Tower?!

Dear Diary,
I write on a piece of paper because you are lost! I feel desperate! My parents have took me out of Englihs School and lock me in my room. They've took my loved things and forbid me use English! I need help, Diary! Help me, please! Why I am bounded? Why?
I don't understand.

The Bounded

The 4th Path Speaks
Take my path, Children of the One Light
I am the Stem of Stems, the Core, the Heart, the Snake of Snakes
I swirl and fuse and merge and spiral
Fly up the Stem, sparkling Winged-Ones and Little Bird
Follow my trail to the Violet Path
Bring the Blueness that is not to be forgotten
The Bounded need the Gift of Remembrance
To See the Violet, To Be ARIASA
Ah... This Golden Greenness I am
I strengthen and heal
Follow my Dazzle!

Hear This! Hear This!
She comes holding the Staff
The Trumpets sound!
The Bells ring!
She is the Unbounded Rainbow Flower
Sustained by the Stem of Strength
The Staff of Staffs
ARIASARIASAA

Prepare Ye!
She comes
to
Walk
the World!

PART 16

The 6ᵗʰ Path of the Rainbow
The Violet Path of Lavender Healing:
The Bridge to ARIASA

AASAIR, IASAARAASAI and AIRAAS stood still. Around them, the silence bubbled with iridescence while the Golden Greenness swirled and spiralled, creating a transparent tunnel of glittering rainbow colours.

The One Voice said,

"Take the Violet Jewel to the Bounded.

With the Blueness, wake their senses to hear the Magic Wand of the Word.

Firmly placed in their Hearts, the Jewel of Jewels, the Violet Path,

frees the Bounded from their Towers.

ASAIRA Am, for ARIASA Is."

Below IASAARAASAI, AIRAAS and AASAIR, the sound of a Tibetan long horn groaned and whirred as IRAASA pushed the Stem out of the earth. When the Stem arrived at the feet of the 3, it bloomed into a heart-shaped purple flower: a Violet! Its quilted petals embraced the Three Gods of ASAIRA who, standing in the centre of the flower, felt themselves covered in the Violet's sweet, powdery fragrance.

AIRAAS's wings pulled a little. She arched her back so that the Sacred Thread from the wings could separate into its twelve strands of golden-red, silver-blue, white, pink lavender, purple and green. Slowly, the silky strands wove themselves around the 3, in and out of the petals of the Violet.

AASAIR raised his hands. From his fingertips a vaporous coil of lavender flowed up into the air and found AIRAAS's pink strand of lavender healing. AASAIR's lavender essence and AIRAAS's pink lavender strand intertwined, deepening the fragrance and healing power of the lavender.

The 3 that were One breathed in the lavender and the violet and felt their bodies vibrate and hum. Gradually, AIRAAS, AASAIR and IASAARAASAI faded away into the fragrant vibration, turning into three others.

Helen Rose-Hip, Jack Lavender-Sprig and Sparrow found themselves sitting inside the Violet. Taking a deep breath, the 3 nodded at one another; they knew what to do and where to go. With the Violet Jewel imbued in lavender inside their hearts, Sparrow, Jack and Helen took flight in a different direction through the Rainbow Realm.

Jack enters the Red Path and the Orange Path

Jack merged with Keon and Jeanne. The 3 of them knew themselves as AASAIR.

Both Keon and Jeanne looked at their sides and saw IASAARAASAI in the form of a cat and a dog. The animals lovingly nudged the woman and the man.

As Keon picked up Carlitos into his arms, and Jeanne knelt down to stroke Baxter, all 4 sensed the Golden Greenness, the 4th Path, slither into their awareness. It brought the English language to be used as a Wand of Healing. The Spanish and the French languages bowed and stepped back.

Helen enters the Blue Path

Helen knew exactly where to find Aye and plunged directly into Aye's troubled dreams.

Helen's wings brought her face to face with Aye's Consciousness. "Aye, can you hear me? I am here to help. I speak to you, Aye, in the English tongue, the Magic Wand you know of. I've come to help you remember and free you from the Tower. Take this Blue Flower that I deliver to you."

Aye's eyes looked at the fairy-like creature. The humming of the wings that seemed to be made of ice mesmerized Aye.

Sparrow continues on the Yellow Path

Sparrow could feel Lily's agitation grow and grow. She flew to Lily's house in earnest.

The Reader looks up from the page. Lily is so innocent and so unaware of everything… what's going to happen to her?

"Do you want to help Lily?" a familiar voice says.

The Reader sees the forget-me-nots.

"Yes, I do! Sorry. For a moment, I'd left!"

Aileen heard a noise. She raised her head. Oh… there's a tiny slit in the wall. She peered through. Outside of the Tower, far below, there was a man staring up at her with some sort of animal in his arms.

Evelyn shivered, his eyes tightly closed. He heard a sniffing. Something cold and wet touched his hands. Evelyn jumped up. It's a dog! Fear transmuted into surprise, darkness into light. He'd always loved dogs. A tear of love, an ancient tear of joyfulness ran down his cheek. He was transported to a forest where Evelyn felt the presence of two old friends. He stroked Baxter who gave him a long lick.

Keon that was AASAIR that was Jack flew up to the top of the Tower and hovered in front of the tiny window. He had a blue flower in his hands. "Forget-me-not!" AASAIR said with a chocolate-eyed smile on his face.

Jeanne that was AASAIR that was Jack approached Evelyn and Baxter very slowly. She carried a bouquet of the most lovely blue and yellow forget-me-nots. Their nocturnal scent filled the air and

"So beautiful," Aye said, and took the forget-me- not. "It's the flower from my diary!" She paused. "The Blueness?! But now I have lost my diary!" Aye's face turned grave again.

Helen said,"Your diary is in your Heart, as is the flowered blueness. This you must realise to be free."

Of course, everything Aye had written was what her heart felt, and no one could take or steal that! "Yes," she said. "That's true! But… I'm not free."

"Aye, listen to me. Do you wish to be free and unbounded? If you do, you will have to speak and act from the Heart. Do you wish this to be so?" Helen's wings sparkled.

Aye didn't really comprehend, but she did know that the truth was in her heart. "Yes, I want to be free!"

"Take this Violet Jewel that I give you, Aye, and together with the forget-me-not flower, put them securely in your Heart. It is your mission now to protect this and never forget. I am a reflection of your real self, and you can speak to me whenever you choose. My magical name is AIRAAS. It's also yours!"

Aye took the luminescent Violet from Helen's hands and placed it inside the forget-me-not. In awe, Aye laid the flowered gem on her heart. It felt like ice. "Ahhhh…."

It was night time in the 3rd Path of England, and the weather was warm. Lily's bedroom window was slightly open, and Sparrow managed to squeeze in. Lily slept, her face crunched up into a frown, her body tense and tight.

Perched on one of the bed knobs facing Lily, Sparrow started chirping, for she knew the child was lost in a suffocating nightmare. The dark Tower had left Lily paralysed, speechless, alone and terrified. Seeing a child suffer was unbearable. IASAARAASAI, feeling the pain acutely now, chirped more loudly.

Lily sat up. Her eyes fully open, she stared at the sparrow who, knowing what to do, flew right up to the child with a little blue flower in its mouth.

"Oh!" Lily said.

Sparrow dropped the forget-me-not into Lily's lap and flew back onto the bed knob. Lily picked up the flower. Sweetly, she lifted it to her nose. Sparrow could feel the salty tears and sweat that ran down Lily's cheeks: Lily was relieved by Sparrow and the forget-me-not, but not healed. The dark Tower was strong still.

IASAARAASAI knew the Word, the Wand of Healing Energy, was

lit up the room. Evelyn could only see the desolateness of his Tower, not the real colours of this ancient abbey chamber, but as he stroked Baxter, Evelyn's body relaxed. The fragrance of the Blue enveloped his senses, evaporating the pungent smell of rot.

Aileen's nightmare could not withstand such a funny picture of a winged Keon grinning, holding a flower in one hand, and with Carlitos squirming a little under his other arm! Aileen burst out laughing. The walls of the Tower cracked. Keon quickly handed Aileen the forget-me-not. The Blueness pierced Aileen's senses, and the dark walls crumbled into the earth. The air quivered with freshness and lavender.

"AASAIR!" Aileen said.

Aileen and Keon kissed and hugged each other in a timeless merging of worlds, realms and paths. Carlitos meowed in rapture!

Evelyn's body gave a jolt when Aileen said AASAIR. Evelyn dared to look up. There was the woman; she was so lovely, so familiar, such warm brown eyes. "Who are you?" he said.

"I'm Jeanne," she said, handing him the flowers.

Aye opens her eyes.

What a dream…

A calming perfume of lavender surrounds her. Mmmm… she smiles, her whole body tingling and buzzing…

Mmm… thank you…

thank you…

The Eagle flies over the 5th Path, the Blue Path of the Bounded. As the Eagle flies, it creates a multicoloured stellar trail of rainbow colours behind it.

There are 7 colours that are 6 Paths that are 1 Rainbow that are 1 Bridge to Freedom and ARIASA.

Faces of suffering look up at the sight: an eagle pulling a rainbow across the sky!

All who see the wondrous colour-filled miracle find peace and solace in each colour.

The Towers imprisoning the Bounded become less solid… some crumble, some even evaporate.

For this was the Gift of the Violet Path, a path of bridges and rainbows that heals all wounds.

Lavender words of comfort, of wisdom, of understanding, of freedom, and of healing, spiral through the air acting as the Magic Wand that frees the Bounded.

required. But IASAARAASAI had no idea how to speak. Sparrow closed her eyes, sensing ASAIRA Am, listening for the right way to move.

Lily got up from her bed. She went to one of the shelves at the side of the room and chose a doll. She showed it to the sparrow. Then, in adorable innocence, she gave the doll the blue forget-me-not, whispering words of love, "It's all right. Mummy's here now."

IASAARAASAI's body started to expand! Ohhh! She practically fell off the bed knob. What…? IASAARAASAI felt two human legs that were hers root themselves to the floor.

"Mummy! Mummy! Are you a sparrow?!" Lily giggled.

"Oh, yes," IASAARAASAI's clear voice said. "I can be a sparrow and lots of animals. Every time you see an animal, you can bet it's me looking out for you, Lily!"

Lily beamed, a smile of wonder at her mother's power. The realisation swept all fear away in one lavender swish of the Spoken Word Wand!

IASAARAASAI was amazed. Twenty-six words had healed the child's fear of losing her parents, maybe forever! And the words were true, so true!

"Forget-me-nots," whispered Evelyn, and the Spoken Word waved itself, Magic Wand that it was. Whoosh! The Blueness spun around them, dissipating the heavy energy. The Abbey, relieved, drew the curtains open and let in a scent of lavender.

Evelyn heard a woman inside of him say, "Ohhhh!" followed by a laugh and knew it to be him!

Jeanne said, "You're AIRAAS, my love."

A pause.

"AASAIR?" said Evelyn.

Jeanne and Evelyn laughed so much it nearly hurt. Baxter wagged his tail in satisfaction!

And when all was silent, the Violet Jewel passed from AASAIR's hands to AIRAAS's, 4 hands that were 8, that were 12, that were 14, that were One.

Flowers bloom, and the Path of the Bounded becomes the Path of the Unbounded, full of poppies, marigolds, primroses, forget-me-nots, lavender, and violets!

ASAIRA AM

I sigh

in

colourful

vibrant

fragrant

healing

ecstasy!

The Reader looks up again for a second, elated. They pause to smell the lavender wisps that float out of the pages…

"Lily, **Sweetie, here's a little present** I want to give you… It's something that belonged to your Abuelita Violeta."[35] IASAARAASAI put the necklace around Lily's neck. "It's a magical violet stone called an amethyst. It'll protect you always, even in your dreams."

Touching the pretty stone, Lily looked up into Violet's eyes. The little girl smiled, then yawned, peaceful sleep beckoning.

IASAARAASAI smiled back, astonished as she realised that Lily's mother was called Violet and Violet's mother, Violeta.

The Reader's Heart feels the miracle of interconnection that every person, every Being is. Their Heart beating fast, the Violet Path sinks into their body and soul.

---

35 The Story Translates

Above, Lily's mother makes a reference to 'Abuelita Violeta'. This means 'Granny Violet' in Spanish.

Discovering ARIASA: RIASAA, the Stem of Stems, grows Rainbow Roots

Aye is awake. She sits up, flicks her hair from her face and realises she's not concerned about being locked in. Someone will come soon! She looks around… Oh, a notebook! She jumps out of bed. White pages! Perfect! And a blue pen. Perfect! Perfect! She sits down. The pages open. Aye writes:

The Promise

Here I am
I'm alright!
A room full of light
Full of Hope, full of Love
I take the Blueness
And write on the Whiteness

My name is Aye
This English Tongue I promise to use
As my 2nd Mother Tongue
It is the Magic Wand of Freedom
And when I doubt
I will listen to the Purple Jewel
My Blue Forget – Me – Nots
That are my Heart

It's all a Mystery
I don't really understand
But I Promise

Grateful I am
I wish to help others
So I use the Spoken & Written Word
From the Purple Blueness of my Heart
To Free Myself & Others
From the Dark Towers of Fears!

I love You
♡   Sweet Heart of Hearts   ♡

Aye xxxx

Oh! It's like other voice, other person, but it's me, too. Hmm… it's like a poem. Can I write poems? In response, the Violet flutters its silvery blue wings. An effervescence of delight leaps into her throat. Aye laughs. Must be so!

Lily is playing outside in the meadow. The primroses move to and fro in the breeze, open and jolly. Helen Rose-Hip and Jack Lavender-Sprig fly merrily around. Sometimes they stop on one of the yellow beds to bask in the sunshine. A sparrow chirps from one of the branches; she can see a woman in the distance. The woman is carrying something and walking towards Lily…

Aileen is on the airplane. Her eyes close. Images of her beloved animal friends display themselves in her mind: Bruxa, my little lamb, I'll see you soon! Missed you! And Bagha, too. I'll be home soon. And I brought a new friend, Carlitos is his name. Oh, Big Bear… yes, you're here, too!

A woman's voice, gentle and strong, rises from deep inside, "Aileen, we're here, Aileen, we're here. Can you hear me? I'm your mother… Aileen… I'm Mia, your Mother."

Aileen remembers a black and white photo of a woman with a baby girl in her arms.

"Yes, that photo. The woman, she's my mother, Violet. She's holding me in her arms. But I couldn't hold you, Aileen, and you so felt that loss. My mother, your Grandmother Violet, had the same experience as you. Her mother, Violeta, died giving birth, too. Aileen, we're here, we're here to tell you, we're so sorry not to have held you in our arms. But we've always been here close to your heart. Can you feel us now, my love? Can you feel us?"

Aileen breathed in deeply… Yes… Yes… Yes… Mama…

"Sweet Aileen, your mother, your grandmother and great-grandmother and all the lineage are here with you. We are one… we are one… always here, Aileen, always here…"

The voice turns into a violet-coloured line and draws itself into a tree… The Tree of Jewels! Rainbow threads sprout from the bottom of the Tree and root themselves in Aileen's heart.

Aileen feels Keon's gaze upon her as a tear rolls down her cheek. Her eyes still closed, she squeezes his hand.

IASAARAASAI pants and takes a sniff… fun powerful nose… cosy and warm in woman arms… happy… happy… little girl… little girl… yes… Lily…

Lily's mouth drops open. Her eyes dart from the soft creature to her Mother. "Is that a doggy?"

"Yes, my sweet. It's for you, he's your new friend."

Lily stares at the fluffy brown puppy. She opens her arms and says, "Bear!"

Evelyn is walking in the grounds of the abbey with Baxter at his side. The fields are full of marigolds and lavender. The orange and purple awaken his senses… mmm…

Evelyn stops and looks over his shoulder. There's Jeanne sat under a tree, writing in her little green notebook. Smiling, Evelyn looks up into the sky and takes in the blue.

A wispy thought playfully comes into the mind and says, "So… now what, my friend…?"

El Pregnero

Escuchadme

Traigo Noticias

Noticias de Ella

ARIASA

El Arcoiris Viviente

Ha decidido

Caminar por este Mundo

Ha llegado Ella

¿Oís sus pasos?

¡Escuchadme!

The Story Translates

The Town-Crier

Hear ye

I bring News

News of Her

ARIASA

The Living Rainbow

Has decided

To Walk through this World

She has arrived

Can you hear her steps?

Hear ye!

Keon miraba los poemas en su libreta. Este último y el resto eran todos poemas anunciando la llegada de ARIASA. Agradecido, Keon cerró los ojos mientras notaba a ARIASA crecer dentro de él… ¡Sí!

The Story Translates

Keon looked at the poems in his notebook. This last one and the rest were all poems announcing the arrival of ARIASA. Grateful, Keon closed his eyes as he noticed ARIASA grow inside of him... Yes!

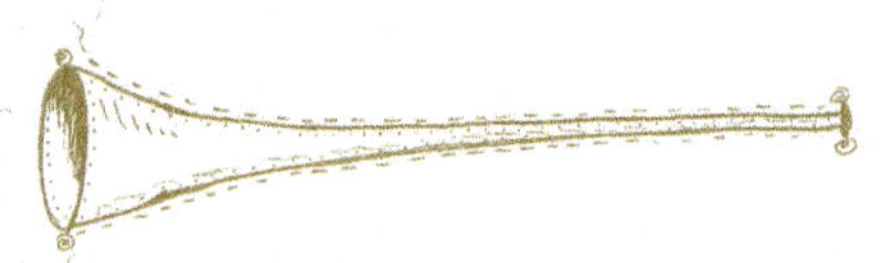

Le Crieur Public

Elle est ici

Elle Marche solidement

À travers le Monde

Ses pas sont silencieux

Mais son Arc-En-Ciel illumine tout

Écoutez, Écoutez

Elle est arrivée

C'est le moment de

ARIASA!

The Story Translates

The Town Crier

She is here
She Walks solidly
Through the World
Her steps are silent
But her Rainbow illuminates all
Hear ye, Hear ye
She has arrived
It is the moment of
ARIASA!

Jeanne a regardé les mots. Soudain, elle a tout compris sans pouvoir écrire un seul mot de plus. Oui, ARIASA est arrivée! Jeanne sentait une émotion qui circulait dans tout son corps… Oui!

The Story Translates

Jeanne looked at the words. Suddenly, she understood everything without being able to write another word more. Yes, ARIASA has arrived! Jeanne felt an excitement that moved throughout her body... Yes!

The Town-Crier

I have to speak

So listen all!

I am the Town-Crier

Of Olden Times

Come to tell you

That She has arrived

ARIASA Is

The Luminous Rainbow

Listen well!

She is Here

To Walk All Paths

To Walk the Worlds

Of ARIASA!

Jack Lavender-Sprig rushed through the meadow, flying high and low as he announced ARIASA's arrival. All who heard and saw were astonished!

ARIASA
ARTIST AS
ARIASA
SPEAKS
ART
I am ARIASA
1 2 3 4 5 67

I am the Living Energy of ASAIRA
In Action & Word, In Silence & Song
I am the Heralded and the Herald of
Heralds
While I walk the Paths of ASAIRA Am
My Rainbow Spirals transform the Bounded
My Diamond Void,
The Black Hole of the Heart of Hearts,
Is the Healing Alchemy of ASAIRA Am
RIASAA is ARIASA is the Stem of Stems
The Solidness that upholds
The Flower of Flowers
JOY TO ALL WHO HEAR ME
AND PICK UP THE STAFF,
THE SACRED WAND,
TO HERALD MY ARRIVAL!

PART 18

Discovering ARIASA: The Walls of RIASAA create a Tower of Stemmed Solidity

* All the characters have a sense of something solidifying inside them: this is ARIASA finding her feet.

* Each feel they have to 'do their own thing, complete their vocation in life'.

* Some of them know more, can see more, but everyone feels their connection with something freeing and real within: this is ASAIRA.

* Heralds are what they are!

The Writer looked up from the page.

She laughed at seeing the words 'The Writer'.

Fun! And she laughed again, amazed at the Universe's sense of humour. How could it be any other way?! The words crossed the page in a silky flow of light-heartedness, and the Writer absorbed that magical moment where the letters join together to make words and sentences and stories…

She stopped writing.

It totally dawned on her! This is where I am too! Exactly the same as everyone else in the Story; something is solidifying inside of me as well…

ARIASA!

Her eyes smiled. Then, the Writer looked straight in front of her, put her pen down… and shyly nodded at the Reader.

All the characters, including the Writer, feel a rippling inside the area around the heart. They lie down to rest… and fall asleep.

A hummingbird dashes in to feed from the feeder and takes off…

A fragrance of burning incense whiffs in, whirls and wafts out…

A foghorn makes a groaning sound in the distance; it echoes for a while…

Notes of lavender freshness caress each character's forehead…

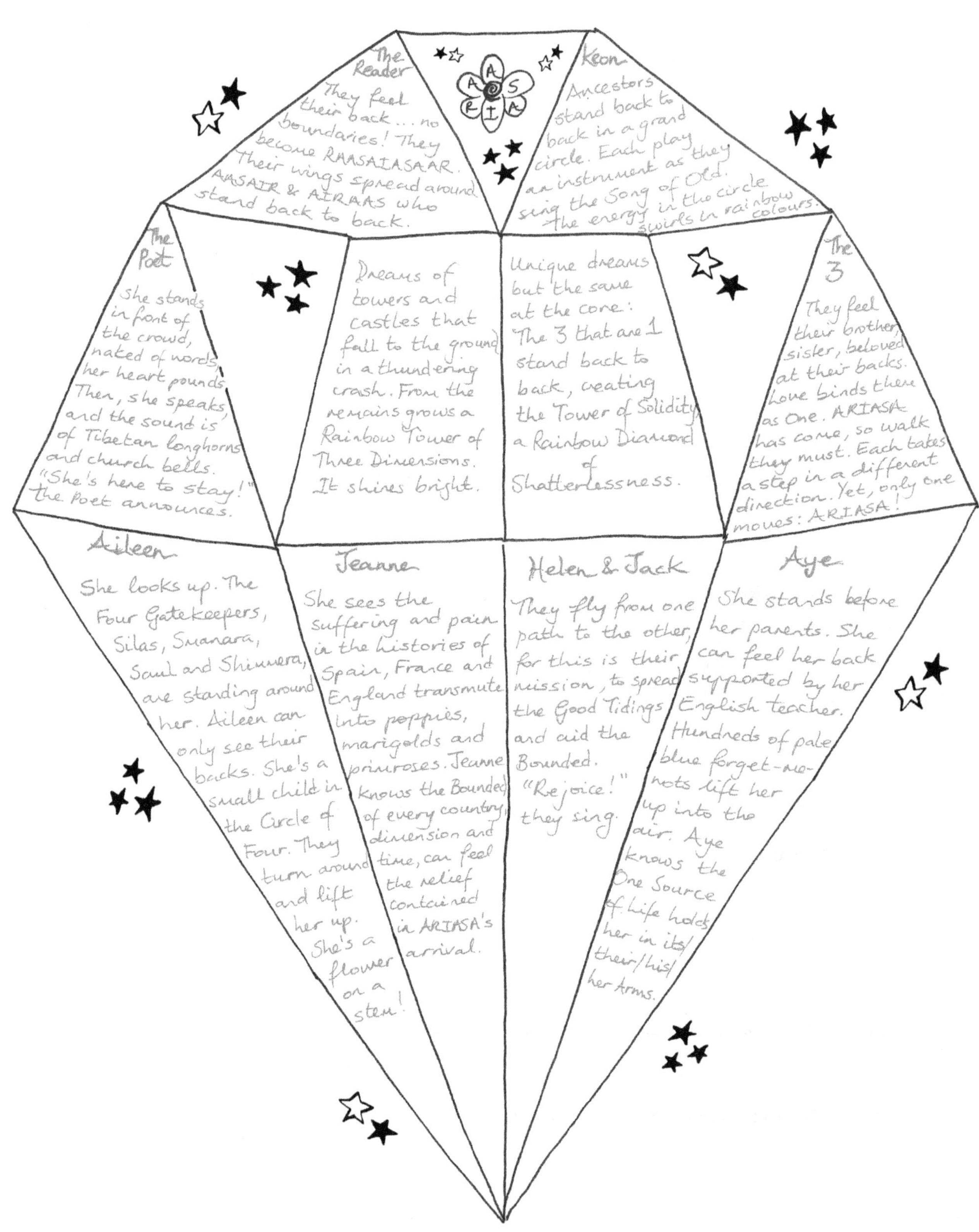

The Reader
They feel their back... no boundaries! They become RAASAIASAAR. Their wings spread around AASAIR & AIRAAS who stand back to back.

A A S R I A

Keon
Ancestors stand back to back in a grand circle. Each play an instrument as they sing the Song of Old. The energy in the circle swirls in rainbow colours.

The Poet
She stands in front of the crowd, naked of words, her heart pounds. Then, she speaks, and the sound is of Tibetan longhorns and church bells. "She's here to stay!" the Poet announces.

Dreams of towers and castles that fall to the ground in a thundering crash. From the remains grows a Rainbow Tower of Three Dimensions. It shines bright.

Unique dreams but the same at the core: The 3 that are 1 stand back to back, creating the Tower of Solidity, a Rainbow Diamond of Shatterlessness.

The 3
They feel their brother, sister, beloved at their backs. Love binds them as One. ARIASA has come, so walk they must. Each takes a step in a different direction. Yet, only one moves: ARIASA!

Aileen
She looks up. The Four Gatekeepers, Silas, Smanara, Saul and Shimmera, are standing around her. Aileen can only see their backs. She's a small child in the Circle of Four. They turn around and lift her up. She's a flower on a stem!

Jeanne
She sees the suffering and pain in the histories of Spain, France and England transmute into poppies, marigolds and primroses. Jeanne knows the Bounded of every country, dimension and time, can feel the relief contained in ARIASA's arrival.

Helen & Jack
They fly from one path to the other, for this is their mission, to spread the Good Tidings and aid the Bounded. "Rejoice!" they sing.

Aye
She stands before her parents. She can feel her back supported by her English teacher. Hundreds of pale blue forget-me-nots lift her up into the air. Aye knows the One Source of Life holds her in its/their/his/her arms.

Am

All

The Earth

The Water

The Air

The Seed

The Root

The Stem

The Bud

The Branch

The Leaf

The Flower

The Petal

The Perfume

The Seen

The Unseen

The Certainty

The Uncertainty

I

Am

ASAIRA

PART 19

Discovering ARIASA: The 3 that are 12 feel the One Path of the Rainbow Mystery

AIRAAS

In the cool of the forest, Aileen rested with her back against the Beloved Tree. Bruxa and Bagha slept in her lap, emitting little snore sounds.

A tingle suddenly swept Aileen's body, and she felt herself transported into the silence. She could feel another presence in the background.

Evelyn stopped and breathed in Aileen's energy.

At that very moment, Helen Rose-Hip whispered into Aye's ear, "You are much more! Don't forget!"

The 4 that were 1 that were 7 closed their eyes to enter the vast silver Sea of Seas inside themselves. Evelyn and Aye had to sit down where they could and found a shady tree, while Helen, rather enjoying her privileged view of the Rainbow Mystery, lay back on one of the branches of the Wise One.

The Ancient Tree of Lands contemplated the Children of the One Light and rustled his leaves.

AIRAAS, **Butterfly Goddess,** sang a song of healing lavender notes. Through the Twelve Sacred Threads from her Wings, the scented notes travelled to every Being in the Realms and Dimensions of ASAIRA.

IASAARAASAI

Lily stroked **Bear's** fluffy head. She giggled because he was jumping up and trying to eat her Grandma Violeta's necklace.

IASAAR **in animal form**, grateful forever, watched over all the Children of the One Path.

ASAIRA the Book quivered in the **Reader's** hands. The Reader's eyes twinkled.

RAASAI Eagle of Eagles, flew over the One Rainbow that was a centillian rainbows. The Eagle's eyes were able to see beyond where there was only One Colour, One Path: the most glittering transparent Stem, a Diamond Tower. RAASAI flew to the top and opened his Wings of Violet.

AASAIR

Keon **and** Carlitos wandered the Green Meadow, observing the insects and the primroses. Fascinated by all the different yellows, Keon crouched down a moment to take a closer look. Jack Lavender-Sprig thought it quite amusing as he was lifted to Keon's nose to be smelled.

"Hey Keon! It's me, Jack! Can't you see me?"

Keon, wide-eyed, laughed.

"Hmm…" said Jack, laughing back, "That laugh of yours, of ours… sounds like that Ancient One… you know… what's his name?!"

"All-Seer?" pondered Keon, chuckling away.

On hearing the familiar laugh, Jeanne glanced away from the computer. She closed her eyes: an image arose of the chocolate-eyed man and the little fairy man…"Ah, je me souviens de vous deux!"[36] Jeanne laughed, too, a sound of deep bubbling in the belly.

Then, the 3 who were 1 who were 4 and many more said,

"All for One and One for All!"

"¡Uno para Todos y Todos para Uno!"

"Un pour Tous, Tous pour Un!"[37]

And AASAIR's **roaring laughs** filled the Universe, sounded the Trumpets of Old and woke up all the Messengers and Heralds, from the Star of Heavens & All Seer to the Town-Crier, prompting them to announce:

---

36 The Story Translates

"Ah, I remember you two!" (From the French language).

37 The Story Speaks

'All for One and One for All', here in the languages Spanish and French, too, is a motto that has echoed through all the dimensions and times of ASAIRA. It has been sung by the 3 in many different moments. Although its exact origin is not known in the Earth Realm, the Story wishes to honour the Storyteller, Alexandre Dumas from France, who used it for his famous book The Three Musketeers in 1844, and also to honour the people of Switzerland who have this motto for their country.

☆★ PART 20 ★★

Discovering ARIASA: ARIASA Looks into the Rainbow Mirror

She Walks

The World

She Treads

With Love

She Speaks

The Word

ARIASA

ASAIRA

Mirrored

Are They

Mirrored

Is She that is a He

That is a They

Mirrored

Are You

I

Am

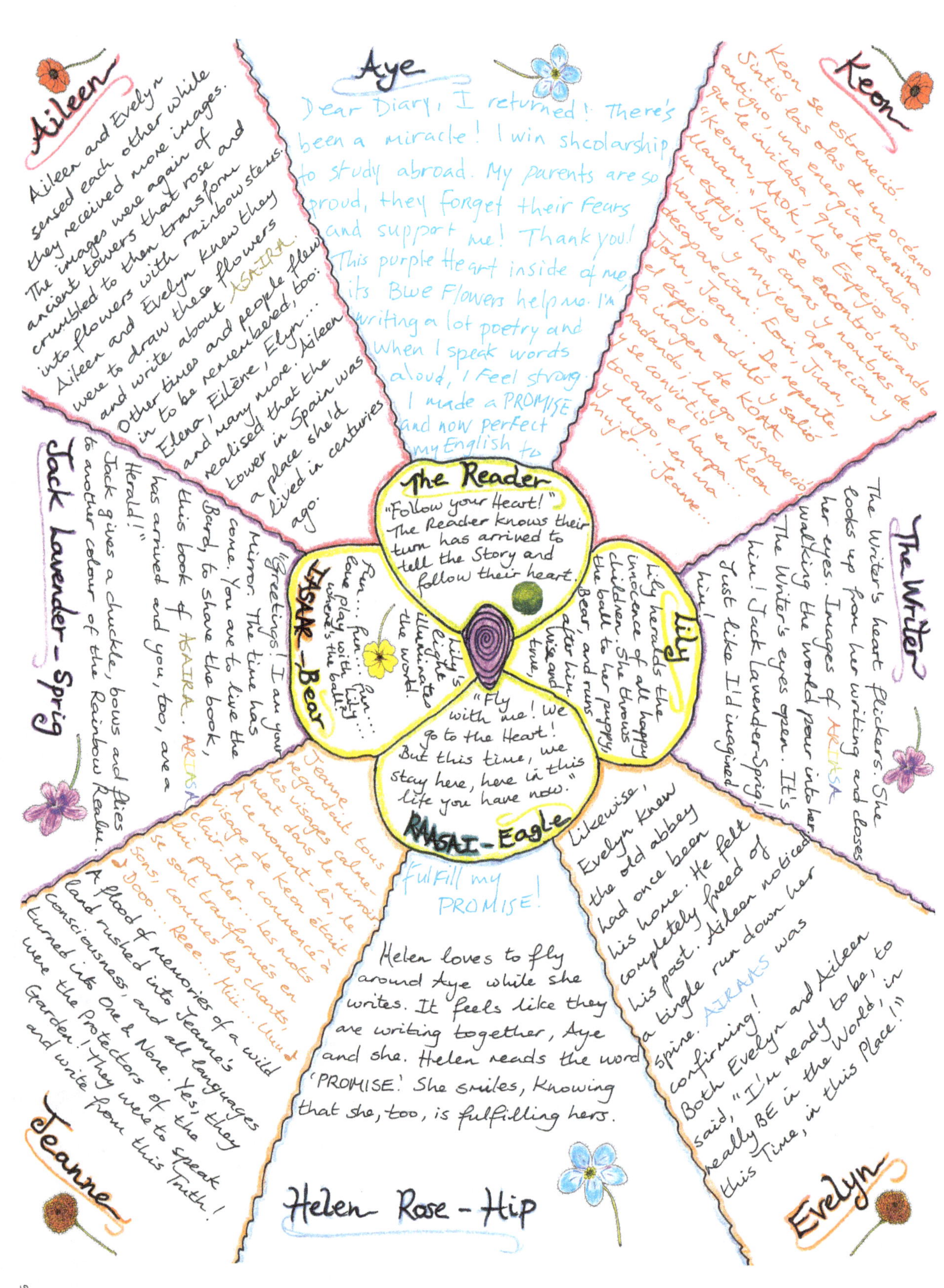

Aileen

Aileen and Evelyn sensed each other while they received more and more images. The images were again and again of ancient towers that rose and crumbled to then transform into flowers with rainbow stems. Aileen and Evelyn knew they were to draw these flowers ASAIRA and write about them, too. Other times and people flew in to be remembered. Elena, Eilène, Elyn... and many more. Aileen realised that the tower in Spain was a place she'd lived in centuries ago.

Aye

Dear Diary, I returned! There's been a miracle! I win shcolarship to study abroad. My parents are so proud, they forget their fears and support me! Thank you! This purple Heart inside of me, its Blue Flowers help me. I'm writing a lot poetry and when I speak words aloud, I feel strong. I made a PROMISE and now perfect my English to

Keon

Keon se estremeció. Sintió las olas de un océano antiguo, una energía que le amaba. que le invitaba, Las Espejos nos "ikeonn", AhOK, se encontró mirando llaman, "Keon". Las caras y nombres de un espejo. Las caras y mujeres aparecían y hombres y mujeres. Eoin, Juan, desaparecían. Eoin, Juan, De repente John, Jean... De repente, salió el espejo onduló y salió la imagen de KORR desapareció dando, luego... se convirtió en Keon el harpa... en una ...ndo, en una ...go... Jeanne...

The Reader

"Follow your Heart!" The Reader knows their turn has arrived to tell the Story and follow their heart.

Lily's eight illuminates the work.

Lily

Lily heralds the innocence of all happy children. She throws the ball to her puppy, Bear, and runs after him. Wise and true.

"Fly with me! We go to the Heart! But this time, we stay here, here in this life you have now."

RAASAI - Eagle

fulfill my PROMISE!

ISAAK - Bear

Fun... fun... Lily... love play with Lily... where's the ball?

Jack Lavender - Sprig

"Greetings! I am your Bard, to share the book, this book of KAIRA. ARIASA Herald!" Jack has arrived and you, too, are a Mirror. The time has come. You are to live the book. Jack gives a chuckle, bows and flies to another colour of the Rainbow Realm.

The Writer

The Writer's heart flickers. She looks up from her writing and closes her eyes. Images of AKIISA walking the world pour into her. The Writer's eyes open. It's him! Jack Lavender-Sprig! Just like I'd imagined him!

Jeanne

Jeanne regardait tous les visages calmes. A ce moment-là, le visage de Keon était clair. Il a commencé à lui parler... Les mots se sont transformés en chants! Hiii... Uuuu... Reee... DOOO... sons, comme les chants.

A flood of memories of a wild land rushed into Jeanne's consciousness, and all languages turned into One & None. Yes, they were the Protectors of the Garden! They were to speak and write from this Truth!

Helen Rose - Hip

Helen loves to fly around Aye while she writes. It feels like they are writing together, Aye and she. Helen reads the word 'PROMISE.' She smiles, knowing that she, too, is fulfilling hers.

Evelyn

Likewise, Evelyn knew the old abbey had once been his home. He felt completely freed of his past. Aileen noticed a tingle run down her spine. AIRAKS was confirming! Both Evelyn and Aileen to be, to said, "I'm ready really BE in the World, in this Time, in this Place!"

The Story Translates Keon and Jeanne in the Rainbow Mirror

Keon shivered. He felt the waves of an ancient ocean, a feminine energy that invited him, that loved him. "Keonnn, AAOK, the Mirrors call us." Keon found himself looking at a mirror. The faces and names of men and women appeared and disappeared: Eoin, Juan, John, Jean... All of a sudden, the mirror rippled and an image of KOAA swimming arose; then she disappeared and turned into Keon playing the harp... and then into a woman... Jeanne...

Jeanne looked calmly at all the faces in the mirror. At that moment, Keon's face was clear. He began to speak to her... The words transformed into sounds, like chants... ♪ Dooo... Reeee... Miiii... Uuuuu... ♪

A flood of memories of a wild land rushed into Jeanne's consciousness, and all languages turned into One & None. Aaah... Yes, they were the Protectors of the Garden! They were to speak and write from this Truth!

PART 21

Discovering ARIASA: Accepting the Forgotten & the Unknown

RAASAI... Can you hear me? It's IASAAR.

Yes, I hear you.

RAASAI... I have an idea... I'd like to meet in person and have a conversation face to face, like we did in the past.

"Wow, that was fast!" IASAAR stares at the middle-aged woman with wings that stands in front of her. "RAASAI, I presume!"

"At your service, Perceiver of All."

"Who are we this time? I don't recognise myself." The young fairy-like girl glances down at her body. She turns her head and catches a glimpse of her transparent wings.

"You have forgotten; but it is of no importance to forget some things, or not to recall the once known. We are Gods of ASAIRA, but when we inhabit the form of a certain Being, a temporary body, we adopt some of its limitations. Is this not why we are here? To talk of what we know and do not know?"

IASAAR sits down in the grass. "Yes. Since I began to be aware of the Story, my function has been to help others remember the forgotten, know the unknown… and it's how it is right now, as well. But there are moments I see so much and know so much that I can't retain it. It's like the memory has its own life, it comes and goes… And then, I feel I should be sharing everything I know about the Rainbow Paths with Keon and Aileen…" The young girl looks into the older woman's eyes.

The woman dressed in rainbow colours takes out a magic wand, makes two circular loops and pushes the wand downwards through the air. There's a shimmer, followed by a pop, and an armchair appears! "That's better," she laughs. "Let me ask you a question, IASAAR? Do you know who I am in this form?"

"You look familiar… but, no, not really."

"Is it important right now to remember? Is it the moment to enter this new Story? I could get even more comfortable and tell you all the details."

IASAAR smoothes out some creases in her sky-blue frock and grins. "OK, I get it. No, it's not essential to remember this now. "

"Exactly, my love. You and I are One and have travelled the Realms watching over the Children of the One Light since the Forgetting. Our mission is always the same one: to help those that have forgotten remember. However, we were also included in the forgetting, and we, too, experienced the same help from AASAIR and AIRAAS… and ASAIRA who, in her way, also forgot, for she is Us!"

RAASAI leans over and takes IASAAR's hands in her own. "ARIASA, ASAIRA's Mirror of Living Energy, wishes to walk… wishes to take the Staff. In this moment, this is what we support, Sweet IASAAR, because we are all ARIASA, too!" RAASAI stands up and helps IASAAR to her feet. "Keon and Aileen, as you do, have their own paths in their Keon and Aileen lives. We are not aware of everything about them because it is not essential for us even though we are One and Together. This is also part of the lesson that ARIASA brings."

"Ah, RAASAI, thank you. When you speak, I always feel my IASAAR nature strong again! It's obvious now. Forgetting, then, can be okay. It's like I'm learning to relax in the forgetting, accepting it as natural and even fun. And I don't need to be trying to save everyone all the time! I suppose I knew this, and then I forgot again!!" IASAAR smiles.

"IASAAR, there is huge strength in this accepting: we will never know or remember all in one given instant. We soar through the worlds, they ever-change. There is nothing to retain, nothing to understand. And when we must know we'll remember, or there will be one of the 2 at our side to tell us the Story needed. As for sharing the things we know, it will happen naturally; you will know. Trust that feeling. And I am always here!" The woman hugs the girl, both of their frosty wings a-glitter. "Now to help ARIASA take the Staff and walk the World!"

☆★ PART 22 ★★

Discovering ARIASA: ARIASA Takes the Staff!

As she walked slowly through the empty hall, the Writer felt a peaceful joy that pervaded her every movement. She knew she was walking a familiar world and yet distant, ancient. Around the hall, the fire-lit torches blazed, emitting a red and orange hue that warmed her soul. There was no one, and at the same time, there was a profound fullness of there being many.

A huge door turned visible at the far end of the hall. No sooner had she seen it than she found herself touching its surface! Her fingers moved across the timber panels carved with spiralling vines and leaves. The door creaked a little and began to open. She took a step back. Inch by inch, a world of ancientness came into view: long wooden tables filled with food and drink, women and men feasting, talking, serving… all bathed in a smoky blur and smelling of broth and pinewood. It felt welcoming and so familiar…

The door was completely open now. She stood still, taking it all in. No one can see me… I'm the privileged observer!

A memory rushed in. She swallowed with difficulty and felt like she'd gone deaf. The door slammed closed while from nowhere a chair materialized in front of her! Shaking, she sat in the chair which faced the door.

To her right, someone else in a similar chair turned to look straight at her with a mix of incredulousness and inquisitiveness.

"Who are you?" she who was dreaming asked the curious on-looker, awed by their appearance which was fuzzy and continuously changing.

"I'm the Reader."

"The Reader?"

IASAARAASAI's face rippled in a flux of faces and Beings, creatures of now and lost lands. They/He/She/It grinned. "And you must be ARIASA."

Silence descended like smooth silk and opened the timber door.

Inside the ancient hall, a tall man climbed onto one of the tables. He carried a harp-like instrument and was clad in earthy-coloured garments.

"Eoin!" both Reader and Writer said.

Eoin gently plucked the strings on the harp. His hands and fingers were full of musical notes from which emanated a mesmerizing melody. The sound vibrated and bounced in sweet-tasting waves around the room. "I am Eoin the Bard, and a song I have brought for you this night." The words were said in an ancient tongue, but the Magic Wand of the Spoken Word transmuted all words into one language, the True Language of ASAIRA. Every Being that was ready could understand. "This winter night, if you open your Heart, ASAIRA will enter into your Soul. Through this humble bard, She sings the words of the Legend of Legends."

Eoin's voice deepened. The Song had commenced.

The Legend of the Living *ARIASA*

There was an Ancient Time

A Time of No-Time,

A Realm of No Beginning, of No End

Where Yesterday was Today

Tomorrow, Yesterday

Here was There

And Nowhere, Everywhere…

Aeons after, yet in Timeless Eternity,

Was the Promise Revealed

And ASAIRA known again

Her Green Meadow

Remembered, Felt & Seen

The Three Gods

The Gardener of Creation

The Butterfly Mother

And the Eagle Guardian

Themselves did find!

Yes, my Friends!

And this snow-lain night

Is a Night of Nights

For SHE is here as never before!

SHE that contains HE

The Queen & The King

In One

ASAIRARIASA

The 12 who are 1

The Diamond Rainbow

A Flower who is the Stem

ARIASA

RIASAA

For One cannot be without the Other

Is here to fulfill

The Promise of the Promise Fulfilled

The 3 awakened have

But only when they walk together as One

Can they free the Towers of Desolation

Of all Realms & all Times

SHE is here, my Friends!

ARIASA, the Walking ASAIRA, the Flower of Flowers!

Then, this Night of Nights

We honour & welcome ARIASA!

Never has she walked the Realms before

In a Real Seeing of Herself

Even now

She looks around

Wondering if I speak of her or another...

The Listeners and the Bard felt the words pierce through their bodies, their souls, their past lives and their future lives…

Eoin breathed in, then pushed the harp strings downward. On the out-breath came a deep bellow,

And thus…

Here ends

This Legend of Old

For

All Good Hearts to Hear

Darkness.

Overwhelming loss.

Fear.

Confusion.

It's okay, it's okay… it's okay…

Trust.

Warmness, from the sun… mmm… fresh air.

Hope.

I open my eyes. I'm outside and it's daytime… I see a woman, a man and a tree. I recognise the man as Eoin and realise the woman is Elyn! The tree is massive. It's a yew, but its molecules seem to be visible and bouncy… wow, it's IASAARAASAI!

It feels like spring, freshness on the skin. Everything is still and slow and tingly, a greenery all around… It's a meadow! The Meadow?! I glance at the ground. Primroses and poppies! Yes!

Happiness.

A slow-motion movie.

A thick, palpable silence, golden and enveloping.

I close my eyes.

Someone takes my hand. My eyes open again.

"Come," Elyn says and leads me to the Tree.

IASAARAASAI the Tree is glowing! Elyn smiles, and it warms me. She looks like someone I know, and I feel like crying. Eoin joins us, and the 3 of us stand around the Sacred Yew. It's a circle.

Eoin and Elyn make sounds with their voices. They're toning… everything is vibrating:

♪ "Uuuu… Oooo… Ohhh… Ahhh… Aiiii… Eiiii… Eeee…" ♪

Eoin & Elyn go fuzzy, and they change. They look like ancient warriors… UT and

SAIRAA!

The sounds of the toning come out in colours! It's so incredible… the colours shine and glitter, and the trunk of the yew turns into a rainbow! I have to close my eyes, it's too bright, too much…

Silence.

Do I dare look?

The 3 are enormous! I have to look upwards and my neck… it strains… I step back in order to see them.

It's okay, I whisper…

The eagle-winged man grins and crouches down to shake my hand. It feels hilarious for him to do that! The butterfly woman is so bright, her wings are sparkling, blinding, she sings to me… it's so beautiful.

The sweetest man I've ever seen comes closer and says, "Welcome." His brown eyes are full of love and peace.

RAASAI is kneeling in front of me. "You know us, don't you?"

"Yes… of… course…" I look at all three. My body buzzes.

"And you remember when you created us?"

"Yes… you… you just appeared on a page… one day…"

"So you know everything because you created the Story?"

"I suppose so…"

A nervousness.

There's a little girl next to me. She says, "Hello." And I know it's Aileen. "What's your name?" she asks me innocently.

Blankness.

"I can't remember!"

Panic.

"I'm going crazy!"

"No, you're not," says Aileen. "We forget who we are, but then someone comes and reminds us, helps us to remember. We're here for that. We're here to help you remember who you are."

I look at her and see myself.

Can't grasp it.

Can't understand.

It wants to be said, but I can't say it.

"You created us!" AASAIR says. "And then we forgot, but you forgot, too! It's time to completely remember, so we can walk fully as ARIASA, who is You, who is Us, to move in this Earth Realm!"

A smell of lavender.

RAASAI the Eagle-God stands up. I feel taller now, the same height.

RAASAI shows me a wooden staff. He says,

"This is the Staff of Staffs: The Stem of ASAIRA

I have guarded it throughout the ages

But now the Time has come

For the Living ASAIRA

To Walk the World in full Consciousness

ARIASA wishes to Be

We shall all Be

She

That is He

That is They

That is I

That is It

That is We

That is You!"

Everything stops except for the air that is alive with little bubbles and sparks.

An unmovable eternity passes by.

The bubbles in the air burst into tiny blue flowers.

"Will you take the Staff?" says the little Aileen. She looks up at me with excitement.

I'm filled with love. "Anything for you, Aileen!" A tear falls down my cheek.

I reach out and see three other hands as we, 4, take the Staff, point it upwards and slam it down into the earth.

ASAIRA finds herself in countless different bodies, in countless different forms.

She feels the body that she has been given. And she knows who she is.

ARIASA moves one leg, then, the other. She walks! Her rainbow-spiralled Staff supports her. At each step, poppies, marigolds, primroses, blades of green grass, lavender and violets grow and bloom behind her, scenting and illuminating the Path. Light and solid, ARIASA feels the golden groundedness that she is.

She smiles.

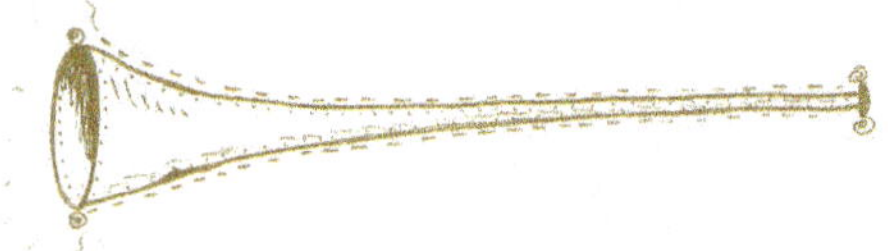

Tibetan Long Horns Bellowing

Trumpets Sounding

Deafening Silence

The Sacred Stem

I Am

Solidified

The Ever-Flowing Flower

I Am

My Petals open

In this Jubilee

My Roots of Eternity

Unravelled

Pull down

Into the Earth

This Sumptuous Tower

I Am

As I walk in slow step

Through the Worlds

Through the Stillness

I Am

ARIASA

ASAIRA

Am

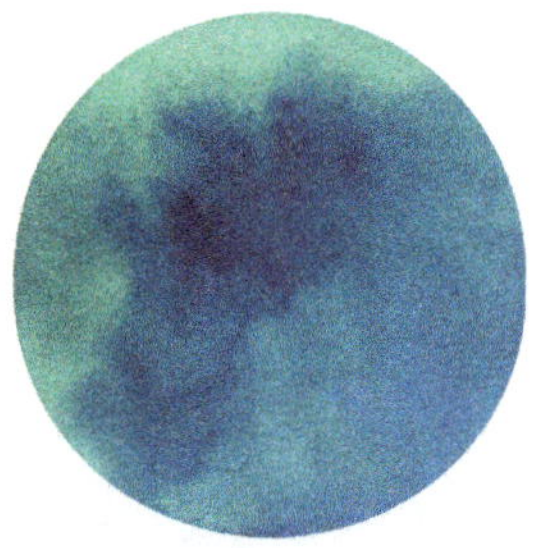

Earth: In the Green Meadow

Her eyes alight, Aileen came to a halt and smiled. Before her was the Meadow: a golden-green ocean bursting with poppies, their red heads bobbing up and down like joyful hearts.

A cool breeze ran through from the Meadow and moved Aileen's hair. Bruxa barked. Aileen bent down and stroked the fluffy white dog, who licked Aileen's hand profusely. Aileen laughed.

"Let's go in, Bruxita," Aileen said.

The woman and the dog entered the silent Meadow. A vibrating stillness hummed in the air. Aileen let her body drop into the poppy-strewn grass. Mmm… She lay down and closed her eyes. Lovingly, Bruxa nestled her head against Aileen's side.

The grass was warm and dry, the earth soft and inviting. Aileen could smell incense. She breathed it in and sank deeper into herself. A warmth of forever-welcome seeped up from the depths and merged with Aileen.

"Thank you, Mother of Mothers," Aileen whispered.

The sense of gratitude expanded and expanded, setting off sparks of gold that danced around her.

An awareness of simply existing floated in, tenderly insisting, through the back of Aileen's head and body. The Awareness settled in front of Aileen and gently engulfed her in its golden light… embracing… widening… mmm… so bright, so beautiful… ahhh, my never-ending Wings of Love…

A sweet memory surfaced. She was a little girl, running in the Meadow with her dog, Big Bear, then meeting the Beloved Tree and hearing the Star's message, "*Follow the Heart and All shall Change!*" That's where the journey had all started; the search for the Light of Love, for ASAIRA the Mother of All, the search to fulfill the Promise of the 3, to create the Garden of Paradise here on Earth…

Cloud-like, the memory dissolved.

The Golden Light spread out even more. Aileen, AIRAAS, all memories and lives, felt themselves melt into the alchemic Goldness.

Just this Light, came the thought.

Then, like a burst of a trillion bubbles, words from another of the Star's messages poured into the One Heart, the Heart of all the Realms, the one and only Heart of ASAIRA, "*And You will know who You really Are: The Light of All Lights!*"

A single tear falls down Aileen's cheek.

The voice that is Her and is not Her says, "ARIASA walks is THIS."

The Wings of a Goddess flutter.

A soft fragrance…

So much Love… Love… Love… Love…

Light beyond Light, beyond Light, beyond Light…

Space… Space… Space…

Silence.

"I Am."

The Goldness of a Trillion Names and No Name shimmers in recognition of Itself.

ARIASA takes another step.

- ✸ The Writer wakes up.

- ✸ A neighbour chuckles.

- ✸ The Reader starts a project.

- ✸ A rainbow paints itself across the skies.

- ✸ Bruxa cuddles up to Bagha, who is Tiger Bright in disguise.

- ✸ A hummingbird stops and hovers in front of the lonely child's face.

- ✸ Evelyn & Jeanne hug each other and then hug Baxter.

- ✸ Mothers and Fathers sit down and read a story to their children.

- ✸ Lily gives her dog, Bear, a new toy.

The Sparrow chirps while sitting on a window-sill.

Helen & Jack fly onto the Tree of Lands to say hello.

Six eagles circle in the sky… No, wait, seven!

Aye writes a poem.

A woman looks at the meadow full of forget-me-nots and forgets her troubles.

Aileen kisses Keon. Carlitos, who is on Keon's lap, purrs.

A bird is let out of its cage.

Keon plants flowers and vegetables in the garden.

A grizzly bear, forced to dance for entertainment, is unchained. The bear is taken to a lush open-spaced place where it rests and is taken care of.

The Reader finishes a drawing. It's called 'The Six Knowings of ASAIRA and Her Twelve Sacred Names'.

A girl who was lost finds her parents.

A fragrance of incense pours out of the pages of the book, 'The Six Knowings of ASAIRA'.

An imprisoned man is pardoned and set free. He is given love and support for his new life.

The Ancient Tree of Lands watches over all the Children of the One Light, knowing them no longer as children but as ARIASA.

ARIASA takes another step.

❊ People in the Earth Realm wake up from their sleep with a sense of respect
and understanding for each other regardless of sex, age, gender, race, religion,
colour or culture. The comprehension feels new and fresh yet ancient and true.

❊ A wave of everlasting love for nature and animals and all living Beings travels
through the Earth Realm and settles in every heart.

ARIASA takes another step.

❊ All Beings that are bounded are freed. Through the Realms and Dimensions
and timelines, the Bounded forgive their perpetrators, who in turn forgive their
perpetrators, who in turn forgive theirs, who in turn…

❊ Wars and prisons suddenly make no sense and cease to be. The bells of freedom
and celebration are heard in every village, town and city of the Earth Realm.

ARIASA takes another step.

❊ Life in the Green Meadow spirals and spirals, creating new out of the old.
The Earth Realm shines with a shimmering golden Light. All its Beings are
unrecognisable for they know themselves as the One Light.

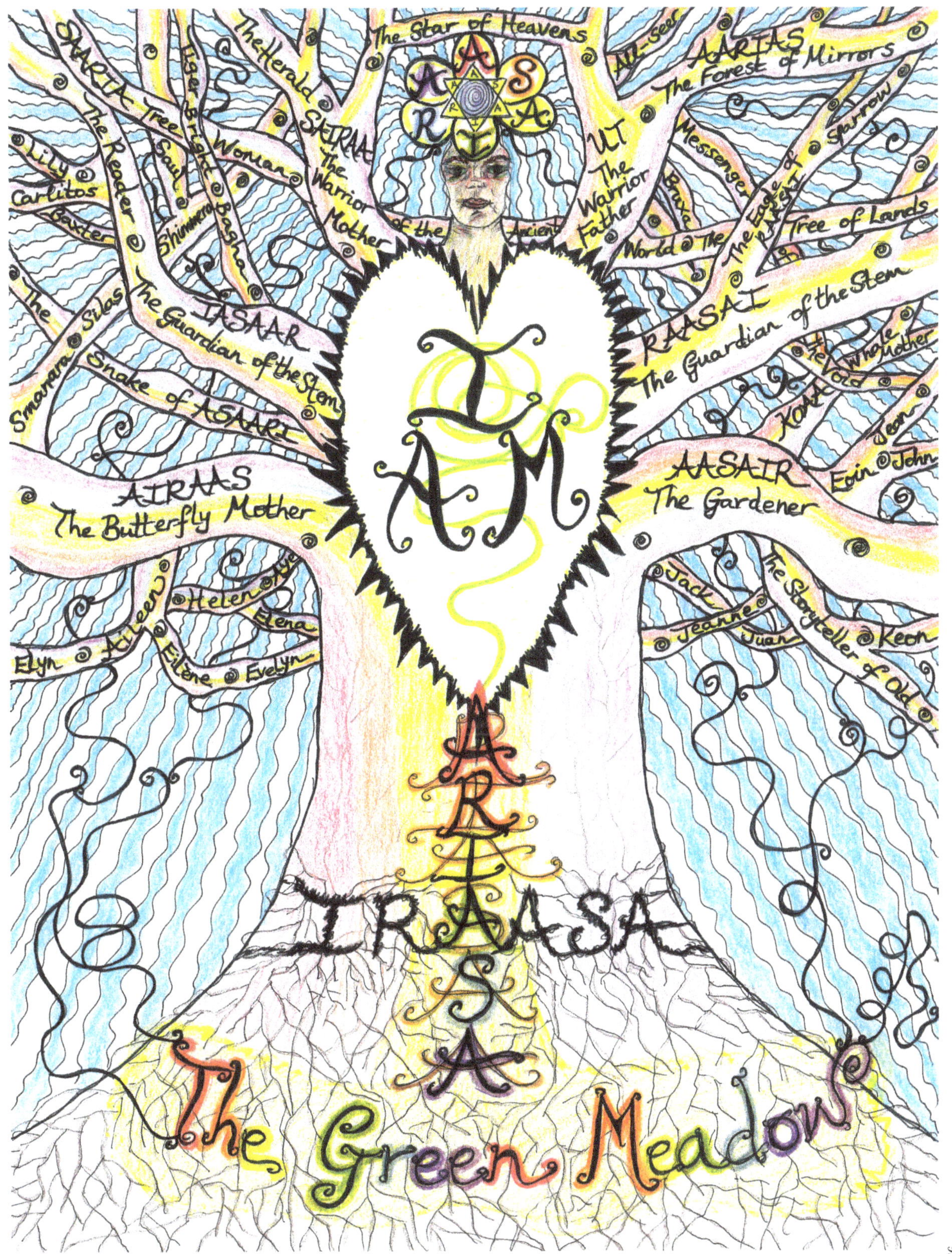
The Star of Heavens
All-Seer
AARIAS
The Forest of Mirrors
The Herald
SEIRAA
The Warrior Mother
SHARIA
The Reader
Tiger Bright Soul
The Women
Shimmering Basho
Lily
Carlitos
Baxter
The
Smanara
Silas
The Guardian of the Stem
Snake of ASAAR
IASAAR
UT
The Warrior Father
Messenger
Buxa
World
The Eagle of Sorrow
Tree of Lands
RAASAI
The Guardian of the Stem
The Whale Mother
Korra
Old
AIRAAS
The Butterfly Mother
AASAIR
The Gardener
Eoin
John
Jean
Helen
Ava
Elena
Elyn
Aileen
Eilene
Evelyn
Jack
Jeanne
Juan
The Storyteller of Old
Keon
IAM
ARIRAASA
The Green Meadow

I am

I am the Essence of Essences

I cannot be spoken of

And yet I am

I cannot speak

And yet I do

I am described in a billion trillion words and pages

My voice is loud and clear in the Open Heart

Yes, Mystery is my name, if I had one

I am the Light of Lights

The Mystery that Clarifies All

I am the Untold of

And the Retold

I am This that Forgot

I am This that Remembered

This Story of Stories

I am

ASAIRA

She, who is I, who is He, who is It, who is We, who is They, who is You,

Who found the Green Meadow

Who returned to the Mother

Who sang the True Song

Who fulfilled an Ancient Promise

Who discovered the Rainbow Path

Yes, She who saw Herself in the Mirror as ARIASA is I is

You

Are

The 3

Am I

Jump for Joy, Child of the One Light!

I AM

And we walk

The Realms of Existence

Together as

ONE

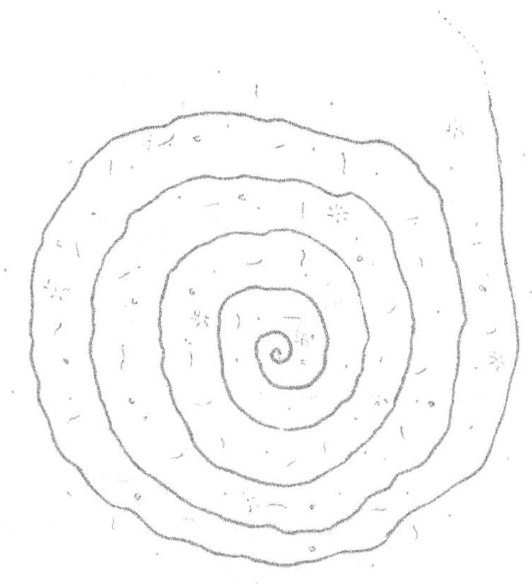

THE END

✦ ACKNOWLEDGEMENTS ✦

*The journey that has brought The Six Knowings of ASAIRA has been miraculously
supported. Over the twelve years that it took to bring 'her' into book form, every
time there was some kind of obstacle, I would receive the help, support, love and
encouragement that was needed.*

*From the short story that was the 1st Knowing, which turned amazingly into six
knowings and six notebooks that had to be typed into the computer and edited,
to working out how to do the illustrations and complex page format, and to finally
deciding how to get the book ready for publishing, at each step I'd miraculously be
offered confirmation and support, despite all the doubts, fears and challenges.*

*The original intention had always been "a beautifully decorated book with magical
illustrations" and that the book would be the "best possible version". And it
happened! So, yes, I am humbled and grateful, and in absolute awe of the mystery
and magic of this creative journey, that is, of course, my own journey of discovery to
ASAIRA.*

THANK YOU SO MUCH TO…

✦ *Antonio, for your incredible patience and understanding, especially in these last
five years, to give me the space and time to focus on the writing and editing of the
book. And also for being the inspiration for the kind, chocolate-eyed Gardener from
ASAIRA! Antonio, I couldn't have written ASAIRA without you, and I certainly couldn't
have finished the book without the love and generosity you gave me and always give
me so unconditionally. Te quiero, Amor.*

✦ *Moni Vangolen, for your wisdom, your inspiration, your unending love of the
Divine Feminine and the Truth. The journey that has brought ASAIRA is intrinsically
intertwined and connected with every Satsang meeting and retreat with you, and
very specially with every Women's Satsang that I attended. All your words and
pointers, in and out of Satsang, are a continuous inspiration. Many of the dreams
that are spoken of in the book are based on real dreams that I often had right after
a meeting. As one example, I remember having a dream about a tree with jewels
after one of the Women's Satsangs in Vancouver, which came to be the Tree of Purple
Jewels in the 7th Knowing. Gracias por todo, Hermana.*

✩ Tomas Stubbs, for your words of wisdom and clarity and amazing lucidness when things get really foggy and turbulent, for being so funny and lovable and so supportive. Again, the many, many Satsangs and retreats I attended with you have inspired ASAIRA and are interwoven in the Six Knowings. One example that stands out is the Eagle of RAASAI in the 6th Knowing: the sense of an eagle perched on a tree for hours on end, rested and alert, was inspired after one of the Satsangs with you. Thank you, too, for reading the first completed manuscript of ASAIRA and the words of advice and encouragement. Gracias, Hermano.

✩ Pamela Wilson , for your wisdom, love and kindness, and pointers to the 'Old Ways'. Every Satsang with you has been and is an inspiration to me. One of the first retreats I attended in Vancouver with you was key in the writing of the 1st Knowing. As an example, the scene between Aileen and the Dragon was inspired by one of the meetings in that retreat where I was so touched by your gentle compassion. Thank you for all your words of encouragement and help with ASAIRA. She is so grateful!

✩ Palmi, for your love and complete faith and understanding that ASAIRA would come into existence, for reading the 1st Knowing and encouraging me always, for reviewing and correcting the Spanish used for the 6th and 7th Knowings, and, not least, for organising the raffle in Spain to collect funds for the book design! ¡Gracias por tu amor y tu ayuda incondicional, Hermana!

✩ Isa, for always being there for me. For continuously being excited about what I was doing. For all your love and enthusiasm and support! For so much understanding and inspiration! Hermanita, te echo de menos. ¡Gracias por cada palabra de amor y entusiasmo, y toda tu risa y sabiduría!

✩ Peggy, for your continuous support and friendship and encouragement! You're always there cheering me on! Thank you, too, for reading the first completed manuscript and giving me feedback! I'm so grateful.

✩ Mary, for reading the 1st Knowing, quite a few years ago now! Your words of encouragement and interest inspired and motivated me to keep going! Thank you for your friendship, support and love!

✩ *Jesús G., for reading the 1st Knowing and giving me feedback many years ago.*
¡Gracias por tu amistad y tu apoyo!

✩ *Yann, for reviewing and correcting the French used in the 6th and 7th Knowings.*
Merci beaucoup for finding the time to do that!

✩ *Tessa, for copy-editing the first completed version a few years ago.*
I really appreciate all the work you put into it and all your great ideas!
Thank you, dear friend!

✩ *Tracy T, for reading the first completed manuscript as a beta reader and giving*
really detailed feedback. Thank you so much for taking that time so generously.
It helped me enormously!

✩ *Everyone that participated in the GoGetFunding Campaign, and the Raffle in*
Spain! The book design and the pages wouldn't be what they are without you! Special
thanks to: Peggy, Armin, Tomas & Moni, Suri, Familia Guerrero: Conchi, Antonio, María
& Antía, Deborah, Pamela, Isa & JuanMi, Alan, Karina, Cindy, Donna, Luisa, Olga, Mary,
Amina, Stan & Jenn, Silvi, Palmi, Héctor, Amparo M., Conchi G., Patri, Julián, Nieves,
Isabel G., Paqui, Estrella, Paco, Carmen L., and Ángel. ¡Gracias a tod@s!

✩ *Bruxa's and Baxter's families for letting me use their names in ASAIRA. Both dogs*
touched by heart and inspired me, as did Carlitos the cat, who started off as a stray,
but became a member of our family in Spain.

✩ *Carmen Wright, for making ASAIRA the book she is now by incorporating all the*
texts and illustrations into the format and layout I had envisioned, and thought was
not even possible! The finished book is magical, every page a delight thanks to all of
your many hours of work and wonderful suggestions and ideas. ASAIRA in published
form with this beautiful book design could not be here without your help, know-how
and enthusiasm!

✩ *The Creative Academy for Writers, for being such a supportive and motivating*
online community! Since I joined in 2019, your words of advice and encouragement,
plus the wealth of experience and knowledge about all the different parts of the
writing process helped me find the way to share, and ultimately, to publish the
manuscript in book form. Thank you so much!

✦ All my Friends and Family in Canada, Spain and UK that have supported and encouraged me by asking how the book is going or showing interest. Wow, every time that happened, if I were feeling it was all an impossible task, your interest would bring me right back to the desk!

✦ And last but not least, to ASAIRA, Herself, because since she came into existence, she has guided me and shown me the way. I bow in humble gratitude, full of joy!

I've drawn all the illustrations and symbols in The Six Knowings of ASAIRA, except for the painted shapes used for the realm circles and doors. These can be found at Deposit Photos. Thank you to the artists who created them. They are beautiful! I'd also like to give a special thank you to Siofra Tural and her illustration Tiger Roar which can be found at Deviant Art. Her illustration inspired my version of Tiger Bright in the illustration on Page 186 of the 3rd & 4th Knowing.

And to end, I would like to acknowledge all the works of literature, poems, songs, rhymes, sacred texts, writers, teachers, goddesses and gods, that have inspired me over the years, and that have appeared in the book, either actually mentioned or behind certain words or characters. Also deep gratitude and bowing from the Heart to all the wondrous women of my family lineages.
ASAIRA would not be here without you!

✦ Thank you! ✦

Carmy Stubbs

Port Coquitlam, British Columbia, November 13th, 2022

✦ ABOUT THE AUTHOR ✦

Carmy Stubbs, reader, writer, storyteller and poet, is a lover of the Word and its power for transformation. She is the author of The Six Knowings of ASAIRA, where all her loves ~ the poems, the magic, the storytelling, the creative force of the Heart, the profound mysteries of life and the search for the Divine ~ weave themselves alchemically through text and illustration.

She lives in Port Coquitlam, British Columbia, (Canada), with her husband, Antonio, and the newest member of the family, their sweet little doggy, Milo.

www.carmystubbs.com

Carmy Stubbs

The Alchemy of Story, Poem and Illustration